Verity Rising

A ***Gods of Deceit*** Novel

Book 1

Phil Scott Mayes

The characters and events portrayed in this book are fictitious. Any similarity to real persons, living or dead, is coincidental and not intended by the author.

ISBN-13: 978-1-7351422-0-3

Cover photo by: Josh Hild on Unsplash
Cover design by: Phil Scott Mayes

DEDICATION

This, my debut novel, is dedicated to my dad, Gerry, who motivated and encouraged me through every phase of its creation.

I also owe a special kind of gratitude to my wife, Tanya, who supported me through countless evenings and weekends, carrying my dead weight while I clacked away, oblivious to the world around me.

CHAPTER ONE

I've never liked human beings. As their liberator, I work tirelessly, putting myself in harm's way to set them free, then watch as they race back under the burdensome yoke of deceit. Sadly, after several months of unavoidable contact with them, it seems I've contracted their contagious misery. Last night, when I returned from work, I flopped onto my inhospitable department store mattress and lay wide-eyed and perfectly still for over an hour. I may have been vibrating; it certainly felt like I was. For the third time this week I lay that way, staring at the exposed rafters of my industrial apartment until the vibrations faded.

Sometimes, a quiet, dangerous voice assures me that I have the right to hate humanity. After all, by my nature I only ever see the worst they have to offer. That, and nearly twenty years ago one of them killed both my parents by simply being a pathetic waste of life. But I see that hatred is an ugly, emotional, and extreme illness, a disease that would've certainly killed me by now, turning my heart into brittle stone and boiling the blood from my veins. No, that little voice is wrong.

The great irony is that, despite my feelings toward them, it's my pledged purpose to loose humanity from the invisible chains that bind their free will. Desperately, they seek lives of meaning and fulfillment in a system of lies designed for their unwitting enslavement. These ignorant fools don't even notice as their freedom is ravaged with each headline, each advertisement, each conversation, and each insidious thought. My only consolation is that most of the dirtbags I deal with end up dead.

"That's thirteen dollars and fifty cents, sir," the young driver says, interrupting my thoughts without disrupting his discreet headbanging. For almost the entire commute, he's rather enjoyed the grunge rock station playing quietly on the radio. I've mostly tuned it out.

I pay him fifteen dollars and pull the door handle.

"How tall are you, man?" he asks before I can clear the door.

"Tall."

Stepping from the white Prius taxicab, I shut the door and tip my head to the sky. Milburn Tower, a square building with slightly rounded sides, stretches toward the scattered, wooly clouds that bathe in morning light. From this perspective it has no end, like a country road that shrinks into the distance until it finally disappears. Its nicely proportioned fretwork of steel and glass makes it one of the most handsome structures in all of Port Ellis, especially after the semiannual cleanings to remove the salt and exhaust residue. For the first few weeks, it juts up like a giant crystal shard in the center of the city, cloning every helicopter, cloud, or seagull that passes by. I enter through the heavy glass doors of the main entrance as I have every day for the last six months.

"Good morning, Tyson," I say with a smile and half-wave to the security guard. I pass his desk near the front entrance at least twice a day, sometimes four or more, so I've grown used to the routine pleasantries.

"Mornin', Mr. Verity," he cheerfully replies.

It's not difficult to detect fake geniality. The way the corners of the mouth hesitate to curl upward, the hardness of the eyes, and the comfort of one's posture offer insights into the true state of a person's heart. Tyson is genuinely jovial and manages to maintain it with unprecedented regularity, a well-known trait of his Scandinavian heritage, he claims.

I lunge for the closing elevator door and enter to find a rare treat: it's empty. In a building bustling with constant human activity, a private elevator is an unexpected delight. With any luck I can bask in this tranquility all the way to my floor. The elevator briefly surges upward only to come to an abrupt stop. It was too good to be true.

The shrill squeak of the elevator door assails my ears and strangers cram tightly against me in all directions. I can't help but feel nauseous. On top of the offensive odors emanating from their various orifices and poorly washed crevices, they're also toting breakfast from the food court. Egg sandwiches, sweet pastries, and bitter coffee copulate with their natural stench to form a truly grotesque pollutant. Bathing in perfume has done little to disguise their decay, and their repulsive attempts to achieve beauty are pathetically transparent. It isn't difficult to diagnose the diseases they carry through a few simple observations.

Take the woman in front of me as an example. Her self-consciousness is likely rooted in the humiliating words of a bitterly insecure high school classmate, or perhaps those of an equally insecure boyfriend who made her feel ugly so she'd never realize she was too good for him. The lies she believes have shaped her identity. Her dense makeup, flirtatious personality, and revealing dress desperately cry for validation from everyone she meets. If approval can't be won, she'll settle for jealousy.

To the left you'll see a floppy patch of hair taped atop the head of a man who clearly didn't grow it. His magnificent wristwatch and designer suit suggest that he is a successful and important man, distracting others from the miserable loneliness in his eyes. At home, thick dust collects on the objects he holds so dear with the exception of his $50,000 liquor collection, which now gets the nightly attention he never gave his ex-wife and kids.

It's not that I know all these details to be exactly true, but it doesn't matter. Different strains of the same epidemic afflict every person I see, and with every new person I meet I am ever more thankful for my own immunity to this condition. I am different.

As a vapor I weave through the human herd, fully aware of the deceptive forces at work but playing along as I maneuver to strike. My awareness of their trivial reality is the only reason I spare them the soul-crushing awakening I could bring. The elite and the celebrities who have sold their souls to achieve their wildest dreams only to be met with the emptiness of such pursuits serve as prime examples. It's then that burning sulfur floods their nostrils and the suicidal escape softly beckons. Suicide is not the end I seek, but it's often the result of my work.

The elevator lurches to a stop as I prepare for my daily marathon. It's draining to embrace the people with whom I interact throughout the day. My most bothersome reflex is the face's tendency to display the mind's contents. Thankfully, with much practice, I have managed to disconnect this inconvenient function.

Joel is hustling down the hallway as I step from the elevator. He smiles and makes eye contact with me, nodding in place of a verbal greeting.

"Hello, Joel, how are you today?" I ask.

I may not like humans, Joel especially, but I was trained to treat others with respect regardless of my feelings. After six months of socialization with humans, I have adapted well to their customs and courtesies and know what behaviors are accepted as "normal" and expected. Beyond that, until this operation is complete, I'm stuck with these people. Making enemies before the appointed time would only hinder my efforts to collect information and get close to my targets.

Joel's suit pants are wrinkled and hanging crookedly from his hips. His curly ginger hair is more unkempt than usual, and his mangy, patchwork stubble makes it obvious he hasn't shaved in days and that he couldn't grow a full beard if he tried.

"Where are you headed?" I ask.

Without slowing down, Joel responds, "I'm fine, Ted," but ignores my second question.

His stride is subtly weak but not much different from most humans. In a truly Darwinian system, most of them would perish. However, their collaborative spirit defies such a system to their detriment. The weak survive on the backs of the strong and the cancer of society metastasizes. I decide to follow Joel.

Each person has a scent, a combination of pheromones and elements beyond the range of human perception. Actually, that's not entirely accurate. Many people are capable of sensing these elements but can rarely interpret them. It often presents as a gut feeling about a person that can be positive, producing immediate trust and attraction, or negative, producing distrust and a warning. My perception of these elements is honed so that I can read them in detail.

Joel's trail is that of disappointment and frustration. He's never measured up and he knows it, but he wants nothing more than to truly matter. This combination of forces makes him the vice president's lapdog, a role that he believes positions him as the logical successor. In many ways he has become indispensable, but his forfeiture of dignity has cemented this power dynamic. He will watch as his peers accomplish the dreams that have always eluded him.

He looks over his shoulder and sees me five steps behind. "Do you need something from the storage room? I'm grabbing a notebook for Dave." Joel's submissive nature is on full display.

"I'm good, thanks," I reply with a polite smile to soften the rejection.

Soft people need coddling, so I've coddled Joel at each opportunity. This has nurtured a one-way relationship that is useful. He is not my friend, but he sees me as *his* friend, and this allows me to siphon the information I need about the dishonest dealings of this company. If Joel knew the true nature of our relationship I suspect that he would feel betrayed and used. Ironically, his role as my agent makes his life more meaningful than most. He would thank me if he could only see, and he will see soon enough.

Joel turns left and enters the windowless storage room as I quickly scan the hall for witnesses. Only two others are within line of sight, but with both fixating on their phone screens the coast is clear. I turn and casually enter the storage room, close the door behind me, and quietly lock the knob.

Joel's suspicious eyes meet mine as I enter. "I thought you said you didn't need anything," he says with a furrowed brow.

"I don't need anything from this room, but you and I need to have a conversation." My ominous tone lands heavily on Joel's ears.

"Okay. What's up?" he asks, pretending not to notice.

People like Joel are always nervous. Undoubtedly, he's flipping through the catalog of wrongs he has knowingly committed looking for my name among its thousands of pages. *Did Kimberly tell him what I said behind his back? Did he figure out I forged his signature on that memo? What if he knows I stole that box of drugs that was missing during the audit?* It's none of these things in particular, and yet it's all of them. I want to talk to him about the catalog itself.

I maintain eye contact while slowly moving opposite Joel to the other side of the waist-high metal cabinet. Each step brings a shift in Joel's expression from confusion to anxiety and eventually to fear. Still staring into his sad eyes, a soothing blanket of peace falls softly over my spirit. This repose assures me that now is the proper time. I press ahead, confident in the necessity of what I must do.

"Have you ever told a lie?" I ask, knowing quite well the answer.

"What kind of question is that, Ted? Who hasn't told a lie by the time they reach our age?" he scoffs.

"So that's a yes?"

I know it's a yes. It's always a yes. Most people tell their first lie within months of learning how to speak. To humans, lying has proven as inevitable as death. They get so good at lying to themselves they can hardly tell when they're lying to others, the most damaging of which are often never even spoken but simply transmitted from heart to heart. Joel's scared expression is taking on notes of defensive aggression, undoubtedly due to the notion that he's being unfairly, hypocritically judged. But I have caught him in many deadly lies, and my judgment is anything but hypocritical.

"Yeah, of course it's a yes, but it would be a yes for anyone. I don't make a habit of it, but everyone lies," he retorts defensively. "Anyway, what gives you the right to judge anyone, Ted? You know what they say about people who live in glass houses."

Humans always think the bad behavior of others somehow pardons their own. At the very least, they take comfort in the fact that they are part of a wretched collective and not just a lonely outlier. I lean forward, propping my elbows on the cabinet and interlocking my fingers.

"You are correct. You have lied, like everyone else, but do you know the cost of those lies?"

"Ted, this is getting weird, man," Joel says with a nervous chuckle. "Is there a point to this?"

"Of course there's a point to this. After all the frivolous conversations we've shared, it's time to have one of great meaning."

"Okay. I'm just saying, it's off to a weird start and you don't seem like yourself."

"That's where you're wrong, Joel. At this moment, I'm more myself than you've ever seen me. Are you being true to yourself? Is this selfish, desperate, pitiful, and dishonest human your true nature or are you acting outside of your nature—a victim of forces beyond your control?"

"I don't know, Ted. How much control do any of us really have? I'm just trying to make the most of the hand I was dealt. I'm doing what my boss says and trying to be who he needs me to be. Don't we all put our best foot forward and try to be who we're *supposed* to be, what people want us to be?" pleads Joel in the hope I'll be satisfied and the discussion ended.

"Most people do from time to time, Joel. Some people say and do whatever it takes to enrich themselves regardless of the damage of those actions and statements." Joel breaks eye contact, looking downward and fiddling with the notepad in his hands. I continue, "It's apparent that you don't see the harm that your behavior has caused. There would be no way for you to fully know how destructive it has been. But I assure you, you have left a wake of irreparable damage in the lives you have touched."

Joel pauses, again perusing his catalog of wrongs for some trace of the destruction I mentioned. Finding none, he meets my gaze with a playful smirk and replies, "You caught me, but you know what? I sleep like a baby every night on my thousand-dollar sheets." His irreverent attitude is an obvious ploy to conceal the fear swelling in his chest.

Sternly, I reply, "You don't seem to grasp the ultimate importance of this moment." At this, Joel's gaze lifts to meet mine. I pause and focus my mind as I glare through his pinhole pupils.

I lift my elbows from the cabinet and stand upright. Already more than a foot taller than him, I stretch my spine a few inches closer to my true form, and as my body extends before him, Joel's face resembles that of a child realizing just how small and powerless he really is. His craned neck and hanging jaw exude both terror and wonder as I reveal a taste of my divine nature. I relax my vocal cords to deepen my voice to its innate, rumbling timbre. I now have his undivided attention.

"Joel, this is not a trial. Your verdict is decidedly guilty. It is now time for your sentencing. I will act as your reflection and you must pass judgment on what you see."

His tangerine locks tremble as sweat seeps from his skin, beading and rolling down his neck. His body appears rigidly frozen in its awkward stance. Only his eyes move to track me as I walk around the end of the cabinet. The fluorescent bulbs overhead begin to flicker as if to match his quivering. I retrieve a small vial of plum-red liquid from my left pocket. Removing the cork, I lift the vial above Joel's open mouth, turn it nearly horizontal, and give it one gentle tap.

This is my favorite part. The drop has exited the vial. I'm captivated by its graceful descent, intently observing its brilliant red sparkle with each splash of flickering light. The orb warps and wobbles as if alive. Undeniably beautiful and mysterious, Joel's helpless eyes wet with tears at the wondrous sight. It dives between his teeth and into his empty tomb of a mouth. When the drop meets the back of his throat he reflexively swallows, emits a faint, haunting whimper, and drops limply to the floor.

As I step over Joel's motionless body, I constrict my stature and tense my vocal cords back to human range. I grab the cold metal doorknob, glance over my shoulder at Joel's motionless body, and exit the supply room.

Despite the inevitability of that drop entering Joel's body, the outcome of this moment is still uncertain. As this is only the eighth sowing of my life, I have yet to find a reliable predictor of the human response. Some who I believed would overcome the torment of the truth didn't, while others who seemed doomed found the strength to prevail. I fully expect Joel to end his life, but this is his sentence to deliver. For the first time in decades, maybe ever, Joel is truly free.

CHAPTER TWO

Freedom is a pipe dream. Humans cherish the illusion of free will but too deliberately compromise each other's freedom of choice for it to ever be a reality. Take, for example, a big pharmaceutical company like my temporary employer Pentastar Pharmaceuticals. In a sterile boardroom, executives were warned about the dangers of the drug they've been developing—they call it Fosillix—but with many billions of dollars invested in research, it's too late to turn back. Unwitting trial participants, already suffering from early onset Alzheimer's disease, sign on with renewed hope of relief only to suffer debilitating side effects and death.

Certainly no one making an informed decision would choose to participate in a drug trial with a 94 percent failure rate and an 83 percent prevalence of drug-related side effects. Executives' suppression of this information effectively stole participants' free will—their ability to choose for themselves based on the facts of reality. Humans often misrepresent the truth in order to manipulate the choices of others.

"Ted, what are you thinking about?" asks Dave from the head of the conference table. I snap back to the moment and scan the half dozen faces of the Fosillix trial task force. Assembled to strategize in the wake of the trial's fiasco, I made sure to be selected for a seat. Admittedly, it wasn't a competitive process. Most employees are doing everything they can to distance themselves from Fosillix, some even requesting transfers and resigning when they get denied.

"Sorry, what was that, Dave?"

"I asked what you think about the plan," he says, gesturing to the PowerPoint slide on the monitor behind him.

Public Relations Recovery Plan

- *Exaggerate trial success through flattering statistical analysis*
- *Downplay severity and frequency of side effects*
- *Attribute widespread peripheral side effects to patients' poor health*
- *Imply that the trial's 5% mortality rate is traceable to patients' underlying conditions*

"I think we need to go back to the drawing board."

"Ted…YOU'RE HILARIOUS," bellows Dave, and his flunkies chuckle in compliance. "In all seriousness, the drawing board is not an option. If we can't make it to market well before the patent expires, we'll never make back our costs. Our only hope then would be lining doctors' pockets to make sure they prescribe Fosillix instead of the generic, but that's a losing battle. We need IDEAS! Do you all like having jobs?"

The bobble heads around the table nod mindlessly.

"We've spent seven years and over five billion dollars in research and development. People have died testing this drug so that others can one day enjoy a healthier life. Failure is not an option. Let's reconvene in two days. I have another meeting in an hour." Dave gathers his notes, places them in a file folder, and slides it back into his briefcase. "Ted, I need to talk to you. Walk with me to my office."

I stand from my chair, gather my notes, and hustle to get ahead of Dave. He loathes the copious time wasted moving from point to point, so whenever he's on the move he hurries and he multitasks. Outside, I stand near the door with a view down the main hall. On the left side, at the far end, is the supply closet where I left Joel about an hour ago. I turn to check on Dave, who should've bolted past me by now, and watch as he gets caught in the web of chatterbox Terry. Twisting back to the main hall, I catch a glimpse of Joel at the far end trudging from the supply closet to the stairwell. His sowing is complete, and we now await the results.

Dave, a medium man in every way—medium age, medium height, medium build, medium brown hair, and medium green eyes—manages to make shockingly quick work of Terry and escape in under two minutes. His nature is complicated. He believes his statement about lives being lost and patients having a healthier future, but he ignored the warnings he and the other executives received from the research team that the drug wasn't ready for trial and could be lethal for some. This troublesome fact makes him the reason that those patients died. Painting them as martyrs eases Dave's conscience, or at least what's left of it.

"Ted, follow me," Dave blurts as he jets through the door and toward his office.

"What did you want to talk about, Dave?" I ask, surprised that he hasn't already begun. Conversations with Dave typically require little more than nods and mm-hmms from those being talked at.

"Have you seen Joel?" His question lands like a gut punch. *Does he know?* He continues, "I sent him to get me a notebook this morning and I haven't seen him since. He was supposed to be at that damn meeting."

I guardedly reply, "Yes. I had a conversation with him in the supply room. He was still in there when I left."

No lies, but I am forbidden from revealing anything about my species to a human unless it's during a sowing. The neurological strain of the sowing causes the loss of roughly an hour of memory prior to the implantation of the seed. Whatever is said during that time is of no consequence.

"Alright," Dave says, "well I need you to track him down. He was more squirrely than usual this morning and I want to make sure he's not getting itchy about all this Fosillix stuff. Did he seem normal to you?"

"He looked a little frazzled, but mostly normal for Joel. I don't think you have anything to worry about from him," I say, comforting my future target.

"Did he say anything about the drug trial? I don't need him having some crisis of conscience." This question comes as we pass the open door of the CEO's corner office. Jan is at her desk, pen in hand over a short stack of documents, but her upright posture and leering, hazel eyes latch onto me as I pass, giving me an unpleasant notion, the same one I felt before the deadly accident.

"TED, I asked you a question," barks Dave impatiently. "What is wrong with you today?"

The same thing as every other day: I'd rather live inside my own head than out here with all these humans. I miss my farmhouse. I miss solitude.

"I apologize. I caught Jan's glare as we walked past and I could almost feel the daggers."

"That's how she's been with everybody these days. It's not personal," Dave assumes, but I know better.

We turn through the door to Dave's office and he takes the position of authority behind his desk. He leans forward onto his hands, fingers splayed open on the desk. His eyes repeat his question about Joel.

"To answer your question, Joel didn't say anything about the trial," I reply. *But a crisis of conscience is precisely what Joel is having.*

Dave pauses in thought. The sharp ring of his office phone shatters the silence, startling both of us.

"Keep an eye on him; let me know if he's getting weird. And when you see him, tell him I need a word." Dave's tone makes it clear that the "word" will be a tongue lashing, something Joel has certainly grown accustomed to by now. His leathery backside endured plenty more punishment than he actually earned, but such was his lot as the lapdog.

Dave answers the call on speaker and as I turn to leave his office, I hear the frantic voice of his secretary.

"Sir, we have a serious situation that you…OH MY GOD, HE'S JUMPING!"

My head yanks back to see Dave's bewildered face looking straight at me. Over his shoulder, through his wall of windows, I see Joel's body plummet past on the way to his concrete doom twelve floors below. Dave immediately reads my horrified expression and vaults to the window in time to see Joel shrink away to a sudden stop. He turns to me, face ghastly and pale.

"That was…was that Joel?" he asks in disbelief. "Could you see?"

I nod, damming the emotional blitz in my throat. Dave slowly returns his gaze to the expanding spectacle below. Red and blue lights approach from several blocks away. Quietly, I slide through the door and move swiftly to the nearest restroom.

Once through the door, I race to a stall just in time to empty my guts. The violent heaving feels deserved; a minute penance considering my role in Joel's suicide. My distaste for humanity does little to relieve the burden of my calling. But, in reality, I do nothing more than facilitate an awakening to their invisible slavery and their enslavement of others. What happens next is a product of the individual's transgressions, their own victimization, and their will to live.

Joel's case serves as a timely example. Three years ago, he engaged in a summer-long affair with Brittany, one of

Pentastar's interns. Joel knew that his wife would leave him if she discovered his transgression, so he lied. In lying, he stripped her of her ability to choose whether or not to stay in the marriage and work through their problems. He controlled the narrative, thereby controlling her and taking away her ability to choose whether or not to remain his wife. She was his captive for three years.

This reality, among innumerable others, haunted Joel in the darkness of the sowing. Facedown on the floor of the supply room, his mind was bombarded with the truth. The impact of every lie he told and every lie told to him afflicted his spirit and eroded his will. He saw the way his lies influenced others' decisions and he saw how his freedom was stolen by the lies of others. He likely saw a far more fulfilling life that failed to materialize because deceit had redirected his path. Perhaps nothing weighed heavier than his role here at Pentastar.

As the VP's stooge, he was often tasked with the dirty work. When documents required "accidental" typos that conveniently hid unflattering data, he was their guy. When palms needed greasing, pockets needed lining, and squeaky wheels needed silencing, Joel eagerly obliged. He'd do anything to please his superiors in the hope of advancing his career, no matter how wrong he knew it was.

A final heave surges through my core, forcefully erupting from my esophagus. Refreshed, I wipe my face, flush the toilet, and wash up before returning to the hall. As the door closes behind me, a vivid and unsettling sensation invades my nerves, stopping me in my tracks. My head pans right to see Jan standing in her office doorway. She says nothing, but her contemptuous glare violates my senses. In this still moment, time has stopped, my skin is translucent, and I am exposed.

Behind me, the stairwell door suddenly swings open with a metallic clunk. Four uniformed police officers enter the hall and divert Jan's gaze. She steps forward to meet them, and I seize the opportunity to escape to the relative security of my office, not that the glass walls do much to shield me from Jan's vision. It's remarkable that a building with so much glass can hide so many secrets.

Sitting in my office, I contemplate the decadence of these halls. How many lives have been ruined to build this empire; how many souls forfeited? These humans feed on the desperation of the needy. The only thing more lucrative than providing cures is creating an ongoing dependency. Titans of industry and governing officials have developed a system that continually rewards them as the masses eat from their hands.

None of this would be possible without lies. Pride is considered by some to be the first sin, committed by Lucifer, who thought himself to be greater than God. However, the origin of his pride was his belief in a lie, the lie that he outshined his creator.

I am part of an ancient people who have lived undetected for millennia. Since before recorded history, we have coexisted with mankind and been called many names. The early Hebrew and Muslim people called us Nephilim, Gibborim, and Rephaim, the offspring of angels and women. The Greeks and Romans thought of us as demigods, the offspring of gods and women. Neither of these are exactly correct, but both suffice for a primitive understanding of our nature. As for our mission, we serve as keepers and guardians of truth. We see and sense the truth, and when it has become distorted beyond recognition, we intervene.

I was summoned to be a reckoning to this place, and Joel was the beginning of their end.

CHAPTER THREE

Being a divine guardian of truth while sworn to secrecy is the type of paradox that's destined to lead to a catch-22. Should I reach that fork in the road, cornered by an inescapable question, I'll be left with two routes forward. When I imagine that moment, the road on my right is asphalt, potholed and crumbling from centuries of neglect. Above it hangs a sign, stained yellow and bubbled with rust. Its message reads *Divulge the Truth of the Nephilim's Existence* in faded letters. This option, appealing in its virtue but nevertheless rife with consequence, would at least preserve my commitment to truth. I don't know of any Nephilim who have chosen this route. In contrast, the road to my left has a smoothly paved and lightly worn concrete surface, well maintained with the tolls of forfeited souls. A bright green sign, adorned in flashing lights and fresh white lettering hangs above it and reads *Lie to Protect Your Secret.* The appeal of this option is the lack of immediate consequences, but the intangible cost is excruciating.

I've never been closer to facing that choice than I am right now. Joel's death could trigger a line of questioning that stretches my ability to protect both the truth and my secret. This isn't the first time that a sowing of mine has resulted in suicide, but in the past I have been tasked to deal with only one target in any given operation. Tackling an entire organization like Pentastar Pharmaceuticals requires me to stay put until the research, planning, and targeting of each evil agent is complete, which greatly increases my risk of exposure.

Dave, my next target, is walking toward my office with the police. Faintly, I hear him say, "Yeah, he's there in his office." He gestures my direction and the officers turn toward my open door. They file in as I stand to greet them with the proper portions of warmth and solemnity.

The closest officer reaches out, saying, "Hello, sir. My name is Sergeant Drake and this is Officer Lewis."

"Ted Verity, head of Pentastar's quality assurance department," I say, extending my arm and shaking his hand. "What can I do for you?"

"Well, Ted, Dave was just telling us that you talked to Joel this morning. We just want to ask you a few questions about that conversation and see what you can tell us about his behavior," says Sergeant Drake in a most disarming tone. The smoothness of his voice belies the intensity in his eyes. He's on a mission and is quite possibly always on a mission, even during an errand to the supermarket or while watching a child's soccer game.

"I'd be glad to help. I knew Joel pretty well. What would you like to know?"

"We're sorry for your loss and to have to do this so soon, but it's best that this is done while things are still fresh in everyone's memory."

He has mistaken my knowledge of Joel to mean fondness for him, although I imagine it's department policy to display such tact and courtesy. Apparently young Officer Lewis missed that day in obedience school. He reaches into my bowl of individually wrapped mints and fumbles noisily with the packaging before popping one into his mouth. He flicks it around with his tongue, clacking it against his teeth, before he notices Drake's perturbed glare.

"I apologize for him. Just think of him as an overgrown child," Drake spits without breaking his glare.

"It's no problem, that's what they're for," I reply with a gracious head bow.

"What time did you see Joel this morning?" he asks as he withdraws a small notepad from his back pocket. He clicks out his pen tip and looks me dead in the eyes as I contemplate the question.

"I saw him as soon as I stepped off the elevator this morning. I'm here at eight most days, but I had a survey scheduled first thing this morning, so I went straight to our production facility. I did the survey and got here a few minutes before nine. I saw Joel walking down the main hallway on his way to the supply room."

"And this conversation you two had, did that happen in the hallway?" inquires Drake, though his tone betrays that he already knows the answer.

"No, I followed him to the supply room so I could talk to him in private."

Sergeant Drake prods, "Tell me about that conversation."

"I confronted him about an issue I had with his misrepresentation of information."

"What kind of information?"

"All kinds of information. He was a dishonest person who regularly lied in his personal and professional life. I told him that I knew about his lies and challenged him to face the truth," I respond calmly, despite Drake's increasingly invasive questions.

It would bring me great joy to elaborate on the specifics of Joel's lies. The declaration of truth brings with it a feeling of freedom, of weightlessness, of relief. The people of Pentastar deserve to be held accountable for their crimes, but an investigation would only hinder my purposes. Once I have dealt with those most deserving of a sowing, the police can root out the remaining corruption.

"Was it heated?"

"Not especially, I simply needed to set the record straight. I left him in the supply room to examine his life choices."

"Did the two of you have a physical altercation?"

"No."

"So, you did not make physical contact with him at all?"

"Again, no, I did not. I don't understand why that question is necessary," I assert as I intensify my gaze deep into Sergeant Drake's skull. It can be extraordinarily taxing to submit to the authority of human beings. Moments like this take me to my limit.

He studies my face closely and says, "Another employee found Joel on the floor of the supply room around ten o'clock, shortly before he jumped."

"I didn't know that," I succinctly respond. At this point I see no benefit in volunteering more information than necessary to answer his questions. He clearly has some suspicions about my possible role in Joel's death and providing unnecessary details could serve to further fuel his speculation.

"He was unconscious. When he came to, he couldn't remember what happened," states Drake. He pauses, still studying my face, looking for a twitch, hoping that I panic as he awaits my response. I give none.

It is exceedingly rare that I find humans worthy of respect. Commonly, even those who choose noble professions are dishonest and do so for the wrong reasons. The purest of intentions stand little chance against systematic abuse and corruption, leading the best people to jump ship and the worst people to embrace their darkest nature.

Police service, being a noble profession, demonstrates this polarizing effect more than any other. The best officers truly give their all to fight a seemingly unwinnable battle while the worst embrace the evil they feel powerless to subdue. They wield their badge as a weapon, empowering themselves as oppressors, and they disparage the profession as a whole.

Being the target of Sergeant Drake's suspicions, I feel his hunger for truth like a hot laser cutting through my flesh, peeling it open to pursue whatever truth hides beneath. I respect that about him. It's in the character of all good cops to expose lies and pursue liars. In this way we are alike. Unfortunately, I can't let him stand in the way of what must happen here. If he gets too close, a sowing may become necessary and his hunger for truth will be fully satisfied. Whether he lives or dies would be his choice.

Drake continues, "Where were you when Joel fell from the roof?"

"I was with Dave in his office."

He turns toward Lewis to see his reaction and transmit some ciphered message over the air waves. Lewis nods slightly in receipt and jots a note of his own. I'm guessing it says *confirm alibi with Dave*, but after what I've seen of Lewis it could very well say *buy breath mints.*

"Alright, last question. Did you notice anything unusual about Joel's behavior this morning? Was he jumpy, sweaty, loopy, did you smell anything on him? Could he have been under the influence?"

"He was frazzled, but that's not unusual. I didn't notice anything else."

"Well, we'll find out when the toxicology report comes back. We have a few more interviews to do so we're gonna move on now. Thanks for your cooperation…"

"It's Ted Verity."

"That's right. Thanks, Mr. Verity."

We shake hands and the officers smile and bow with disingenuous courtesy. No sooner than they clear the door, Dave appears outside my office, blocking my attempts to watch them. I lean right, hoping for a glimpse of their faces to read their lips or looks, but I can't see anything around Dave's medium body.

"Come in, Dave. Sit," I gently demand.

He clears my field of view just in time for me to see Drake motioning in my direction as they wait for the elevator. Officer Lewis glances toward me, awkwardly meeting my gaze, then moving along to play it off. The men lean in and share another secretive exchange. The elevator bell dings and doors slide open. Sergeant Drake turns to select their floor before sniping me with a blatant scowl that I fearlessly return. The gap in the doors narrows to a close and severs our silent war with a temporary ceasefire.

Regardless of my tenuous respect for Sergeant Drake, he is aligning himself as an adversary to my cause and further complicating an already tedious operation. With more sowings to come, his watchful eye will make avoiding detection even more arduous, forcing me into a delicate dance between finishing my work at Pentastar and preserving my own integrity.

Dave scoots to the edge of the chair and asks nervously, "What did they ask you about?"

"Joel," I calmly say, still looking at the elevator. I turn my attention to Dave, whose anxiety is pitiful. Yet another benefit of honest living is that when people get nosey, there's nothing to fear. Clearly Dave is worried about what truths I might uncover.

Dave McConnel's salty brown hair sits impeccably coiffed atop his oval face in a wavy style that gives him a certain boyish charm. His life of plenty has contributed to the slight doughiness of his midsection, but his custom-made five-thousand-dollar suit implies a more chiseled form. In his mind, his bloated annual salary is the proof of a worthwhile existence, one of importance and meaning. This suit and the others in his four-hundred-square-foot closet are little more than sandwich boards that announce his place in the corporate caste. He reclines in my chair the way he does in every chair, as if it were designed with his comfort in mind. In many decades, I have yet to meet a more dichotomous man. The people in his circle are thoroughly convinced of his likeability while outsiders generally find him repugnant. He looks at me with the emerald eyes of a scared child, desperately in need of comfort and escape.

"Obviously they asked about Joel, but what did you say?" he asks urgently.

"I didn't say anything that's going to draw attention to Pentastar, if that's what you're worried about."

"Okay," he says with relief. "I'm just doing some damage assessments so I can get ahead of the narrative on this. No doubt the media will make circumstantial connections between the Fosillix trial and Joel's suicide. I just want to make sure no one here is connecting those dots to the cops or reporters."

"They were only interested in my interaction with Joel this morning. They didn't ask any questions about Pentastar or Fosillix."

"Okay. Okay, good. Just so you know, I wasn't trying to sic them on you, but they asked if anyone else talked to Joel this morning and you said you had. I want answers too. Joel will be hard to replace. He was my go-to errand boy." Dave wags his head sadly before realizing how cold his last statement was. "That came out wrong. I'm devastated for his wife and I'll miss him, but now I also need someone who can fill his shoes, and quickly."

Dave pauses and digs deep. With squinty eyes, he muscles up a dismal display of theater.

"I never thought he'd do something like this. I didn't even notice any warning signs," he whines with a dry sniffle.

I hang my head, hiding my face to avoid offending him with my skepticism. An awkward moment of silence passes, interrupted occasionally by contrived sniffles. After Dave fulfills his quota of public grieving, he stands with a sigh and newfound composure. He clears his throat, buttons his jacket, and tidies his sleeves.

Then, in his most authoritative tone, Dave says, "Ted, I need you to do something."

I know what comes next: this worthless weasel is about to assign me dirty work. It wouldn't be the first time he's suggested I do something disreputable, but his previous suggestions were met with such swift rejection it would be astonishing for him to try again. Nevertheless, his mouth is opening.

"I need you to approve this report," he dictates as he produces a file folder out of thin air and slings it in my direction.

I stoop to retrieve the folder from my desk, flip open the file, and peruse the document inside. It's worse than I expected. This report says that they were given the green light from research and development and quality assurance to initiate human trials.

"Absolutely not!" I protest tenaciously as I slap the folder shut and thrust it back at Dave.

His face crumples into a nasty frown as he says, "I was just going to have Joel forge your signature but now that he's gone it's just easier if you sign it yourself. I'll make it worth your while. I'm thinking of a number between ten and twenty thousa—"

"No," I interject with concrete resolve.

His frown ignites in a flash of red.

"I figured as much you damned Boy Scout! How about this: sign it by tomorrow morning or you're fired! Leave it on my desk when you're done," he snarls as he stomps out of my office.

I sit on the edge of my desk looking at the folder in my hand. The report it contains is an abomination. Not only does it absolve the ones truly responsible for the untimely death of numerous people, but it also inevitably directs the authorities' crosshairs to me or someone in the lab for fabricating results. Signing this is not an option, but I can't afford to be fired before my work at Pentastar is complete. Dave has given me no choice but to expedite his sowing.

Planning a sowing is more a question of timing and location than anything else. In an age of low-cost digital surveillance, the latter is supremely important. I pace to my office window and look out over the vast maze of cement, steel, and glass. In the city, the odds of doing anything outside my apartment without being recorded are probably worse than getting struck by lightning. Every cell phone, doorbell, dash cam, drone, streetlamp, and traffic signal form a global network of eyes, always watching, never forgetting. Unfortunately, attempting a second sowing in this building will draw too much attention to Pentastar and myself, so it can't happen here.

All cities have blind spots, and Port Ellis is no exception. The further from downtown I go, the easier it is to find those places, but luring Dave to the shipyards, or the industrial park, or the Cascade Mountains without sounding his internal alarm would be impossible. Even if it worked, it would leave a trail leading that bloodhound Drake straight back to my red hands. With Milburn Tower crossed off the list and without knowing Dave's plans for the evening, the only predictable opportunity before his ultimatum expires will be tonight, at his home.

The office PA system crackles to life and Jan's velvety voice floods the office.

"Due to today's tragic events, I have authorized early release for the office. Please take the rest of the day off to mourn and decompress. We are providing counselling services free of charge for anyone who wants to stay and talk or make arrangements to do so at a later time. If you require additional time off, please visit with your supervisor for approval."

Profiteering aside, Jan genuinely cares about her people. In that way, and that way only, she and Dave are decent leaders. Unfortunately, like Jim Jones they are leading their people down a path to death and damnation. They wield their charisma like a weapon, incising conscience from spirit and soul from body.

Dave's tenure comes to an end tonight.

CHAPTER FOUR

Even Nephilim like leaving work early; some might say we especially do. We crave escape and find our bliss in solitude, making us introverts by human standards. Early release frees me from the stagnant stench of my office, the oppressive atmosphere of these halls, and the scrutinous overwatch of my "superiors." As I exit the ground floor of the building, the warmth of the midday sun permeates my stony countenance. The strident squawks of hungry seagulls echo off the concrete cliffs as they dive to snatch the bits of hot dog bun that have fallen near the vendor's cart. The rotund man tries to shoo them away, and it works for a few seconds before their courage is renewed. Behind me, the soothing rustle of the potted plants whispers my name, moved by a delicate breeze that weaves through my follicles. I blink slowly, basking in the fleeting serenity.

The moment is shattered as a shoulder jabs into the middle of my back and a car horn bawls abrasively before a stream of obscenity spews from its driver's mouth. I observe the parade of fabric and flesh and take note as they shove and grind past their fellow beings like cattle in a stockyard. If not for humanity, the earth would be flawless.

The fantasy of an entire planet, or even a small community, of my own kind has flitted around my mind on many occasions. We are a beautiful, honest, and stewarding race truly deserving of the splendor of this place. Alas, we must share it with mankind and suffer their company as they squander this most precious gift. They take it for granted, too preoccupied with acquiring money and manmade creations to take the time to appreciate creation around them.

I weave through the flow of livestock toward the curb and hail the approaching taxi. It slows to a stop as a hand stretches into my peripheral vision and a tall, slender woman in a long gray skirt suit steps into view. Her fingers wrap gracefully around the cab's door handle as the same gentle breeze that sways the potted foliage tosses and flips her shoulder-length sable hair to the side. With honest blue eyes and a gentle expression, she is unlike any woman I've seen. None of this excuses the fact that she's taking my taxi.

I clear my throat with a hearty "Ahem," but she doesn't notice as she pulls the cab door open and prepares to sit. "Excuse me"—she looks my direction—"I hailed that cab."

"I did too," she replies with a pleasant, coy grin.

The driver rolls down the front passenger window, so I lean lower to see his face.

"I pulled over for her, buddy. I didn't even see you," the driver says, setting the record straight. I turn back to face the majestic creature to my left.

"I stand corrected. My apologies, I didn't realize. I'll catch the next one. Have a nice day," I say with a friendly smile and half-wave. The woman hesitates for a moment before returning the sentiment. A magnificent perfume of fairness and virtue flows into my nostrils, resting gently against my olfactory receptors. Her elegant neck lowers her head into the car before she pulls the door shut and jets away.

An unnatural amalgam of sensations darts through my body as I watch the taxi dissolve into traffic. The warmth of hope and the exhilaration of beauty swirl with the icy chill of mystery and fear. The resulting force of nature bombards my mind with a debris field of questions and fragmented thoughts. Who is she?

Does she work here? Will I ever see her again? Was she wearing a ring? More than any of that, I want to know why I feel this way. Before this moment I had never met a human in which I detected so much light. There has never been a person that elicited such a positive emotional response. Focusing on Dave's sowing and the greater purpose of my existence suddenly feels like a chore that diminishes my prospects for personal happiness. I have never felt more…human.

I reach to hail another cab but the nearest one is a couple blocks and traffic lights away. I'll be left here to wrestle with my thoughts a few minutes longer. It crosses my mind that, however improbable, this woman may have dropped a clue to her identity, a proverbial glass slipper. While I don't believe in fairy tales, my mother read them to me as a boy, which apparently planted a seed in my heart that's now blossoming into delusion.

I replay the brief memory, amplifying every detail, searching for a nametag, a company logo, anything to direct my analysis. Why didn't I ask for her name or ask if she works here? Listen to me. I sound like a twitterpated, pubescent human. Despite my chagrin, I continue to discreetly check my surroundings, scanning for some hint of her identity.

This leads to the curious but unrelated discovery that I'm being watched. Parked against the curb about a hundred feet to my left is a vehicle whose driver appears to have a special interest in me. I walk back toward Milburn Tower's glass entrance and pretend to read one of the notices next to the door. A casual glance his way confirms that the man is indeed watching me quite intently.

There exists a fine line between vigilance and paranoia, the operative difference being that paranoia is a psychological and emotional state while vigilance is a state of mind. Vigilance demands that I notice the signs when they're real while paranoia drives me to notice them when they're not. As the nearest traffic light turns green, I quickly scoot back down to the street, hail my ride, and waste no time leaping in.

The driver looks back, startled, before asking, "Where to, friend?" with a stout Armenian accent and a smile.

"Uh, can you just drive straight for a couple blocks?"

"Sure, friend. I go wherever you want."

"Thank you"—I lean forward to read his name plate—"Alex."

"No problem," he assures, throwing the gear shift to drive. Alex pulls into the lane and begins to zip ahead before slowing to a stop. The traffic light above burns bright red and gives the slight impression that it's chosen the side of my watcher, who still hasn't pulled away from the curb but now has plenty of time. Then, as we start rolling again, the navy-blue Taurus with dark tinted windows jerks into the lane three cars behind us. It's time for a test.

"Alex."

"Yes, friend?"

"Could you please go straight for one more block, then pretend to make a left turn at the next intersection?"

"Of course, happy to," he says compliantly. "Uh, but just to understand, how do I pretend to turn?"

"When we get close to the intersection, hit your turn signal and move into the turn lane. Slow down, stop if you have to, but don't turn. Then look for an opportunity to get back in this lane and go straight."

Alex nods an uneasy nod and says, "Okay, friend. You the boss."

The tick-tock of the turn signal fills the otherwise silent cab as we veer left and begin breaking. Now just one car behind, the

Taurus changes lanes as well, and as the arrow turns yellow, Alex signals right and finds an opening to go straight.

"That's perfect, Alex. Nicely done," I praise as he slides between a yellow cab and a black Cadillac.

"Thank you, my friend."

A few seconds later, the blue sedan follows suit.

Whoever's behind the wheel of that car is definitely following me, and though there are plenty of reasons why that might be, all of them are bad news. My past is a trail of suicide with the occasional, dramatic recovery, but those footprints have been washed away with the tide. My past is an uncharted constellation of nightmares in which I am the bogeyman. No one affected by my work even knows I exist. No, this person is not tailing me for the sowings of old. This person is tailing me because of my work at Pentastar Pharmaceuticals, and I need to lose him.

"Alex, at this next intersection, can you approach slowly until the light turns yellow, then zip through before red?"

"Sure."

Alex is getting less talkative as he wonders what he's gotten into. He takes his foot off the gas and coasts to the intersection, pushed from behind by honking horns and the metaphysical power of road rage. When the light goes yellow he floors it, slipping through just before red. The Cadillac behind us runs the red, then whips into the adjacent lane and passes us on the right, waving a stiff middle finger on the way by. The blue Taurus got nabbed at the light and now sits behind a Swamp Suckers Pool Service van, their ridiculous winking gator emblazoned on the hood. Distracted by the angry bird to our right, I almost miss the Taurus using the turn lane to pass the pool cleaner's van, then brazenly blow through the cross traffic at Nichols Street.

Another car merges between us and the Taurus, but it's clear Alex has noticed them.

"I watched in the mirror since you made your strange request, friend," Alex says, looking at me in the rearview mirror. "That blue car made every move. Who follows you?"

"I have no idea. He was watching me from the curb back where you picked me up."

"Want me to call cops?" he offers.

"No, I'll think of something. Just keep going straight, please."

I don't know what I'm dealing with yet and don't need to see the police again today. The light turns green, and Alex accelerates forward then suddenly slams on the brakes, pressing me into the back of the front seat. As I collect myself, Alex pops open his door and jumps into the street. He walks to the back of the taxi as the driver behind angrily honks their horn.

With one more step he gains a clear view of the blue sedan's driver. He points his index finger sharply at the man's face before pulling it across his own throat. With both hands he mimes removing his own head and then aggressively drop kicking it. A final pause punctuated with a menacing glare drives his point home. The blue sedan pulls around our stopped vehicles and speeds past.

Alex returns to the car and sits with a triumphant plop.

"There, problem fixed," he says with a chuckle. "Now friend, where to?"

I smile and shake my head before saying, "Comstock, please."

"Oh, nice neighborhood. You live there?"

"No, I'm going to see someone," I reply.

"You are going to do business?" Alex pries.

"Something like that."

"Oh, you are mysterious, my friend," he exclaims with a delighted hoot. "I love this job!"

"I like you, Alex, and coming from me that is a tremendous compliment. What you did back there was as courageous as it was outrageous. I sincerely thank you."

"What are friends for, sir?"

"You're absolutely right. You've been a big help. Did you happen to notice anything identifiable about him?"

"Not really. He looked like Juggernaut, you know? That was only thing."

"What do you mean, Juggernaut?"

He has a belly laugh at my expense and says, "You don't get out much, do you? Juggernaut, like from X-Men. There was internet video. 'I'm the Juggernaut, bitch.'"

"I don't know what any of that means, but thanks again, Alex. Now, if you don't mind, I need to do some thinking while we drive."

"Say no more, friend."

Between downtown Port Ellis and the swanky, foothill neighborhoods that cozy up to the Cascades lies a moat of projects and row houses. Forty feet off the ground, the interstate bridges the chasm of the disadvantaged like a jetway for the wealthy, ferrying them from their heavenly homes to their opulent offices and back. If not for the inconveniently located H.R. Donaldson International Airport, there'd be no reason for them to ever wade into the purgatory of the masses. Even then, most of Comstock's residents fly out of the nearby regional airport on private or chartered planes.

It's easy for me to forget that my genetic code is a mix of angel *and* human DNA. There is a part of me that is very much human, but I've spent my entire life ignoring and suppressing it. On the rare occasions when it has managed to poke through,

I've fought to rid myself of its weakness. The effect of that mystifying woman and Alex's protective actions have emboldened my human side, and for the first time in my life, I am fully aware of my dual nature. It couldn't have come at a worse time.

I said before that the ancient tales of my people are not entirely accurate. It is true that we are part angel and part human, but this did not come about through reproduction between angels and women. That's not to say that Nephilim don't engage in sex with humans. We have, but not as an avenue for reproduction, because we're not compatible in that way. It was deemed necessary to create a hybrid race capable of living covertly amongst humans and tasked as messengers of truth, like their angelic ancestors. We are the product of careful engineering, designed to bridge the gap between deity and mankind.

If I had time, I'd leave town for the night to clear my head. A wide-open space away from people would work well to reset my mind. As it is, I'll have to subdue these thoughts through sheer willpower so I can formulate a plan for Dave's sowing.

"Sorry to interrupt, friend, but do you have address for your destination?" Alex politely inquires.

"No need to apologize, Alex. There is a park and playground at the corner of Heritage Lane and Swanson Street. Can you just drop me there?"

"Of course. We will be there in ten minutes."

"Thank you," I reply as I retreat back into my mind.

Predominantly, my life has been spent in solitude, and I prefer it that way. If not for my calling as a guardian of truth, I would avoid all interaction with human beings. Like a birth defect, I'm bombarded by a neurotic compulsion to see truth flourish. Outwardly I may appear human but, as far as I'm concerned, that is the extent of my humanity. I have a mission, a higher calling, that precedes all else, including my own happiness. And with that reminder, at least for now, I have pushed away any notion of love, earthly pleasures, and humanly living.

Another five minutes pass and we pull up to the small neighborhood park only a half-mile from Dave's house. At the eastern limit of the metro Port Ellis area, nestled against the foothills of the Cascades, is a scenic neighborhood complete with thirty-six holes of golf, a racquet club, and a well-appointed community center. Given the wealth in this neighborhood, one might rightfully expect a far more robust park than this—a sandbox, swing set, slide, and backyard-quality castle playground. But, of course, most of these homes have theater rooms, basement bowling alleys, and swimming pools to keep everyone entertained.

Alex brings the vehicle to a stop and turns to face me. "Time to pay, my friend."

I retrieve my cash and round his rate up to the next ten.

"Alex, keep doing what you're doing. You're one of very few good ones. Thank you."

"There are more of us than you think. I hope to see you again, Mr…" he says, dragging out the end for me to finish.

"Just call me Ted."

"Mr. Ted. It's been nice to meet you. Take my card and call whenever you need ride." He searches his pockets before producing a business card that was obviously designed on his home computer. "Best of luck with whatever you do."

"You as well, Alex. Take care and stay honest!"

With that, I slide out of the cab and Alex drives off, giving a farewell wave from his window. I survey the immaculate, viridescent grounds. It's quiet here. The red maple trees that line the perimeter sway in the shifty sea breeze that's now unobstructed by columns of concrete and steel. The evenly cut blades of grass appear uniform in size, shape, and vibrant hue. Low above the horizon, from southeast to southwest, the strange moon drifts stealthily through the brilliant blue sky. With little imagination I could lie on this lush lawn facing that blue expanse with the candy-red trees all around, the mountain peaks to the east, and the daytime moon lurking through the southern sky and imagine I'm on a faraway planet. One inhabited solely by my own species. It has long been my one indulgence of imagination to stare up at the night moon with its radiant continents and murky oceans and imagine it is such a planet. It's an escape that tempts me frequently these days, but one I can only enjoy sparingly. Regardless, this is truly a serene respite from the chaos of the city and will provide the space I need to think through the next ten hours.

Thanks to Joel, I know where Dave lives, and I expect him to return home sometime this evening. I know he has a wife who may or may not be home, and I can also safely assume he has a monitored security system. Passive video surveillance alone will be onerous to evade, but real-time monitored service with a panic button and cloud storage takes meticulous planning to work around—or the right to be on the premises. Maybe the key is not to evade surveillance so much as to find a legitimate reason to be there. Dave and I are coworkers and it wouldn't be out of the ordinary for me to stop by for a visit. But if he turns up dead and I was his last visitor, as the security footage will show, I might as well have sown him back at Pentastar.

The giggling of children joins the soft flapping of leaves and draws my attention to two young boys, twins by the look of it, one trying to drag the other to the ground by the shirt collar. Their mother watches on from a nearby bench, at first absorbed in their antics, then staring at her open palms as if to question her usefulness. She's old enough to be their grandmother, and rather than invigorating her with their youthful energy, they're siphoning her dry like a reserve fuel tank. I turn away and again try to concentrate on Dave, but their jubilant, infectious laughter invades my thoughts. With no siblings and intense Nephilim parents, I never really played as a child, and I can't say I've ever experienced that innocent joy. Even when my mother read me bedtime stories it was meant to indoctrinate me into nobility and virtue, not fill my head with whimsical ideas about love and happy endings. I was programmed from a young age to slay the dragons of the world, not for true love's kiss, but simply because it is the right thing to do. Settling into my headspace, my musings continue until I realize how badly I've lost track of time.

I don't have time for this! If I can't focus, this operation will be a total failure. Pentastar will get away with wrecking lives, the victims will see no justice, I could end up in jail or, worse still, it could lead to the compromise of my entire species.

"Teddy!"

The woman's voice sends a jolt down my spine. I train my eyes on her, but she's not looking at me. The boys' play is turning rough and she's completely focused on them.

"Teddy, Franky, stop it!" she hollers as the boys wrestle and grunt on the ground.

She stands from the bench and trots over to separate them, but as she approaches, they disengage and scamper away from her. They snicker as the woman desperately orders them to stop, then notice me and veer in my direction. Their jouncing blonde heads and grins full of tiny teeth are equally playful and impish, but there's nothing fun about this for their dispirited mother in sluggish pursuit. I squat down as the boys approach and spread my arms wide to prevent them from entering the road behind me. They grab hold and position my arms like guardrails to keep the woman away.

"BOYS, get over here," she shouts. "I'm so sorry, sir. I'm hopelessly outmatched."

She slides her hand up her forehead to sweep back the strands of gray-brown hair that have escaped her messy bun. She's not young but not old either, nor is she fat or skinny. Wearing leggings and an oversized sweater in this neighborhood makes her look like hired help, but the five-carat diamond on her finger suggests she's right where she belongs.

"It sure seems that way. Are they twins?" I ask, looking down at the kids who are still holding onto me. I raise my gaze to the woman's face and detect an abnormally harrowed subtext in her expression. Yes, she's overwhelmed by these boys, but that's not why she teeters on the edge of tears.

"Yes, they're twin four-year-olds. God save me."

"Boys, go back to your mother," I say, using my arms to tow them in her direction. The boys unlatch from my arms and hop like bunnies back to her.

"Oh, I'm not their mother; I'm their aunt. I help my sister with childcare while she works."

"That's very generous of you. I'm sure these boys are in good hands!" Though this sounds like flattery, her compassionate nature and motherly love for the boys is readily apparent. However frazzled she may feel, those kids are well-off in her care.

Bluntly, one of the twins says, "You're really tall!"

"Are you a giant?" the other one asks.

"People used to think so," I respond. "What do you think?"

Both boys issue big smiles and nod vigorously.

"Boys, what did I tell you about saying things like that?" she asks rhetorically. She looks up to me and says, "I appreciate the compliment, but my husband is the one with the golden touch. The boys adore him so much." She pauses as a lump lodges in her throat. "He's really stepped up since their dad passed away," she says while running her fingers through the boys' thick yellow curls.

"I'm very sorry to hear about their father. It's so important for young men to have strong male mentors. I commend your husband for stepping up."

"He's a complicated man, but he's a good husband and is turning into an awesome uncle. I don't know what I'd do—what these boys would do—without him," she says with a teary smile that twists quickly into a frown. "But he just had a close friend commit suicide at work today and I'm worried how it's going to affect him."

My pulse quickens and plays through my eardrums, my abdomen an acrobatic circus. A piñata of thoughts bursts, dumping more than my mind can process. I sift through in a scramble to find a suitable response, but the confusion has already found its way to my face and she's noticed.

"Oh my God, I'm sorry. That's too much information." She recoils at my horrified look. "I always do this. I'm so sorry. I've just had too much on my mind and no one to talk to. Dave works a lot and he's not even coming home early today after everything that's happened." The tears are now streaming down her cheeks.

"It's okay, really, I understand." It seems impossible that any situation could be more awkward than this. Not only is a total stranger breaking down to me, but she's the wife of my next target.

"I assume that Dave is your husband."

"Yes," she snivels. "Going on twenty-six years this November. Wow, I guess that's next month, isn't it?"

"I'm sure that Dave knows what he can handle. Give him time and space to process and then be there for him when he's ready to open up."

"You're right. That's quite good advice, thanks." After a short pause she says, "I just realized I never asked for your name."

"You can call me Theo," I deliberately reply. Theodonis, my full name, is traditional Nephilim and too conspicuous for public use. Ted and Theo are both suitable, forgettable nicknames, and I don't want Dave to know I was here. "And you are?"

"Bridgette," she answers meekly.

"Well, Bridgette, it is very nice to meet you and these rambunctious boys!"

"It's nice to meet you too, Theo."

"I don't mean to run off prematurely, but it's just dawned on me that I left some unfinished business back at the office. I really need to get going. Are you going to be okay?"

"Oh yeah," she says with a brave face. "We'll be fine, but didn't you just get here in a cab?"

"I did. I was going to meet a coworker here, but we may just have to reschedule."

"Well, alright then. You have a blessed day, Theo."

"Thanks. You too, Bridgette."

As she and the twins walk back toward the playground, I rifle through my pockets for Alex's card. The boys' voices are fading but I can still hear them ask why she is sad. The tender empathy of children is one of humanity's most endearing qualities.

Such an unlikely meeting has stirred a warning in my spirit. The tranquility that reassured me about Joel's sowing has vanished. This feels like a sign. Beyond that, when I shook Bridgette's hand and looked into her broken eyes, I saw a lifetime of tragedy and pain. She and those kids have been through too much for me to sow Dave and risk a suicidal outcome.

I need to get to Dave before he returns home. For the first time in my life, I have to make sowing someone my backup plan. I remain faithful in my commitment to truth, but perhaps there's another way to show him the truth. Tonight, I will try a new, more human approach.

CHAPTER FIVE

Alex is still nearby and responds quickly to my call for a journey back to the city that's very different from the drive out to Comstock. Removing wicked people from the world may be an improvement in the lives of those who don't know them, but it can still be devastating for the family and friends left behind. This time I've actually met one of them, and it's challenged me with new doubts about the morality of my mission and my methods. I stew quietly with the hope that Dave will make the right decision for Bridgette and the boys. Verbal confrontation: such an approach would not typically suffice, but my sincere desire is for Dave to be the exception.

Alex pulls to the curb and we share another warm farewell. Outside, I stand at the base of Milburn Tower staring up to where Joel's end began. This time each evening, the tower's top two floors are set ablaze by the sunset's final rays. It is the lighthouse of Port Ellis, but certainly no beacon of hope. I don't want to confront Dave inside this building. The offices that loom overhead are his territory and this confrontation will be most effective if held in a public, neutral place. The presence of witnesses will delay Dave's volatility and provide leverage if he's unwilling to see reason.

All around me the bustle becomes a saunter. Businessmen and women with ties loosened, shirts untucked, and blazers slung over their arms no longer check their watches with weary eyes. The enchantment of twilight slows the pulse of the city. Radiant oranges, pinks, and purples paint the blue sky and bring the concrete and glass to life. The streetlights' soft glow marks the onset of their nightly battle against the darkness. Chaos and clamor dull to a soothing hum, the overture of the urban lullaby.

Despite the workday winding down, the budding social scene maintains the metro movement. Instead of hurrying to meet deadlines, people stroll leisurely down the sidewalk on their way to restaurants and bars, galleries and shows. Their smiles and laughter steep the atmosphere in joy and enthusiasm for life. Inviting Dave for a drink at The Downspout could create the disarming setting I need to break through to him. I dial Dave and plan my words in a way that I know will grab his attention. Three rings later, I'm greeted dryly by his voicemail.

"You've reached the voicemail of Dave McConnell. Leave me a message and I'll be in touch as soon as possible."

"Dave, it's Ted. We have a problem. Meet me at The Downspout as soon as you can."

I hang up and drop my phone back into my pocket. A glance up to the Pentastar offices confirms that the lights are still on, but I'd be surprised if they ever get turned off. Dave's work hours regularly exceed those of the single employees, but it's hard to imagine him plugging away at his to-do list on an evening like this. Then again, most people gladly welcome any distraction from grief and fear. It would make sense for Dave to self-medicate with more work.

I can't imagine more time in the office being therapeutic. Growing up, my parents shared all the responsibilities on our small family farm and took turns doing everything whenever the other was drawn away for a sowing. My mom or my dad would be gone for a couple days—never longer than a week—and would return revitalized. Nephilim eat about half as much as humans, so the farm was able to sustain our family without much trouble, but there were times when Dad took the occasional carpentry job and Mom sold some of our harvest at the local farmer's market to get cash for the things our farm couldn't produce. No matter what my parents were busy with, it was only after a sowing that they seemed to thrive and the same is true of me. It's only by doing that thing I was born to do, the thing that fulfills my purpose and makes an impact, that I can overcome any loss, any pain, any crisis. That is Nephilim medicine. That is my therapy. It's how I survived my parents' death.

I turn and begin the three-block walk that will take me past some of the finest restaurants in the city. Gemini Bistro, Palace Square, Cape—the people who dine at these establishments are more than happy to pay hundreds of dollars for a single meal. The food is skillfully prepared by highly trained chefs, the wine is aged for decades, and the customer service is unrivaled, but in a world stricken with so much poverty and hunger this lifestyle seems grotesque to me.

Large glass windows give me a glimpse into a fantasy that most people would sell their souls to obtain. Beautiful people with sharp jaws, flawless teeth, and sculpted noses lounge in trendy designer clothes to enjoy a lavish meal—one of thousands they will eat in their carefree lives. Who wouldn't want such a perfect existence? It's no wonder people buy the lie. But on the other side of that glass, their clothes are uncomfortable, they're stressed by the impossible expectations of their stratum, and they still don't like their noses.

Those people think that a new vacation home in British Columbia, the latest model of their luxury coupe, or that next surgery is the only thing that stands between them and enlightenment. What they don't know is that they drift nearer to a black hole with each extravagant purchase and otherworldly experience. Closer than most to having everything they dreamed of, they feel emptier than ever. All human beings spend their lives trying to fill the same void and find fulfillment. The more earthly things that fail to deliver on the promise of lasting happiness, the less hope they have of ever being made whole. The world has offered them everything, but their emptiness remains.

One block left to The Downspout and the sun has almost completed its descent below the horizon. Soon the dome of night will seal off the city, inviting the insects and rodents to fill the streets. The appeal of this block takes a sharp nosedive from the previous two. It's fascinating that a single street—Folsom Street in this case—can form an invisible barrier between classes. Despite being on the other side of the tracks, The Downspout has become a favorite of Dave's and several other Pentastar employees.

It's not a dive bar, but it's the most blue collar stop you'll ever see a downtown suit visit. Whenever he's around the working-class employees, Dave talks proudly about being raised by a steeler who taught him how to work hard and how to play hard. I doubt his father, if he were still alive, would approve of the way Dave has handled the Fosillix trial so far. My phone chimes in my pocket and I slide it out enough to see the name.

"Speak of the devil," I quietly quip to myself.

Dave's text reads, *I'll see you there in fifteen minutes. This better be important.*

A couple of storefronts away I can already smell the fatty meat sizzling on the grill. The atmosphere is different here. It's a strange, bipolar brew of motivation and surrender. People want the best life possible, the life they see just one block away, but their subjugation stands in the way. Unwilling to compromise their values in order to gain the world, they yield to the output of an honest day's work. With rare exceptions, principles and fortune are mutually exclusive.

I elect to sit on the bench outside the bar as I wait for Dave. The relative quiet allows me to collect my thoughts while I plan a deliberate appeal to Dave's sensibilities. He seems to genuinely care for Bridgette, which sadly can't be said of all husbands, so appealing to her best interests may get him partway there. If he cares at all about those boys he'll need to avoid prison, which may prove impossible without a miracle transformation. These are good starting points, but it will take something more to convince Dave to change his ways and forsake his career.

A black town car slides up to the curb.

"What are you doing out here?" Dave asks as he emerges from the back seat. "You should be three drinks deep by now." Before I can respond, he leans back in to address the driver, saying, "Don't wait here. I'll call you when I'm ready."

"I wanted a clear mind and it's too chaotic in there," I say, gesturing toward the red metal door that does little to muffle the bedlam inside.

"Well, I need a drink. Let's go," he orders with a head tilt.

I stand from the bench and straighten my pants, casually confirming that my vial of blood is still in my pocket where I left it. *Just in case.* Dave is already two steps ahead and holds the door with an, "After you."

The sound of music and voices escapes through the opening like air from an untied balloon. Stale sweat, motor oil, and cheese greet me as I cross the threshold. Maybe this is more of a dive bar than I remember. His love for this place certainly paints Dave in a curious light.

The door closes loudly behind me, drawing looks from around the room. I offer a friendly nod of apology then look over my shoulder toward Dave.

Dave leans forward and half-shouts, "I'm gonna get my drink," then veers toward the bar.

I scan the room and spot a booth toward the back that'll give us some privacy and put some distance between us and the blaring speakers. This won't be a conversation for the general public.

"I'll be back there in that booth," I yell and point.

Gliding, bumping, and twisting, I make my way across the crowded floor to the booth and slide into the seat. Dave is propped on the bar, chatting with the bartender and a couple of nearby customers. They all burst out in laughter and Dave pats them on the back before he scoops up his drink and heads my direction. I can't help but wonder if they'd still like him if they knew his secrets. They'd probably like him more. His sins would make them feel better about their own.

Dave reaches the table and slides into the seat across from me. He stares at the brown bottle in his hand, presses it to his lips for a few slugs, and slowly places it back on the table. He raises his eyes from the table to meet mine.

"So, what's this about, Ted?"

"This is about you," I respond, doing my best to adopt the tone of a concerned friend.

"What about me?"

"I'm worried about the path that you're traveling. It won't end well."

"What the hell is this, Ted, an intervention?" he scoffs irritably. "If this is why you dragged me down here, you're a bigger idiot than I thought!"

"Dave, I'm trying to help you. You don't have to go down with the ship. There's a mountain of damning evidence piling up at Pentastar and the lawsuit with the Fosillix patients is going to bring it all to light. The truth always comes out."

"I don't have anything to hide, Ted. I did my job and I did it so that those patients' kids won't have to suffer from their parent's awful condition," he righteously professes.

He tips his bottle high and sucks down several ounces before pounding it down to the table. I study his face as he winds up to regurgitate more of the lies that help him sleep.

"Those people are heroes for being brave enough to take the risk. They knew what they were getting into when they signed the waiver. I'm a hero too for persevering through their tragedy and continuing our work for a cure!" he passionately spits. "My dad had early onset Alzheimer's for God's sake. He forgot who I was before I even made it down the aisle."

That's yet another thing I didn't know about Dave. HIPAA makes family medical history especially hard to research. Still, Dave's crooked halo glows like a neon bar sign as his lies of self-preservation and personal enrichment morph into hollow hymns of glory and virtue.

He continues, "You know what your problem is? You're weak. You don't have the balls to push through this pain for the greater good. People get hurt and your heart bleeds and you give up, making their death meaningless!"

He's hit full stride now. Slowly he rises from his seat as if looming over me will increase the validity of his argument. I spread my arms out across the back of my chair and watch with one raised eyebrow as Dave completes his application for sainthood.

"The world needs more people like me. I see the bigger picture and I don't let little setbacks derail progress. I carry the burdens of the masses on my shoulders as I try my damnedest to help the sick and needy."

I slowly stand from my seat. Even without extending to full Nephilim height, I'm eight inches taller than Dave. He looks up at me and offers a momentary silence.

"Sit down, David," I demand slowly and calmly with a slightly deeper voice than he's used to hearing. He sinks down into the booth and sweeps the room to see how much attention we've drawn. Several people awkwardly look at their food to avoid making eye contact.

I drop down onto my seat and ask him with a sigh, "Are you done?"

"Ted, all I'm trying to say is that you and the people who see this stuff from your perspective don't get it. I always end up defending myself because no one on either side of this understands the pressure," says Dave with a quick hand signal to the bartender.

He grabs the bottle from the table and drains what's left in a single gulp. He looks at me earnestly and says, "When I started at Pentastar I really wanted to make a difference. It was my dream to be a part of curing cancer or even the damn common cold. Two decades later and it's all about profit margins, minimizing losses, and covering our asses."

"Dave, I believe you, but it's not that simple. How do you think those decades-old good intentions hold up in a courtroom when dozens of sick people and the families of dead patients take the stand against you in your designer suit?" I ask. "You will lose, you will be disgraced, and you will probably get locked up."

The bartender delivers Dave's second round to the table. He gives me a quick look before turning back to Dave and asking, "You guys all good here? Looked like it was getting a little heated."

"Yeah, Matt, we're good. Thanks for the drink," Dave replies.

Matt walks away and I continue, "Dave, you have to get ahead of this and do the right thing. Tell the truth before it's too late. Do you really think the board and Jan are going to have your back and risk the downfall of the whole company? When the axe drops, they'll all be pointing the finger at you. You'll be the bad apple that spoiled the bunch. At least, that's how the headlines will read."

Dave sips his fresh beer. His contemplative silence births renewed hope that he can change. If Dave McConnell can change, there is hope for the rest of Pentastar.

"Nope. I'm not doing that," he blurts suddenly.

"Dave, don't be a fool. Listen to reason," I counsel.

"No. The company's lawyers have this whole thing covered. I've worked too hard to have my career end that way."

"The company's lawyers will lose their biggest client if Pentastar goes down. You are the easy out, Dave."

"There are emails and memos from Jan and the board of directors documenting their marching orders to me. I'm not the mastermind behind this. If anything, that proves I'm a puppet just like Joel."

"Dave…"

"I said no!" he cuts me off curtly. Dave takes another swig from his drink, then pushes up from the table. "I gotta piss."

He walks off, rounding the corner to the bathroom as my hand immediately finds the vial in my pocket. I sit, transfixed on the open beer across the table. While not totally at peace, much of my resolve for Dave's sowing has returned. If he is unwilling to choose the truth, I have no choice.

One drop of condensation absorbs another before cascading down the side of the glass bottle and splatting on the table. The image of Joel's body falling along the side of Milburn Tower flashes through my mind. An uncharacteristic impulse drives my arm to remove the vial, pop the cork, and tap a drop into Dave's beer.

Before I can even replug the vial, regret invades my skin. I've acted rashly and that's not the way my parents taught me to do this sacred job. Dave could still make the right choice. More so, what happens when he passes out cold for an hour in a crowded bar? I have to get rid of his drink! As I reach across the table, Dave's figure enters the corner of my eye.

"That's mine. Get your own."

In an act of convenient ineptitude, my arm clumsily recoils, tipping the bottle to its side. I stand to grab napkins and Dave retrieves his bottle.

"Damnit, Ted. Lately you're more trouble than you're worth!"

My head turns to Dave just in time to watch him take a drink. His face turns sour as he grimaces and spits the mouthful back into the bottle.

"Gross, it's already warm," he explains. "I wasn't even gone two minutes."

I say nothing and continue cleaning the spill. Dave stomps off to the bar where Matt retrieves the bottle from him and drops it into the trash. Above the noise I hear Dave's booming voice say, "And this time, give me one from the fridge!"

I can't help but wonder if any of that drink made it down his throat. A single, concentrated drop is strong enough to cause immediate unconsciousness but I have yet to discover the effect of a miniscule exposure. Will there be a delayed effect, a diminished effect, or no effect at all? So far, Dave seems fine and, with any luck, he'll stay that way.

Dave arrives back at the booth and hoists his beer above the table as he slumps heavily in the seat. He looks at me with a crooked head and irked brows. After another long slug, he sets his beer on the slightly sticky table and focuses his gaze on me.

"Where were we?" he asks.

"You had just refused to do the right thing."

"Ted, when this whole thing blows over, history will remember us as the farsighted trailblazers who weathered the storm and overcame controversy. If we stop now, we'll just be remembered as failures."

"The more often you repeat those lies, the more obvious it becomes that you don't truly believe them. You were warned that people would die, you withheld that information from trial patients, and patients died."

"I was ordered to withhold that information. Jan told me to press ahead with the trial or I was a goner. Now I'm caught in the middle and it's too late. The only way to salvage this fiasco is to press on and hope we can put a stable product on pharmacy shelves."

Dave's version of events is eroding my confidence in this entire process. It's not that he's innocent—he knew he was crossing a line when he followed those orders—but his eye contact is intense, his tone is resolved, and his posture is consistent; he's telling the truth, or at least he believes what he's saying. I need to grab his attention and increase the stakes. His lack of total responsibility for the drug trial fuels my desire to see his redemption.

"If you don't put a stop to this now, Dave, the only time you'll get with Bridgette and the twins will be spent talking through plexiglass."

"Have a little faith, Ted. You're such a pessim…" he trails off. The gears behind his face begin to turn as he processes my words. "How do you know about the twins?"

I deepen my voice to a soft rumble and draw Dave into my gravity. The fluorescent bar lights by our table gently flicker. Confusion turns to nervousness as he questions his senses.

"How I know about them doesn't matter. If you value your relationship with them, you will make the right decision now," I press with finality.

Dave's breathing hastens and fine droplets of sweat appear on his skin. He searches for something on the table, then the seat, then on his person. Clearly agitated, he yanks his arms out of his suitcoat sleeves and tosses the jacket to the wall.

Standing as he removes his tie and undoes his top shirt button, he offers a breathy, "I need some air. I don't feel right."

He stumbles across the crowded room, pinballing off of tables and people along the way, and barges through the door. Numerous possibilities enter my mind, all of them catastrophic. My gravest concern is that he consumed the seed and is having an unprecedented reaction. Such a possibility is especially disastrous since I sensed him opening up to the idea of confession.

After this morning's events, I don't want to be too close to Dave if something happens, but it's too late for that. Everyone in the bar has seen us together and witnessed our argument. It's best that I check on Dave and try to prevent the inevitable.

I slide out of the booth and politely weave through the crowd. Before exiting, I stop and shout to the bartender that we'll be back.

My hand touches the door just as the crack of a gunshot penetrates the brick walls of the bar. My pulse quickens, vibrating my entire body. I punch the door open and scan the sidewalk for Dave, but there's no sign of him.

Remembering the alleyway next to the bar, I take off in that direction. As I round the corner, I'm stopped in my tracks by the grisly sight of Dave, back to the wall and lying on his side in a rapidly expanding puddle of blood. Light from the far end of the alley gleams off the nickel revolver resting just inches from his hand as the oozing scarlet engulfs its silhouette.

CHAPTER SIX

The bar's patrons gather behind me, gawking at the morbid scene and mumbling in horror. I carefully approach Dave, tiptoeing around the crime scene, and feel for a pulse that I know I won't find. I look back toward the onlookers and see Matt approaching with his phone to his ear.

He motions my direction and asks, "Is there a pulse?!"

I shake my head no as I crouch by Dave's side, eyes filling with tears that I blink hard to hold back. Sometime later this evening, an officer will arrive at the door of Bridgette McConnell's house. This officer will knock not with the startling force of a battering ram, but with a tenderness that's far more frightening. Bridgette will open the door and see no officer at all, but a courier of the grim reaper himself, come to deliver secondhand death. Her existence will shrivel to a skeleton of its former beauty and those boys will once again be fatherless. Dave's hand twitches slightly and I lean back in to check his pulse but there's still nothing.

"There's no pulse," Matt tells the operator. He nods and offers several yes and no answers. Angling the phone away from his face, he says, "The police are on the way," then returns his attention to the operator.

This isn't my first time being this close to death. When devoid of animation, the human form is unsettling. Sunken cheeks and nebulous orbs replace the trademark features we are conditioned to recognize. Death never quite feels real because the dead don't bear the likeness of the souls they once carried.

As I look soberly upon what remains of Dave, death is different than I remember. The color has yet to fully leave his face. He sleeps a dreamer's sleep, haunted by a never-ending nightmare. If not for the exposed contents of his skull, I might expect him to lurch awake at any moment. He'd look at me through tearful eyes and beg for my help exposing Pentastar. The fact that such an opportunity is gone weighs heavily on my heart.

The ear-prickling, staccato screams of an approaching police siren pull me back to reality. Tires chirp as the squad car grinds to stop. The sea of gawkers parts and the familiar faces of Sergeant Drake and Officer Lewis emerge from the gaggle. Lewis turns to the crowd and directs them back from the scene so he can roll out the yellow tape. Drake heads straight for me.

"Sir, I need you to step away from the scene," commands Drake. "Wait over there, please."

I shuffle back to the opposite wall of the alley and watch as Drake checks Dave for a pulse or breathing. He turns to Lewis, who is already collecting witnesses contact information and shouts, "Lewis, he's gone."

Withdrawing Dave's wallet from his pocket, he perks up slightly as he reads the name on the driver's license. Studying Dave's face, he seems to have made the connection between Dave and Pentastar. It won't be long until he makes that same connection with me. Reaching across his chest to his radio handset, he squeezes the button and makes a call to dispatch.

"Dispatch, seven-seven."

"Go for dispatch."

"Dispatch, I'm ten-seven. Go ahead and send OMI to my location," says Drake, referring to the Office of Medical Investigators.

"Dispatch copies. OMI is en route to your pos."

An ambulance and second squad car arrive. The EMTs remove a gurney and a body bag from the back of the ambulance and wheel it over toward Dave's lifeless body. Drake halts them with raised palms and walks over to brief them. Their heads bob in understanding and as they part ways, the medics cart their equipment to the side, down the wall from me.

Drake hones in on my location and approaches with fiery eyes and taut lips that forewarn of the storm he brings. Several onlookers snap photos that blast the alley in white light and burn a carbon copy into my retinas. The flash stops Drake in his tracks and spins him around.

"Lewis, make sure those get deleted and move them around the corner!" he shouts angrily. He turns to the officers that pulled up in the second car and yells, "Make yourselves useful. Help him! And get that barrier moved! Come on people, move! Let's get this scene secured!"

The officers scurry around, eager to comply with their sergeant's orders. They collect the phones from those who took pictures and make sure they're deleted, then hand them back. Whether opportunists hoping to sell them to the *Port Ellis Tribune* or sadists taking them as proof that they were at the scene, it makes no difference. Drake won't have any of that. Not at his crime scene. He pivots and continues his charge in my direction. Five feet away, he aims a ferocious finger at my face.

"You! You're the one from the jumper at Milburn Tower this morning." His inflection matches his quizzical expression. I offer no response while I inspect the topography of his face. His light brown skin is tinged red with anger, blushing at the ridges but leaving the creases and valleys dark. At an age that can't be north of thirty-five, the premature onset of crow's feet paints a very different picture of him than I've come to know: a smiling Drake.

"What in the actual hell is going on here?" he exclaims. "Two deaths in the same day and you're at the scene of both of them." He takes a moment to process the situation. "This time it's your boss who told us about your conversation with Joel and gave you an alibi—shot in the head. Let me guess, was he threatening to come clean about you and Joel? Did he try to shake you down?"

"I didn't kill Joel and Dave was telling the truth about my whereabouts. There was nothing to 'come clean' about."

"Well, you're out of luck this time. I don't believe in coincidence and I'm definitely not going to take your word for it."

I look over to Dave's still body, then back across to engage Drake's accusatory stare. His golden hazel eyes smolder intensely in the glow of the alley's streetlight, his combative stance ready for a physical altercation. Given that I'm bigger than nearly every human I meet, it's quite rare to find one that isn't blatantly intimidated by my presence. Within Sergeant Drake resides a valiant and laudable sentinel, a noble guardian prepared to rebuff all threats. Rather than glare at him down my nose like I would with most adversaries, I lower my face and offer a pacifying look.

"I didn't kill him."

"Of course you didn't. Any idea who *did*?"

"I don't know. I was inside when it happened. I think he did it to himself."

"Another suicide…right after you talked to him," he says with a curious tone, a break in his tough-cop character. "You're gonna have to do a little better than that. Let's go, hands against the wall," he grunts with a rough hand to my back.

I spread my arms wide and touch my palms to the ruddy bricks that still hold some of the sun's residual warmth. The gritty mortar grates the tips of my fingers as Drake swipes and pats his way down my sleeves. His rough search of my torso bumps my chest to the wall, but it's the realization that he's about to discover the vial in my pocket that brings frenzied thumping behind my sternum. A rush of adrenaline sweeps from my scalp to my toenails, bringing every follicle on my body to attention.

He pulls the phone from my right pocket and places it on the nearby dumpster before continuing to my ankle. Moving to my left leg, he slides his hand over my pocket and down to my knee before returning to the small bump of the vial. Every muscle tenses, ready for action. I close my eyes and exhale a slow, calming breath as his hand fumbles around my pocket and withdraws the glass tube.

"What do we have here?" he asks with a gunslinger's swagger that's far more cocky than intrigued.

I look back as he lifts the seed in front of the light. Shimmering crimson and violet hues churn and caper in the whites of his eyes. Mesmerized by its luminescence, Sergeant Drake is frozen in awe. Traces of joy flit across his cheeks, raising his brow and creasing his eyelids. The ethereal splendor of truth pervades the confines of the vial, drawing a tear that wanders down to Drake's jaw then drips to his shirt.

He shakes himself loose from the wondrous clutch of the seed and lifts his shoulder to wipe his cheek. Eyes moving like scalpels, he visually dissects my appearance for confirmation of something, but what? Could he know of the Nephilim, or is it something else? My height is not the only hint of my true nature. The prominence of my cheekbones and strength of my jaw allude to my structural differences while an atypical combination of brilliantly blonde hair and deep mahogany irises paint me with an exotic palette. He seems to find nothing actionable during his scan and returns his attention back to the vial.

"Let's go. I'm bringing you in," he says abruptly.

"Why? I was inside when this happened. You can ask the bartender, Matt. I heard the shot, came outside, and found him like this."

"You can stop talking now. Your connection to all this is more than a coincidence. Normal, healthy people don't just walk out of a bar to blow their brains out in the alley and there's nothing to suggest a third party. Hell, I've never even seen a crazy person do something like this. You're behind this and now you're coming with me."

He presses into me with his shoulder as he pulls my arms down behind my back and squeezes hardened steel handcuffs around my wrists. The cold metal shackles link my arms in bondage in the way my tongue is bonded to the truth. In moments like this, my calling becomes my burden.

I understand what drives humans to lie. The right lie could get me out of this mess entirely. If I hadn't told Dave that I saw Joel this morning, the cops would never have caught my trail. In fairness, telling the truth about the Fosillix trial could also get me out of this. But then I wouldn't be able to finish my work here and I'd have to rely on human beings to investigate the truth and enforce justice, and they'd screw that up. Pentastar would spend a fortune on lawyers and those most deserving of wrath would escape unscathed. That's an unacceptable outcome. I must be sure they suffer the consequences they so callously earned.

Sergeant Drake escorts me to his car and pulls the door open. He pushes my neck low and I stoop awkwardly with both hands locked behind my back until I settle into the seat. Looking through the open door at Drake, I can't tell if he's the flipside of my coin or a servant of something darker. If he somehow knows of the Nephilim and knows us well enough to figure me out, I can only imagine who's supplying him with information.

There have been rumors of rogue humans that have adopted the role of Nephilim hunter. Convinced by the ancient books that we are real, that we still exist today, and that we are the root of most earthly problems, they look for telltale signs of Nephilim activity, like suicides, and then stalk and attack their target. They would be brave and bold with pure intentions, like Drake, taking action to rid their world of a perceived evil. Oftentimes, those are the most dangerous people. Police officer is the ideal profession for such a zealot.

"Ask Matt. I was inside when Dave died," I tell Drake, repeating my defense.

"Just like you were in Dave's office when Joel jumped off the roof of a skyscraper? You may not have pulled the trigger and you may not have pushed Joel off that roof, but that doesn't mean you weren't the cause. Something tells me a lot of people die after talking to you. Oh, and you didn't answer me about the vial, but I'd rather you don't," he says with a salty smirk. "I already know it's blood."

With that, Drake shuts the door and walks back to the dumpster to bag my belongings. He heads over to Lewis, who is still taking witness statements, and sets the evidence bag in the passenger seat in front of me as he passes. So close, but it might as well be on the other side of the Cascades. I may be strong, but I can't rip these cuffs open, and even if I did, I'm still caged in the back of this car. From a criminal's vantage, I watch as he checks in on his protege. He listens to Lewis's questions and looks over his shoulder for a moment, then gestures toward Lewis's notes. Sergeant Drake scans the crowd, then locates Matt and pulls him aside.

The Office of Medical Investigators' van arrives at the curb and several people jump out wearing hooded white coveralls and latex gloves and carrying cameras and toolboxes for documenting the macabre exhibit. Dave's body remains undisturbed, preserving any evidence that could point to a shooter other than himself. I doubt they'll find anything, but if they do it'll be my hair, or my blood, or a skin cell, or some microscopic parasite that will worm its way into Drake's mind and whisper accusations about me. After his comments about people dying around me and the vial containing blood, I have some grave concerns of my own about the hypothesis he's forming. If he knows about the Nephilim and thinks himself a hunter, I may have no choice but to do the unthinkable.

The muffled voices of first responders, rubberneckers, and journalists form a hypnotic white noise. Enclosed in this wheeled lockbox, I'm sequestered from the pandemonium that epitomizes human existence. Call it drama, call it thrash, or call it chaos, I call it prodigal. So much time and energy is wasted scurrying around, getting in everyone else's business. *Just let me do my job as a Nephilim, Drake, and I'll turn it over to you when I'm done.* I close my eyes, hoping to find a moment's solace from the surrounding mess.

As my eyelids touch, Bridgette stands before me. She drops to her knees and wraps her arms tightly around herself in crushing agony. From my peripheral vision, Teddy and Franky run into their aunt's embrace and all three weep bitterly. Their anguished wails rattle in their lungs and bring a flutter to mine.

The only comfort I could hope to offer is that I tried to avoid this end. I didn't want Dave's death and even allowed myself the vain hope of his redemption. The possibility of survival and redemption exists even in the sowing process, but I have never been emotionally invested in the outcome before Dave. This time was different. This time I cared.

The flashing red and blue lights reflect sharply off the metal on Drake's uniform as he talks to the bartender. Those lights, much like my presence, mean drastically different things to different people. To some, my presence is a flag of liberation, flying at the front lines of the battle against deceitful oppression. To others it is the dreadful beauty of a tornado barreling towards them. Of course, no one knows which perspective to hold until I have revealed myself, but by then it's too late.

My perspective of Sergeant Drake is shifting with each interaction. Another wag of blue glints off his badge and nameplate, and for an instant I detect how heavily they press against his chest. However passionate he is about catching bad guys, police work is not his life-giving pursuit, it is a means to an end. There's something else, something of greater importance in his life that pulls him from sleep each morning. I just hope it's not hunting Nephilim. I would love to believe that an explanation of my mission would align our efforts, but it seems ever more likely revealing my purpose here would only solidify our adversarial relationship.

After finishing a short talk with Matt, he strides back toward the squad car and takes the driver's seat. The car wiggles side to side as he plops heavily onto the weathered black leather.

"Bad news, Ted. It's not looking good for you."

"You talked to Matt. Surely he told you I was inside when this happened."

"He did, but he also said that you two were arguing before Dave came outside and wound up dead. From our interview this morning I know that you were also arguing with Joel before he ended up falling to his death. So, again, it seems that you argue with people and they die. I'm taking you in."

Drake recites the Miranda warning with the enthusiasm of a mortician, and Lewis pops open the passenger door and takes his seat as Drake reaches the end.

"Do you understand these rights as I have explained them to you?"

"Yes."

Drake aggressively shifts the transmission and begins the relatively short drive to the Twenty-Seventh Precinct. There are several police stations in the downtown area to shorten the response time to emergencies and quell the rampant crime that has swallowed other cities whole. This strategy seems to have had an impact as the violent crime rate here is markedly lower than comparable cities.

That's not to say they're doing any better at prosecuting criminals. Eyewitnesses here still have sudden changes of heart. Paper trails disappear in the form of confetti or smoke while ones and zeroes are wiped away. As much as technology has helped in the investigative process, it has also empowered the tech savvy with new ways to elude authorities and manipulate information. In my case, it's not manmade technology that will exonerate me, but ancient foresight.

Long before toxicology reports existed, my kind were designed with blood that is indistinguishable from humanity. If they test the contents of that vial, they'll discover that it contains a few milliliters of my blood. There may be abnormalities, but nothing that can't be explained by several hereditary conditions or certain dietary habits. They'll never have anything more than circumstantial evidence of my involvement in these deaths. Nevertheless, my greater concern is not the justice system, but Sergeant Drake. When I get released, and I'm confident I will, he will continue hunting until he's satisfied. I've met his type before.

There are still six potential targets remaining at Pentastar, and this attention from the police will make them virtually impossible to sow one at a time. My only chances of evading arrest while I complete this operation are to carefully execute these sowings so that they aren't immediately discoverable, or to sow all of my remaining targets at once and then disappear. Of course, it would help if some of my targets survive their sowing.

Just three blocks north of The Downspout, we pull into the Twenty-Seventh Precinct parking lot. This stately two-story concrete building houses the department with a field-level forensic lab and a lock-up suitable for scoundrels and drunkards. I know this because one of my previous targets was a morally bankrupt police lieutenant. I never worked at the department, but my extensive research for that sowing delivered plenty of insider knowledge.

I don't belong here—an angel, shackled by men, placed in a criminal's cage, and about to enter a structure that reeks of mankind's self-importance. How many fiendish men have worn this jewelry and warmed this seat? How many devils have earned this humiliating treatment with their evil deeds? Drake opens the back door and stands aside as I slide out.

"Let's go," he urges impatiently. "My shift's almost over and I don't want to be stuck here dealing with your paperwork."

"The only paperwork you'll be filling out is for my release," I curtly counter.

"We'll see about that," says Drake, pointing toward the staircase.

We traverse the concrete steps to the large, wood doors with squeaky old hinges. The corners of the glass panes are embossed with decorative detailing and the brass handles are tarnished with character. The concrete blocks are arranged in the decorative manner one might see on a centuries-old college campus, but the beams of light glancing off its facade give it a more gothic personality. Many decades ago, someone took great pride in the construction of this bastion of justice. Such meticulousness is a rarity in work and in life. If people put as much effort into developing their character as was put into this building, I would need a new line of work.

As I enter the station, the results of such neglect are on full display. All around me sit people bearing literal and metaphorical chains. The curvature of their spines and rotting of their teeth are outward expressions of their decaying spirits. Desperate eyes latch onto me as I walk through the lobby with Drake and Lewis. A sowing wouldn't reveal anything new to these miscreants. They live fully aware of their wreckage, and it owns them. Too scared to end themselves and too weak to fix their messy lives, they choose numbness as they resign to the abyss.

"Nice suit, pretty boy," cracks a balding, mostly toothless vagrant.

I'm being mocked by a meth-smoking zombie. I try hard to think of a clever rebuttal to neutralize my humiliation but Drake intervenes, saying, "Shut up, Washburn! Did you run out of meth and rob someone again?"

He laughs like a dolt and says, "How'd you know? You watchin' me?"

Drake ignores him.

Humiliation is a disgusting feeling. With every new surge of human emotion I find myself swinging further from the principles that define my kind. Drake's rebuke was not in my defense. His dirty glance my direction reassures me that, to him, I'm no different than the ragged stranger on the hallway bench. We turn into an office area and Drake sits me down at the end of his desk. Lewis props himself against the neighboring desk, securing me within the confines of his watchful eyes.

"You're gonna love your sleepover in lock-up," drawls Officer Lewis. "Them boys can get a little rowdy when the lights go out…prolly won't be much sleepin'."

My blood tingles at the idea of spending the night in a cage with this societal excrement. It's not that I fear humans. Even without revealing my angelic stature I'm still longer and stronger than nearly every human. The problem is that if I fight back, it'll give Drake a real reason to keep me here, but not fighting back means taking hits and bleeding. What happens if my attackers accidentally ingest or absorb some of that blood? The last thing I need right now is to be the only one left standing in a holding cell full of dead men.

I flop my head back in frustration. My breathing steadies as I apply my mind to finding a solution. Without lying, my options are extremely limited. I haven't used my phone call so I could call a lawyer, but that would only make me appear more guilty. Complying with an interview could satisfy Drake's misgivings and get me out of here tonight, but one unfortunate choice of words or cornering question and I could end up in worse shape.

The clacking of high heels approaches from down the tile hallway. Swift, important steps broadcast their resolute movement in my direction. They quicken, then suddenly stop. An odd arrangement of clacking precedes another pause. Instead of thinking of a way out of my increasingly dire circumstances, I find myself fixated on the sounds of an invisible woman. Despite my imminent incarceration, her presence brings a strange comfort.

The image and goodness of the mystery woman from this morning flood my mind as the clacking starts again. The light I noticed in her could make perfect sense. Maybe she has a larger role to play in all of this and is about to come through in the eleventh hour.

As the footsteps reach unobstructed clarity, Jan enters through the door, shoots a disappointed scowl at me, and beelines straight to Drake, who is in his captain's office. She interrupts their exchange with a knock on the door, her beauty immediately grabbing their attention.

"May I help you, miss?" the captain politely inquires.

"Yes, you can. You boys want to explain to me why my client is chained up like a criminal when you have zero evidence that he's guilty of anything and are here, standing before my very eyes, conspiring about what to charge him with?" Her warm, beguiling voice dresses her venomous words in flowing silk.

Drake speaks up. "I know you from Pentastar. Jan, right?"

"Mm-hmm, Jan Lucero," she says with a patronizing nod. "What is it, exactly, that you suspect Mr. Verity of having done?"

"Ma'am, two men have died today. Your client was the last person to speak with both of those men before their deaths and, in each case, those conversations were hostile in nature," replies the captain.

"Sounds like you're just adding to my client's woes after a devastating day in which two coworkers committed suicide. You have nothing but circumstantial evidence. There is nothing that even remotely implies that my client violated any laws in either of these horrific tragedies," she spins masterfully. Briefly pausing, she adds, "We will accept your humble apologies and be on our way," playfully flicking her short, platinum hair.

Oddly softened expressions wipe across the men's faces before they oblige. After offering up mindless and insincere apologies like scorned children, Drake tosses the handcuff keys to Lewis to free my wrists.

"We're just gonna let 'em go? This is bull, Cap'n!"

"Lewis, shut your—"

"Officer Lewis," interrupts Jan, "did you not hear what I said to these fine officers?" Jan raises her eyebrows condescendingly to the young man.

"Ma'am, honestly, I don't care who you are. We know he has somethin' to do with these deaths and I ain't gonna watch him walk outta here and slip away. We can hold him for twenty-four hours without chargin' him."

"Young man, that's not the way this is going to work. Before you lock people up, you should at least have some actionable evidence for the DA to bring charges. You have absolutely nothing. If you put this grieving man in a cell for any amount of time without being able to bring charges in the end, I will drop a backbreaking lawsuit on this department and make sure you never work as a cop again."

An emasculated Lewis looks at Jan, then at his captain, who offers no support. The captain's slowly shaking head advises Lewis to desist. Lewis examines the keys in his hand, frustration wrinkling his forehead. He returns his gaze to Jan.

"Good. So, we're done here?" Jan asks with a coy smile.

"Yes, ma'am. I'm sorry for the misunderstanding," Lewis says through his teeth. "Have a lovely night."

Without breaking his stare at Jan, he retrieves my personal belongings and drops them on the desk near my hands. His shoulders twist toward me to fumble with the cuffs for a few seconds before he turns his head to see what he's doing. The emptiness in his chastened eyes is pitiful, like a scorned child. As my hands are freed, I snatch the bag and leap from my seat. Jan extends her hand toward the door.

"Let's go, Mr. Verity," says Jan.

As we round the corner, Drake hollers, "I'll see you later, Ted," and for reasons I don't fully understand, the words make me wince.

I stride toward the exit with Jan at my side. Everything about this day feels hideously deformed and bleak. Dave is dead, Bridgette is widowed, the twins are once again fatherless, and my wrists bear the red stripes of a criminal. I have become Drake's primary suspect and would have spent at least one night in jail if not for Jan, one of my principal targets at Pentastar. Villain has become victim, enemy has become ally, and hero has become criminal. Nothing about this operation has been orderly, and each step forward takes me farther into a labyrinth designed for my demise. With each new intrigue, new affliction, and new horror, I feel like one piece in a dynamic, unsolvable puzzle. It's becoming apparent that unnatural forces are at work in this city.

CHAPTER SEVEN

Defying reason, Jan has aligned herself as my advocate, and by helping me elude captivity, she has unknowingly facilitated her own undoing. Once again I face doubts about the pervasive darkness that I came to eliminate. I was able to read Joel and Dave quite easily at first, maybe too easily. Their wickedness seemed absolute but, at least in Dave's case, it was only the oily residue on the surface of a murky puddle. If one were to step in that puddle, as I have, they would fall straight through into a sunless, twisting, stinking sewer and look up to find that the hole through which they entered has closed behind them. Such is my plight. My only hope of finding daylight is to follow the slithering air, and right now it's moving with Jan.

Jan has always been challenging to analyze, partially due to hierarchical barriers and partially due to something just beyond my mind's outstretched fingertips. We don't attend the same meetings or share conversations in the halls or cafeteria. We don't socialize, and there are virtually no records of her on the internet other than some educational and employment history. Ironically, she is well-known for not being known at all. I can sympathize with her desire for privacy, but it's unusual for a human to be so reclusive, and it's left my investigation in the mud. This is one of the main reasons I had to gain employment at Pentastar rather than just target them from the outside. In a company this size, it's unlikely that their problems stem from just one person, even if that person *is* the CEO.

I've seen the degrees on her office wall: bachelor's degrees in business administration and biochemistry from the University of Michigan, an MBA from Wharton, and a JD from Georgetown. Graduating at or near the top of her class, she landed a few lucrative upper-management positions before Pentastar, but in spite of all of that prominence and achievement, I know almost nothing about her personal life. Social media is an easily accessible fount of information, but Jan has no accounts.

After my exhaustive efforts, all I really know about her is what the framed, gold-leaf embossed papers hanging neatly on her wall tell me. I suppose the same thing could be said about me. I am formally educated, which can be verified through University of Washington records, but in every other way I have also remained inconspicuous. Even my education was entirely online so I wouldn't have to sit through lectures surrounded by hundreds of people. The only reason I was able to secure my position with Pentastar was due to an eloquent and adamant letter of recommendation from a Port Ellis City Councilman named James Hudson—an old friend of my parents. I suspect even the recommendation wouldn't have been enough if Pentastar leadership actually wanted a capable quality assurance division. But they jumped at the opportunity to hire an inexperienced fellow like myself, someone they thought they could push around, someone they thought wouldn't give them trouble. Little did they know.

But no matter her secretive nature, no matter her insulting reasons for hiring me, no matter her status as a potential target for sowing, she's the reason I'm not behind bars and for that I am grateful.

"Jan, I don't even know where to begin."

"You're welcome," she replies abruptly.

"How did you know I was here?"

"One of our other employees was at the bar. He called me when he saw what happened."

"Well, I'm grateful that—"

"Ted, I don't want to dwell on this."

I stop as we reach the foyer and turn to face Jan, who slings me an openly aggravated expression. Her blatant irritation suggests some wrongdoing on my part, but after her defense of my innocence just moments ago, it seems unlikely to be related to Joel and Dave. In an attempt to diffuse her hostility, I drape my eyes with humility and lean in with gentle gestures.

"I'm just trying to say thank you. I would've been locked up if you didn't swoop to my defense."

She scolds me with her eyes as she scans the room. Her hand lands heavily on my shoulder in a quasi-shove as she directs me outside. We push through the squawking doors and descend the steps to the parking lot where Jan's town car awaits at the far end, engine running. She stops on the sidewalk and responds tersely.

"Thank yous are cute, Ted, but I didn't defend you because I believe in your innocence or because I like you. I didn't do it for you at all, actually. I did it because it's what's best for the company, for me, and for my employees right now. We can't afford to attract any more attention from the media and authorities. We need to unite and close ranks, and if that means I have to stick my neck out to save yours then that's what I'll do because I'm committed to my people. Are you committed, Ted?"

"Yes, ma'am, I'm very committed to my purpose at Pentastar. That's why I met with Joel and Dave."

I cringe at my own mention of their names. Before the words escaped it seemed like an opportunity to address the elephant in the room and paint my involvement innocently for Jan. In hindsight, the inclusion of their names added nothing and only served to highlight the connection between myself and the day's morbid events. I need to shift the focus.

"I'm sorry, Jan. I've been completely insensitive. I can't even imagine how you're feeling right now—"

"Let me just stop you right there. I didn't get to my position by pouring out my feelings to my employees, and I'm definitely not going to cry on your shoulder now. I'll grieve in my own time and my own way, and you will not be a part of that process."

CEO or not, she's only human, and being snapped at by a human always pings an aggressive reflex that I can't afford to indulge. Instead I offer a contrite nod: message received. She appears to accept this atonement, exchanging her air of untouchable superiority for the firm warmth of a mentor.

"Ted, another reason I saved you is that I want to see you live up to your potential. I've been watching you lately. You are not average in any way, and yet your performance is markedly inferior to that of your peers. It's wasteful."

Wasteful? I'm baffled. The peers she's comparing me to are all human. No human could outperform a Nephilim in any task. Besides, I'm the Director of Quality Assurance, a job they expected me to fail, and I run a tighter operation than any other department. I'd think she was playing mind games if not for the sincerity in every aspect of her delivery.

"I don't understand why you think I'm falling short, Jan. I do exemplary work and run an efficient and talented team."

"Those are true statements, but you don't seem to truly grasp the magnitude of your potential. A man of your immense ability should be accomplishing so much more at Pentastar and, eventually, beyond."

Jan pans her gaze up to the now overcast night sky. A news helicopter chops around above the spires and antennas. The electric glow of the city highlights the underside of the clouds. With a little imagination, the distant whoosh of overlapping vehicles sounds like the gentle purl of the ocean. She rolls her lips in between her teeth then levels her eyes on me. Her lips release and, as the warm mauve color returns to their surface, she continues.

"Ted, everyone is dealt a different hand in this life. Some people are born into poverty. Their limited opportunities prevent them from gaining the experiences and making the connections that would change the course of their life. Malnourishment compounds their woes and stunts their cognitive development. Even if their bodies were strong, their underfunded school districts struggle to retain quality teachers who will battle through the behavioral problems of students whose parents work multiple jobs just to put food on the table."

She stops and examines me from my shoes up. Her light hazel eyes, glowing under the inky night sky, linger on my hair before looking warmly into mine. The indirect light from the police station emphasizes her pert cheeks and smooth, tan skin while her platinum hair gleams twofold in the cool twilight. Surprised by the empathy of her previous remarks, I can't help but wonder what depth of character I could unearth with more time and less barriers. After what I saw in Dave, such an investment seems prudent to my mission. With every sincere interaction, humans continue to defy summary judgment. If it's my goal to find and sow only those who are ultimately responsible, I have to get closer to Jan.

"Then there are people like us, Ted. Born talented and intelligent, we were nurtured by parents who offered us the world. Our bodies grew strong as we shopped from a catalog of bright futures, knowing they were ours for the taking. The measure of success is not the same for us. We were meant for greatness from the moment of our conception. Don't settle for mediocrity, Ted. This world belongs to us and we owe it to others to make it a better place for them."

I nod in receipt of the lesson, but Jan's assumptions about my beginnings are far from accurate. It is true that I was cut from a different template—one of greater strength, intelligence, and talent than humans—but I was not raised with earthly wealth. My simple upbringing reinforced the values that my parents taught. Regardless, she is correct about one thing: my measure of success is vastly different from humanity's.

"I'm going to focus on the veiled compliment in all of that, Jan, but you don't know me as well as you think. You and I have many differences, and I'd guess that our definitions of potential and achievement are among them. I gauge my successes according to my own priorities. My life's goal is not to amass wealth or status or to make the world mine. I have a higher purpose."

"Look at that, you do have a spine," she says with a chuckle. "You misunderstood me, Ted. I don't have wealth, comfort, and notoriety because they're priorities and measures of my worth. My goal is to make the most of my life, my talents, and my opportunities, and to use them to better the world for others. Surely we can agree on that."

I take a second to think not about her words, but about whether or not she means them.

"You're right, we can agree on that," I admit. "But I will never compromise my principles to gain the world."

"These material luxuries are not the object of my pursuit, Ted, they're just byproducts. I'm lucky that my self-actualization has brought worldly riches and pleasures, but I'd still be just as committed to my work without them."

Jan's eloquent words juke and jockey through my defenses. Unlike with Dave, it's difficult to establish the boundary between true conviction and convenient fiction. His empty mantras were filled with guilt and appeasement, but she's on a roll like a gospel preacher turned politician. Her words are fiery and impassioned, and though she's clearly given them thought, they still feel unrehearsed. Those qualities alone don't make them true, but the art of deceit is not an exact science, and if she's lying, I would know.

"You might be right, Jan. Maybe there is more I could be doing."

"Of course I'm right, Ted," she says, laughing sweetly. Jan looks deeply into my eyes as she enjoys a weightless breath. "I'm really glad that you're receptive to what I'm saying. I think we would make a formidable team."

I don't sense the darkness in Jan that I expected to find. She is either the most talented liar I've met or she's another collateral victim of the greater evil I'm here to combat. After Dave, I'm more willing to consider the possibility of the latter. If she is caught in the shadow of something or someone diabolical, I feel a responsibility to break her free from its grip before assessing her need to be sown. The development of this "relationship" will offer me the perfect opportunity to be more than a truth-wielding assassin.

"Well, you made me think. Perhaps there is more I have to offer this world than what I've been giving. I don't want to look back on my life with the regret that I could have had a larger impact," I concede.

"I don't want that for you either! You're remarkable, Ted. Together, we can be a light in this dark world."

"That's exactly what I want," I exclaim, surprising myself with my own enthusiasm.

"Excellent. I want to start working closely first thing tomorrow morning. I'll teach you everything I know, and you can teach me what I don't know. How does that sound?"

"That sounds great."

She turns toward the black town car and I open the door. Striding into the back seat, she thanks me with a warm smile, and before I shut the door, she calls my name.

"Ted, I'll send you a car."

"That's not necessary, Jan. I'll just catch a cab."

"Nonsense. You're with me now and at our level, we have personal drivers."

I sense the futility of further argument and reluctantly accept. It's going to take a lot more than a personal driver to buy my loyalty, so I'll play along for now in order to get close to Jan and closer to the truth. As unlikely as it seemed this morning, Jan may serve a larger role in the proliferation of my angelic nature and its impact on this broken world. If this experiment takes a turn for the worse, I can always just sow her like I had originally planned.

"Thanks again, Jan. I'll see you tomorrow."

"You're welcome. Now stop thanking me and get some rest. It's been a long day," she consoles.

I shut the car door and step back as the wheels begin to roll. It *has* been a long and challenging day that's forcing me to rethink much of what I thought I understood about humanity's relationship with evil. The truly diabolical does exist, I'm convinced of that, but Dave's dishonesty and others like him is far more pitiful than malevolent. They turn to lies in the hope of preserving their status quo, but those lies only multiply their hardships.

Could the same be said for Jan? Each step higher up the ladder at Pentastar has to lead closer to the origin of their decay. Her supposed interest in the betterment of her people and belief in each person's responsibility to maximize their existence brings me hope that she is not the source of evil. But if not Jan, if not the CEO, then who or what is the root of Pentastar's evil?

CHAPTER EIGHT

Like a serpent trying desperately to swallow its living prey, today has found me continuously subduing my disdain for people for far longer than usual, and it's been exhausting. A rodent that refuses to die, it has clawed up my esophagus to the back of my throat only to be washed back down with a stiff shot of restraint. My typical one-off missions have only required that I research my potential target (which can be accomplished mostly from home since the advent of the internet), plan the mission, sow the target, and then retreat back to my rural farmhouse east of the mountains. It has never been necessary for me to secure a job and live in the city before Pentastar, and all this time around people is taking its toll. My only oasis until this operation is complete is the seclusion of my empty apartment.

Sitting on the woven metal bench outside the police station brings a much-needed lull. The sleepy night air caresses my neck as I prop my head in my hands and embrace the relative silence. A trail of ants meanders alongside my foot. I trace the dotted line to a dime-sized piece of glazed donut. Faced with an insurmountable problem, they band together to bite, tug, and drag with determination, their tiny movements blending together in unified purpose. It's possible that ants are more respectable than most human beings. They demonstrate commitment on a level that has to be admired. Nothing deters them from risking their lives to return a single bite of food to their queen and colony.

Humanity would thrive with such dedication to the common good. Instead, their personal safety, security, and benefit take on supreme importance. But in their dishonest attempts at self-preservation and gratification, they erode the very security they desire. Each selfish lie pushes their most valued relationships and accomplishments ever closer to ruin, and yet they still do it.

It would take the concerted effort of many more Nephilim than actually exist to have any hope of changing this behavior. Each sowing transforms the most corrupt either into an honest soul or into a corpse, but the rate of positive change can't match the rate of decay. It's a losing battle and I recognize that fact, but it's still a battle worth fighting, if only for my own sake.

I've never believed in mankind's ability to improve themselves. The only instances of revolutionary human change I've witnessed have been the byproduct of external forces. Catastrophes often force people to rethink their perspectives and make positive changes to behaviors and attitudes. For Dave, Joel, and my eight prior targets, the sowing was their catastrophe, and I was its herald.

Stones grind and pop under the weight of an approaching vehicle, bringing an end to another session of mental congress. Initially expecting my town car, I straighten my hunched posture and prepare to stand, but instead watch a green cab draw near. The brakes squeal slightly as it slows to a stop in front of the staircase. Staring covertly, I watch in bored curiosity as the cab door opens and a woman steps out. Her familiar heel and slim ankle are visible beneath the cab door before she rises from her seat to reveal her identity.

My heart knocks against my ribs as I see the sable hair and breathtaking upturned eyes of the woman from this morning. But as providential as this meeting seems, I can't bring myself to call out to her. Not only am I not in the mood for a resurgence of human emotion, but this day has devoured all of my best-laid plans, and I don't want to add her to the list of casualties. I twist, hiding my face to avoid contact. Still, my eyes are lured to the corner of their sockets for another glimpse.

In a sudden breath of wind, she wrestles with hair so dark it absorbs light and frames her pale, oval face in a flowing silhouette. She's an incarnation of my black-and-white view of the world. The streetlights bow as if to concede their inferiority to her overpowering radiance and the air ripples as it passes around her presence. My veins tickle the inside of my flesh as I feel the pressure building in my neck.

She leans down and thanks the driver, then closes the door and heads for the stairs. One step later her head does a double take as she senses my presence. Freezing in her tracks, she squints at me curiously. My pulse stops during her examination, as if perfect stillness will render me invisible.

"I know you," she says, her voice an unforgettable melody to my ears. "Well, I don't know you, but I've seen you before. Don't tell me…"

I'm not planning to. Even if I were, my nervous system is too overloaded to command coherent speech. It's unfortunate, but it offers the byproduct of finding out just how memorable she finds me. I turn sideways on the bench to face her as she works out the details of her memory.

"I saw you this morning outside Milburn Tower," she says with a clever grin. "You tried to steal my cab!"

I laugh a little too hard at her joke before responding, "I don't steal. It's not in my nature."

Replaying the words in my mind, I immediately cringe. I've never felt this nervous before, and I find it to be another disgusting human emotion that belongs on the list right below humiliation. I need to tap into the sociable part of me that's helped me fit into an office environment for months. Then again, at the Pentastar offices my stomach isn't in active freefall and my tongue isn't swollen inside my mouth like it is now.

She begins a graceful stroll toward the bench, and I detect a hint of delight in her gate that I hope is more than just wishful thinking. My soul burns hotter as each step closes the distance between us. Her allure is not just in her physical beauty because, despite leaving me speechless, it's rather understated. It's the kindness of her countenance, the peace of her presence, the strength of her spirit that wrap their fingers around my neck and pull me in.

"Well, that's good. Stealing is dishonest," she replies as if talking to a preschooler.

"I'm surprised you remember me."

"It took me a second to place it, but you're a unique looking fellow. Memorable…in a good way," she says.

"That was a nice thing to say. My name is Ted Verity," I say as I reach to shake her hand.

"Melody Galanis, but my friends call me Mel."

Without knowing a thing about her, it's evident that she's seen her share of hardships. She carries herself with the humble confidence that only comes from victory through terrible adversity. It's rare. I've seen it before in first responders, firefighters, and military members, but no one like her. Something tells me she's not to be trifled with, the type to walk softly and carry a big stick.

"Melody…I like that name."

"Thank you! I can't take too much credit; it's not like I picked it out."

"True, but it suits you."

"Well, thanks again," she says with a charming grin.

"You're welcome. So, how is it that we've crossed paths twice in the same day in a big city like this? What brings you here?"

"Oh, I'm a journalist. I'm working a story about today's Pentastar deaths. Well, it was just one death until a couple hours ago. Their VP shot himself or someone else shot him, I don't know. That's what I'm hoping to find out," she replies. She interprets my contorted expression as a response to her flippant mention of the dead. "I'm sorry, it's kind of morbid. TMI?"

"No, it's not that. I work for Pentastar. I already knew about their deaths."

"Oh, geez. I didn't mean to be insensitive. It's been an eventful day for you," she says, sending an electric jolt through my spine. *You*? Why does she think my day was eventful? Does she know something? Did Drake tell her I'm a suspect? I cork my emotional geyser just enough to play off my next question as nothing more than one of clarification.

"What do you mean?"

"I mean it's been an eventful day at Pentastar."

"Oh, right," I affirm with a silent sigh of relief. "Yes, it's been exhausting."

I break eye contact and look to the road. The passing cars and pedestrians make me think of chance meetings and missed opportunities. As water flows over and around stones, these travelers move through life completely oblivious to what they're missing until the fateful day that their lives intersect with providence. My collision with Melody is beginning to feel less providential and more cataclysmic.

"So, you never told me why you're here," says Mel.

"I'm waiting for my ride."

I know that's not what she was asking, but journalists make their living poking around in messy business, looking for answers. The last thing I need is another busybody interfering with my work. Her journalistic instincts could lead to a line of questioning that exposes me and my kind, changing the course of humanity. I can't carry on with her and take such a risk. Perhaps our future is not as bright as I hoped. Worse yet, I hate how disappointed that makes me feel.

"No, I was asking why you're at the police station in the first place."

"Are you asking off the record?"

"Not sure why that clarification is necessary, but sure, we're off the record."

"I was with Dave at the bar before he ended up dead in the alley, and I was the last person to talk to Joel this morning before he jumped from Milburn Tower."

Mel processes this data for a second before her face turns up excitedly. She stifles her expression and instead looks at me with a question on her face. Her eyes look deeply into mine as she forms words.

"Are they treating you as a suspect?" Her inflection suggests the ridiculousness of the question.

"It seems that way."

"Is that strictly based on you being around them before they died?"

"Yes, but I wasn't there when either of them died. There are witnesses to that fact."

"What did you talk to them about before they died? Did you talk about the Fosillix trial?" she pries enthusiastically.

"What do you know about the drug trial? Are you writing about that too?"

"Ted, everybody who watches the news, much less *works* for the news, knows about the drug trial. I know you're being sued and they're talking about felony charges for whoever's responsible. Level with me; is Pentastar responsible for those patients' deaths?"

Her home run swing lands squarely on my jaw. She knows I can't discuss such things, especially with a member of the press. As much as I'd love to, corporate policy says I can neither confirm nor deny Pentastar's responsibility in the death of drug trial patients. Not that policy would stop me. I respect no agreement, no policy, no law that prevents the truth from being spoken. My compliance with the non-disclosure is temporary and self-serving. I need time to finish my sowings and leave town before Pentastar crumbles and takes me down in the rubble.

"Melody, I don't mean to be rude, but I can't talk to you about that."

"I figured, but it was worth a try. So, were Dave and Joel involved in what happened with the drug trial? Is that why they killed themselves…I mean, *if* they killed themselves?"

Mel's interest in me is obviously more professional than personal. Each question about Pentastar, the drug trial, and my targets' deaths shatters my naive attraction and raises my defenses. Beyond that, she's painting herself as a potential threat to my mission. I look upon her enchanting face with further disappointment.

"You don't seem to get it. I'm not going to answer any of your questions about Pentastar, the trial, or any dead or living coworkers. Honestly, this is pretty distasteful of you."

"Alright, alright, I'm sorry. You're right. Sometimes my quest for answers overpowers my better judgment. I'll save those questions for Julius."

"Who's Julius?"

"Julius Drake; he's a cop I pester when I need information for an article."

Each evolution of this situation is a step further into a lion's den. If she works closely with Sergeant Drake then it's only a matter of time until I say the wrong thing, she takes it to Drake, and I end up behind bars. Even if she and Drake aren't close, no journalist is going to pass on scooping the identity of a vigilante serial killer. I've never killed anyone myself, but that's not what the headlines will read. Those outcomes seem almost preferable when I consider the possibility, however unlikely, that they work together as some kind of Nephilim hunting duo.

"Do you work closely with Sergeant Drake?"

"Julius and I go back years. We've worked on a lot of investigations, officially and off the books. You know Drake?"

Off the books?

"We've met. He's pretty enthusiastic about…justice."

"Yeah, he's a good cop and has been a great friend and ally."

As much as that stings, it makes my path forward clear. I have to play it safe. Drake is hunting me—at least as a cop, if not as a Nephilim hunter—and if Mel isn't already, she'll be hunting me for a story or for my head soon enough. Whatever delusions I entertained about Mel, I'm back on my own. Though I've never seen my loneliness as a personal liability, I now recognize it as a tactical one. It isn't a part of the Nephilim code to live in solitude, it's a conscious decision I made years ago based on my view of the world and my place in it. Now, in the midst of a complex operation, I find myself desiring such relationships. There is no one to watch my back, no one to help me, and no one that I can trust. I have no such ally.

The squeak of the department door and the familiar drawl of Officer Lewis invade the cool night silence. Drake's uproarious laughter implies a sense of humor that's hard to imagine after our interactions thus far. They skip down the steps with a peppy gait, eager to embrace what's left of their evening. Lewis spots us on the bench and points us out to Drake, whose face rapidly sours at the sight of me.

"I should go. I want to catch them before they leave. Until next time," Mel says with an apologetic expression.

"Oh, you think we'll meet again?"

She stands from the bench and offers a dainty wave before she turns toward Drake and Lewis. She hustles a few steps away before responding.

"Ted, we'll meet again. I'm confident of that," she replies with total conviction.

"How can you be so sure?" I ask, hoping she tips her hand.

"There's just something about you, Ted. You could say my journalistic instincts are lighting you up. It's as if *you're* the story here. Either way, I know where to find you."

I watch as she greets them with cordial hugs and smiles. An irksome twinge tightens my jaw as I observe the only woman who has ever caught my interest cavorting with a man who has become my leading opposition.

The three of them chat in front of the station, tension building in my muscles with each hostile glance from Drake and Lewis. I'd really like to be gone when they get to the part of the conversation where Drake tells Mel that he suspects I'm a murderer or a Nephilim or both. That's a sideways glance I could do without seeing.

What is taking this driver so long?

Just as my imaginary countdown nears its end, headlights bounce into the parking lot. A black town car pulls up and veers around Melody's cab, stopping right in front of me. I hustle from the bench to the car in the hope of making an unnoticed exit, but they've been watching the car from the moment it turned in. I can feel their sour eyes tracing my every move as I zip inside and lean to close the door.

"We'll do this again soon," hollers Lewis as the door slams shut.

"Take me to Rockefeller Park, please."

"You live way out there?" he says curiously. "If you don't mind me asking, sir, why?"

"I don't like people."

He accepts my answer with a satisfied nod and lifts his foot from the brake. The vehicle starts rolling and I feel relief with every revolution of the tires. It's funny how a little geographic separation from a problem can bring peace of mind. Nothing about my situation with the police and Melody has changed, and yet the problem still shrinks away in the rearview mirror.

I'm humiliated. The *idea* of a "Melody" has lurked in my blind spot my entire life but, somehow, I never realized I was capable of such naive twitterpation. My father harped on the importance of self-awareness on a weekly, if not daily, basis. He said that the greatest threat we face as Nephilim is our own humanity quietly driving our choices and steering us away from our purpose. He would be disappointed to see me so utterly blindsided by these desires.

The drive to my apartment in the industrial district can't pass quickly enough. I lean my head against the glass as the streetlights pass in a blur. Melody seems to be more trouble than she's worth. After just two brief meetings she's disturbed my sense of identity, diminished my self-respect, and likely now shares Drake's suspicions about me.

With each block traveled, the buildings look less like places where no one wants to live and more like places where no one wants to work. Warehouses with broken windows and walls crusty with decades of graffiti line both sides of the four-lane boulevard. Tight jets of white vapor spiral from the tops of distant smokestacks before billowing into plumes of fluffy gray.

A city initiative has slowly pushed the industrial district farther beyond the outskirts of the city. Every couple of years, the properties closest to town are rezoned as residential or commercial properties, but the local land developers remain mostly unconvinced of their viability. The cost involved in tearing down these old warehouses to build new apartments and condos requires rent pricing beyond the reach of the nearby factory workers. That alone isn't the problem. The real problem is that Rockefeller Park is an inconvenient commute for the "downtown folk" who can actually afford such high rent.

One developer invested in a few of these properties, but instead of demolishing the existing structures they repurposed them into large urban-industrial studio apartments at a very reasonable price. They did little more than raise a few walls, install some plumbing and appliances, and add some new windows, but I don't need much and it makes for an adequate temporary living space. More than anything, it's quiet and isolated from the arterial flow of the city.

The landowner's desperation to find tenants offered the added benefit of getting into a paperwork-free, cash-based arrangement. I prepaid one year of rent in cash and they don't ask me questions. It's not home, but it'll suffice until I've dealt with Pentastar.

"It's up here on the right. You can just drop me off in front," I tell the driver.

"Yes, sir. Do you need to go anywhere else tonight?"

"No, thank you. I'm just staying home."

"What time do you need a car in the morning?"

"Seven o'clock will work."

"Excellent, sir. I've already entered the reservation in the system. A driver will be here at seven in the morning. Have a good night, sir."

"Thanks. You too," I reciprocate as I climb out of the vehicle.

I hurry up the lighted walkway. Modern glass entry doors replaced the building's original metal doors, but it still feels distinctly like approaching a high school gymnasium. Warm, amber light emanates from industrial fixtures on each side of the entrance. I pull the door open and hurdle up the stairs to my top-floor unit, but as I traverse the final flight, my kicked-in apartment door comes into view. Splintered bits of wood sprinkle the ground from the jagged, cracked door frame and a cluster of dirty boot prints mark the painted white door.

My fatigue suddenly vanishes as the fight surges through my body. I release my constricted posture and extend to my full Nephilim stature. Blind rage vibrates through my muscles as I maneuver my neck and head for a look inside. A strobing lamp lies broken on the floor, providing moments of visibility that cast imposing shadows all around the room with each flash of light. My heart skips a beat as a flicker reveals a figure standing motionless behind the table. Then the next flash highlights the vase responsible for the figure. Without being inside, I can't see into the dark corners that could easily conceal my intruder. I have to go in.

I tense my jaw and stoop as I barge through the door and sweep my hand up the switch plate, turning on the ceiling lights. The door slams against the wall with a deep thud that I feel in my body, then slowly returns with a gentle pat against my shoulder. I feverishly scan for movement but find none. The room is still and silent. Gently, I push the door shut until it scrapes loudly against the protruding shards of the door frame.

Bits of wood crunch underfoot as I slowly step, wide-eyed, into my ruined sanctuary. The drawers and doors of each cabinet, chest, and dresser hang from their stops and hinges.

Like massacred bodies, couch cushions lay strewn on the floor with their fabric slashed and insides on display. Piles of snowy fluff speckle the laminate faux-wood flooring, a typical early spring landscape in the North. The walls are stripped bare of my minimal décor, which is now torn and tossed around the room. Of my décor, one piece in particular had the special responsibility of guarding something sacred. I panic at the realization and race to the bathroom to find the framed photograph broken on the floor and the brick missing from the wall where it hung.

"No, no, no," I exclaim aloud as I search the empty compartment. I kick away the mess on the floor to rifle through the vanity and medicine cabinet but find nothing. Having yet to check the kitchen, I head that way in the desperate hope that whoever did this was unaware of the value of their discovery.

As I charge toward the kitchen, the familiar object grabs my attention. Placed neatly on the kitchen counter is a small metal case containing several full vials of my sacred Nephilim blood. To the untrained eye, the case might look like a pack of diabetic supplies. Six vials rest safely in pre-cut foam in one half of the case, while the other half holds several syringes and a rubber tourniquet. To most, it would mean nothing. To me, it's something symbolic, the hope of righted wrongs and freedom in truth. It's not only the lifeforce of my body, but the essence of my identity and the substance of my spirit.

I race to inspect my most valued possession. With horror I discover a broken, empty vial resting beside the case. Nausea wrenches through my gut as I read the words that are scrawled on the countertop in my blood: *WE KNOW*.

CHAPTER NINE

The squawk of my alarm rips me, gasping, from exhausted sleep. My heart throbs, sluggishly moving my thick blood like a motor chugging through a sleepy climb. I fumble with the phone beside me, silence the incessant chirping, and flop back onto the mattress until my pulse settles. East-facing windows drench me with hot morning sunshine in defiance of the cool morning air. I sit up in my bed and peer out over Southwest Port Ellis. The massive rainwater culvert dividing the residential sector from Rockefeller Park sparkles with blinding intensity.

Despite its lack of affluence, this neighborhood enjoys the wealth of community. Here, shop owners see their customers as more than a means to wealth. They didn't start their businesses to get rich, but to provide a service or products that their community needed. They care more about their customers and even give food to the local homeless. Neighbors share with one another and dine together. No one has enough to be self-sufficient, creating a codependency that fuels compassion and cooperation. Of course, there are exceptions to every rule. For some, this level of need brings desperation, and desperation, selfish lawlessness.

Break-ins are an occasional problem, mostly committed by youths looking for a quick score. They usually target parking lots, looking for cars with loot in plain sight. Ever so rarely, they'll seize an opportunity for a home invasion or burglary, but last night's break-in was no such crime. Whoever broke in knew what they were looking for and already suspected my true nature. Nothing was missing because it wasn't a crime of desperation, and there was no need to make it look like one. They knew I wouldn't contact the police.

I throw off my comforter and make my way to the bathroom. A minefield of debris still litters my unit, forcing me to tiptoe beyond my early morning agility. Before reaching the bathroom, a staggering step leads me off course and onto one of my broken picture frames. I release a pained yelp as a thin sliver of glass pierces the sole of my foot. Awkwardly hopping, I wince and suck the air through my teeth as I pluck the transparent needle from my flesh.

The morning radiance of the nearest star bombards the crystal shard as I lift it for inspection. Golden light shines through the bloodstained glass like a slide under a microscope, alive with movement. Within the thin red film I can almost see the microbes responsible for the wonder of the sowing. It is not the Nephilim blood itself that is the seed, it's these microbes that invade the mind of the sown, activating dormant parts of the human brain. In the blackness of the sowing, the human mind is stimulated well beyond its typical ten percent workload. Observations that never consciously registered, hidden memories in long-forgotten files, and connections beyond their mental acuity are all logged away in their limitless cranial storage. The seed defragments the entirety of the mind's filing system, revealing the truths that people tried to forget as well as those they didn't realize they knew.

Gravity stretches a drop loose from the glass splinter that falls to a syrupy splat on the very frame that stabbed me. The photo inside is one of the only photos I own of my parents and me all together. I toss the piece of glass into the trash and crouch near the broken frame. Carefully, I pick it up and slide the photograph free from the debris.

A man and woman sit on the worn wooden steps of an old farmhouse porch. Between them, on the next step down, is a lanky fourteen-year-old boy whose face is perfectly masked by my drop of blood. I grab a tuft of couch stuffing and try to wipe it away, but it mostly smears. Several more swipes and I can make out my features. My wispy blonde hair flaps in the light cross breeze and my mom's dirty-blonde locks sway like willow leaves. Dad's chiseled jaw and dimpled chin were the first things anyone noticed about him, but it was his wisdom and patience that I remember most.

There was nothing truly remarkable about the day of this photograph, but I still recall it quite vividly. Almost every day from my tenth birthday until the day of his passing, my father and I enjoyed a daily lunch routine. The day of this photo was no different. After all the morning farming duties were complete, we broke for a small lunch consisting of an apple, a few berries, the vegetable of the day, and a couple slices of meat for protein. We then moved to the living room and sat on opposite sides of the oak coffee table—me on the couch's floral upholstery and my father in his wooden rocking chair. The early-afternoon sun baked the front yard, which shone brightly on the other side of the sheer curtains and made the dim living room look even darker. Sipping on glasses of fresh milk, we spent thirty minutes playing chess. Of course, I use the word "playing" loosely—it was strategic training. Some days my tactical blunders brought swift defeat in under thirty minutes, and we'd clear the board and head back outside for an afternoon of callus-forming labor. But on that day we were finishing a game that we had started the day prior. Being our second day of play, I knew that the game would be over quickly and remember feeling both dismayed, because I'd soon be gripping the weathered shovel handle again, and elated, because I was only a few moves from defeating my father for the first time. Checkmate came five moves later, turning up the corners of my father's mouth and bringing a beaming grin to mine. He told me that before we even finished yesterday's play he knew I was going to win and there was nothing he could do to stop it. He said that if I approached sowings the way I played that game, I could maneuver people like chess pieces and make myself as inevitable as death. That afternoon, we set the camera on a tripod and took the photo to mark the occasion.

It is the last picture we took together before they died. Even so, it's not a great picture. Like the photos from the early history of the camera, none of us are smiling because it isn't customary for Nephilim to smile. It would be a stretch to make it a matter of principle, but faking smiles for the sake of a camera is somewhat disingenuous. Despite having a pleasant upbringing, no one in our little family unit appears happy. Their emotionless expressions would be unsettling if not for their kind eyes.

It's hard to know what my parents would think of me now. They were tough, leathery Nephilim inside and out, like hardened war veterans, my dad more than my mom. There were times that she was affectionate simply for affection's sake and, like I said before, she read me stories. Other than that, softness and sensitivity had no place in the life of a truth warrior. Yet here I am, struggling with infatuation, doubt, anxiety, and more. I doubt that the fact that I'm still accomplishing my calling would do much to ease their disappointment in how human I'm acting. They challenged me to be more, to tap into the strength of my supernatural marrow and to build my identity around my angelic lifeblood.

Though Jan couldn't have been referring to my abilities as a Nephilim, she was right that I'm not living up to my potential. At the very least, I've taken for granted the certainty of my success at Pentastar and failed to approach my work there with the same tactical mindset as those countless chess matches. My casual "watch-and-sow" strategy is like blindly sliding my queen around the board, neglecting the rest of my pieces, and expecting to stumble upon a checkmate. That may have worked during the simple sowings of the past, but it hasn't been working at Pentastar, and after yesterday's break-in I get the feeling that my evil opposition are making some moves of their own. It's no coincidence that it happened on the exact day that I began sowing my targets. Ignoring their brash tactics and continuing with my nonchalant approach will almost guarantee failure, if not worse.

It's time for me to use all the pieces on the board, starting with Jan. I can't lower my guard entirely with her; target-turned-ally is an unlikely conversion. Nevertheless, she rescued me from a night in jail and has proven her usefulness. My mind is open to the possibility that there is more to learn about Jan and the gripping evil that leaches through the mortar of Milburn Tower. If nothing else, maneuvering her properly could make her a powerful piece in my strategy.

I press on with my morning routine, hopeful about what the day holds in store. As much as I don't want to return home to this intolerably messy apartment, I need to prepare for my first day with Jan. She is clearly a high-functioning person and, if not morally bankrupt, may have much to offer.

I finish showering, dressing, and grooming myself, then grab a breakfast bar before I head to the door. I wedged a bed-frame rail against the door last night that thankfully held strong while I slept. The door slowly creaks open as I remove the rail and toss it aside with an off-putting clang. I'll put in a repair order with the landlord on the way to work. Having hidden my vials in my briefcase, there's nothing of any real value left in the apartment anyway.

Outside, the chilly morning air dries my nostrils with each breath. A black town car idles in the parking lot, billowing puffs of vapor from its tailpipe as morning dew evaporates to a fine mist from its hood. Distant car horns crow softly, heralding the new day and the possibilities it presents. I trot down to the parking lot and climb in my ride.

Morning drives into the city are rarely quick, but today's flies by and I find myself ascending the bowels of Milburn Tower once again. My palate somewhat cleansed of yesterday's foul taste, even the humans riding beside me on the elevator are more tolerable. Their coffees and breakfast food create an early-day potpourri that today seems rather pleasant and reminds me of the countless pre-dawn farmhouse breakfasts I shared with my parents. Dave's exploited position in all of this and Jan's exhortations are shifting my opinion of humanity. Seeing them as wayward children in need of strong leadership not only makes their sins forgivable, it also motivates me to be the leader that they need. I realize now that there are people in this world who either don't know any better, can't help themselves, or are unwilling envoys of the same heinous evil that lurks the halls of this company, stalking its next victim.

The elevator dings and several of us shuffle around the human pylons, spilling into the hallway. An unusual magnetism draws my attention to Jan awaiting my arrival on a boxy leather sofa, the type of modern furniture that says "We want you to feel at home" but fails to deliver on its claim. As we make eye contact, she lifts herself weightlessly from the seat. Her hands smooth the ripples from her dark gray pant legs and she moves to greet me.

"Jan, I hope you weren't waiting long. I made sure to be here early."

"It's fine. I wasn't waiting long," she notes tranquilly.

Jan dissects me with her famously intense eye contact. Most people can't handle such prolonged engagement, but she feeds off it. It establishes her dominion over those she meets by assuring them that she's supremely confident, indomitable even, and I like that spirit. Amongst her circle of monumental men and women, I've seen this result in more than one impromptu staring contest. In those battles of will, many legendary men have attempted to silently force her submission before averting their gaze in red-faced defeat.

"Let's talk," she says as she walks briskly through my bubble and toward her office.

I follow the mesmerizing mirage of her slinky strides reflecting off the spotless white tiles. Each step forward could be one closer to my death, and yet I care not. A pied piper of sorts, Jan's mysterious charisma has attracted a fiercely loyal flock who can't hope to understand the subliminal forces that leave them spellbound. People believe in her, follow her, and work hard to please her; in many ways, this is a strong model for the relationship I could someday have with humanity.

Stretching my gate, I catch up to Jan and walk by her side. What I need is an interrogation—an opportunity to shine a light in her face and ask all my questions. I need to read her without distraction as she responds. As much as I'd love to dive into such a conversation, if I move too quickly it could spook her, and then she'll be of no use to me. First, I need to earn her trust.

"I'm interested to hear your take on maximizing my potential and expanding my influence," I offer to both initiate and direct the conversation. Flattery, in moderation, is an effective catalyst for trust, and I am genuinely curious about her thoughts.

"Ted, let's just wait until we reach my office. We can't have a meaningful conversation while we're speed-walking down a crowded hall. Besides, there's something else we need to discuss first, privately," Jan gently corrects.

"Alright. I can wait," I reply, intrigued.

Eleven steps later, we enter her corner office. The sun is at just the right angle to reflect off the windows of the adjacent building in a blinding array of orange and yellow. Jan presses a control panel button on her desk, lowering motorized window shades. A linear darkness cuts across the room and wipes down the walls, erasing our shadows inch by inch before meeting the floor. Vertical glints of sunlight peek around the edges of the shades but dissolve when Jan turns on the bright overhead lights. She presses another button that instantly frosts the clear glass doors and walls of her office.

"Please sit, Ted."

I lower myself into one of the sleek black-leather chairs and set my briefcase on the floor between my feet. It won't leave my sight until I find another suitable location for the seed. Jan takes a seat in the chair next to mine. As I raise my gaze back to her, I'm greeted by a pleasant smile. I've heard rumors of its existence but have never seen it before. It's actually delightful.

"I wanted to start the day with an informal conversation. A lot has been going on here lately and if we're going to partner up, we need to clear the air and find a way to understand each other. I need you to see exactly what we're up against."

Sounds like I'm about to get my interrogation after all.

I adjust my position in the chair and lean into the space between us before replying, "That sounds like the perfect way to kick off this relationship. I have plenty of questions that need answering."

"Good. I'm glad you agree and I'm eager to answer your questions and bring you up to speed on our dilemma," she says, subtly reiterating our unavoidable union. "First, though, I have a question for you. The document that Dave asked you to sign, did you sign it?"

After a beat of anger, I draw a deep, cleansing breath and respond with resolve.

"No and I will never sign it," I declare while burning holes through her skull with my fiery eye contact.

Jan chuckles playfully at my intensity. "Look at you…so serious all the time. I'm glad you didn't sign it. I told Dave not to do that but he was too eager to be a good soldier and cover his ass with this whole drug trial thing that he ignored my direction. That report wasn't my idea, but it made for an excellent test of your trustworthiness. You just gave the perfect response."

Her lighthearted demeanor is making it difficult to analyze her honesty. Joking can very effectively disguise lies. In fact, liars often claim that they were only joking when caught in a lie, and people believe them. Many forms of humor require some level of deception, and the speaker's body language and tone of voice are usually more of an act than a reflection of their genuine state of mind.

"Interesting, but Dave's version of events was quite different. He said it was you and the board of directors that were forcing him into that position. He was very convincing," I rebut as I remember his earnestness at The Downspout.

"Of course he would say that, Ted. You're an imposing figure and you were confronting him about criminal behavior. People will lie every time in such a situation."

"Jan, I have…a knack for discerning when people are lying. You could almost say that I can read them like a book. Dave didn't display any of his tells last night and he spoke with conviction," I assert as I interlock my fingers and prop my elbows on the chair's armrests.

I watch closely as Jan takes a moment to contemplate my words. Her gaze drops to the floor and her head shakes slightly from side to side. The results of this deliberation could end up being a genuine explanation of how her and Dave's versions of truth could coexist, or it could be calculated misdirection. She meets my gaze with a look of staid vulnerability.

"Maybe he was telling the truth that someone pressured him to falsify the report, but it wasn't me. I've been at odds with the board about how to handle the Fosillix situation, and it's entirely possible they cut me out of the loop and told him to blame me. Either way, I think I would remember telling him to falsify a report, and I don't," she asserts vigorously. "Besides, you weren't even the quality assurance department head at the time of the drug trial. That would've been sniffed out during an investigation anyway. It was an idiotic plan."

Even in the absence of playfulness, Jan's words are still believable. But through the murkiness of Pentastar's ambiance, my extraordinary relationship with truth is still unable to confirm or deny her statement's veracity. The dynamic between truth and lies is uniquely absolute. Truth exists only in the complete absence of lies. There are varying degrees of dishonesty ranging from fibs to total falsehoods, but there is only one degree of truth. Something cannot be mostly true. It is either wholly truth or it is, to some degree, a lie.

If not for the nuance of individual perception, the discussion of truth and lies would stop there. Unfortunately, each person views events from a limited vantage that creates an incomplete understanding. Each unique interpretation of events further diminishes the universality of truth. This is why it's vital to process the speaker's personal conviction in their words. One who says something untrue is not necessarily a liar if they sincerely believe it to be true. Jan's message clashes with my data, but her bearing, tone, and posture are telling me she believes what she's saying. If I detect even an inkling of wavering belief, then the message has become a lie.

"Let's say I believe that you aren't the driving force behind Pentastar's culture; how do you think the drug trial's aftermath should be handled?"

"People need to be held accountable for their actions. Just because I'm the CEO doesn't mean I exercise absolute control over everything that goes on here. There are members of the board of directors that pull my strings, and even they have powerful majority shareholders who pull theirs. Ultimately, I can't control anyone but myself—Dave and that stupid false report as case in point—and lately even that feels limited," she says with visible frustration.

I look at Jan Lucero through my skeptical brow. The predator at the top of the food chain who prowls these halls and strikes fear in the hearts of all says she's little more than a figurehead. Not many CEOs would so freely acknowledge their own impotence. It requires tremendous humility and a healthy dose of desperation, both of which are apparent in Jan. Though I can't wholeheartedly trust her yet, the desperation that I'm sensing will make her more pliable and, therefore, useful. Either way, we agree on one thing: whoever is responsible for this avoidable tragedy must be held accountable. No matter who it is, I will look into their eyes as they face the reckoning they deserve.

"Are you saying you didn't order the drug trial to proceed or are you saying that you did, but you were provided with bad information?"

"I didn't order the drug trial, Ted. The data showed a high rate of dangerous interactions with some very common drugs and harmful side effects for patients with common, minor health conditions. The drug wasn't ready."

I turn to clear my head, breaking from the exchange. Floating blobs of color bounce along on the other side of the frosted glass. Indistinct voices vibrate through the walls and heels clack against the hallway floor. Straight across the hall sits Jan's secretary answering the ringing phone. Jan's words don't feel calculated, but they're exactly what I'd need to hear to join her cause.

"Why didn't you stop the trial when you found out they went behind your back?" I ask pointedly.

"When I found out that they were proceeding with the trial I was livid, but stopping it would have cost me my job and drawn a lot of unwanted attention from the FDA. I probably should've resigned immediately to punish the board for their overreach. If I had, I also would have avoided this mess, but I still believe in this drug's potential to help suffering people. There's time to get the formula right, and I don't want to give up on all our work here, especially with the price that's already been paid."

Jan's passionate response offers some appeasing concessions about her handling of the situation and also touches on the same noble themes as Dave's. Both claimed some level of victimhood while professing their desire to contribute to the greater good. Either they're working from the same playbook or people in their position all tell themselves the same lies.

"So, do you know who, specifically, is puppeteering the company?"

"The board, in general, has usurped my authority, but I suspect only a few specific directors are pushing their agenda through submissive pawns like Dave and Joel. It's unclear if they're acting under the direction of the shareholders I mentioned. We need to deal with the board first. Once the board stops interfering, we'll have control of the company again, but we may still be under fire from the shareholders."

"I appreciate your candor, Jan, but everything I've seen and heard about the drug trial paints a pretty ugly picture of Pentastar and of you, in particular."

"What happened with the drug trial was sickening. Many of us have been carrying a weight ever since and I've been looking for a way to make those responsible pay for their crimes, but they've been covering their tracks and setting up others to take the fall. They had you in their crosshairs. That's why they sent Dave with the false report. I'm definitely in their crosshairs too; who better to take the fall than the CEO? They've had their minions drop my name with every dirty deed."

"It seems to be working. I can't speak for everyone, but I've definitely thought of you as a ruthless profiteer," I concede.

Jan's shoulders hang heavily. Her downtrodden gaze drifts away. "That's why I need your help, Ted. I can't win this fight without you. There are some truly evil, deceitful people calling the shots here. They make the rules, and they're writing their own version of history. The only reason I haven't been fired is because they want to pin everything on me so it's my neck that ends up in the guillotine."

"Why don't you just resign now?"

"It's too late for me to resign. If I quit now, they'll just tell whatever lies and forge whatever documents they need to absolve themselves and shift the blame to me, you, and numerous other innocent employees. I'm the only one holding the truth together, I mean, whatever is left of it."

Holding the truth together.

Those enchanting words are exactly what I needed to hear. Anyone could say them, but everything I'm sensing in Jan tells me that she's sincere. Beyond that, she knows by reputation that my integrity is incorruptible. If she is the source of Pentastar's wickedness, asking me to help would only increase her likelihood of exposure and worsen her situation.

An excited shiver races up my spine. The idea of maneuvering her as an ally in this operation, even a human one, multiplies my hope. I have never appreciated companionship, perhaps because I have never found a worthy companion. Humans are weak and corrupt and the few Nephilim I have met are reclusive like me. We often use our innate ability to read others as a tool to ensure our own privacy. We stay hidden even from our own kind.

"You're not the only one here who's fighting for truth. I take great pleasure in tearing down the lies that most people hide behind. My work here gives me an opportunity to man the front lines in this war. I'm already actively working against the corruption in this company."

"Is that why you were talking to Joel and Dave before they died?" she asks.

Carefully, I reply, "Yes, I confronted them about their part in all this. Rather than do the right thing, they killed themselves."

"It was honorable of you to try to get through to them," she commends with a comforting look. "Men like them aren't interested in denying themselves and becoming better people. We're a rare minority, Ted. I can't right this ship alone."

"As long as righting the ship means bringing to justice those responsible for all this, then I want to help," I reply while prodding her for confirmation with my eyes.

"I'm so glad to hear that and, yes, that's what I mean by righting the ship," Jan says through a beaming smile. "When you refused to sign that report I knew I could trust you with what's been going on around here."

She looks like a kid on Christmas morning. Her already-high cheeks squeeze her almond eyes to slivers and her body language is relaxed and unguarded. The longer we talk, the more her integrity and warmth cut through the dense atmosphere.

The possibility of having an ally in this fight has me giddy too. I am elated to have found a worthy knight to complement my queen: educated and intelligent, fierce and powerful, and passionate about fixing this company. This exuberance, unexpected and uncontrollable, opens my eyes to how deeply I've longed for this moment. It's doubtful that this reaction is even a credit to Jan as much as it is a release of my bottled-up loneliness. I must be careful to prevent these emotions from influencing my plans for her. She is first and foremost a pivotal piece in a cosmic chess match whose purpose is to be useful in executing my strategy. Any other roles she could fulfill are subordinate to the first. In many ways, Jan isn't even the ideal accomplice. She's too close to the situation and has yet to earn my complete trust. But, at the very least, her education as a lawyer makes her a terrific defense against the human legal system.

Jan will be the high-powered attorney who protects the vigilante from entanglement in the web of human "justice" while also using her formal authority at Pentastar to aid my investigation and targeting. Between the two of us we may actually have a chance to complete this mission and leave Pentastar in capable and trustworthy hands. Once the dust has settled, she will rebuild and restore Pentastar to the lifesaving glory it once enjoyed.

"Ted, there's a board meeting in two days. I'd really like for you to be there. If nothing else, you can be a fly on the wall...see for yourself how corrupt they've become. In the meantime, I'd like to brainstorm tactics with you. We need a long-term game plan, but if there's an opportunity to act quickly, I'd hate to see it go to waste."

Great, she's already trying to take charge. I'll fix that soon enough.

"Dragging this out will only bolster the board's position and increase the chances that we take the fall. I'm prepared to act as soon as we know who's responsible, and I'm eager to put this whole situation in the rearview mirror and move on as soon as possible," I assure, although she can't know exactly what I mean.

Jan and I spend the next several hours discussing the Pentastar Board of Directors and our ideas for righting the ship and restoring the Fosillix trial participants. Occasionally a word or phrase brings some small talk about ourselves or our past, and by the time I head back to my office for the afternoon, I not only feel like I know Jan quite well, but that I actually *like* her. I never thought I'd be able say that about a human.

I log into my computer to review some of my departmental responsibilities. Each day my employees observe the members of the production and maintenance teams performing tasks to ensure that they're following safety and procedural protocol and that product quality meets regulated standards. Their reports are entered into a database and reviewed by auditors who compile the data into a daily rundown that I am expected to know inside and out. If ever a divine guardian of truth is to be relegated to a desk, this job is a suitable alternative. Holding people accountable to these rules and standards is similar enough to holding them accountable to the truth.

Still, I can't release my mind from the fantasy of a rehabilitated Pentastar long enough to concentrate on my work. A hunger grows in the pit of my stomach. It bubbles and growls with ravenous desire to see the shimmering rouge seed put evil on its back. As I stare blankly at my monitor, I imagine the approaching confrontation with the board of directors.

WE KNOW.

The thought makes me sick. Someone, something, knows that I'm Nephilim. A part of me still longs to just sow these devils and be done with it. It would satisfyingly punctuate this operation and ensure its success. My initial brainstorming with Jan got the ball rolling toward a non-sowing solution, but with each passing minute I'm increasingly convinced those options won't work. I need to do this my way, and I need her to accept her role as a piece in my game. If I should need to toss her into the water like chum, I won't tolerate her resisting and dragging me overboard too. The question is, how do I convince Jan to surrender to my authority when so many before me have failed?

CHAPTER TEN

The next several hours of work are anything but productive as I spend them plotting the end of this regrettable chapter in Pentastar's history and engaging in a series of rousing internal debates about Jan. The overcast evening sky obscures tonight's sunset behind dreary, sherbet-infused clouds and as my car delivers me to my apartment building, specks of rain tap out a rhythmic prelude to the upcoming downpour. I arrive at the top-floor landing and see my repaired but unpainted apartment door standing strong before me. The unnerving memory of last night's invasion creeps into my mind and rattles the peace that grew during the day's distractions.

WE KNOW.

I have lost the advantage of anonymity. No, I didn't lose it; it was taken from me.

My keys sway and jingle as I fumble for the right one. Thankfully, Norma, my landlord, just had my locks moved over from my original door. It's become normal for me to have to overwrite muscle memory since I started performing sowings. I instinctively go for the tarnished key with worn teeth that unlocks the family farmhouse, but each of these operations draws me into new spaces that never feel like home with new keys that I never fully break in.

On the other side of the door I expect to be greeted by yesterday's untouched wreckage, but as I enter my apartment I find things much tidier. The pleasant surprise soothes my nerves and brings a smile to my face. The couch cushions are returned to their proper place with the torn side down. Although not in the correct spots, the intact wall décor is rehung and the other unbroken items are all set neatly on the coffee table. All the bits of glass, wood, and porcelain are swept and dumped in the trash.

On the counter, a piece of notebook paper trembles downstream of an air vent. It lies on the exact same spot as last night's bloody message. As I approach the note, the blue cursive handwriting comes into focus.

Mr. Verity,

Gerald and I just want to say that you seem like a nice man and you've been a great tenant. We're saddened that anyone would do this to you and feel some responsibility since this is our building and we care about our tenants' security. We were more than happy to clean things up the best we could and we upgraded your door so everything is steel. I appreciate you offering to pay for the repairs but we've got it covered.

We're happy to report that our hallway and entrance security cameras recorded the intruder. From the video, it doesn't look like he took anything. We would be happy to provide you with a copy of the video so you can file a police report, but we know you value your privacy so we'll leave that to you.

We don't want to pry into your business, but if you've gotten yourself into some kind of jam and need to talk to someone, our pastor would be happy to listen. Let us know if you need anything.

Sincerely,

Norma and Gerald Thompson

I set the note back onto the counter. Norma is the brave developer who bought, owns, and manages this property with her husband Gerald. They're a kind elderly couple who decided late in life to dabble in land development. If I was forced to say good things about humanity, I would start with them. I can't imagine ever seeing humans as family, but they treat everyone in their life as though they're a cherished relative.

The rain has gradually increased from a soft drizzle to a steady shower the sound of one drop indiscernible from another. I grab my phone and check the time: 7:15 p.m. Late, but not too late to call Norma. With the board meeting less than two days away, I need to have a look at that surveillance footage as soon as possible. Any insight into the intruder's identity will help me devise a better plan of attack for Pentastar. I dial Norma's number and wait two rings before the line opens up.

"Hello?" she answers.

"Hi, Mrs. Thompson. This is Ted Verity."

"Mr. Verity, how many times do I have to tell you to call me Norma?"

"I'll call you Norma when you call me Ted," I argue playfully. Maybe it's a byproduct of prepaying a year's rent or maybe it's something else, but we've clicked ever since we first met. Our rapport developed organically and effortlessly.

"Fine, fine. Ted, I take it you got our letter."

"Yes, I got your letter and I want to thank you for everything you did today."

"It's our pleasure. They did quite a number on your place. Is everything okay?" she asks. Her use of the word "they" grabs my attention, even though it makes sense. The bloody note said "we" and there was enough destruction to assume it was caused by multiple people.

"Yes, as good as it could be under the circumstances. I was wondering, though, is it possible for you to send that surveillance video to me via email?"

Norma covers the microphone poorly as she relays my request to her husband. The phone picks up Gerald's distant voice as he explains how to attach the video to an email. Norma, confused, tells Gerald he'll have to do it himself because she doesn't know how. She puts the phone back up to her ear and continues.

"Yeah, Ted, we can do that. I'm going to have Ger do it because I don't meet the ten percent rule. Do you know that rule, Ted?"

"I think I know the one."

"The one that says you have to be ten percent smarter than the computer? Well, I'm not!" she hoots and hollers with a healthy belly laugh.

"Oh, cut yourself some slack. Computers are impossible to keep up with no matter how smart you are," I respond through my smile. They remind me of the grandparents I imagined as a kid. I never met mine.

"Okay, okay. Ger wants to know if we should just use the email from your rental application or if there's a different one?"

"The one from the application will work fine. Thank you, Mrs. Thompson. Your kindness has had a greater impact than you could possibly know. You and your husband are good people."

"NORMA. And you're welcome, Ted. We pray for you, son. Every night lately."

"Thank you for that."

"Okay, okay. I'll watch Gerald send this video through the email as soon as we hang up. That way he won't forget! We'll talk soon."

"Talk soon, Mrs. Thom…Norma. Tell Gerald I say hello."

I hang up and set my phone on the counter. Patience is not my forte, and waiting for the Thompson's email will be torturous if I don't find something to keep me busy. Organizing the remaining clutter from the break-in serves as a suitable diversion for a whole five minutes before I find myself sitting in my armchair, twiddling my thumbs. I'd eat something, but the thought of looking upon the one who knows my true identity has ruined my appetite. Anxiety holds my stomach in its gnarled grip and, outside, the rain shower becomes a historic downpour.

In the stillness of this empty room, my solitude removes its mask and again reveals itself as loneliness. It's not that I want someone else to be here with me. I'd be happy just knowing there is someone out there who has my back the way Melody has Drake's. It feels like a betrayal to suggest the fallibility of anything I was raised to believe. But after spending the day with Jan and experiencing Norma and Gerald's thoughtful kindness, it has never seemed more apparent that my life is lacking. I switch off the cracked, shadeless table lamp and leave my chair for a better view of the storm. As I look out at the blurry yellow rectangles checkered up the nearest high-rise apartment, I imagine the people within sharing a meal around the dinner table, curling up on the couch to watch a movie, and helping their kids with homework.

Behind each window lies a different story, none of them perfect, but all of them sewn together with a common thread: love. I don't know much about love, but I do know that it requires vulnerability and sacrifice to obtain, neither of which I'm accustomed to doing. I'm not seeking romantic love with Jan. I don't even fully know if I can trust her, but I am craving companionship at some level. At the very least, Jan is the enemy of my enemy and, therefore, my friend.

Love? Companionship? A human friend?

Thoughts like that bring my shameful inner conflict into the spotlight. But no matter how real those feelings are, they're always met with a warning. In a voice that is more my father's than my own, I'm reminded that my sacred mission is best accomplished free of entanglements, that to even consider fraternizing with humanity is a violation of everything a noble Nephilim stands for, and that me pursuing love is no different than a dog chasing its tail. However enraptured I become with its buoyant flicking and wagging like a summoning index finger, the whimsical promises of love will wither in reality's corrosive atmosphere. All I'll have to show for my time and energy are my own teeth marks and the humiliation earned in my foolishness.

No, Jan is not a friend and don't need her companionship. What I need is for this operation to be over. I need to return to the farmhouse refreshed by the crisp, clean flavor of justice served. Jan is nothing more than a means to that end.

Barely audible over the volume of water smacking my windows, a blip sounds from the kitchen counter: my email. I turn from the window and race to my phone. It's from Gerald. My tablet's larger screen will let me see more detail so I pop the latches on my briefcase and slide it out. The attachment opens faster than I can stifle the shivers of excitement in my spine. My fingertip thumps with each pounding heartbeat as I touch play.

The tablet screen glows with a grayscale still life of the parking lot. I tap the screen to confirm the movement of the progress bar. Eerily motionless given last night's breeze, the young shrubs and trees extend rigidly from their roots. Being a mostly empty building, only three cars sit slotted in parking spaces. Bright stars glimmer where the streetlights reflect off their glass and metal. In the distant background, a set of headlights move slowly from left to right across the frame. Contrary to the timestamp, it looks more like midnight than 8:07 p.m. When this video was recorded, I was on my ride along with Drake and Lewis.

A streetlight suddenly cuts out, leaving half of the screen black. The bushes and trees on the bright side of the parking lot begin to shake before that streetlight also flickers and dies. Total darkness. I lean closer to my tablet, hoping to make out any variation in the deenergized pixels. My eyes are bombarded when both lights reignite at once, washing the camera in blinding white. I reflexively snap my eyes shut then spy through my eyelashes as the camera adjusts its exposure, revealing three dark figures who walk swiftly and smoothly through the parking lot. Their backlit position leaves their features shrouded in shadow, but their silhouettes reveal their tremendous size—broad enough shoulders and long enough bones to intimidate even me.

The outside footage catches several frames in which the faraway figures' faces are partially lit, but the small handful of dots only reveal a gaunt, human-like appearance that could just be a Halloween mask. With each step closer, it becomes apparent that they're wearing long coats with hoods over their heads and seem to have knowledge of the camera's location. The closer they get the more downward their gaze, concealing their identities until the entrance lights flash and the video dissolves into static.

The recording, now colorized, switches cameras flight by flight, and I watch as they ascend the stairwell to my floor at a leisurely pace. This was no hasty smash and grab. Still facing downward and shrouded by their hoods, one of them takes a post at my door while the other, the biggest of the three, moves straight to the camera's position in the upper corner of the landing. Without looking up, he draws a blade from within his jacket and slams the pommel straight into the lens. It cracks in webbed lines that render parts of the video unintelligible.

He slowly removes the hood from his hairless head and looks directly into the camera. I pause the playback. There are no masks. A gaunt, fractured, and distorted face fills my tablet screen, a taunt that even when I see him I won't *see* him. Black-and-white or color, it makes no difference, because his flesh is gray and his eyes black and soulless. Unable to make a positive identification, I take a screenshot and move on. I can barely make out the creature's blurry, mosaic movements as he kicks my door repeatedly until it relents. He's inside.

An uneventful twenty minutes follows during which the one guarding my door never even flinches until the other two exit my apartment. The big one stops a step outside my door and, before the largest unbroken piece of camera lens, raises his right index finger that is darkened with my blood.

WE KNOW.

He recoils his finger straight into his mouth and pulls it out clean. Unafraid of and unaffected by the seed, the being walks past his accomplices, who follow him down the stairs. The recording switches cameras back to the main entrance, which is once again working, and I stare in fascinated horror as the three figures move across the asphalt. The lights over the parking lot strobe rapidly. The bushes and trees violently whip to and fro. As the figures step into the shadows, I look ahead to the next pool of light, but they never emerge from the darkness. They simply vanish into the night, bringing a sudden stop to the flickering and swaying.

A full progress bar marks the end of the playback. I open my gallery and look again upon the face that will skulk around every blind corner and slink in every twitching shadow within my mind. The enormous size and exotic features of the man, the flickering lights, and the man's immunity to the seed scream Nephilim, but I've never seen a Nephilim like him. It's not just his physical appearance, but also his behavior. The point of Nephilim existence is to be able to walk amongst humanity without detection, but that man walked along a public street into an occupied apartment building and allowed himself to be recorded in his full Nephilim form. Such unhinged brazenness is beyond irresponsible, it's downright reckless. Of course, in the larger context of a Nephilim breaking into and trashing my apartment, such brazenness appears to be in his nature.

The intruder's dead eyes watch me through the screen, and for a moment I feel as though he can see me now. I glare back boldly to overcome the knot of fear that's lodged in my chest, but it doesn't work. Why is a guardian of truth breaking the law and risking the exposure of our race's existence? What led him to me and what does he want? He broke in, took my secret for himself, and spoiled a sacred vial, and here I am left with no answers, no privacy, no allies, nothing.

It occurs to me that an ancient prescript as oppressive as gravity is at work and can be seen throughout reality: the good guys always play from a disadvantage. Our respect for authority and our self-imposed limitations form a barrier between us and our goals. If we dare cast aside our limitations to win by any means then we've entered the wasteland of moral ambiguity. Those who wander here see themselves as the good guy of the story, forced by a broken world to employ evil methods in the hope of fixing it, but in so doing they forfeit their goodness and bow to the broken system; Dave is a prime example.

In that sense, good versus evil has always been an underdog saga. As long as I refuse to bend the rules, abominations like this rogue Nephilim will always have the upper hand. Lucky for me, some of my self-imposed limitations have nothing to do with morality; they're simply pragmatic. It's not impossible or immoral for me to reveal my true nature to humans. We aren't bound by anything more than the warnings of history. The last time the Nephilim lived out in the open it nearly brought about a global extinction. But that was millennia ago, and humanity has changed. Clearly my enemy has no fear of such consequences, and he's using it to his advantage.

At this point, they haven't divulged my true nature to the authorities, but they also gave me no hint as to what they want from me. It's entirely possible they don't want anything from me at all, that their goal was just to intimidate. They know I'm Nephilim, they know where I live, there are several of them working together, and they don't fear my angelic blood. I *am* intimidated. I also feel confident that this creature is the malevolent force behind Pentastar's evil. That's why he made himself known as soon as I started sowing targets. If he's trying to run me off, he failed. In fact, he's piqued my interest. If he's the source of evil, then Jan was telling the truth and is just another victim of his game.

My path forward has become clear. I need to level the playing field and I can't do that without recruiting more pieces to be maneuvered. I also know just how to make Jan one of those pieces, eager to do my bidding and sacrifice for the greater good. Before the board meeting, I'll reveal to Jan that I'm Nephilim and invite her to be my ally. The risk/reward analysis is simple. She either accepts the role as a piece in my game, or she becomes a threat to my confidentiality and I sow her, which was the original plan anyway. If she's as innocent as she says, she'll come out of the sowing better for it. If not, she'll kill herself, an acceptable risk when the reward is completing this mission and returning to my farmhouse by the end of the week.

CHAPTER ELEVEN

The same dreary rain clouds that unleashed a torrential downpour ten hours earlier still blanket the Port Ellis skyline. Snagged on the city's spires and antennas, they failed to make their escape in the night and are now smothering out the sun's light and warmth. Each manmade summit of sufficient height gradually fades into the floating droplets that pulsate slowly with red iridescence. The lethargic crimson strobes are beacons mounted atop the titanic landmarks of earthly empires.

Of all the mornings for a sewage problem on Sixth Street, today is most inconvenient. The remnants of last night's storm force my straight and narrow path into a dizzying dance around and over enormous puddles. Then again, such a sewage problem would only happen after a historic rainfall overwhelms the city's dilapidated infrastructure. My driver could only make it within two blocks of Pentastar, so I walk in the cold mist with the foul odor of human slop in my nostrils.

Each nanoscopic bead releases a tiny arctic chill as it bursts against the skin of my face and neck. To describe the air's motion as a breeze implies a certain weightlessness, but this morning's atmosphere is far too dense and putrid for such a refreshing adjective. Despite the ground-level cloud's hurried movement, it's going nowhere but still circulates a fresh chill with each redundant puff.

There is something exciting about this brief stroll down the mystical sidewalk. Instead of the same boring scenery, my surroundings have taken on an otherworldly ambiance much like that of the Pneuma Rigma, or so I've heard. According to Nephilim folklore, the angelic dimension, the Pneuma Rigma, exists on the same plane as ours but is shifted out of phase. My father explained it to me in terms of three-phase electricity and sine waves, but that was only mildly helpful. I would equate the dimensional relationship to holding two saw blades flat against each other with the teeth aligned, then shifting one blade so its teeth are evenly spaced between the points of the other blade.

I have no intention of ever grasping it fully because Nephilim are not meant to enter it, and so I have no need to understand it. It's the expanse through which angels and demons move undetected amongst humanity and only they possess the power to generate windows—to bend the saw teeth into alignment—in order to pass between realms. This is exceptionally rare.

There's a silly children's story about an ancient Nephilim named Verdonos whose blood was almost purely angelic. As the tale goes, he was extremely powerful and learned to pass between dimensions. He used this ability to move stealthily throughout the world, sowing the seeds of truth and vanishing without a trace. When in the Pneuma Rigma, Verdonos always made sure to move swiftly to avoid being detected by those who truly belonged there and who would not look kindly on his presence. One day, he opened a window like he had hundreds of times before, but as he passed through, he was met by several demons who took issue with his use of their territory for the spreading of truth. The legend ends with him making a valiant stand against a small demonic horde. They tore him to shreds before the angels could come to his aid. He's the closest thing to a superhero the Nephilim have, and the story still inspires young ones to this day.

For the shortest of moments, I allow myself to swoosh, like Verdonos, through the mist before I turn to enter the villain's lair. Inside the lobby of Milburn Tower, I depart from my usual path to the elevator in order to ask a favor of Tyson Ander. He sees me weaving toward the security kiosk, immediately stretches his lips into a genuinely thrilled smile, and waves cheerfully. There's no other person in this building better suited to be the first face everyone sees on their way into work.

"Splendid morning to you, Mr. Verity," he starts.

I glance over my shoulder and back outside just in case the weather has miraculously cleared since I entered. Still cloudy. "You really think so, Tyson?"

"Of course, sir. Every day we wake up breathing is magnificent!"

"Tyson, don't change," I say with a smile.

"I couldn't if I tried," he exclaims with a laugh. "Positive by nature; it's a curse. Now, what can I do for you, Mr. Verity?"

"Well, I can't go into much detail—the nature of my problem is confidential—but I have a threatening situation and could really use your help."

Tyson's expression betrays his excitement at the prospect of doing something other than manning this desk. A subtle grin and slow head bob prophesy an affirmative answer before a question has even been asked. This is his finest hour.

"I can't abide threatening situations in my tower, Mr. Verity. I'm all ears. Please continue," he casually prompts while eating his smile. I can see it in his eyes. He's hooked.

I lean in and motion for Tyson to come closer, reeling him in. I lower my volume and dial up the intrigue. "A couple of days ago, I'm sure you're aware, two of my coworkers committed suicide; one of them here and one of them in an alley next to The Downspout."

"I saw the jumper hit the sidewalk…and I heard about Dave," he whispers sadly.

"Yes, it's very sad. Well, there's something sinister going on at Pentastar and I'm trying to get to the bottom of it. I need a totally secure place to have a meeting. A place without cameras or microphones, without potential spies, and with no chance of interruption."

"Anything you need, sir. Did you have a place in mind?"

"Yes, actually. I know they reinforced the door and replaced the lock since Joel—the jumper—but I was hoping you could get me on the roof," I say.

Tyson winds up to shake his head no.

Before he can respond, I continue, "There aren't any cameras or microphones up there, no one will see us in this thick mist, and no one else will accidentally wander by. It's perfect."

Tyson releases his coiled-up wag of disapproval.

"Sorry, Mr. Verity. No can do. I would lose my job if anyone found out, and if something bad happened up there I could be held legally responsible." Tyson's tone is a cocktail of remorse and disappointment. His moment stopped before it started.

I nod in understanding and lower my head in a bit of a pout that I'm not proud of.

"Actually, I might know an even better place, sir," Tyson offers. "The roof actually has cameras in a few places so that wouldn't have worked well anyway, but one of the boiler rooms would be perfect!"

"That might work. Where are they?"

"There are two downstairs and I have the keys right here. There are no cameras in the rooms and the only people with a reason to go down there are maintenance, but the boilers were just replaced last month and these sewage problems will keep them occupied elsewhere."

"Okay, Tyson, that sounds like a decent option. Good thinking. I'll need you to show me where it is, though. When can you go?"

"Hey, Barry," Tyson calls to the man seated next to him at the kiosk.

Tyson turns to his shift partner who's deeply involved in a game of solitaire. Barry clicks the deck repeatedly, cycling through every card. "Crap," he grunts, then begins clicking through the deck again. For the first time since I've known him, Tyson is visibly displeased, probably because this human dough ball is hampering his heroic fantasy. He watches Barry begin clicking through the deck a third time when he finally snaps.

"Barry!" Tyson quietly shouts.

Barry startles slightly then turns to face the heat of Tyson's glare.

"What, man?" Barry asks.

"No matter how many times you click through, the cards aren't going to change without you playing one."

"Duh, bro. I know how to play solitaire. Stay outta my biz, man."

"You're the reason no one takes us seriously, you rent-a-cop cliché," Tyson slashes.

"Well, we are rent-a-cops and you're welcome, douche. Thanks to me they expect so little of us that we can play solitaire at work," Barry retorts with a smirk.

"That's only because I cover for your lazy ass! They'd fire you in a second if they knew."

"Hmmm, I suppose thanks are in order. I do enjoy getting paid. So…thanks, Tyson," Barry says with a glib shrug.

Tyson pauses, trying to steel his irritated expression, then lets out a bottled-up giggle.

"Good...you're welcome. Now, I need you to cover the desk for five, maybe ten minutes. I have some business with Mr. Verity."

"What kind of business?"

"The kind that's none of yours. Now get off your ass and start greeting people."

Barry reluctantly leverages his overweight frame from the desk chair.

"Now smile," Tyson orders.

Barry's natural smile is more infectious than tuberculosis, but this one, this grotesque attempt, is an atrocity. I'm not sure what I just witnessed during their interaction. At first it seemed like a lecture, then a fight, but by the end it was something of a playful quarrel between old pals. Tyson and Barry have worked together for some time now and have accumulated just the right balance of comfort and bitterness to stand the test of time.

"You ready, Tyson?" I ask, trying not to end up in the crossfire.

"Yah, Barry's got this. Let's go."

Tyson leads the way to the stairwell where we descend one flight and arrive at a red metal door. As he unlocks it and pushes through, the long corridor exhales a rush of stale breath that feels like a warning to turn back. The door closes behind me with a metallic *ka-chunk*. It's too late now. In this dimly lit and dank unnumbered circle of hell, I half expect to find black ooze bubbling up from the drains, angry specters patrolling the hall, rotting corpses being eaten by rats, and any number of other horror movie tropes.

One thing's for sure: Jan is going to think I've lost my mind when I tell her to meet me down here. This environment will definitely set an ominous tone for our meeting. I just hope it's not too much. In the end, I think she'll understand why I chose to do it this way. There's also the added benefit that no one will be able to hear her scream from down here if she freaks out.

"So, what was all that about with Barry?" I ask as we move toward the first dull splash of fluorescent light.

"Oh," he says with a spirited laugh, "I guess that does require an explanation. Barry says I'm too nice, so he's challenged me to be meaner to him."

"Ah, I see. That makes more sense. For a minute, I thought you finally blew your top."

"No, no. I really am this nice. I'm not even bottling anything up. I'm not very good at being mean and I don't see the need to improve, but Barry insisted and it's kind of fun to pretend. Plus, he is really lazy and it's nice to finally tell him," he bawls loudly, chasing it with a sturdy laugh.

Tyson's overpowering positivity is radiating off the cinder block walls, bringing an inviting warmth and light to this dungeon. The thought crosses my mind to have him escort Jan down to meet me. He might even prefer it that way to keep an eye on us "unauthorized personnel," although he seems to inherently trust me. He slows down and veers to a set of large double doors on the left.

"Here's the first boiler room," Tyson announces. The jingling of his keys comes from behind me as it echoes up and down the hall. The lock tumblers grind as he inserts the key with a slight jiggling motion. "Voila," he says as he pulls the door open.

Shockingly intense light spills into the hallway. Tyson looks back at me with squinty eyes as he beckons me to enter.

"Don't be shy. The lights are bright but they don't bite." Tyson's expression asks if I noticed his rhyme. "I just made that up on the spot. See what I did?"

I can't help but chuckle. "Yeah, I see what you did. Impressive. They *are* really bright!"

"The technicians complained about the dim lighting during the boiler installation, so the maintenance director had these bright flood lights installed on both walls. It makes their boiler maintenance easier too, once your eyes adjust anyway."

The fixtures flood the room with clarity. Massive, glossy green cylinders flank each side of the double doors with plenty of room to move around. Straight through the doors, in between the boilers, is a large open space perfect for revealing myself to Jan. With any luck, the process will go as smoothly as a routine medical procedure under these operating room lights. Like showing her an oddly bent finger or an unsightly mole, I'll briefly prepare her for what I'm about to do, then release my posture and reveal my true form. She'll react with fear, confusion, maybe even shock, but eventually accept her new reality and take her place at my right hand.

"Tyson, would you be able to do one more thing for me?"

"Sure. What do you need?"

"Will you meet Jan Lucero in the lobby and bring her down here?"

"Absolutely. It can be kind of creepy in that hall. Besides, it's probably better if I'm involved, at least at that level. For security reasons, you know? Is she headed down now?"

"I know. I figured you'd say as much. I'm going to call her down now. Thanks, Tyson."

I pull my cell phone from my pocket but, as I should've expected, there's no service in hell. I see a phone installed on the wall near the doors. "Tyson, is this networked to the rest of the building?"

"Not sure, sir. You could try," he replies with a shrug.

I grab the handset and lift it to my ear. There's a dial tone, so I punch in Jan's direct office number to bypass her assistant. She may not answer the direct call, but for all I know her assistant could be spying for the board of directors or that rogue Nephilim. Without knowing who to trust, the fewer people who know of our budding alliance, the better. It's 8:04 a.m. I'm officially late for work, which means Jan will have been in her office for over an hour already. Some days, it seems she never leaves.

"This is Jan Lucero," she answers in the middle of the first ring, catching me unprepared.

"Uh, hey, uh, good morning, Jan. It's Ted."

"Ted? Why do you sound like an idiot and where are you calling from? I don't recognize the number."

"Sorry, I was caught off guard when you answered," I explain.

"Why would you be caught off guard? You called me not expecting me to answer?"

Jan is in a fun mood. Already I'm questioning my choice of allies. Maybe the enemy of my enemy is just another enemy.

"I wasn't sure you'd answer a direct call from an unfamiliar number." Unsure if our newly forged relationship affords me the privilege, I delicately approach my next question. "Is everything okay this morning?"

"There you go sounding dumb again, Ted. Of course everything is not okay. This company is teetering on the edge of—" She pumps her brakes mid-thought and sighs. She's definitely not in the same state of mind as yesterday. "I'm sorry, Ted. It's the board meeting tomorrow. I'm a little stressed. We don't have a good plan and I'm just really tired of being in this position. I'm ready to be done with all of this."

"A *little* stressed?" I think. Thankfully the thought never makes it to my lips. Instead, I commiserate. "I completely understand, Jan. Anyone would be unbearably stressed in your situation." My stomach does a somersault as I prepare the next sentence. "I need to show you something that I think will tip the scales in our favor and put your mind at ease."

"I like the sound of that. By the way, you never answered earlier. Where are you? I'll come meet you," she offers excitedly. Undoubtedly, she won't anticipate my answer.

"I'm in a basement boiler room." I pause as I realize how creepy that could come across. "I know this sounds weird, but I need you to trust me. I need you to meet me down here."

Jan is silent. I may have overestimated her trust in me.

"You're right, that sounds really weird, but I'm intrigued. When should I come down?"

"Tyson Anders from security will meet you in the lobby in five minutes and bring you down. We need to discuss something of critical importance. I need you to keep an open mind. Sorry, I can't be more specific than that over the phone."

"Okay. I'll head that way now."

The line dies, and Tyson looks at me with inquisitive eyes.

"She's on her way," I say to him, but his face is still asking a question. "What is it?"

"I'm just really curious what you're going to show her…down here…in the boiler room," he says, both asking a question and insinuating the apparent impropriety of this clandestine meeting.

"Tyson, you're being extremely helpful and I'm truly grateful, but I can't bring you in on this. I can't put you at risk too."

"At risk? If this is so dangerous you should call the police," Tyson says, and he would be correct if it wasn't for my presence. They could come in and flesh out all the evidence, maybe even forensically identify some of the fraudulent documents and signatures. Still, innocent people will get caught in the crossfire, Jan will likely still fall, and the ones ultimately responsible for this will get little more than a slap on the wrist, if they're even caught. That's an unacceptable outcome.

"You're right, but it's too complicated right now to bring in the police. We need to untangle the situation before the police get involved. If they investigate now, they're going to build a case against the wrong people."

"I'll take your word for it, Ted. I just don't want anyone else getting hurt."

"Well, you don't have to worry about Jan and me. We'll be fine. Speaking of Jan, she should be halfway down to the lobby by now," I prompt Tyson.

"Yeah, you're probably right. I'll head up there. Just wait here and I'll bring her down."

And with that, Tyson heads back down the gloomy corridor to the stairwell, jingling with each step. I stand propping the door open with my foot and looking between the brightened boiler room surfaces into the shadow. Tyson disappears through the red metal door with a shrieking clunk that reverberates and swells off the cold, concrete walls. A spasm in my abdomen reminds me of what comes next. I'm going to violate the principles that have defined my entire existence, and Jan is going to have her understanding of the world blown to bits.

CHAPTER TWELVE

Five long minutes trudge by. My only distraction besides the hissing and thunking of the giant green boilers is a rampaging pill bug that's been scuttling aimlessly back and forth. Looking out from my vivid enclosure, the hallway shadows appear to sway and jitter, but there's still no sign of Tyson and Jan. My ears perk sharply at the muffled sound of a stairwell door somewhere above the surface. I watch the end of the hall, hopeful that Jan will appear so I can get this over with and settle the boiling acid in my stomach, but the door stays closed. Behind me, a pump kicks on and hums deeply, grating at first but eventually rather soothing. The droning rumble relaxes me like road noise to a stir-crazy toddler.

No amount of watching will bring Jan here any faster, and I don't need her to find me waiting for her arrival like an anxious dog. I step back inside to channel my anxiety into a boiler room walkabout and the door is pulled gently shut by its closer. With the darkness of the hallway closing in around me, I had failed to notice just how high the ceilings are down here. It looks like twenty feet to the intricate highway of piping and conduit strapped to the ceiling.

"Good thing for the extra headroom," I quip to myself. "I'm going to need it." Although I definitely won't need all of that space. At full extension, I measure eight feet, two inches; hardly a giant by angelic standards. Even by Nephilim standards I'm on the short end, but this has proven more of an asset than a liability. It allows me to compress my stature to a modest six feet, eight inches, easing my integration with humanity. Of course, that's still extremely tall, but there are plenty of full-blood humans even taller, enough to avoid being the tallest "person" most people have met.

Nephilim skeletal structure varies from human beings in a number of ways. The shape of each of our vertebrae resembles a cam with peaks and valleys on opposite sides. When we tense special muscles in our back, the vertebrae twist so that the peaks align and extend our height significantly. Our hip sockets have a similar design that raises and lowers our pelvis relative to our femurs. I can only imagine a human doctor's morbid fascination with our anatomy if we were to stroll into a clinic. Thankfully, Nephilim rarely suffer from illness or injury so the need for traditional medical care is minimal. If it's ever necessary, there are a handful of Nephilim who have adapted human medical practices and a few basic medicines for our bodies.

My stroll around the boilers reveals the expected: various dead insects, shriveled spider exoskeletons, cobwebs, stray metal shavings, and a couple of forgotten screws and washers. A folding metal chair leans, collapsed, against the wall at the end of the tank. There are several low points in the concrete floor that bear the chalky mineral scars of evaporated leaks, one of which can be traced back to the far wall. Panning up, I find the culprit. A brand-new stretch of four-inch pipe, probably one foot in length, is installed between two couplings. It must've rusted out and burst as the adjacent bulging pipe looks prepared to do. Examining the deformed pipe reveals an otherwise healthy stretch of plumbing. If not for this single point of corrosion, it would be in top shape.

A clear memory from nearly twenty years ago comes to mind. It was a sunny fall day, hotter than usual, as my father and I were clearing a section of the yard to build a new shed. An old stump, the diminished legacy of a tremendous oak tree, sat stubbornly in the perfect place for our new building. Realistically, there was probably another suitable location for the shed, but the old stump was matched in its stubbornness by my old man. It took a full morning and most of an afternoon digging, picking, cutting, and tugging to make any progress on the firmly entrenched trunk.

It was nearly dinnertime when my father and I found hope in our battle. We wrapped a chain around the stump and hitched it to the back of our rusty four-by-four pickup. Father gradually increased the tension with the truck in first gear. Initially, it didn't budge, so he let off the gas. He had me double-check the chain before he gassed it again, this time harder than the first, but still nothing. On the third heave, the oak trunk peeled upward from the earth by more than six inches. Tasting imminent victory, he pressed the gas pedal half an inch farther but the stump doubled down, snapping the chain with the strangest jingling crack. I can still remember the sound to this day. It recoiled in a blur straight toward the back of the truck and smashed the rear window of the cab, flinging glass that embedded itself in the right side of my dad's face.

The wounds were superficial but painful and bloody nonetheless. After he and my mother tended to his injuries, we both went back outside to survey the damage. A single chain link gave out under the pressure, a metaphor that my father employed wisely. He taught me that we, as Nephilim, must be vigilant to inspect ourselves, to know our weaknesses and our vulnerabilities in order to prevent such catastrophic failures. He said that no matter how hard we work, ignoring even a single weakening link in our integrity or our emotional and psychological health could be our undoing. He said I have to be honest with myself and take care to address my personal weaknesses.

This timely reminder comes as I'm more aware than ever of my own desire for companionship. The effects of last night's fatherly pep talk from beyond the grave were short-lived, and I'm once again faced with the inner battle that threatens to split me in half. Continuing in this loneliness seems unsustainable, and the more of an island I become, the more susceptible I'll be to wayward thoughts and actions. I need to remedy this growing chasm in my life, but I can't let this loneliness motivate my actions with Jan. I don't fully trust her yet and probably never will. She's human, prone to deceit and certainly contaminated by their usual filth. That being said, I've never fully trusted anyone, and that won't change if I can't allow someone the opportunity to earn my confidence. Not only does recruiting Jan provide the ally that I need, it's also low-risk practice for learning how to trust. That way, when I someday meet a proper Nephilim companion, I'll have some experience in building a relationship. Besides, revealing myself as a divine being should correct any of her undesirable behavior. And, again, if she doesn't clean up her own act, a sowing will do it for her.

Voices reverberate from the far end of the hall, ripping me from my introspection. I fly back to my post at the door and prop it open slightly. Though the familiar jingle-clink, jingle-clink of Tyson's wad of keys obscures their words, I recognize Jan's voice. A shot of mania pelts my skin. I draw a deep breath then release it slowly through a pinhole in my tight lips.

"He's up here on the left," Tyson says like an assistant delivering a client to my office. He speaks calmly, naturally, as though it's perfectly normal to walk through a dark, dingy tunnel for a one-on-one meeting in a boiler room. They enter the trapezoid of pure light that's escaping around me as I push the door slowly to avoid startling Jan.

"Thank you, Tyson," I say before turning my attention to Jan. "Thanks for meeting me down here. I know it's a bit…unconventional, but you'll understand soon enough. I'll take it from here, Tyson. Are you good with us just showing ourselves out after the meeting?"

"Uh," he hesitates, "I guess that will be fine, sir." He nods a goodbye and heads back the other direction as I pull the door to make sure it's completely shut.

"DAMN, it's bright in here!" Jan exclaims. "I can't see a thing after being in that dark hallway."

"Yeah, the light is overwhelming at first, but you'll adjust," I say, accidentally speaking in metaphors.

Jan blinks tightly and rubs her eyes. She opens them a touch, staring at the floor to avoid the direct blast of the floodlights. Gradually, she raises her head and scans the room.

"Okay, I can see again." She puts her hands on her hips and surveys the room. "Well, this is homey," she snarks.

"Sorry, it was the only place Tyson could think of where we could have total privacy." As I say that, I remember the phone on the wall. "Actually, hold on a second." I reach to the back of the phone and unplug the cable. "Okay, now it's totally private."

"I assume that's the phone you used to call me?"

"It is. There's no cell service down here. Speaking of, would you mind turning your phone off and setting it on that ledge? I'll do the same." I remove the phone from my pocket and hold the power button until *Samsung* appears on the screen. Jan holds her power button and shows me the black screen before placing it gently on the ledge.

"You sure you aren't being a little paranoid there, Ted?" she asks rhetorically. "I don't want to spend any more time down here than I have to, so what game-changing information did you want to show me?"

I draw another deep breath and squeeze it through taut lips. My pulse slows for a few beats before a surge of electricity enters my chest and jolts my heart into overdrive. If I can't subdue my nerves, I'll just have to fight through them.

"I wouldn't necessarily call it game-changing *information*. It's more of a game-changing revelation of reality. Yes, information, but, more importantly, cosmic truth."

"What the hell are you smoking, Ted? There are few things I hate more than listening to people say things that don't mean anything. Stop telling me about what you're going to say and just say it."

"Fair enough," I concede. That was a clumsy start. "Jan, are you a religious person?"

"No, I'm not *religious* but I believe in the spiritual, the supernatural."

"By 'supernatural' do you mean God, angels, and demons or do you mean ghosts, vampires, and werewolves?"

She lets out an impatient sigh then humors me. "I'm not entirely sure. I just wouldn't be surprised if humanity isn't alone and life doesn't really end when we die."

"Good. Have you—"

"You're not about to tell me that God's on our side or some religious garbage like that, are you? If you are, you can save it," Jan spits.

"No, that's not what I'm trying to say. Have you heard the story of Noah, from the Bible?"

"Yes, when I was a young girl and again when I dabbled with church during my college years. I was curious, I guess. I didn't want to dismiss it without giving it a try." She smirks sheepishly before saying, "You know, that story is a lot more R-rated than I remembered from Sunday School."

"Indeed it is. So, is it safe to assume you're familiar with the concept of the Nephilim?"

"I know the word," she says, pausing to search her memory. "They were the offspring of angels and women right? Weren't they giants? Wait, never mind. What the hell does this have to do with us and Pentastar?"

"I'm getting there," I say, intently watching every twitch of her eyelids, every stretch of her lips, and every movement of her pores. Under these lights, it's like looking at her through a magnifying glass. She seems a little nervous but no more so than anyone would be during a private meeting in a basement with a large man asking strange questions. "Would you believe me if I told you that the Nephilim are real and walk amongst us to this day?"

"I would say it's possible, potentially believable, but I would need more than your word to accept it."

"What if I could show you?"

"I don't know what that means. Are you about to offer up some blurry Bigfoot photo or are you saying you actually know where to find them? I'll just tell you now that I'm not going to believe a photo. Any hack with a computer can doctor a picture. I'd have to see it in person."

"Well, that's the idea."

"So you're claiming to know the identity and whereabouts of an actual angel/human hybrid, and that is somehow relevant to our situation here…"

"I realize how it sounds, but I asked you to trust me, and the fact that you're down here in the underbelly of Milburn Tower means that, at some level, you do."

"I was starting to trust you quite a bit, but right now you sound insane."

My ribs tighten when I realize the only way forward is to show Jan my true identity. I remember the chair leaning against the wall and grab it for Jan to sit on. I don't want her head bouncing off the floor or anything else if she faints. I don't know how she'll react. I've never done this before unless it was part of a sowing. No matter how this goes, I need her to accept this reality, vow to keep my secret, and commit to being my ally in this fight.

"Jan," I say, pausing heavily. "What I'm about to show you will be frightening but I promise that you are not in danger. This will not hurt and I will not harm you."

Jan glares at me like I'm an extraterrestrial. It's now apparent that I'm talking about myself, that I'm claiming to be Nephilim. Her cynical expression takes on notes of sizzling fascination. She knows I don't lie and have never before given her reason to doubt my sanity. She's inspecting my face and my stature, doing the math. I don't look like most humans, a fact she has undoubtedly noticed, but one that's taken on new significance during this conversation. Suddenly, her face opens to the possibility.

"Show me," she urges with a flick of her eyebrow. It's a hungry *show me*, as if she has buried the need for such a revelation her whole life and now it's breaking free. It's proof that there's something more to this existence, the answer to whether or not humanity is alone. "Come on, prove it," she gently pushes, as one would say to a friend who said he could do the impossible. I can almost read her mind: *He sounds crazy, and maybe he is, but it would be amazing if it were true.*

I cock my head as I look down at the feisty woman who's still surprisingly tall despite being seated. "Okay, then. I'll show you," I say calmly.

I remove my suit coat and hold it up to Jan. "Would you mind laying this across your lap?"

"Sure, whatever helps get this show on the road, Ted."

Next comes my tie, then my dress shirt, button by button. Jan looks at me, annoyed, from beneath a growing pile of laundry. "If you get naked, I'm leaving…and you're fired."

"Noted," I reply while kicking off my loosened shoes.

"Is this really necessary?"

I respond stoically, "It is."

While extending to full Nephilim form, I have ripped the seams on more than one dress shirt. Most of my growth is vertical but my overall proportions also change, putting stress on the shoulders and typical cut of human shirts. It's also just really uncomfortable to grow over a foot in clothes that weren't made to stretch. Some situations, like Joel's sowing, don't require full extension, just five or six inches. After a sowing like that, I can simply tuck in my shirt and go about my day, but this is different. If I want to make sure Jan knows her place, it'll require a stronger dose of humility, one that only my full stature can impose.

The pumps grumble to life again, providing a convenient pillow of sound to stifle any gasps or screams from Jan. With my eyes closed, I carefully tense the muscles along my spine, twisting my vertebrae to their full extension. My disks pop and crackle like chafing leather as they uncoil, raising my head even with the top of the tanks. Every inch stretches my skin tighter around my skeleton. Through my eyelids, I can see the room's dazzling lights flash sporadically. Three flickers…pause…two flashes…a bright blast…darkness…four flickers.

The microbes in my blood dance against my tingling veins which are now quite visible through my thinning skin. As on a roadmap, the dark trails extend in major thoroughfares and tiny back roads, zigging and zagging along and around my limbs, torso, neck, and face. Waves of adrenaline sweep across my body with every pulse. I lift my face to the ceiling as a surge of strength passes through my clenched jaw. The pressure in my ears makes it difficult to hear more than the muffled rumbling that originates in both my quaking bones and in the droning utility pumps that surge on.

Each and every hair flees the surface of my skin only to be stopped by its follicle. A tumbling, metallic trickle approaches from behind me. I snap around only to find the loose screws, washers, and metal shavings from the floor caught in my electromagnetic field and jittering along the side of the boiler tank. The lights are now flickering with frantic intensity like an epileptic nightmare, their moments of darkness almost indistinguishable from their moments of light. I spread my arms wide to bask in the raw exposure of my angelic glory.

A vulgar, carnal euphoria washes over me; the sour satisfaction that can only be found in the flesh of forbidden fruit. For the first time in my life, I've broken one of my rules and it is a big one. Taking my true form in front of a human who will live to retain the memory violates my personal code but exhilarates my body. I revel in the debased liberation of this moment.

"Jan," my voice rolls in an earthquake whisper, "the Nephilim are real and I am one of them."

No response.

Slightly panicked, I look down to the door—it's still closed—then pan over to Jan. Still in her chair, she is the embodiment of dread, frozen in time. Like the immortalized dead of Pompeii,

Jan's body is stiffly contorted on the metal seat. Her face a ghoulish grimace, both pained and horrified. Her mouth, agape and twisted, releases a breathless shriek. The possibility that I've actually hurt her confronts my conscience. A face like that is enough to inflict pain on passersby; I can only imagine what she must be feeling.

I relax my spine and instantly settle back into my human form with a crackle like twisting bubble wrap. Lunging toward Jan, I grip both of her shoulders firmly.

"Jan…Jan. Snap out of it."

No response.

"Jan," I call, snapping my fingers, "come back to me."

She takes a series of audible, labored breaths, then a gasp as she reanimates. Still dazed, she hangs her head and collects herself before looking at each of my hands on her shoulders.

"Do you mind?" she asks. I release her shoulders and stand upright. She props her elbows on her knees and rests her forehead in her palms. I maintain the silence in the vain hope that she'll speak first. After thirty seconds of Jan's groaning, I decide to speak up.

"I'm sorry. Did it hurt? I didn't mean to hurt you."

"Holy shit, Ted. What the hell did you do?" she shouts. "I feel like I got hit by a truck. My whole body is sore."

"I didn't even touch you. You were pretty tense though, muscles locked up and everything. It was like you were frozen. That's probably why you're sore." It's a guess, but it makes sense. She starts massaging the knots out of her legs. "Do you remember anything?" I ask, almost reluctantly.

"Yeah, Ted, if that's even your real name. I remember."

"Actually, Ted is my nickname. My full name is Theodonis. What, exactly, do you remember?"

"I remember everything up until I blacked out. The lights started flashing, you grew like a foot taller, then I guess I blacked out. The next thing I remember is you waking me up. How long was I out?"

"I don't know. The whole thing only took a minute or so. You might have been out for ten, fifteen seconds. I wasn't really watching you."

She moves her massaging fingers up to the back of her neck, still winding down and processing what she just witnessed. I gently retrieve my dress shirt and tie from her lap, then my coat. As I reassemble myself, she looks at me with hopeful uncertainty.

"So…you're part angel, a Nephilim?"

"Yes," I chirp quickly, not wanting to interrupt the flow of her thoughts.

"Aaand what? You have some kind of angel powers, I assume."

"In a way."

"What kind of way?"

"I'm a divine agent of truth. I can reach into the minds of men and set them straight."

She spends more time in silent, jumbled thought, then says, "You were right. This changes things. It changes my whole damn understanding of the universe. But how does it help us at Pentastar? Surely you can't just angel-Hulk smash all the bad guys."

"You're right, I can't. That's not how this wor—"

"Wait a second, did you actually kill Joel and Dave?" Jan interjects incredulously.

"I didn't kill them and that's not how this works. That's what I was about to explain. They actually committed suicide, but my involvement led them to a crossroads. With enough residual integrity and will to live, they could have chosen a fresh start. It's the morally filthy and the spiritually weak who usually choose to end their lives, but there is no way to know for sure what the outcome will be when I sow someone. You knew Joel and Dave even better than me, you knew their dirty deeds and corrupt hearts. The more evil that people have to overcome during a sowing, the harder it is for them to continue living."

"You said 'sowing.' What's a sowing?"

"There's a lot I need to explain before you're going to fully understand our options and my role here. We can have this conversation here or somewhere more comfortable. Now that I've shown you what I needed to, we don't have to stay down here."

"No, you were right. I see why we're down here now and I don't want anyone overhearing us or finding out about you. Let's just hash this out here and now," she says.

"Okay. Fine by me," I reply.

Jan stands from the chair and arches backward with her palms pressed into the small of her back. Still working out the kinks. She seems to be handling all this surprisingly well, probably aided in part by her newfound position as an angel's sidekick. It really doesn't matter to me why she's taking it well. In the darkest corners of my imagination, this moment had ended with ear-piercing squawks of terror and me having to pin Jan down and force-feed her my blood. Anything short of that fiasco feels like a win, but *this* outcome feels like a grand slam. The upcoming conversation is simply my lap around the bases that leads to the victorious embrace of my teammate.

"So, you were saying something about sowing?" she asks, but the subtext barks *out with it, I don't have all day*. Even in the presence of a divine being, Jan is still bossy.

"Yes. Nephilim were created to be agents of truth who expose the lies that hold mankind captive, stealing their free will. Contained within our blood is a wondrous microorganism that impacts the electrical field of the human brain, temporarily supercharging it. That organism is also the reason that the lights flashed when I showed you my true form; their excited movement can affect electromagnetic fields in the surrounding space. Anyway, when the human brain is stimulated this way, it extracts many realities that people know to be true without actively knowing. The lies they tell themselves melt away and the cues that went unnoticed during conversations with others become highlighted in their memories, revealing the lies that others have told them. The limitless alternate endings of life parade before them and they are confronted with how their dishonesty and that of others has destroyed lives. Then they're left with a choice: embrace the truth and start fresh or collapse under the weight of ruined lives."

My response seems to have answered several of Jan's questions before she could ask them. Her unplugged eyes look through me as she nods to herself, but then her nose crinkles.

"How does the organism get from your blood to theirs?"

"That's a good question," I say, hoping my positivity will fuel hers. I reach into my pocket and produce my small vial of blood. The intense lights blast through the red syrup, casting a faint magenta *X* on the floor. Her eyes are gripped by its magnetism. She looks on in wonder as I continue. "Every time I've sown someone it has entered through their mouth, but any avenue to the bloodstream will do. During a sowing I usually reveal my angelic nature, and while the subject is literally frozen in fear, just as you were, I release a drop into their mouth. They reflexively swallow it and it absorbs quickly before ever entering the intestines. It travels straight to the brain and goes to work."

Her head bobs with wonder then suddenly stops and tilts crookedly.

Incredulously, Jan asks, "Wait, did you sow me?"

"No, Jan, I didn't sow you. You would almost immediately lose consciousness and stay that way for a half hour to an hour."

"I did lose consciousness! Ted, Theo-whatever your name is, what the hell?"

"Jan, you weren't unconscious, only frozen for a few seconds, and that was just the fear. I didn't sow you. You're going to have to trust me. I only risk the outcome of a sowing with those who truly need it; those who are too far gone to choose repentance."

As she processes this new information, the corners of her mouth lift and her cheeks squeeze her eyelids to that sliced almond shape. She looks squarely into my eyes and though she may only be a human, she's a smart one and she's finished filling in the gaps.

"Hmm, okay, I think I've got this. You sowed Joel and Dave and they chose the coward's way. That's the reason you're here at Pentastar. You came as a judgment to those whose selfish dishonesty with the Fosillix trial cost innocent lives—and that's the game changer. You're going to sow whatever board members and shareholders are responsible. Am I close?"

"More than close; that's pretty much dead-on. Now, I have a question for you. Can you get on board with this or are you going to be a part of the problem?"

"I'm already on board, Theo-whatever it is."

"Just keep calling me Ted."

"Okay, Ted. Let's do this. Honestly, this is the most badass thing that's ever happened to me."

Through the giggle in her throat, she sounds uncharacteristically childlike. Little Jan Lucero has met her hero and he's taking her as his sidekick. A subtle sense of celebrity approaches, which I reluctantly rebuff. Still, she's not wrong. It is pretty badass moving stealthily from place to place, taking down the irreparably depraved, pursuing justice for their victims. As shameful as such fantasies make me feel, it serves my purposes for Jan to see me this way. Her admiration will be the catalyst that aligns our efforts and keeps her clear of my path.

"It hardly seems 'badass' to me now. It's been my meaning, the purpose of my existence, since I was a child. I was raised to live this life."

"Maybe so, but you're like a supernatural vigilante." She tries unsuccessfully to wipe the smile from her face, embarrassed by her own gaiety. Clearing her throat, she flattens her lips briefly before a charming grin reappears. "I just can't believe I get to be a part of what you're doing here. Why me, though, really?"

"In a lot of ways, you're the ideal partner for this venture. You're smart and capable, are intimately familiar with what's happening here, and you're in the perfect position to help rebuild Pentastar. Once I remove those responsible for the present state of this company, you'll be free to make it the beacon of hope that you've always dreamt it would be. You can make restitution for the tragedies of the Fosillix trial and move forward, leading Pentastar toward a future of prosperity and lifesaving success."

Jan's smile is now molded permanently on her face. I've never seen such a transformation in someone's countenance. The stone has been kneaded to putty, the ice liquified. With certain victory fast approaching, she's sucking the pure scent of her impending freedom deep into her perfectly proportioned nostrils. She levitates, weightless at the prospect of free rein. Better yet, she doesn't even have to do the heavy lifting anymore. She has me for that.

"Ted, you don't know what it means to hear you say that; to suddenly be so close to waking from this nightmare. How sure are you that you can deliver that outcome?" The question spews out convulsively. She draws back and puts her fingers to her lips. "Sorry, Ted. I don't mean to question you or your abilities so much as to protect myself. I don't want to get my hopes up."

"I understand, Jan. I'm absolutely certain. I've never failed a mission and I don't intend to start now. But we're going to need to have a no-holds-barred conversation. I need to know everything you know about the board and the shareholders so that we can build a foolproof plan, maybe several plans."

"I can tell you right now who needs to be sown from the boar—"

"I told you before," I interrupt sternly, "I only target those who are truly deserving. Only I can make that determination, but your input is invaluable. I'll need to do my own research to be convinced, but I'm trusting you to point me in the right direction. Can you do that?"

"Sure, Ted. I would be honored, and I'm sorry if I overstepped."

"Of course, no apology necessary," I console. "Now tell me about the board first."

We spend the next hour in the boiler room scouring the gritty details of several board members' personal and professional lives, at least those that Jan already knows. The frequent deep hum of that utility pump keeps us company and secures our privacy. Though still astonished by Jan's ready acceptance of my divine nature, these feelings take second chair to the fact that she has seemingly embraced her subjugation. After all the tenacious rumors, all the accusations of maleficence, all the human cockroaches scattering upon her approach, she is merely mortal. Her soft eyes and eager body language beg for my approval, and I grant it to her in doses but, like an addict, she keeps returning for another fix.

The names that receive special attention are Thomas Sanford, the son of David Sanford, who inherited his father's blood-built conglomerate and now sits on several boards, including a company who was recently investigated by the Securities and Exchange Commission; Stacy Meyers, who knifed her way to the top of a tech startup before it was eventually bought out by the resident giant; and Trent Jameson, who has more HR complaints filed against him for sexual harassment and workplace violence than seems remotely possible. This stellar group of human trash is less than half the total number of directors on the board. Thankfully, the other six directors have relatively benign stories, making it easier to highlight the few worthy of my attention.

After our detailed chat, we decide that it's best to not be seen around each other any more than usual. Triggering suspicions during this heightened state of security will only complicate matters more. According to Jan, the board wants a full report on the recent deaths and a preview of Jan's media release at tomorrow's meeting. She claims they're rattled by the coincidental loss of multiple high-level foot soldiers and want to be sure they aren't next. A demon would relish the opportunity to dwell in that room and feed from their trough of fear and sadness. For me, it will be an exercise in invisibility. Their hypersensitivity and vigilance could draw attention to anything out of the ordinary, including something as simple as my presence at the meeting. Even so, Jan assures me that she can manage their paranoia and promises that my presence will be entirely forgettable.

Tomorrow's board meeting will provide an invaluable opportunity to assess firsthand the nature of these suspects. It may be the only chance I get for the next few months to wrap up this investigation and get out of Port Ellis. Jan can weave whatever tall tales she wants about the board, but I should be able to detect any lies and, so far, her account aligns with my preliminary research of Pentastar's board. All I really need is a few minutes face-to-face to read them and make a decision for myself, but Jan's input gives the inside story, the behind-closed-doors edition. By tomorrow night, I'll be on the inside of those closed doors, stalking my prey.

CHAPTER THIRTEEN

My first three sowings as an actively operating Nephilim went like clockwork. The first target I pursued was a con artist named Patrick Smyth who had been swindling elderly women out of their life savings. It required little research and was as clear-cut as a sowing could be. The perfect icebreaker. On a mild winter evening, knowing he was home alone after watching his movements all day, I gently knocked on his bungalow door. As soon as I saw the twisting of the brushed nickel knob, I plowed through the door shoulder first. Patrick stumbled back, grabbing his nose, and flopped over an ottoman. I calmly closed the door and revealed my Nephilim form, to which he responded with debilitated horror. I knelt beside him, tapped a drop from my vial, and went on my way. The next night's evening news led with the story of a con man who walked into the local police station with a broken nose and a suitcase of money in tow. He confessed to his crimes as well as a humiliating history of lies and generally bad behavior. Strange, because I had him pegged as a suicide candidate.

On my second outing, I tracked the owner of a family of car dealerships, Troy Bailey. He amassed a tremendous fortune by lying to customers, lying to banks, and even lying to his employees. He regularly downsized and withheld commission checks from salespeople, citing dwindling margins. "Would you rather have a full commission check or have a job come this time next month?" he would ask them before adding, "We're all in this together and if we don't make sacrifices, we'll all be unemployed." Of course, there was no financial crisis and there were no sacrifices for Troy.

At the end of the year, his dealerships posted record profits which he used to justify his personal six-figure bonus. His employees, many of whom were struggling to make ends meet and facing collections on important accounts, each received a whopping twenty-five-dollar prepaid gift card. In the end, Troy awoke from a sowing, jumped in his late-model hot rod, and slammed it into the concrete support of a highway overpass. The driver's front corner hit first at ninety-six miles per hour. With no seatbelt, the airbag could only hope to slow his two-hundred-pound body enough to keep most of him inside the car, and it did just that. On impact, his head punched straight through the windshield, stopping at his shoulders. As the car spun sideways and rolled several times, he was nearly decapitated by the jagged glass.

Out of the first three, the third was the most satisfying. A charismatic preacher by the name of Jeremiah Daniels had grown progressively unorthodox. Somehow, his popularity and influence grew in direct proportion to his heresy. His doctrine became aggressively self-serving, and although congregants left in droves, new, more vulnerable ones always took their place. Like a frog brought slowly to a boil, thousands of people became cult members without noticing. That in itself wouldn't necessarily demand a sowing, but as his ego swelled, his behavior became increasingly manipulative and sadistic.

A self-proclaimed prophet, he spoke under the authority of God Almighty, directing his followers to do increasingly unhealthy, dangerous, and even violent things. Husbands gave him their wives and daughters, people scourged themselves and scourged each other, some stopped taking vital medications, and others took life-threatening risks under the belief that God would save them. Some acts were said to be a form of penance, some tests of obedience, and others were God's orders of divine retribution against neighbors. Hundreds of people sold all of their possessions, moved to the Daniels Commune, and donated everything to Jeremiah, acting on the faith that they would be blessed tenfold. By the time I got involved, the official death toll read fifteen, but I believe it was more than twice that.

On a beautiful, spring Sunday morning, I infiltrated his worship service and concealed myself in the robes of those serving the ritual wine. Head down, hood up, I ambled step-by-step up the red carpeted aisle. Rays of golden sun beamed onto the seas of brainwashed marionettes standing on both sides of me, desperate for Jeremiah to pull their strings and make them feel alive. Just before I reached him, I emptied a whole vial of the seed into his chalice. He took a large swig and immediately buckled. During the commotion I wandered to the back of the sanctuary and, despite the unnecessary risk, stayed to watch the outcome.

His congregants gathered around, frantically trying to wake him to no avail. They were scared, but since his pulse was strong and breathing steady they obeyed his teachings by praying, ripping out tufts of their own hair, and cutting themselves instead of calling for an ambulance. Surely God would hear such anguished cries and see their pain. After thirty-seven minutes, he awoke.

Without making a sound, Jeremiah stood, wiping the drool and snot from his face. His congregation hooted and hollered their jubilant praises. They danced and tried to pat his shoulders and give high fives, but he urgently and robotically walked to his office at the back of the platform. The room settled somewhat until he reappeared about thirty seconds later chugging clear liquid from a gallon water jug, only it wasn't water he drank. It was the poison he had been saving for a very special service during which God would invite the congregation to join Him in heaven.

Jeremiah drank a liter, maybe more, before he dropped the jug and clawed violently at his abdomen. He cried out in agony and tore his shirt open. His continued clawing smeared the blood from his incessant scratching all over his chest and stomach. Then came the vomiting. He dropped to his hands and knees and started heaving dryly, then productively, over and over. First came his breakfast, then eventually a swirled mixture of blood and a mucus-like fluid, and, finally, chunks that looked like the important soft tissue of his internal organs. During a brief pause in the retching, he sat back on his heels and with blood seeping from his eye sockets and nostrils, drenching his chin, tried to say something. He ended up choking on his own blood and collapsing as he drowned in his liquified insides. During the weeping and gnashing of teeth, I walked away unnoticed.

Despite a few minor hitches in the sowings between Jeremiah Daniels and my arrival at Pentastar, all of those missions were entirely one-dimensional. A lone, irrefutably devious person was ruining lives—one target, one sowing, no mess. It wasn't just the simplicity of only performing one sowing that made them go so smoothly. It was the emotional distance.

I never mingled with my targets during those missions like I have with this one. I didn't take a job at the Bailey family of dealerships, I didn't join the Daniels cult and live amongst them, and I didn't interact with any of my previous targets the way I've had to with Joel, Dave, Jan, and everyone else here at Pentastar. Getting involved with humans complicates things. Everything about them is messy and their mess is contagious.

Unfortunately, there was no way for me to diagnose the specific sources of Pentastar's evil without such immersion.

My efforts to untangle the lines of deceit from the inside have led me here. After a restless night's sleep with repeated appearances of the gray-faced, black-eyed, rogue Nephilim, I'm back in my Milburn Tower office with only one hour to go before the board meeting. My only interactions with Jan since the boiler room have been the crooked, co-conspirators' smiles we've exchanged in the hallway. Fortunately for me, I'm not the CEO and have had a light workload, affording me several hours to research the board. I've discovered even more unscrupulous behavior from the three prime suspects as well as some shady dealings involving two others. Bribery, ethics violations, pocket-lining politics, and infidelity make the short list. Still, I have yet to find a smoking gun that connects any one of them to the Fosillix trial, much less the evil of the rogue Nephilim. The dirt I'm unearthing is entirely garden-variety human muck. What I'm looking for is the diabolical foulness that emanates from a perverse, blackened, and decaying heart.

Interestingly, the three directors of principal interest are the only holdouts after a recent period of serious turnover on the board. It's as if they've been cleaning house, getting rid of the do-gooders and conscience laden. The newer members of the board are only evil to the extent that their spinelessness allows the evil around them to flourish. Not enough records exist about any of them to indicate a strong pattern of behavior, much less one of habitual corruption. For tonight's meeting, I'll mainly focus on the three candidates that Jan and I discussed, but if I can't confirm their guilt by the end of an evening of direct observation, then I may have to go back to the drawing board.

The fleet clacking of Jan's heels funnels into my office, each step slightly louder than the one before until she's framed in my doorway. She pauses and asks, "May I come in?" then proceeds to my guest chair without waiting for an answer.

"Make yourself at home, Jan," I offer sarcastically.

"Sorry, Ted, but my assistant is running an errand to prep for tonight's meeting so I only have a brief window of opportunity."

"It's fine. What do you want?"

"I've been thinking about the board and looked back over some of our past meeting minutes and vote results to refresh my memory. I don't know how all that sowing stuff works, but I think you should focus on two people in particular tonight," she asserts.

"Okay. Who are you thinking?"

"Thomas and Stacy. Trent is a nuisance, but he's really just a petulant asshole. Thomas and Stacy are the insatiable ones that fight me at every turn. They've formed a little axis of evil and have been trying to recruit some of the newer board members. It's gaining momentum."

I give a nod and say, "Okay, they'll be first."

"Wait, just like that? You said yesterday that *you* have to decide. Now you're going to sow them? Honestly, that would be great. We can just get this over with and start the rebuilding tonight!"

"I didn't say I'm going to *sow* them first. I'm going to *read* them first."

"Read them?" she says with disappointment. "How do you do that? Do you have to touch them physically or is it something you do…psychically?"

"There's nothing particularly mystical about it, Jan. When I observe a person, I can recognize even the slightest nonverbal cues—the wavering output of their lungs while speaking, the interplay between their eyes and the rest of their face, the level of tension in their posture—and determine whether or not they're lying. More than that, actually. I can often detect their emotional and psychological state as well. Human pheromones have a lot to say about a person's body chemistry and even more to say about their guilt. Men like Joel emit a rotten odor. These are all things any human can detect and some do, at least subconsciously. But most people aren't observant enough to pick up on the blatant cues, much less the miniscule ones. If anything, the ability is basically hyper-observance."

"So you're like a lie detector?"

"You could say that, but it's not always that simple."

"Well, the only reason I asked is to find out if there's anything more I can do to help. Like, if you needed to physically touch them I would make sure to introduce you face-to-face so you could shake hands, stuff like that."

Despite our fledgling alliance, I'm beginning to find Jan's involvement meddlesome. Clearly she wants to play a larger part in this process, but I have all the information I need from her at the moment and the more I depend on her, the more I risk failing at Pentastar because of her. Jan's involvement provides three major benefits: (1) It gets me a seat in the board meeting, (2) it provides information about the targets that I couldn't find elsewhere, and (3) it helps lure my targets into position once I've selected them. The first two advantages have played out and now I need her out of the way until I'm ready for the third. If her behavior spooks my targets, this will be over before it starts and the last few miserable months will have been a waste.

"No, nothing like that. It can help to be closer to the subject so I can see their face in greater detail and differentiate their pheromones from everyone else in the room, but I usually still need to spend some time observing them as they speak and interact before I can be certain about anything."

"Okay, then I'll find an excuse to get you close to them. I'll also be sure to address them directly during the meeting so you have opportunities to study them while speaking. Anything else?"

"No, don't do anything out of the ordinary. Let's keep it simple. I was prepared to take on Pentastar without you. It's helpful to have you on board, but I'm not used to it. I usually work alone, so let's not overdo it with some harebrained scheme."

Jan recoils with an insulted expression that twists into a sarcastic, patronizing nod. "I understand. I'm not used to this either. This is the first time I've joined forces with a Nephilim—which I didn't know existed until yesterday—on a covert operation to rid a company of *eevill*," she bites mockingly. "Might I add that you revealed yourself to me voluntarily and invited me to be a part of your work here. Sorry if I'm not doing it right!"

She's right. Maybe my nerves are getting the best of me too. I longed for companionship, for an ally, and now I've got it. However, this isn't exactly how I envisioned things working, and in the post-euphoric valley I have some regrets, though I know it's unfair to her. With no point of reference, any expectations I brought into this partnership would have been unrealistic and probably left unfulfilled.

I clothe my face with an apology and lean toward Jan. "You're right. Believe it or not, I have some nerves about tonight too and I guess I'm not handling them very well."

"You're nervous?" she asks in disbelief. "That's a little hard to believe."

"Well, you know I'm not lying. I put a lot of pressure on myself in everything I do. My main concern about tonight is that it's probably my only opportunity for the next couple of months to see the entire board of directors in person. If I can't identify the culprits, this operation could get even more drawn out and I'm already tired of it."

My words seem to have no impact on her nerves. In the background, the elevator dings, reminding Jan of her assistant's imminent return. "Crap, I have to go. Hopefully that's not Angela yet." She stands abruptly and turns for the door then doubles back, saying, "I'll see you in the conference room in twenty minutes. You don't have to do this alone, Ted. Let me know if you think of more I can do. You may be an angel, but I'm Jan Lucero, CEO, and the apex predator around here. People know better than to underestimate me. I'm not useless and I'm not to be trifled with."

She turns and walks out without waiting for a response.

With the day shift winding down, the next ten minutes zip by, second hand ticking as frantically as the footsteps of the thirteenth floor exodus. The board meeting is scheduled for the end of the workday, allowing the participants ample time to prepare throughout the day and ensuring no disruption to standard productivity. Conveniently, this means that outside of the conference room, the entire floor will be empty with the possible exception of the contracted cleaners, but they aren't scheduled to come in until after the meeting would normally end.

I rise from my chair and stroll to the doorway. The flow of bodies is now only a trickle and the stony hallway is eerily still. I take the opportunity to make my way to the conference room before the arrival of the board members. If I can inspect them one at a time as they enter the room, that will give me a head start which could mean the difference between nailing down targets and leaving with doubts.

From the end of the hall I can see the conference room lights shining through the glass doors, reflecting off the polished tile floor. Jan is already inside setting up her presentation. She glances over her laptop monitor, her eyes stopping momentarily on my approach, which she pretends not to notice. I reach the door, give it a single knuckle-knock, and enter.

"Jan, I thought about your offer. I want you to help me get close to Thomas and Stacy without forcing it. What do you have in mind?"

She releases a big, pent-up smile.

"Well, it's not glamorous, but I was thinking that when everyone gets settled, you could work your way around the table and hand everybody their drinks. We preordered for everyone from the cafe on the second floor. With the cool weather and evening hour, they all like a little shot of caffeine to start the meeting. The seating is assigned so you'll know who's who. It would give you access to each member's personal space without there being anything strange about it," she says triumphantly.

"That's a good idea. I already know who's who, though. I've done my homework."

"Of course you have, and thanks. Normally I'd have Angela do it, but it's exactly what we need to get you up close and personal. You should be able to pick up the scent you're looking for and then confirm it with observations from the far wall." She motions to a row of chairs against the wall that should provide a clear sight line to everyone at the table depending on which chair I select.

"Jan, it is a good, simple plan. Thank you," I reaffirm.

The ding of the elevator sings through the empty hall followed by the scrape of the doors and the clucking of several voices. Footsteps patter their way closer, bringing them around the corner and into view. Three men—two quite round—and a squatty woman shuffle and laugh at their own jokes like a group of old friends. The first four directors have arrived.

The round men, one white and one black, are Eric Granger and Carl Packard, respectively. The slender, boyish towhead is none other than Thomas Sanford, but the squatty female is Justine Steinberg. Thomas's sandy blonde hair flicks back as he guffaws at himself then settles into a new, stylish position. His well-tailored suit adds inches to his average height and adds shape to his lean frame. It's not difficult to imagine him eating Gerber from a silver spoon.

I inform Jan, who is looking down at her laptop, that they're here.

She says, "Okay. Go ahead and open the doors." After a beat, she adds, "Sorry, old habits. I'm not used to not being the boss."

"Well, for this meeting you are the boss and I'm just a guy handing out drinks."

"Ah, that's right. Well, get those damn doors open, Ted!" she playfully demands.

I snort a laugh and shake my head as I prop open the glass doors and take a seat nearby to screen them as they enter. With any luck, the other members won't be far behind. Sitting in a room with just these four feels like a good way to be noticed and approached for an introduction; although, at the moment they seem to be pretty enamored with each other and themselves.

Before they even reach the conference room threshold, another elevator ding cuts through the chatter. Finally, things seem to be lining up nicely. Six more men and women in suits round the corner, except this group is far more stoic than the first. I recognize Stacy among the gaggle, but divert my attention to Thomas and the first group as they pass in front of me.

A relatively standard blend of guilt enters my nostrils: body chemistry affected by lust, greed, anger, and regret. Such a bouquet is the scent of humanity as far as I'm concerned. It's impossible for me to be around any group of people and not detect varying combinations and intensities of such internal torment. It is the self-inflicted human condition. A subtle, sour, fermented tinge settles heavily on the receptors of my nose, one not very common at all. I have smelled such a pheromonal stench before, but in that case it was the product of a man's sexual deviance. Unfortunately, the board members entered the room stacked against one another, making it impossible to identify the specific perpetrator. Even if I did, such a particular iniquity may bear no connection to the problem here at Pentastar.

The second group made up some ground on the first and is only a few steps from entering the room. Francesca Arroyo, Christopher Nguyen, Bjorn Jansen, Stacy Meyers, and Trent Jameson reach the doors with minimal ceremony. Christopher's head dangles toward his phone the entire length of the hallway, Francesca and Stacy freeze each other out with upturned chins like high school rivals, and Bjorn and Trent share a brief exchange before appearing absorbed in their own thoughts. The sixth fellow is a very large man in both height and girth who I don't recognize, but I would certainly remember. His suit is stretched tight around his chest and biceps and the patch of dark hair on the top of his head is slicked back into a short ponytail. He meets my gaze and holds it for at least twice the socially acceptable length until his head twists toward Jan.

Once again, with the exception of the mystery bodybuilder, they begin to pass me with no real acknowledgment of my presence. The air shifts in swirls as they file through the door and across my space. I draw a deep breath in each person's wake and detect more of the same, that is until the ponytail walks by.

The scent of darkness, of genuine evil, is difficult to describe. It is the odor of decomposition, of bile, of dirt, of heat, and at the same time it is the absence of scent itself. It's a vacuous stillness that stifles the sense of smell and burns the sinuses. Though the body reacts to the stench of evil with goose bumps and the tongue can nearly taste the rot, the nose draws an empty breath and reports nothing. Such is my body's response to the beast's overwhelming odor.

A tingling ignites within my network of blood vessels and veins, the same feeling that happens during a sowing, only I'm not causing it. The seed within my body has made its choice between fight or flight and, if it could, would pierce through my skin to lash out against this evil. Suddenly, I realize that I have a dreadful problem: the same roadmap that marked my skin in the boiler room is streaking across the backs of my hands and probably my face as well. I hang my head to the floor and slip my hands into my pockets while I frantically search for an off switch within my mind. I have to control the seed.

Breathe in. Hold. Breathe out. A peek at my wrist confirms that it's going to take more than breathing techniques to calm this storm. The lights flash once. *No, no, no, this can't happen now.* I have seconds before the people in this room start looking around and see me like this. What is it my dad taught me about self-discipline? Control of self is the only true freedom. That's not helpful. Another flicker and I feel the muscles in my back tensing without my consent.

A flash, this time within my mind, conjures a strange medicine with no time to spare. Wind from the front moves smoothly around my face, then along my neck from behind. I'm drifting, floating back and forth like a ship trimming fore and aft. A giggle, *my* youthful giggle, fills my ears. Hands push against my back, but instead of falling I fly forward and upward. I'm on a swing. I'm playing and I'm happy. Peace flows through my spirit and evaporates my gathering storm, but it also brings with it many questions—questions that will have to wait.

I check my hands and the skin is clear, so I look up to meet Jan's concerned glare. Her eyes ask if I have a problem, to which I respond by motioning my eyes toward ponytail. She ignores my gesture before training her sight on Angela speed-walking down the hall with a tray of Joe S'Mo's signature blue coffee cups with names written in chalky white.

Angela's nasally voice filters through the walls and into the room ahead of her. "Sorry that took so long. There were two large orders in front of ours. Apparently we aren't the only ones working late tonight," she says.

She rounds the doorway and sets the tray on the side table against the glass wall that separates the conference room from the hall. Grabbing two cups, she turns toward the table but Jan interrupts, nearly shouting, "That will be all, Angela." The chatter of the board members immediately ceases.

"Oh. Well I'm just going to—"

"Did you do exactly what I told you to do?" asks Jan.

Angela looks confused. "Wha…uh…yeah, yes. I did."

"Then that's enough, Angela. You're dismissed. Go home for the night," Jan demands sternly.

Angela blushes and says nothing as she replaces the cups on the tray then hangs her head in humiliation and scurries from the room. Jan shakes her head in aggravation before giving me my cue. I head to the tray and grab the drinks two at a time, starting with the members about whom I have few suspicions. Giving them to the rest of the directors first will establish a baseline for comparison. Any substantial anomalies in Thomas's and Stacey's demeanor and scent may confirm Jan's conclusions. Then there's the guy sitting by the window, behind my prime suspects.

I make laps to and from the tray and around the conference table, handing out the various coffees and teas. As expected, I detect nothing extraordinary from the first three recipients: Francesca, Carl, and Christopher. They take their drinks with a polite nod but no genuine expression of gratitude or interest in my identity. To them I'm just another hired hand unworthy of a moment's attention, and for the next hour I wouldn't have it any other way. Their nonverbals exude confidence and security spoiled by discontentedness, and their scent is that of hopeless bitterness. It's a slightly abnormal secretion, but hardly a red flag. I've sensed it before, typically in people who feel stuck between a rock and a hard place.

Trent, Bjorn, and Justine are bottling the same hopelessness as the others, although Justine has a dwindling lightheartedness about her. It's an intrinsic positivity—it could be thought of as optimism—and not a byproduct of any specific set of circumstances. She is the type to make the most of any situation, and if she can't find the silver lining, she'll paint one on. Eric is similarly optimistic and is truly appreciative when I hand him his coffee. So far, there's nothing alarming about anyone, aside from the golem across the room.

The real surprise comes as I offer Thomas and Stacy the paper cups on which their names are written. I hesitate slightly as each one reaches for the cup, creating an awkward moment in which I can sample any attempts to hide their inner reaction. Once I release their drinks, each one smiles with genuine kindness. Thomas responds with a "Thank you, sir," while Stacy offers a "Thank you kindly." Their eye contact is direct but gentle, their tone sincere, and their posture is neither defensive nor offensive. In these ways, Thomas and Stacy are the opposite of what I have come to expect from evil people.

Ponytail serves as an ideal sample of what I expected to find to some degree in the two of them. His nauseating stench is wafting over from the wall and his crooked grin is arrogantly corrupt. I don't need a closer look to see his evil. He wears it with pride like a rack of military ribbons.

I return to my seat near the door. The angle works well enough to see Thomas and Stacy but, more importantly, it gives me a perfect view of my new person of interest. I sit, see that Jan is engaged in small talk with Francesca and Carl, and wait for her to catch my gaze. She looks around Carl's melon-sized head and sees the empty tray, then leans clear of Francesca and meets my eyes. I shoot Jan a subtle head shake about Thomas and Stacy, then try to direct her attention to the mystery man. She briefly glances his direction, then addresses the group.

"I'd like to call this meeting of the board of directors to order," she announces. The pockets of chatter quiet down as the board directs its attention to her. "Today we have the full board, all nine members, in attendance. You all received the meeting agenda sent two weeks ago, but there have been a few last-minute additions due to recent events. I have taken the liberty of printing copies of the amended agenda for each of you."

Jan opens a file folder on the table and begins passing around freshly printed sheets of paper.

"Please take a moment to review the agenda and the minutes from the previous meeting," Jan requests. For ten seconds, the group skims the documents before Stacy's voice shatters the silence, drawing the attention of everyone in the room.

"I'm sure I don't speak for everyone here, Jan, but I don't give a crap about the previous meeting minutes. I want to start with your explanation of what the hell is going on here," she says, shooting lasers at Jan.

"I second that," Thomas adds. The rest of the board freezes, then braces as they slowly pivot their attention to Jan.

Stacy, still shooting lasers, questions, "How is it possible that we have two upper-level employees, who you accused of sharing most of the responsibility for the Fosillix shit show, kill themselves on the same day?"

Thomas and Stacy have certainly formed an alliance against Jan, that much is clear, but to what end? The two directors share a quiet elbow bump, satisfied with their collaborative confrontation, then reach for the drinks they have yet to taste. Perhaps they were saving their first sips for this moment. A toast to victory, or at least a celebration of having put Jan underfoot. They watch Jan squirm for a few seconds, then look at each other from the corners of their eyes and exchange a smirk before tipping their cups.

The bouncing thud of a bowling ball detonates through the room, startling everyone as Stacy's head dives onto the table. Her cup hits the table's surface, popping its lid and spattering its contents onto the nearby papers and people. The agenda and minutes that lie beneath her head wrinkle with a white-brown ombre as they absorb the spreading pool of foaming coffee. Around the table, everyone's eyes are transfixed on the motionless woman. Everyone except Thomas.

Thomas's head is hanging, draped backward over his chair, and his cup lies in a puddle on the floor. I scan the reactions around the room—shame, fear, regret, sadness—then watch as they turn to their leader standing at the head of the table. Jan stares at the two motionless directors, then aims a condemning scowl toward me. As if connected by a string, every able head follows Jan's scowl, turning slowly in unison to my position.

"Ted, what the hell have you done?" Jan rebukes.

"I didn't do anything," I insist indignantly.

"Did you sow them?"

"Shut the hell up, Jan. I'm telling you, I have nothing to do with this!" I insist defensively. Fear grips my neck at the mention of sowing in front of the entire board. If she doesn't shut her mouth, this operation is finished, I may be finished, and the global secret of the Nephilim could be blown.

"That's not what I saw. In fact, I'd wager that everyone in this room saw your actions. You're the only one who handled their drinks. You tampered with them! Did you all see that too?" she asks the remaining directors, scanning the table for their consensus.

They all nod together, not like brainwashed minions, but like scared human beings who are trapped in Jan's web and know there's only one answer that will keep them alive. *The rock and the hard place.* Their unusual scent makes perfect sense now.

"I didn't do anything to their drinks other than hand them over! What are you doing, Jan? What is this?" I shout.

"Ted, we all saw you put something in their cups. From what you said yesterday, this is exactly what would happen during a sowing."

"Jan, you need to stop talking about that," I admonish fiercely. "I didn't put anything in their drinks. They need medical attention, and what I don't understand is why no one in this room is doing anything!"

"Trent, check their pulse," Jan orders.

He reaches over and grabs their wrists. "Got a strong pulse, boss."

"See, Ted, they're just unconscious…for now."

As if that was his cue, ponytail stands from his chair and moves behind Stacy. He runs his thick fingers through her hair then grabs a handful and lifts her head from the table. With every ounce of strength in his monstrous frame, he slams her head into the table. Everyone jolts violently at the sound and winces at the sight. The impact of her head travels down the table legs and across the floor, thumping in my shoes.

I jump up from my chair to stop this sickening act, but as quickly as I reach my feet, ponytail brandishes a revolver from his waistband. He aims it directly between my eyes—no trembling, no jitters, just a steady hand. My veins tingle with activity and with rage. My flesh tightens as I reflexively prepare to unleash the fight, but at this distance I'll never get to him before he squeezes the trigger.

"Sit down, Ted," the man orders. He knows my name. Despite having never seen him before, his presence is familiar to me as well. The Juggernaut. "I said sit, boy."

Boy? I should feed him that gun one round at a time. I slowly back toward my chair, sit, and watch helplessly. Without lowering his revolver, he lifts her head again and slams it once more, this time with a crunch.

Looking toward the ceiling, he releases a sigh as he withdraws his hand from Stacy's head and leans to retrieve the dangling right hand of Thomas. He lays his hand over Thomas's and uses it to grab a pair of scissors from the table. With all the frivolity of a high five, he plunges them deep into the flesh of Thomas' neck. The movement is swift and precise, severing his right carotid artery. Removing the scissors brings a shower of blood and a wave of horrified gasps. Jan watches every moment frigidly.

As the stranger plops back into his chair, I scream, "Jan, what are you doing?"

"Killing three birds with one stone, Ted. I lied. Thomas and Stacy weren't the source of 'evil' around here. I am."

She strolls behind the recently deceased on her way around the room, then sits on the corner of the table nearest to me and crosses her arms.

"They were my opposition, working on leaking the truth to the authorities and the press. They were the first two birds. You may be the third, but that's up to you."

"How so?"

"Tonight, the nine of us saw you tamper with those drinks. We didn't think much of it at the time, but when they lost consciousness we all thought back to that moment. When they awoke, Stacy began slamming her head on the table until she cracked her own skull open and Thomas jammed scissors into his own neck. Your fingerprints will be found on the cups and a toxicology report will reveal the same abnormalities as Joel's. Reject my offer and I dial nine-one-one. However, if you shed the constraints of your archaic beliefs and join me and Harvey, my friend with the gun, these bodies will disappear and we will become everything we were meant to be. We will be the king and queen of whatever we damn please."

"You forgot Dave's toxicology report," I respond, hoping to buy more time to find a way out of this.

"You stupid simple boy. Did you even sow Dave?"

I pause and brace for the worst. "I thought so until you just asked," I answer.

"Did he lose consciousness?" she asks.

"No."

"Then you didn't sow him. Of course, I already know this because I've had Harvey following you ever since you sowed Joel. He saw you and Dave talking at that bar. We weren't sure if you could flip him or not, but we weren't going to leave anything to chance. I had Harvey shoot him in the head using his own hand just like what happened to Thomas tonight. Harvey stole the revolver from Dave's office earlier that day."

"*You* killed Dave?" I cry, stunned, disgusted, and shamefully relieved.

"Well, I didn't kill him myself. That's what Harvey's for, and I pay him handsomely to do it. It's good to have big, strong friends and I'd like to have another. Will you still be my friend, Ted, now that you know everything?"

My world is spinning. I feel relief that Dave's death was not my doing but guilty that I feel relieved. As the body count continues to rise, I consider that my presence is the catalyst of death. I have never been more blindsided by anything than I have by Jan. How could any human be so diabolical right under my nose without my noticing? Sure, I had my suspicions at first, but she massaged those away without breaking a sweat.

"I don't know everything. Right now I feel like I don't know anything. I don't understand how you could go invisible right under my nose?" I ask, feeling more lost than I ever thought possible.

"Aw, Ted, I almost feel bad for you," Jan says with the utmost condescension. "So powerful, yet so confused and impotent. I guess it's only fair that I show you mine since you showed me yours."

With that, she stands from the table corner and removes her suit coat. As she untucks her shirt, the lights begin to flicker. The sound of chafing leather emanates from her expanding flesh. Her veins glow darkly through her skin as she stretches toward the ceiling. I crane my neck back to take in her immense height, at least six inches taller than me in full form. She is Nephilim.

In this moment, so many things about my time at Pentastar make sense, but with those answers come more questions about Jan and about the Nephilim. It explains why she was able to deceive me, why she was so difficult to read, and why the source of evil had remained so well hidden. But it also defies everything I've ever believed about the Nephilim, about our purpose and our relationship with truth. And if she's the source of evil here, then what is the dead-eyed, rogue Nephilim's role in all this?

"Ted," Jan continues in a hissing rumble, "I used my blood to knock them out. I had Angela add it before she brought in the drinks. The police will never identify its source because they don't know what it is, so all they'll know is that the abnormalities in their blood match Joel's. This will draw Drake, Lewis, and the whole crew straight to you."

Jan pulls her cell phone from her pants and dials three digits. She turns the phone to me so I can read the screen: *9-1-1*. Her finger hovers over the green dial icon.

"So, what's it going to be, Ted? Are you going to take your rightful place with me as gods amongst men or are you going to continue to waste your time fighting a losing battle against their depravity? They don't even appreciate what you do. They are insignificant, meant to be ruled. Join me if you want to live up to your potential, your true calling. If not, you'd better start running."

CHAPTER FOURTEEN

The quarter inch between Jan Lucero's trembling, veiny thumb and her phone display measures the thread from which my freedom hangs. She broods over me with hungry eyes as she waits rather impatiently for my answer. Still in Nephilim form, she is the ravenous monster that crawls beneath the beds of the directors: their bogeyman.

As the lights continue to strobe, the room has become a stop-motion horror scene. Each frame, each exposure of my retina, gives just enough time to observe one of many atrocities. A murderous beast reclines, comfortably seated near the windows, shades drawn. A man lies lifelessly in a still, red pool. A woman twitches faintly, forming ripples in a small red and brown puddle of her own. The faces of seven prisoners watch in terrified suspense, waiting to find out if I'll join Jan and multiply their woes.

I scowl with every ounce of strength my face can muster and say, "You're an abomination. We're supposed to be guardians of truth but you lie, steal, and murder for your own sick gratification."

"An abomination?" she asks. "You really are a pitiful waste; a blind guardian of truth who was all too easily deceived."

"Deceived by you, yes, but that's only because you've embraced deceit and betrayed your kind. You've turned your gift into a weapon!"

She chuckles ominously then settles into a sly grin that sends a shiver through my bones.

"You really don't know?" Jan asks in disbelief. "How can you have made it this far into life and not know?" Her chuckle turns to howling laughter which appears to have a shrinking effect. Gradually, with the jiggling of her shoulders, she returns back to her human form and leans back onto the corner of the conference table. The phone still rests securely in her grasp, her thumb close enough to the dial icon to reflect its green color.

"What could you possibly be laughing about as you sit on a table next to two people you just murdered?" I ask, sickened by her irreverence and concerned about what new darkness her answer will bring.

"Your whole life is a lie!" shouts Jan before bursting out in another round of hooting. Harvey has joined in, folding forward in his chair. His whole skeleton shakes stiffly, heavily like it's made of steel beams. They're out of their minds to find humor in such a moment and, worse yet, the feeling in my gut says this is only the beginning of my carnage.

"What the hell are you talking about?" I shout over their laughter.

Jan sighs. "You don't know anything. The Nephilim are not guardians of truth, you fool. All you have to do is read the ancient stories to know that. Read the Bible, the Quran, the Book of Watchers, the Book of Giants; it doesn't matter which you choose because they all say the same thing. We're the reason for the debauchery leading up to the flood. We revealed God's secrets. We taught humans evil magic. If any of those stories are even true, he sent the great flood to exterminate our kind. I'm just staying true to the nature of the Nephilim. We are gods of deceit, Ted, agents of chaos. You have to see that at this point."

"It's also written that we were sent to act as judges; that we had a noble purpose, whether or not our ancestors always lived up to it. Humanity cannot shift the blame for their misdeeds entirely onto the shoulders of supernatural beings. Whatever temptations they face, they make their own choices and tell their own lies. I have only ever known good Nephilim in my life and we are still fighting for truth."

"I'm surprised you've known any Nephilim in your life," she bites.

"What is that supposed to mean?"

"As easy as it was for me to deceive you, you must barely be Nephilim at all. You've got that weak blood, diluted nearly to the point of irrelevance. You're obviously far more human than angel." With each word her posture is increasingly aggressive and her tongue more venomous. She continues, snarling, "That's why I'm taller. That's why I'm stronger. That's why I'm twice the Nephilim you are! I'm a saint for even giving you a chance to join me. I should snuff you out where you stand."

Every word is a detonation of my worldview. Her verbal hacking and slashing has failed to cause pain, but it has produced fear. What if she's actually telling the truth? What if my entire life is a lie? I'm not sure that's something I could survive, and I hate her for feeding such doubts. My prickly instincts of self-preservation activate and hatred swallows my self-control whole.

Like a hissing stovetop burner, my brain is consumed by the electric snapping of her lips, each word one spark closer to my flashpoint. In a moment of blind rage, I rapidly tense the muscles along my spine and I lunge for Jan's throat, grabbing it with my right hand. My veins ignite, providing a rush of strength that allows me to lift her clear off the ground. The phone drops from her hold as I take the high ground.

"I'm tired of this game," I growl. Her feet dangle as I squeeze with all my might and snarl like a rabid dog. Harvey pounces from his chair, but before he can even reach us, Jan's feet are no longer dangling and I feel her lengthening neck stretch within my grasp. Her left arm swings wide, pushing the hulking Harvey back into his seat as if he were a mere child.

She barks to Harvey, "I'll handle this," then grabs my wrist with her right hand and peels herself free. Crushing pressure nearly snaps the bones in my forearm and drops me to my knees. From the corner of my eye I see the board, looking on in bewilderment at this battle of otherworldly beings. I imagine they're rooting for me, hoping to be set free from Jan's tyranny. Another pump of her vice-like grip drops me closer to the floor, bringing to my attention the scissors that lie below Thomas's right hand and well within my reach.

I snatch them up and swing violently and recklessly in Jan's direction, hoping to hit any part of her. She releases my right arm and twists her torso, bringing her right arm across to block the scissors while also landing a strong left hook to the side of my head. Her fist hits like a sledgehammer. It knocks me over and slams the other side of my head against the edge of the conference table on my way down. I collapse to the floor, disoriented and bleeding from a gash where my head met the table.

Lying on the floor with bits of wood strewn around my throbbing head, the knot in my throat heralds a burst of vomit. The ringing in my ears subsides and my eyes regain their focus just in time to see Jan grimacing as she extracts the scissors that are lodged straight through the back of her hand and out of her palm. Her pain becomes fury as I attempt to stand and find my footing.

She charges me and pins me to the wall. It takes a second of frothy grunting and struggling from both of us before I recognize the feeling of sharp metal against my skin. The scissors straddle my throat, splayed wide and pressed tightly to each side of my neck. The steel, warmed with the blood of multiple victims, threatens to add me to the list. I'm certain she can't sever my head entirely with these paper-cutting implements but, as strong as she is, she could come close. I knew she was taller than me, but in my wildest imagination I never would have expected such a difference in strength.

"THAT'S QUITE ENOUGH OF THIS LITTLE TANTRUM," she screams, spitting on my face in the process.

I raise my hands in surrender. A drop of blood blends with sweat in a swirling trickle down my left temple. Each pounding pulse is a battering ram trying to breach my skull. My heavy breathing settles with the scissors forcing my compliance. Jan hardly seems winded in the slightest as she asks, annoyed, "Are you going to behave now, Mr. Verity?"

The return of my sanity brings the realization that I would never win a straight-up brawl with Jan, much less one with Harvey ready to pounce the moment I have the upper hand. I give her a reluctant nod. She withdraws the scissors and we both return to our human form. My hand stops to rub my neck on its way to my throbbing temple.

Harvey chimes in with his gravelly voice, "Ma'am, he touched the scissors, you touched the scissors, your blood is on them; this is getting messier."

"Oh, Harvey, you worry too much. All of that is easily explained with the right lie. Three sets of prints are on the scissors along with two victims' blood, neither of which is his. I don't know about you, Harvey, but as I recall we tried to subdue him after we realized what he had done to Thomas and Stacy. He grabbed the scissors and fought back, stabbing me through the hand."

"Yes, ma'am. I remember it the same," he responds.

Jan bends down and retrieves her phone, then faces the conference table. "What about you, cowering leeches? How's your memory?"

Their disappointment in me is painted on their faces as they quickly calculate the outcome of rejecting their oppressor. Jan dials the same three numbers on her phone and turns the screen toward me without breaking her glare at the board of directors. Like popcorn, scattered nods begin to jitter from around the table. They each mumble their own version of "We see whatever you want us to see" and Jan aims her smug mug back to me.

"Well, Ted, it's your move and I wouldn't recommend resorting to violence again. Next time you pull that shit, Harvey and I will race to see who can kill you first. I may not be faster than a bullet, but I can guarantee you I'll win," she taunts with a sideways glance to her pet monster.

"Don't count your chickens, ma'am," the monster replies. "I could kill this one with my bare hands. You're right. He's soft, almost human." He forces a proud chuckle at the insult he's added to my injury.

I ignore his cheap shot with a snort before I lock red-hot eyes with Jan. Never before have I felt such a volcanic eruption of primal rage. It's not just her wholesale disregard for life and virtue, it's personal. She attacked the very essence of my identity, the truths that inform my purpose and, by extension, she defamed my parents' integrity. Still, she's a practiced liar and her willingness to say or do anything for her own benefit means I'll never confirm those claims here. I scrape the last of my self-control from the bottom of its hollow reservoir and respond to Jan calmly.

"You know my answer. You've always known what it would be, so this little charade was just a stage for you to make a fool of me. No trap could convince me to forsake everything I hold true. I will never join you, I will never reject my calling, and I will never forget what you did here tonight. You and whoever else is like you are a disease to the Nephilim race and to the world, and even if it takes the rest of my life, I vow that I will find a cure. When I find it, you can be damned sure I'll return and, with great pleasure, I will wipe you out."

"Ooh, good speech," she snarks. Jan looks at Trent and, as her thumb taps the phone screen, orders, "Take off your dress shirt and smear their blood on yourself and the shirt. Touch their wounds and leave plenty of bloody fingerprints. I don't want the cops asking why we didn't try to save them."

From a couple feet away I can hear the muted ringing through the earpiece. The voice of an operator answers the call as Jan dials up the drama.

"Please help. I've been stabbed and two other people are dead!" she shouts tearfully into the phone. The panic in her voice is incredibly believable. She truly is a master of her craft. The patient, methodical voice on the other end of the call speaks its reply as I stand, prepared to make my exit. My movement draws everyone's attention, the board clearly hoping that it's the start of another attack, one that I win this time.

"We're on the thirteenth floor of Milburn Tower. You have to hurry. There's a lot of blood and the maniac is getting away!" she says, raising her eyebrows at me as if to ask whether or not I'm getting away.

Of course I'm going to escape. My mission can't end with me in cuffs and Jan roaming free. She has made herself my new obsession. If I fail to accomplish anything else in this life, it won't matter as long as I take her down. The thought crossed my mind to just sit right here in this room until the cops arrive. Staying put certainly looks less suspicious. I could pit my narrative, the truth, against the nine of them and let the evidence speak for itself. Except that Jan is right: whatever evidence they find will point clearly in my direction after Joel and Dave. I'm already on their radar and they'll just see this circus as confirmation of their suspicions, even if they can't fully explain my involvement. I have to run, to regroup.

It has to be worth something to have the truth on my side. Famous quotes aside, I believe and pray that *truth* is the great equalizer. No amount of evil or deceit can forever subdue the truth. Like the delicate tendril that grows from a concrete slab, truth will always work its way into the light of day. It is resilient and it is immutable.

I didn't kill Thomas and Stacy, I'm not responsible for the Fosillix trial, and Jan is downright diabolical. Layer upon layer of dirt cannot bury these facts forever. All I have to do is survive tonight and hold out long enough to find the antidote for their evil. Until then, I will run.

CHAPTER FIFTEEN

Suddenly, the choice between the elevator and the stairs has taken on unusual gravity. I wipe the blood from my head with my dark coat sleeve and decide that the staircase is the more logical option. My stronger bones can handle the beating from leaping down each flight of stairs, which makes my descent faster than the elevator and gives me the option to exit quickly if needed to dodge the authorities. At this stage, speed is of the essence. Escaping the building before the police arrive is probably the only chance I have at avoiding capture. There aren't enough avenues of escape and no amount of ducking behind doors is going to help me once the cops have the building locked down.

As my feet stomp onto the fourth-floor landing, the metallic report of a stairwell door resonates from below. My exhausted heart stops entirely as I lean over the center handrail, trying to catch a glimpse of who's approaching, but I can't see anything. They must be staying close to the wall. Over his flat-footed plodding up the stairs, I can hear his whiny voice blabbing about his client's inalienable rights—he's not a cop. I bound down another flight, then take it one step at a time to avoid suspicion as we pass each other.

The balding, bespectacled stranger nears and I offer a courteous head-tilt greeting. He gives me a buggy look through his gold, wire-rimmed glasses, ignores my greeting, and returns to his important call. "I gotta call you back," he says as he reaches the next landing. I glance back and finding him looking at me before dialing another number on his phone. Does he recognize me? Probably another of Jan's spies. I go back to leaping down the stairs.

My shoes slap against the second-floor landing as another metallic *ka-chunk* echoes up the chamber. With nowhere to hide in the stairwell, I push through the nearest door, entering the bustling second-floor food court. For the average employee on the go, this level provides an assortment of dining options. Everything from a smoothie cabana, to fast food, to a full-service sports bar surround the elevator shafts and stairwell at the core of Milburn Tower. Those with more refined palates and discriminating eyes typically dine at Orchid Song, the four-star restaurant on the sixty-fifth floor. The only local restaurant that can boast a higher elevation and better views of the Pacific and the Port Ellis skyline is Talon's Landing situated at the top of the Pika Crest Tramway, but their food isn't nearly as good.

The late evening hour is a popular time for the Milburn workaholics to either grab a bite before returning to their offices for more work, or eat their dinner before embarking on the hour-long commute back to the suburbs. On the other side of the stairwell door, several pairs of heavy boots tramp hurriedly toward and past the second-floor exit. I bob clear of the window then, as the thudding fades, take a quick peek that reveals what I hoped not to see. A uniformed police officer grips the handrail as he turns the corner toward the third floor.

I scan my surroundings, looking for any avenue of escape or at least a place to lay low. Each of the restaurants has its own front counter with a small kitchen behind it. Most will have walk-in freezers and refrigerators, ingredient pantries, or other places to hide, but as busy as this place is I wouldn't stay hidden for long. About a dozen tables stand between me and any of the restaurant counters, and half of them are occupied by men and women in suits. A quick survey of their faces registers several that I've seen in passing—no one that's likely to know my name, but some that could know I'm from Pentastar. To my right and at the north end of the floor is an open dining area with plenty of seating and windows that overlook the building's main entrance on Sixth Street.

From where I stand, the view through those windows would normally be the bland, concrete wall of the building across the street. Only when seated at the window bar can one see the street below with its honking cars, drab suits, and balding heads. But tonight that bland wall dances with colors like a Vegas billboard. Reds, blues, and purples wag and prance along the porous concrete, lighting up the mostly vacant tables and chairs of the dining area like a dance club. I make my way toward the window to assess the severity of my circumstances.

An abstract masterpiece, eight squad cars sit motionless at all angles in the street. Their flashing emergency lights are blinding even from twenty-five feet up. The police have responded en masse to lock down Milburn Tower and apprehend a killer, and there is little hope that I'll make it out of here without steel bracelets tightened around my wrists.

I desperately brainstorm for a solution as more and more people scurry to the windows from around the dining room. Two more squad cars arrive, sirens screaming, and a couple of satellite dishes move into position atop white news vans. The longer I wait to act, the tighter they'll have this place sealed. In less than a minute, it seems that the whole second floor has flanked me at the windows, hoping to catch a glimpse of the mayhem or, better yet, get a dramatic video for their social media followers. A large flock of cell phones migrates overhead as their owners offer up ignorant commentary about the unfolding drama. To avoid starring in their recordings, I make a hasty retreat from the crowd.

The sight of such a multitude of phones reminds me of my own phone that spends the majority of its week swimming around in my pocket, forgotten. Ordinarily, I find it to be a rather useless device. I have no social media accounts and never will. The only reason I even own a phone is because of my position at Pentastar. Outside of Milburn Tower, I have no real friends and can't imagine that ever changing after my horrifying experience opening up to Jan. That said, I may yet have a single friend in this world willing to help.

Only one person I know could possibly help me get out without detection, but it's a huge ask and he could just as easily turn me over to the cops. I slide my phone out and dial. After three rings, I begin to lose hope that he'll answer. I hold out for the answering service, but the line is answered on the fifth ring.

"Milburn Tower Security Desk, this is Barry," he answers, sounding much more professional than expected.

"Hi Barry, I'd like to talk to Tyson, please." I close my eyes and hope he doesn't recognize my voice.

"Tyson is occupi—, actually he's headed this way now. Hold just a moment," he says politely. Then in a quieter voice as he reaches for the hold button, he mumbles, "No one ever asks for Barry. Why can't Barry get no love?" Then the line mutes.

"This is Tyson with Milburn Tower Security."

"Tyson, it's Ted. Before you react, I need you to hear me out."

A long pause follows, during which I find a seat at a back corner table with a clear view of the elevators and stairs. The gaggle by the window chatters loudly enough for me to hear their conjecture about which Pentastar employee killed themselves this time. Sordid chuckles follow as several names are thrown out, none of which are mine.

Tyson finally speaks in a hushed tone, "Sorry, I had to get a little space from these curious ears. Mr. Verity, where are you? The police are sweeping the building looking for you. They're locked and loaded and saying you're some kind of monster."

"Do you believe what they're saying?"

"I don't know. You've always been kind and honest with me; not exactly monstrous qualities. Plus there's that sense you get about a person. I've always thought of you as a good man. Honestly, when I heard what happened upstairs I half-expected to hear that Jan did it. I've always had a bad feeling about her. But lately you've been acting strange and your relationship with Jan is concerning."

"You're on the right track about Jan. She betrayed me, set me up, played me at every turn. Tyson, she's evil. She's responsible for all of this darkness. Between her and that juggernaut she trots around on a leash, they account for the Pentastar drug trial disaster, Dave's death, and the two murders in that conference room tonight. Who knows what else they've done. I'm the only one who knows what she really is and I'm the only one who can take her down, but not if I'm behind bars. I need you to help me get out of here."

"Let's say I believe you. The cops have the building surrounded and if I get caught helping you, I'll be charged as an accomplice. It won't matter whether or not you did what they say. If Jan has you as dead to rights as you claim, the evidence will give them all the proof they need to put both of us away for life. The truth doesn't matter, only what you can convince people is true."

I sigh. He's right, and it pains me to admit that the truth is meaningless. It should always be supremely important, the only thing that matters in situations like these, but is instead impotent without the ability to prove it. Still, as much as I hate putting

Tyson in this position, I'll never make it out of here to gain the proof I need without his help. I press a little harder.

"You're right, and I don't want that for you. I'm not asking for your help so I can run away from Jan and leave you hanging. I need you to help me get free of this mess so I can regroup and formulate a new plan of attack for Jan, to gather the evidence I need to convince people of the truth. This city needs to know the truth, and I have to bring an end to Jan's reign."

Tyson sighs as he considers my request—a good sign. I wasn't sure I'd even get the chance to finish my bit, much less earn his contemplation. Before he can answer, I speak again to lighten the load.

Pleading calmly, I say, "Tyson, all I need is information. You don't have to stuff me in a laundry cart or walk me out in a trench coat and sunglasses. You know this building better than anyone and you have access to all of it. I've done my research, but I only know of the two primary points of entry and the service entrance in the side alley, and there will probably be police watching all three. Is there another way out that's less likely to be guarded and, if so, how do I get there?"

Tyson makes a popping sound with his lips as he processes. "There really isn't anything else," he says. He lowers his voice and continues, "The freight elevator is probably your only hope. I don't know how you'll make it free once you get outside the building, but if you can make it to the second or third floors you can catch that elevator down to the basement and out through the service entrance."

I ask him, "Won't I need a key or badge to operate the freight lift?"

"I can override the badge reader from the main security office. It lets us give access to third parties that are making deliveries or open it up in an emergency situation."

"I'd call this an emergency," I say, hoping to tip the first domino.

"No doubt, but I'm not sure what kind. I hope I'm on the right side here. You better not be screwing me over."

"I can't promise that you won't face any backlash, but I promise you that I'm telling the truth about being framed. I wish I could offer you more than that."

"I wish you could too," he says sadly. Then, with determined resignation, "Either way I have to go with my gut and do what I believe is right. If you can get to the second-floor food court, there are double doors marked 'Authorized Personnel Only' leading to a back hallway and the freight elevator. Those double doors are never locked. Go through them and make your way to the elevator. I'll head to the main security office to bypass the badge reader. That service entrance lets out into the side alley. I highly doubt you'll be able to walk free from there, but with any luck, you'll find a way."

Though nothing about the circumstances deserves one, a smile forces its way across my face. It feels good to have Tyson's help, and not just because it gives me a chance to make it out of this situation. It's more than that. After all this time spent feeling alone and longing for companionship, I failed to realize that I've been planting the seeds of friendship all along simply by being a kind and honest being. Tyson sensed it strongly enough to risk everything to help me, and there has to be others.

"Tyson, thank you. You have my sincerest gratitude," I gush as I stand from my seat. A loud honk from the chair legs scooting against the floor echoes through the dining hall, startling several people and drawing a couple of disdainful looks in my direction. With no time for apologies, I ignore them and leave the chair where it stopped, striding hurriedly toward those double doors.

The doors are positioned out of line of sight from the elevator shaft at the center of the room. As I reach to push the door open, I can hear the stairwell door swing forcefully ajar followed by the sound of boots and loaded riggers belts. This draws the attention of the gaggle in the dining hall who swing their cameras toward the police, nearly including me in the frame as well. I slip through the doors with panic in my spine. Even if they didn't spot me, the cops will canvas the crowd and someone will remember the loner who sat at the table while everyone else gawked and who spooked a stiff jolt from them just seconds ago. It's time to make my move.

I sprint down the wide hall and make a left turn as directed by the arrow pointing toward the elevator. Eighty feet ahead and to my right is the large opening of the freight lift. The door is closed, so I press the call button and pray it opens. Nothing. I look back down the hall and repeatedly mash the button as voices filter through the double doors to the food court.

I quietly urge, "Come on…come on."

I notice the red status light on the elevator badge reader. Only seconds away from being arrested and I can imagine Tyson having a friendly chat with the guys in the security office, trying to act casual in his attempts to override the lift's security controls that are an important part of lockdown protocol.

"Let's go, Tyson. You can do this," I cheer to myself.

A heavy thunk startles me. I stare intently down the hall but no one rounds the corner. As I turn back toward the firmly shut lift doors, the status light, now green, catches my eye and my ears vibrate with the quiet wheeze of the elevator's movement. The wheezing stops, the doors open, and I dart inside. As I push the basement button, another heavy thunk rattles my nerves. This time it's not the elevator. I hammer the button to close the doors and pray they shut in time.

Voices, unobstructed by metal or sheetrock, echo down the hall. Through the closing lift doors, I hear a shout, "Over there!" Their heavy footsteps thump with the staccato mayhem of a carpet bombing toward the nearly closed doors but fail to reach them in time. The lift jerks to life and delivers me smoothly to the ground level.

At this moment, my pursuers are surely racing down the stairs and making radio calls that the killer is in the freight lift. They won't be far behind, and more will rush to reinforce the exit to the alley. Even without taking Nephilim form, I can run as fast as most Olympic sprinters and can do so for longer distances. Speed is my only chance. As the lift door opens, I bolt.

I make short work of the fifty feet between the lift and the outside world and burst through the doors, spilling into the side alley. Skidding to a stop, I pause briefly to get my bearings. The police presence on Sixth Street is far heavier than I care to take my chances with, so I opt for a sprint to Fifth Street. I turn, lean, and start to lift my foot.

"Hello, Ted."

The familiar voice stops me in my tracks.

Then, in that still moment, a small clap rings out. My whole body ignites in scorching, seizing pain. I'm paralyzed, locked within my burning flesh and deaf to the world. My brain vibrates violently against my skull that's still tender from Jan's pummeling fist. No amount of effort coerces my muscles to move. A dry, frail moan emits itself from my esophagus—a formless mayday cry to the celestial bodies that hover above, watching my demise in silence. It's only as my body settles into a numb agony that my hearing returns enough to recognize the rhythmic snapping of a taser. Like twigs, my legs buckle under my weight, and as I fall, the world fades to black.

CHAPTER SIXTEEN

Deep rumbling and sporadic tinking tugs me gently back to consciousness, but it's not until my head bounces off my hard plastic pillow with a crack that I fully come around. My skull is pounding even worse than before, and when I try to reach for the back of my head, both hands move together. Through my blurry vision I can make out the moonlight's reflection off the shiny handcuffs that bind my wrists. I sit up with a groan and a wince and as I open my eyes, my vision is clear enough to see the cage between the driver and myself.

Sergeant Julius Drake adjusts the rearview mirror to make eye contact.

"Morning, Sunshine," he quips.

"Drake. What are you doing? Where are we?"

"You don't recognize it? Has it been that long?"

I look to my right, but apart from the moon-soaked treetops and shimmering silver fields, I can't make out much. Even if I could, there appears to be little in the way of landmarks.

"I'm not seeing very well at the moment. We're not in the city. I can see *that* much," I reply.

"Well, don't worry. You'll get your bearings soon," he says rather ominously.

I turn my head and lift both hands to feel the hot spot on the back. Sticky blood wets my fingers and a sharp jolt of pain zaps my scalp. I grunt, withdrawing my fingers and taking a look at them.

"Yeah, sorry about that. You fell like a tree when I tased you back there. Hit your head pretty hard," he snickers. "It bounced off the asphalt."

I give him a scornful look, wanting to yell, to lash out, but knowing that I'm depleted. Feebleness has set in, and I have never felt so close to death. Emotionally, I'm spent. Physically, I'm a shell. Spiritually, I'm severed. Now I'm being dragged out to the middle of nowhere by a cop who should've put me behind bars. He would be lauded for his heroism, receive commendations, and be the frontrunner for the next promotion. Instead, he's forfeited all that to take me far from civilization as his personal prisoner. I can only imagine the horrors this Nephilim hunter has in store.

"Why didn't you take me to the station?" I ask, hoping for a hint of his intentions.

"You don't belong at the station," he says flatly.

It's an answer that answers nothing; not exactly what I was fishing for. Allowing a short silence, I wait for him to continue but he doesn't. I lean forward, closer to the metal grid that divides us.

"Where *do* I belong?"

"Not sure yet. A hole in the ground. A pile of ash. A bear's digestive tract. The pits of hell. Maybe someplace else. That's what we're going to find out."

"We?" I ask, a question he ignores.

Now would be the perfect time for my abilities of observation, my "sixth sense" about human honesty to be banging on all cylinders. He's being secretive, but with hazy vision, tinny hearing, and a bruised brain, I'm incapable of verifying anything. I'm stuck. Even at full strength I wouldn't be able to rip apart these hardened steel cuffs or kick the door open, and the windows are all caged. I can't read him, I have no idea where we're going, and I'm still in a lot of pain. I'm a trifling human trapped in a cage. I just hope I'm not actually being led to my death. It's not so much that I fear death, it's that I refuse to die until I destroy Jan.

I look out the window again, searching for something familiar. On the right is a double-wide manufactured home, beloved by its owners. Resting on a cinder block foundation, the elderly couple has installed shutters and gutters, built an awning over a beautiful front porch, landscaped the grounds with trees and flowers (most of which are surely wilting in this cool, early-fall weather), and wrapped it all neatly within a white picket fence. I know this not because my eyesight is back to normal, but because I can make out enough to recognize our location. We're heading to my farmhouse.

"Drake, how do you know about the farmhouse?" I demand.

He ignores me and flips his left turn signal. Hand over hand he turns the wheel, and hand over hand I lose my patience.

"Drake! Answer me!" I shout, slamming my hands against the cage. My head throbs with the surge in blood pressure and my ears ache at the volume of my own voice.

Drake looks through his eyebrows and into the mirror, then speaks. "I have some associates who have taken quite an interest in you over the last few days. Between their resources and my sleuthing, we've learned more about you than you know about yourself."

"Who?"

"Who what?"

"Who are your associates? What do they look like?" My fear is that Drake is somehow involved with that gray-faced, rogue Nephilim.

"Don't worry, Ted. If we decide not to kill you, we'll be glad to answer all your questions."

That's not exactly a comforting assurance. Drake's in bed with some people capable of murder, and I'm currently incapable of defending myself. I've never been tased before, but I know that humans can be tased and be back on their feet within minutes. Their soreness the next morning might be the worst part, and yet here I am over an hour after being tased and my muscles have degenerated to the point of uselessness.

Feeling desperate, I try to appeal to Drake's morality, saying, "I really had you pegged as one of the good ones. I could actually *sense* your integrity. Handing me over to murderers is the end of all that. You'll never be able to return to the city, much less the police force. If you take me back now, there's still time."

"It's not murder when you're fighting a war," he says dryly. "Soldiers kill the enemy every day without the stigma of *murder*. It's killing for a cause. For the greater good and to protect innocent lives. Besides, my career was over the moment I drove you out of the city, but there's something much bigger at stake. Something I'd be willing to die for."

"And what would that be?" I pry.

"That's enough questions outta you. We're almost to your crappy farmhouse. Then I get to do the asking." After a beat, he says, "Make that *interrogating*," with a satisfied grin in the rearview mirror.

Drake flicks the right turn signal and veers onto the half-mile gravel path leading up to the crappy farmhouse—my beloved home. In business with murderers and this guy still uses his turn signal on a country road at night…to turn into a driveway. In the distance, the white farmhouse to the left of the driveway looks more like a dollhouse. With our approach, the dollhouse grows and takes on more haunting features. The second-floor shutters hang crooked and the wood siding is molting a layer of paint. It's amazing what a few months of neglect will do to an otherwise charming property, or maybe it wasn't so charming when I left for Port Ellis.

My dad's old pickup truck is right where I left it, parked just in front of the detached garage that's too full of farming equipment to be used for its intended purpose. It, too, is looking sadly forlorn, leaning wearily on one-and-a-half flat tires. The silver moonlight washes over the top of the house, but leaves the covered wraparound porch cloaked in shadow. I can only make out the front door and windows, because the first-floor lights are already on and the front door is swung wide open. I painfully twist for a look behind, but the only thing following us is a cloud of ruddy dust, no headlights.

Drake's squad car exhales a tired shriek as it comes to a halt. He hops eagerly from his seat and pulls my door open.

"Let's go," he orders.

I sigh and scoot across the seat as fast as I can, which isn't very fast at all. Drake may be eager to interrogate and subsequently kill me, but I'm not looking forward to it. Besides, after being electrocuted I couldn't move any faster if I wanted to. My slothful legs nearly buckle as I try to stand, but Drake grabs my arm and keeps me upright.

"What if I refuse? Are you going to kill me right here?"

"I can tase you again. Got a fresh cartridge with your name on it."

Dear God, I'd prefer death.

"That won't be necessary. Let's get this over with," I yield.

As we walk across the front yard, a tall silhouette in the dining room window catches my attention. Backlit and featureless, the figure watches me closely all the way to the screen door, but when I step inside, there's no one. The old wood plank floors creak under the weight of each step as Drake leads me to the living room. A dining room chair awaits, positioned in the center of a blue square tarp. The lamp near the window is turned on, but the room is still fairly dark. Drake drags me to the chair, pushes me down onto it (not that he needed to), and recuffs my hands through the slats on the seat back.

"You ready for this, Ted?" asks Drake.

I say nothing and glare at him through my eyebrows.

"I'll take that as a yes. Let's get started," he says as he leans toward me and pulls something from his pocket. The familiar snapping of arcing electricity fills the room, the same searing pain ignites within my body, and my vision goes black.

I awaken again, this time much faster than the first. The blobby hands of the grandfather clock have spread farther apart, marking the passage of maybe ten or fifteen minutes, though it felt much longer. Despite having no way to measure time after I was tased at Milburn, the drive to where I awoke takes about an hour and forty-five minutes without traffic. I force my eyes wide then squint, but my vision is still as blurry as ever. I can make out the familiar form of Drake sitting in front of me, but as I attempt to turn my head, I can't. Someone's large hands are holding it firmly in place.

Drake stands and says, "Welcome back, Ted. I had to zap you again. My associate insists on anonymity for the time being and needed an opportunity to get into position without you seeing. It also helps to soften you up a bit more so you won't try anything foolish. That time it was just my stun gun. The first time it was my department-issued Taser."

My mouth tastes like iron and my throat is sandy and dry. I open my lips to speak, but only a raspy squeak and jet of hot air escapes. Drake takes a couple steps my way and crouches in front of me.

"I'll give you one for free," Drake offers. "Tasers work really well on you Nephilim because of those little organisms in your blood. They amplify the effect of the electricity while also taking a beating themselves. It hits your kind a lot harder than humans."

That confirms my suspicions. He knows I'm Nephilim. The bloody writing from my kitchen counter flashes in my mind.

WE KNOW.

Drake grabs something from the coffee table and holds it up to my face. "We're going to need you to be able to speak. Drink some," he says, pressing a straw to my lips. "Come on, Ted. You said you wanted this over with. It's just water; drink up."

I take a sip, then another, and another. Only after drinking some water do I realize how dehydrated I am. I guzzle half the glass before Drake pulls the cup away and sets it back out of view. He leans back toward me, locking his blurry face in my direction.

"Okay, now, let's start with a control question or two. What is your name?" he asks.

"Ted Verity," I reply, but as the words leave my mouth my brain is riddled with deep, penetrating needle pains in multiple places. It's a violating pain that tingles, burns, and stabs within my gray matter. There's something kinetic about it, as if information is being extracted straight through my skull. I want to fight it, but I'm completely powerless. I doubt I even have the strength to take Nephilim form right now.

"Your full name," Drake prods.

Here we go again.

I brace for the cranial violation and deliver my answer. "Theodonis Verity."

Drake looks well above my head to the person holding my skull and returns their silent nod of confirmation. Already satisfied that they've got a baseline, he starts with the real interrogation.

"Good. Next question: what were you doing at Pentastar Pharmaceuticals?"

There it is: the unavoidable question with a condemning, honest response. I've feared this moment my entire life, but now that it's finally here, I'm at peace about it. He already knows I'm Nephilim and likely knows I was somehow involved in Joel's death. My mission at Pentastar was noble, and if I'm to die for my efforts, then I'll die honestly, my only regret being my failure with Jan. I have nothing to lose by being honest.

"I acquired a job there to identify targets for sowing. You know what sowing is?" I ask. Drake nods so I continue, "I was there to be a reckoning, to hold accountable those responsible for the Fosillix trial. The only person I actually sowed was Joel Donovan."

His head shifts upward again, waiting for some kind of verification before the next question. I try to crane my head for a glimpse, but it doesn't budge. Drake snaps back to me and says scornfully, "Now, Ted, you're doing well so far. Don't screw this up by getting impatient."

"Drake, I'm already in agony from being tased and every time I answer a question, this vice-gripped wraith lights up my brain with flaming needles. I'm telling you the truth and I'm going to tell you the truth, so whatever this is, it's not necessary."

He gives me a look that, given my blurred vision, I can only imagine is condescending. "Unfortunately, with your kind, Ted, this is entirely necessary. In fact, it's the only way to be sure, so sit still and suck it up, big guy. Next question: what is the nature of your relationship with Jan Lucero?"

I begin my response with a huff of displeasure. "Initially, she was my target—one of many," I say, fighting through the probing pain in my head. "But after a while, I thought maybe I had misread her role in the situation and she proceeded to deceive me with incredible cunning. Tonight she betrayed me after her stooge killed two people. She gave me an ultimatum: join her and rule over humanity or run for my freedom and possibly my life. Of course, I rejected her offer and went on the run. I now see that we have always been adversaries, mortal enemies even."

I wince and clench my jaw as the pain builds, then subsides.

"Very good, Mr. Verity. I mean, it's pathetic that you foolishly fell for Jan's shit, but so far it seems you're an honest fool. We can work with that. Okay, last question for now: what is your purpose?"

He would ask such a crushing question in such a pivotal moment. After everything I've been through with Pentastar, I have certainly lost sight of my original sense of purpose. More than anything right now, my purpose is to pulverize Jan Lucero. If that happens to serve the greater good, then so be it, but this vendetta is personal.

"If you had asked me that question ten hours ago, I would've told you that I'm a divine guardian of truth whose only purpose is to rectify creation's decay through the sowing process. I thought it was the calling and the burden of all Nephilim to walk amongst humanity, denying themselves the pleasures of their flesh that so often lead to corruption and deceit. Now, after seeing Jan for what she is, that belief is shattered. I wonder how many more Nephilim have chosen her path, and I wonder if the things she claimed about my kind are true."

The more questions I answer, the more accustomed I become to the pins and needles in my brain. What was once painful and violating is now just a hair beyond uncomfortable. I realize that I can tolerate the sensation further and that I failed to completely answer Drake's question, so I continue.

"The truth is still all that matters. Being deceived by Jan has only reinforced that belief. But now it feels like I've been wasting my time going after these people when I could have been waging war against the so-called gods of deceit. So, to answer your question, destroying Jan and those like her is my new purpose."

Drake ponders my response and seems to have noticed my strengthening resolve. The strong hands still squeeze my head tightly, but as he cranes toward his associate for authorization, their grip softens and his posture relaxes. He begins nodding, and as the nod gains momentum, he removes his Taser from its holster and trains it on me. Reaching into his pocket, he produces a pair of handcuff keys and dangles them between us.

"Looks like you passed. Now, my friend behind you is going to remove the cuffs, but you're going to keep your eyes locked on me. If your eyes so much as twitch, I'm going to tase you again. Understand?"

I nod and give a plainly annoyed, "Yeah." He tosses the keys and the mysterious mitts release my head to catch them. I stare deeply into what have to be Drake's pupils, although I still can't see well enough to make them out. It's not an exaggeration to say that I'd rather die than be tased again. I'll give him no reason to do so.

My shackles fall free but I remain motionless. Planks squeak behind me, then creak around my right side with each step. I'm still firmly locked on Drake's pupils and will remain so until he lowers the Taser. The figure steps into my peripheral vision and I fight furiously against the temptation to glance toward it. Without looking, I can tell it's not what I expected: tall, but not some behemoth. Maybe the hands weren't as strong as they felt in my weakened state.

Without a flinch, Drake asks his associate, "Are you ready?"

A hand rests on Drake's shoulder and squeezes, then he speaks again, "Okay, Ted. You can relax."

I lean forward and withdraw my arms from between the chair slats. Hanging them loosely toward the floor, I shake them like limp noodles and then bring them together and massage my wrists lightly. As curious as I am at this point, I'm not sure I want to know the identity of his partners. If those questions had gone differently, whoever that figure is would have snapped my neck with their bare hands and probably dumped me in the nearest pond. This ordeal has definitely left me gun-shy and well aware of my limitations.

"Aren't you gonna look?" Drake asks.

"No. I don't want to know. I just want to be left alone. I don't trust you or whoever is standing next to you, and if you're not going to kill me then I have a lot of thinking to do about how I'm going to take down Jan," I say, speaking into the tarp.

"It's okay, Ted, you can look. Why don't we plan that together?" says a familiar, comforting voice.

I quickly snap to its source and, despite my faltering vision, immediately recognize the woman standing near Drake.

It's Melody.

"Melody?" I ask, but my voice cracks embarrassingly. "I probably shouldn't feel this surprised. It's just that I got a pretty dark idea of what Drake was up to and would never have expected you to be involved with that. How do either of you know about the Nephilim, and what's with the interrogation?"

Melody calmly fields my questions. "Ted, when we first saw each other at that cab, I was investigating Joel's suicide, but not for an article. I investigate every local suicide because they can be indicators of Nephilim activity. Not all are, of course. Plenty of people commit suicide on their own, but with the circumstances surrounding Joel's death and you being the last person to talk to Joel that morning, we knew there was a high likelihood that you're Nephilim. When Julius picked you up at the bar after Dave's death and found that vial, we were certain. Jan must've known we were closing in on you with the way she swooped in to rescue you at the station. We figured that she was going to try to flip you, but we didn't know she'd murder in the process or we wouldn't have let it play out. I'm not sure when she identified you as Nephilim, but as strong as she is, she probably sensed it pretty early on and waited to see what you were doing at Pentastar before she took action. Once you sowed Joel, she knew you had to be flipped, run off, or killed."

"That's all great info, but you didn't answer either of my questions. How do you know about the Nephilim and why are you doing this?" I repeat, a little more bothered than the first time.

Drake, still lounging in the chair across from me, turns and looks up at Melody. She meets his gaze from the corner of her eye and they share a moment of silent astonishment at my density. I notice, and don't appreciate the insult.

I speak again in my own defense. "You'll have to forgive me if I'm not at the top of my game. I've been tased twice and had my brain probed during the last couple of hours. My head is throbbing, sizzling, and mostly useless."

Mel looks at me with kind pity. "Right. Well, Ted, I'm Nephilim. I thought you would've figured that out immediately with my little lie detector trick, but apparently you do indeed have a lot to learn about your own kind."

Her look, her light, her effect on me, they all make sense, and at some level I think I've always known. Still, like with Jan, it never fully sunk in and I want to know why. How could I be so close to them and not recognize our sameness? Why didn't the seed within my veins react to theirs?

Melody finishes answering the second of my earlier questions, saying, "The interrogation was the only way to tell if you had been compromised by Jan. Nephilim's inherent relationship with truth can also make us extremely talented liars. When I placed my hands on your head and energized the seed within my blood, it created a small electromagnetic field that influenced the seed in your blood."

"So are you saying that I have a lot to learn because I didn't know that we have supernatural abilities? Like some kind of mind control?"

"I *am* surprised that you were never taught about your abilities, but I don't mean it as an insult. The one I just used doesn't let me see your thoughts or control your mind—nothing like that—but I can sense the electrical impulses in your brain. Also, 'supernatural' isn't the right word. Electromagnetic fields are completely natural. They're a part of creation's design and are harnessed for radio and cellular communication, internet, and television transmission. Some might say that it's our ability to interact with those fields that is supernatural, but we aren't even the only creatures who can do that. Dogs can sense when their owner is going to have a seizure, other animals can sense fear, and yawns and laughter are contagious. Some of this can be explained by social and nonverbal cues, but the underlying cause is those creatures' relationship with invisible but very real and natural forces. With my ability, I was able to determine that you weren't using the creative centers of the brain to fabricate your replies. It can be a very uncomfortable feeling, but we had to be certain that you weren't seduced by their ways."

"Yeah, it felt like needles gliding deep into my brain," I say with a shiver at the memory. "You said *their*. So there are more like Jan?" I ask.

Drake nods, and Mel says, "Many more. But there are more like us too."

"It's not murder when you're fighting a war," I say, finally fitting some of the pieces together in my crippled mind. "So I stumbled into the middle of a war?"

"Not so much stumbled, you were *born* into it. This war started long before you or I were around, but it is *our* war and no Nephilim can avoid it forever. Those who've tried to withhold their allegiance inevitably end up choosing deceit or vanishing."

As her words sink in, the only sound is the ticking and tocking of the grandfather's pendulum. A delicate howl travels down the chimney and out of the stone fireplace. The wind is picking up. Through the drawn sheer curtains, it appears that the brilliant moonlight is now obstructed by cloud cover.

"There's no choice for me. It's always been truth and it'll always be truth. But choosing a side in this war sounds like joining a team and I've always worked alone. It's all I know and, after my experiment with Jan, it seems better that way," I assert.

Drake takes the opportunity to land a jab. "Yeah? How's that working out for you?"

Sick of his attitude, I slash back. "How exactly do you factor into any of this, human? Let me guess, you figured you'd latch on to the first Nephilim you met so you didn't end up eating the muzzle of your service weapon? What's it like being a powerless sidekick?"

"Powerless? I've got more than enough power to handle you. I've dropped you twice with the push of a button. Some divine being you are," he says with a snarky chuckle.

"Boys, boys," Mel intervenes. "Ted, I know this is new for you and you're not sure where you fit or how to make it work. That's totally normal. Most Nephilim who've joined us struggled at first, but it's worth it. I promise you'll be glad you did. Going alone is a good way to end up dead, or worse."

"Melody, no offense, but I'm not convinced. First, you said it yourself that Nephilim are skilled liars. It's going to take more than your noble words to persuade me. Second, if your cause is really worth joining, why don't I see more of an impact in this city and others? If joining the team makes us more effective, multiplies our output, shouldn't I see those results? The reality is that the world is still a cesspool and all the 'Jans' out there are still living like royalty."

"I know how it looks, Ted, but I need you to trust me. We're laying low for now, building a foundation, and preparing. There are forces at work that we don't fully understand yet, and we don't want to reveal our hand too soon. Our numbers are growing and we're honing our skills daily. You could do the same on your own, but we'll only have lasting victory if we work together." Her earnestness is evident and infectious. "There's a place I'd like to show you. I think it will change your mind."

"You've got me curious, I'll give you that. You also haven't killed me yet, but neither did Jan, so that doesn't necessarily make you the good guys. If you really are plotting to take her down, I'm interested, but if I've learned anything from the last few days it's that when things seem too good to be true, they usually are. So, Melody, what's the catch?"

"Oh, we're going to take her down, Ted. Her and all the others like her. As far as the catch is concerned, there is one." She tosses an opaque black hood onto my lap. "I'm going to need you to wear this over your head until we arrive at the settlement."

CHAPTER SEVENTEEN

What feels like several hours pass as we cruise and bump along numerous highways and county roads. At first, I try to stay oriented, tracing our new heading with every turn, but I eventually lose track during a stretch of interchanges that seems deliberately entangled. For a moment, I thought I could make out the sound of a train horn and figured it was the Ellis Trail Line and that we were headed back toward the city, but depending on which way we came out of those confusing turns, it could be any number of tracks. Mel and Drake sporadically talk in hushed tones that I can't fully decipher over the shimmering strings and soaring brass of the classical music they're blasting in the back seat. I'm now lost, not just geographically, but philosophically and spiritually as well.

The blissful beauty of my current circumstances is that my choices are so woefully biased. My best options are obvious, and in that sense my decisions are being made for me. I thus enjoy a lack of control that's almost therapeutic, for now. It will eventually drive me crazy, but until I reach that threshold, I'm reveling in the flow like a fallen leaf caught in a fast-moving stream. All I can do is buckle up, let go, and make the most of the ride.

The comfort of helplessness lulls me into a profound sleep, as rejuvenating as it is long. Absolute nothingness engulfs my spirit, and in that void, I find my health. But that's not all I find. I am visited in my rest by a most unwelcome guest: the dead-eyed rogue Nephilim.

What I first assume is a nightmare takes on a surreal palpability. He stalks my spirit in its comatose slumber. His scent, his presence, his aura so real I can taste its bitterness. He says nothing because he is not there to speak, only to make his presence known. Watching me with soulless indifference, he sits on the seat beside me examining my motionless body. In his silence, his simple, terrifying message is clear: *I see you.*

I lurch from my sleep expecting to see the inside of the black fabric hood. Instead my eyes are scorched by the high-noon sun filtering through the window blinds. Children's voices chatter and whoop playfully amid the cadenced shrieks of a rusty old swing set. I prepare for an onslaught of full-body aching as I attempt to sit up, but none comes. I feel terrific. The round mechanical alarm clock on the bedside table reads 1:33 p.m., meaning I just slept for almost twelve hours. I'm still wearing the same overripe suit pants from the day prior, but I can see my dress shirt and coat hanging in the closet through the white bifold doors that are accordioned slightly open. Leaning forward, I find my black dress shoes placed neatly under the edge of the bed.

"Morning, Sunshine," blurts Drake from the doorway, startling me.

Deja vu.

"Sorry, I couldn't resist," he says while jiggling with laughter. "Feeling better?"

"I feel brand new," I answer, doubtful that he actually cares.

"Mm, yeah, don't care. You better be feeling new after that much sleep. You had me waiting around forever."

"Twelve hours is hardly *forever*, and if it were up to me you would've left a long time ago," I rebut.

"Twelve? Try thirty-six," he says. Then, noticing my shocked reaction, he adds, "That's right, Sleeping Beauty. You've been out cold for a day and a half, and I've been stuck here babysitting your lazy ass the whole time. I had to check your pulse just to convince the others you weren't dead. By the way, that reminds me, your breath reeks."

"Were you smelling me in my sleep?"

"Only when I had to."

I ignore him and stand up slowly from the bed, savoring the revitalized strength of my legs. It takes only one and a half of my large steps to cross the small room to the window where I peer out at the settlement. From here, it looks like a quaint, inviting, rural town; albeit one that was unearthed after fifty years in a time capsule. Hand-painted signs, now scaly and flaking, are mounted above mom-and-pop storefronts, all of which look uninhabited. I guess a secret Nephilim settlement doesn't make for much of a commerce center. A two-lane county road splits the village down the middle, and all of the stores, restaurants, bars, and churches cling to it tightly like grapes to the vine. The houses line up neatly behind them, and it's not hard to tell that the village's growth radiated from the county road outward. Those who showed up late to the game took jobs working at the businesses already established by others and built their homes, their shacks, on the nearest unclaimed piece of land. For that reason, the lots seem to get gradually smaller the farther they are from city center.

The modest home in which I've landed is fifty yards from the one-size-fits-all school building. Ancient playground equipment fights a losing battle against rust at every junction and rivet, but the half dozen or so kids don't seem to mind. In fact, they seem entirely carefree as they spin, slide, swing, and sprint around their personal Eden in full Nephilim form. Though likely just elementary school age, each of them is nearly the size of an average adult human and notably taller than I was at their age.

This is far more than the bare-bones, military-style camp I expected. They're making a life in this haven and living in community.

Even if I had been raised around other Nephilim, it's hard to imagine my parents allowing me to participate in schoolyard play. My father taught me a lot and we shared a laugh or two, but it was always in the course of preparing me for my future mission. To live in the moment was to waste my most precious resource, one I could never replenish: time. I can practically hear him using those kids as an object lesson: "Play, entertainment, and pleasure are the trifecta of selfish indulgence. It makes you soft, erodes your focus, and steals time that you could have spent sharpening useful skills."

Even now, so many years after my father's lectures, their frivolous play still strikes me as a disservice to themselves. As future soldiers born into a divine war, a pleasant childhood will only serve to harshen the blows of their inevitable reality. It's better for them to have never known lightheartedness than to have such a carefree upbringing, only to have it stripped away.

The old saying comes to mind that it's better to have loved and lost than never to have loved at all. The phrase has something to say about love, but makes no claims about loss. I've never been in love. In fact, the only love I can remember experiencing was my parents' rigid, utilitarian love, expressed through their care for my physical health and fastidious sculpting of my worldview. Put another way, they made sure I didn't die and that I knew my place in the world. However, one thing I do know plenty about is loss. Having barely survived the soul-punishing loss of both my parents and their malnourished love, I can't imagine that it would ever be better to have found true love and lost it than to have never found it at all. No, these children shouldn't play. They shouldn't fall in love with the lie of a warm, kind world.

During a momentary break in their gleeful squeals, I detect the low, steady drone of multiple engines—generators if I had to guess. Drake's voice splashes over their droning.

"The town's called Carver."

"I've never heard of it," I reply, looking at him over my shoulder then turning back to the window.

"Very few people have. It's been forty-seven years since it was abandoned. The town lived and died on agriculture and it promised to be a mecca of rich soil, rich crops, and richer farmers. People flocked in droves when they heard about the wide-open, cheap, unsold plots of land with nutrient-rich topsoil. At first, it was everything they hoped it would be, and record crop yields came easily, which only summoned more would-be farmers. Unfortunately, the aquifer couldn't keep up with the town's rapid growth and suddenly went dry. Carver's rural population migrated, taking with it the business owners' customer base. Eventually, the aquifer replenished but not soon enough. No one's coming back."

"What do they do if someone wanders through and gets curious?" I ask.

"Well, the county road gets no traffic because it goes nowhere—it's basically a glorified driveway to Carver—but it *has* happened before. The biggest problem has been curious teenagers exploring the spooky ghost town rumors. I don't live here, but when I met Melody and learned about the Nephilim, I did some investigating into Carver's history. I'm basically on call twenty-four/seven to deal with trespassers or anything else a pocket-cop can handle. It's a long drive, but it's the least I can do for the cause."

I raise an eyebrow. "Pocket-cop, huh?"

"Normally it would be an insult, but I'm proud to be duty-bound to Melody and the alliance, and I'm not even on the payroll," he says piously before adding, "There is no payroll. Before Melody, I spent all my years on the force fighting crime but was oblivious to its source. Kinda like how you were before Jan. Now that you know who's truly to blame for the state of the world, could you ever go back to sowing one person at a time?"

"Humans have to shoulder their share of the blame, Drake." I spin around and point a finger in his direction. "You have the freedom of choice. The ramifications may be unjust, but you can still choose to do the right thing," I counter.

"With ramifications as harsh as death, it's not that simple, Ted," he says, scowling. "When authority figures manipulate the truth and build a false narrative that we all live by and are powerless to refute, all of our decisions are tainted. At that point, our freedom is meaningless. Well, guess who's using their authority to manipulate others' reality these days. Your kind! I'm not saying humans have no responsibility for the way things are, but let's bring the Nephilim meddling to an end before you judge humanity too harshly. If it weren't for the goodness of Melody and the alliance, I'd hate every last one of your kind."

It pains me to admit it, but he makes a valid point. If Jan could mislead even me into taking a different course of action and thinking it was the product of my own free will, then what chance does an ordinary human have? That being said, the number of children playing outside this window surpasses the total number of Nephilim I have met in my life, not including my parents. Such a low Nephilim-to-human ratio would suggest that most humans forge their personal brand of evil with no Nephilim meddling at all.

"You make an interesting point but, for now, I still disagree," I respond.

Drake rolls his eyes and says, "Of course you do. If I had to guess, that'll change after you meet with Reb. Anyway, you need to take a shower because, damn, you stink, and I'm supposed to get you to Reb when you're presentable." He looks down at a pile of clothes lying on the upholstered seat of a cedar chest that's nestled up to the foot of the bed and says, "Put these on when you're done. They're clean and should fit well. I'll be waiting at the dining room table. Bathroom's down the hall and to the right."

He leaves the doorway and ten seconds later is fumbling with the tangled legs of the wood dining chair. They thump against the floor and clack against the other chairs until they eventually break free. I can hear his flustered mumbling and snicker to myself.

Bested by a chair.

"I can hear you laughing. Let's go! Chop, chop," he bellows.

I retrieve the stack of clothes and smile crookedly as I stroll past Drake and down the short hall to the bathroom. The windowless, wood-paneled room is as outdated and dark as they come. Feeble light emanates from the top of the boxy medicine cabinet but is thirstily absorbed by the walnut walls faster than the old bulb can burn. I drop the clothes on the floor and look at my bruised reflection in the cabinet's sliding mirror doors. With the seam of the mirror panels running down the middle of my face, it's divided into two parts, the left one slightly distorted. It's a fitting visual, a glimpse beneath my flesh.

Like royalty in a deck of playing cards, I've spent my whole life living as if I'm one-dimensional, as if there's only one side of my face, only one side of me. I've lived in fear of what I would become if I acknowledged that I'm not only one thing, that I'm not only angel but am also equally human. I can't help but wonder, now, what it would be like to have lived all my years with both halves of my being working in unity. How whole would I be if my dueling natures merged to complete one another instead of my angelic nature lording over my human nature and my human nature lashing out against the oppression of its angelic counterpart?

I unpack the new toothbrush that's lying on the small vanity and squeeze a green-striped ribbon of toothpaste from the little tube. Scrubbing my teeth in small, concentric circles, I can see no difference when I look at them in the mirror, but I can feel the day's grime wash away. I know it will return and I'll have to brush them again, but if I stop brushing altogether, they will inevitably rot. My fight against the deceit and manipulation of mankind is much the same. Whatever progress I make in a given day will be undone by the next, but to quit the fight altogether is to abandon creation to decay that will nibble its bonds to dust.

As the showerhead pelts my skin with the aquafer's icy beads, my body stiffens tightly, squeezing the air from my lungs. I wish my body had reacted this way at the thought of working with Jan, but none of my alarms were triggered. Her words were exactly what I needed to hear, which is true of most lies, but I don't understand how she could knowingly lie and still convince herself and me that it was truth. My feelings may have interfered more with my judgment than I realized, but I can't shake the feeling that there was something more at work. Perhaps, like Mel's interrogation technique, Jan used some Nephilim ability to conceal her deceit. That would be a dangerous weapon, especially against humanity. They wouldn't stand a chance.

The shower's water never warms, but I manage to brave enough breathtaking blasts to get clean. After I dress, Drake and I step out into the open air. Hot sun bakes my face while a chill creeps up my shaded back. We walk in silence, the dry, brittle grass crunching with every step. The denim overalls, long underwear, and brown work boots do indeed fit well because they're mine, plucked from my closet back at the farmhouse some time before the interrogation. I can't remember the last time I wore them, but I'd be ill-prepared to own a farm without such a getup on standby. He keeps looking over at me with a sheepish grin, obviously enjoying the sight of me dressed like a farmer.

"Don't worry, we brought you a couple sets of clothes. I just had to see this," he says with a snicker, gesturing top-to-bottom in my direction.

I ignore the ribbing, instead asking, "Where's Mel?"

"How would I know? She's around here somewhere," he answers.

"You two seem pretty close. I thought maybe there was something there and I figured you'd know, that's all."

Drake's mouth stretches into a sly grin. "Well, I don't know where she is at every second of the day. Even though we are a couple, she's still her own person."

He's lying. Thirty-six hours of sleep has my abilities sharper than ever, and that lie was written across his forehead. "You must've forgotten who you're talking to. That was one of the most obvious lies I've ever seen."

Drake lets out an impish laugh and says, "You're right, we're not a thing. Just testing you. She's a dream to look at, but Mel's not interested in romance. She's pretty focused on the mission. If I were you, I wouldn't bother. You'll just end up feeling like a rejected middle schooler."

"Well, you're not me and we're not even the same species. I don't want, or need, your advice, Drake," I snap.

"How is it possible that you're still this proud after the ass whipping of the last couple days?"

Through gritted teeth I mutter, "Just stop talking and take me wherever it is we're going."

"Gladly," he says with frustrated resignation. Then, pointing to the right, he announces, "It's right here anyway."

We stop in the shadow of a church steeple. The charming wood building, smaller than a regulation basketball court, sits behind the stores and only a stone's throw from the main road. Like the rest of the town, decades of neglect have taken their toll, leaving patches of roof exposed, most of the beige paint worn off, and quite a few of the stained-glass windows broken. Mischievous teens are likely to blame for the windows, but time and nature account for the rest.

"This is your stop, Ted-tastic. Reb is inside waiting," says Drake.

"And who exactly is Reb?"

"He's their leader. The leader of the alliance—the leader of this cell, at least."

"There are other alliance cells?" I ask excitedly.

Impatiently, Drake replies, "You're asking the wrong guy. Just go in there and talk to Reb. He's got your answers."

I trot up the fissured concrete stairs, pull the heavy door ajar, and step slowly onto the dry rotting floorboards of the foyer. The wood flexes under my weight with a delicate crackle, but it holds. Each step brings more confidence in the floor's integrity, and I begin to stride naturally toward the man seated in the front pew of the sanctuary. The sun enters in bright white beams through the broken windows along each side wall and casts colorful holograms where it passes through the intact stained glass. If not for the plant life growing through the floor and the vacant seats, I'd be vividly reliving the memory of the cult leader's sowing.

When I reach the front of the sanctuary, I sit on the first pew next to the still, quiet man. He has a peaceful presence as he remains motionless, locked in a meditative gaze toward the slightly crooked cross that's mounted above the podium. Without breaking his motionless stare, he greets me.

"Hello, Theodonis. My name is Rebarro, but I go by Reb. It's good to see you again."

Again?

His voice is tender, almost fragile, and yet it still resonates with authority. I've yet to even make eye contact with him or see the other side of his face and I already like him. He's smaller than I expected, but that hasn't impacted his immediate command of the room.

"Hello, Reb, it's nice to meet you. I wish I could say that I've heard a lot about you, but I've actually heard next to nothing about you or this place, which makes it even stranger that you said 'again.'"

"I wouldn't expect you to remember me, Ted. The last time I saw you, you were just a toddler. In fairness, I wouldn't have recognized you if I didn't already know who you are from Melodia and Sergeant Drake, and our research."

Melodia?

The Nephilim tradition of choosing odd, Greek-sounding names has somehow persisted into the modern era. It wasn't always that way. Before the proliferation of Greek mythology, Nephilim followed no naming conventions. Goliath is a well-known example. He was one of us but was named shortly before the tradition started. Eventually, Greek mythology went mainstream and Nephilim parents saw their sons and daughters as the real-life demigods of those heroic tales, stronger and braver than men. They chose mighty Greek names with the fantasy of seeing their children's likeness carved into marble effigies and celebrated for their heroism. What started as a trend lasted long enough to become tradition, and now it would feel odd to settle for modern human names. In an effort to blend in easier, we usually ditch our full given names and go by common nicknames, but, for some inexplicable reason, we eventually end up naming our own offspring something unique and Greek-like.

Rebarro, more Hispanic than Greek, finally turns to face me, unveiling a prominent scar on his right cheekbone. White tissue in the shape of a mangled fishhook wraps around his right eye and stands out against his olive skin tone. It's not difficult to look at, but it does make me cringe to imagine the blow he received in order to earn such a scar.

His age is difficult to guess, as is typical of Nephilim. Once we reach adulthood, we age very little for many decades. It isn't until our final, waning years that the common signs of aging set in, but when they do, they hit hard. He could be forty; he could be eighty-five. The only way to know is to ask, but it's not relevant. I have more important questions that need answering.

"How did you see me as a toddler?"

He looks at me with disarming, compassionate eyes as he responds. "Before we start with the question and answer session—to be clear, that's what this is—I need you to prepare yourself. We want you to join our cause, but it's been brought to my attention that you hold some unconventional views about your purpose, your history, and the broader nature of the Nephilim. This is an opportunity for us to set the record straight and make sure you're making a truthfully informed decision. This may be unpleasant for you."

"*Unconventional?* I'm not worried about whether or not my views are conventional; I'm dedicated to the truth even if it's unpopular. My views, my beliefs, are true. My parents raised me in truth and it's all I've ever known."

Reb sighs heavily before he says with reluctant gravitas, "That's as good a place as any to start. Your parents, Dan and Val, weren't who you thought they were. The reason I knew you as a toddler is because we picked you up…when you were an orphan. You were living at the Burkwood Orphanage south of Port Ellis, and we caught wind through a police contact of an incident report involving a young boy whose veins glowed red during a tantrum. We knew nothing about your biological parents, but it was obvious you were Nephilim at some level. So we—Dan, Val, some other alliance members, and I—took you in. As Dan and Val's love for each other grew, they wanted to have a family but were unable to conceive. They asked for our blessing to adopt you as their own and we granted it."

His words hit like lidocaine. Numbness spreads from my brain to my lips then everywhere else. I want to cry out in denial, but an eerie crimp rolls forward from the back of my abdomen. It is the horrifying gut feeling that Reb speaks the truth and that more disturbing news is to come.

"Take a moment, Ted. I know this news is not easily digested."

I impulsively decide to put my numbness to work for me and keep the shocks coming. I just need to absorb the information and process it later.

"What happened to Dan and Val? If they were part of the alliance, why wasn't I raised here?"

"We had some strong differences of opinion with Dan and Val when it came to how to best approach preparing the next generation of alliance fighters. They believed it was better to train up traditional Nephilim, but didn't think that was possible without a shift in the narrative. They insisted on teaching you and the other new recruits that Nephilim are all noble creatures, that Nephilim are not actually the byproduct of illicit sexual relationships between angels and women, and more. When we refused to adopt the same narrative, they abandoned the alliance and took you with them to the farm where you grew up." He looks at me with deep concern and pity. "I'm sorry, Ted."

"So you're saying that all of that was a lie?" I ask, staggered by my crumbling reality.

"It's not entirely a lie. The Nephilim were initially noble but, like humanity before them, their nobility was short-lived. We've been fighting to lead our kind closer to our angelic roots and our honorable calling, but we've struggled to have widespread success."

"Jan taunted that I'm more human than Nephilim and you implied that Nephilim really are the product of angels and women. Is what she said true?"

"Yes, the old stories are true. Nephilim were originally the offspring of angels and women, but they can also be the offspring of two Nephilim or even a Nephilim and a human. With each generation, the potency of angelic blood is usually further diluted, so there are Nephilim of various size, strength, and purity. Some people out there have just a dash of Nephilim blood and don't even know it. Others are more angel than human. There is evidence of Nephilim reproducing with angels, thereby increasing the concentration of angelic blood and making offspring of incredible strength. Have you heard the legend of Verdonos?"

"I have. My paren—Dan and Val told me the story when I was young," I respond.

"Verdonos is an example of one such Nephilim and is the most powerful ever recorded, although we also have another such example living amongst us here who may be just as powerful. Verdonos was conceived by an angel and his Nephilim mother, whose blood was already elevated in purity, making him more than seventy-five percent angel. Hence his incredible power and ability to open a bridge to the Pneuma Rigma."

I'm both fascinated and bothered by his tales and information. It doesn't seem realistic for anyone to have such knowledge about things so far removed from their experience. Yet, somehow, I find it unquestionably believable. It just feels true, but so did some of Jan's lies before her betrayal. I have to keep my guard up for now.

"How could you possibly know that? According to the legend, he lived and died centuries ago," I challenge skeptically.

"Ted, the implications of this war are far-reaching. It has attracted the attention of beings well beyond the Nephilim. We have allies in their ranks and I meet with them occasionally. They've opened my eyes to a multitude of truths that surpass my wildest imaginings. That being said, the recent exponential growth in the ranks of wicked Nephilim is a mystery and a grave concern to all of us."

WE KNOW.

Concern wipes across Reb's face as if my nose is gushing blood or a worm just slithered beneath my skin. Those words, the image of that bloody message, is seared into my mind. Its involuntary retrieval, as inconvenient as it is, is beginning to seem like the voice of my subconscious. Based on Reb's reaction to my expression, my subconscious sees it as a warning.

Reb speaks with genuine concern, saying, "I know this has been a lot to absorb. We don't have to do this all at once. There's plenty of time. Why don't we put a pin in this and pick up where we left off tomorrow?"

"You're right, this has indeed already been a challenging session. But if it's all the same to you, I'd like to just get this over with now. Frankly, I already feel numb and that beats having my heart repeatedly steeped in stomach acid with each revelation."

This appears to meet Reb's cautious approval. "Alright then, before we continue, do you have any questions about what I've shared or any specific questions I have yet to answer?"

"Yes I do, but first I'm intrigued to know who here may be as powerful as Verdonos."

"I'm afraid that's a conversation for another time. What's your other question?"

"Is there a way to know how concentrated my blood is?" The question erupts from my lips before I can stop it.

"Actually, there is. We have devised a test that works quite well for determining our percentage of angelic blood. We already took the liberty of scheduling you for that test tomorrow at nine in the morning. Is that okay with you?"

My gut crumples with his response. It's the question that has consumed my thoughts more than any other but, until now, seemed impossible to have answered. With the answer so close, I'm not so sure I want to know.

"I'm not sure yet. What if I don't want to be tested?"

"You don't have to be. It's strictly for your own benefit. I know you're struggling with your identity right now. Answers, the truth, though it may hurt at first, will be the salve that heals your wounds and makes you whole. Take this time to rebuild your foundation and redefine yourself. That's what this place is for. When you're ready, you can start training with the others."

"What kind of training?"

"Honing your Nephilim abilities and learning to fight. That's an oversimplification, but the point is that we are not merely hosts to the seed. It's a part of us and carries our unique genetic code. With practice, you can learn to control and direct its activity."

"Abilities like Mel's mind-reading trick?"

"Yes, amongst others. I'm actually using one right now, Ted. I have been throughout this conversation. Do you have an overwhelming sense of my honesty despite the fact that my statements defy everything you've believed up to this point?"

I say nothing, but it's obvious that the answer is yes. Although, no matter what he's about to say, the rawness of this conversation has left me on edge, and I don't appreciate his secretive use of any Nephilim ability on me.

"You've been secretly using some Nephilim ability on me this whole time? Not exactly the stellar honesty that I would've expected from an alliance leader. If this is the way you're going to do things here, maybe I am better off on my own," I piously declare.

Reb raises his eyebrows, taken aback by my dramatic reaction. "Ted, no one is being deceptive; quite the opposite actually. I'm using the seed within my blood to 'transmit' my state of mind in a small electromagnetic field. Basically, I've made myself an open book so that you know I can be trusted."

"What if you weren't being honest?"

"You would sense it clear as day. All I can do with this skill is make my state of mind transparent. I'm not *telling* you that I'm being honest, I'm *showing* you what's in my heart, my intentions, and they just so happen to be honest."

The discovery of this ability isn't all that surprising. I've always known that Nephilim use similar tactics to stay hidden by closing ourselves off, but I've never considered doing the opposite. My memory wanders back to Jan and how deftly she earned my trust. Sure, I didn't completely buy it, but I never should've bought into it at all. If she knows of this ability, perhaps she used it to make me trust her.

"Reb, is it possible for that ability to be used for deception? What if someone figured out how to transmit a state of honesty when they were actually being dishonest?"

"It could be possible. We're still learning about the full potential of our abilities, and there have been all kinds of rumors over the years. We've heard of Nephilim reading minds, brainwashing people, and even shooting electricity from their bodies. I don't put much stock in those stories, but I believe that there is probably a nugget of truth in each of them that's been greatly exaggerated."

He pauses but clearly has more to say. After a moment, he continues, "For Jan to have done that to you would've required her to lie to the seed within her own veins. In theory, it's possible. In reality, it would seem impossible. But if some evil Nephilim has figured it out, it would be a dark turning point in this war. They could deceive any human they please as well as the many weaker or untrained Nephilim. They really could subjugate the masses and rule over humanity. Imagine Nephilim generals with armies at their disposal. Hundreds of thousands, even millions of highly trained soldiers worldwide brainwashed into believing we're terrorists or some kind of subhuman monsters. We wouldn't stand a chance."

The burdensome thought weighs visibly on Reb's shoulders. Their disheartened sagging betrays the outcome as he plays out the scenario in his mind. He muscles down a strained gulp and lifts his gaze to mine. His disarming compassion is replaced with alarmed consternation, and in a weary, ominous tone, he speaks again.

"Ted, do you believe that's how Jan was able to mislead you?"

The gravity of his question presses me firmly into the worn maroon upholstery. Not only am I not an expert, Reb just drop-kicked my reality with a few simple statements. Now, I feel as though he is relying on me for one of the most valuable pieces of intelligence in his lifetime. It's obvious that my answer to this question has implications for the future of the alliance and maybe even creation as a whole.

"I don't know. I don't know anything anymore." The weight of these revelations about the Nephilim and about my parents starts to wring my heart dry. The protective numbness that gave me strength is giving way to a maddening tingle. I was an orphan, abandoned by my own parents. A divine being of truth, raised on a steady diet of lies. The flood of pain and confusion crashes through my makeshift dam, spilling in streams from my eyes and self-pity from my tongue.

"Reb, I'm sorry, but until a few minutes ago I thought Nephilim could only reproduce with other Nephilim. I thought that we were created this way, not the actual offspring of angels and humans. I thought that I was the biological child of the couple who raised me, and that my one purpose on this earth was to sow people who had irreversibly lost their way. I thought that the Nephilim were all noble beings working toward a common goal. I thought that sowing was the extent of a Nephilim's power. I thought that I was destined to be alone, but now I'm here being invited to join an alliance that I didn't know even existed until a couple days ago."

"Ted, you're being too har—" Reb attempts to comfort, but I'm not finished.

"What *I* think is meaningless, and if you're relying on me for anything critical then this alliance is already doomed. I don't belong here. Whatever small part of me that's Nephilim is of little use to me now, much less to your alliance. I don't know where I belong, but it isn't here. Your time will be better spent training up those children out there than me. I'll just be another mouth to feed." I prop my elbows on my knees and hang my head.

After a long pause, Reb's hand squeezes my shoulder. "I understand why you feel that way, Ted, but I assure you that there's a place for you here. I think that's enough chatting for today. Before you make a final decision, please stay at least one more night. Spend the rest of the day exploring Carver and feel free to introduce yourself to the others, although I doubt you'll have to. We're a friendly bunch, always eager to welcome newcomers. If you have any other questions or needs, feel free to ask."

Struggling to lift himself from the pew, Reb displays an unexpected frailness. He makes enough progress to twist and use the seat back to push himself upright. As he walks in front of me, his steps are slow and deliberate. With a profile view, the curve in his upper back is plainly visible. It isn't a smooth contour due to an abrupt hitch one third of the way down from his neck, and it's not simply a hunch. It's an injury, an old one if I had to guess.

Before he makes the turn down the center aisle he stops in his tracks, disrupting my impolite stare. His once-again gentle eyes have caught my fixation on his back. Embarrassed, I offer a preemptive apology.

"Sorry, Reb. I shouldn't have stared."

"It's an old injury. One from before I joined the alliance actually, back when I was a few years younger than you. I tried to take on a very powerful Nephilim by myself. He was the corrupt mayor of a large city and was a shoo-in for governor. I couldn't allow that to happen, so I confronted him. He broke my spine, and I haven't been able to take Nephilim form since.

The bones don't align correctly anymore. I could paralyze myself if I tried."

I can't imagine life without the ability to take Nephilim form. Reb's fortitude to not only live amongst Nephilim who are everything he used to be, but to train them and lead a revolution is astounding. He is that rare, enigmatic leader to which others are drawn in spite of his apparent disqualifications. It drags me toward him and his cause despite my determination to push them away, to be alone.

"That's awful, Reb. After hearing that story I can tell you that you're stronger than me, and I admire you for it. You said the injury happened before joining the alliance?"

"Yes. It happened when I was a loner. Everything I've achieved as a part of this group, including my position as its leader, has been as a cripple. I may not be as physically capable as Mel or Dan or Pam or even you, Ted, but I am gifted in other ways, and I do my part. That's all we would ever ask of you too: do your part. Anyway, I don't mean to harp. Let's pick this up tomorrow if you're still here. Deal?"

I nod. "If I decide to stay, it's a deal."

We shake hands and exchange a cordial farewell. Reb carefully makes his way out of the church and I settle back onto the pew with a lot of thinking to do.

CHAPTER EIGHTEEN

After an hour of fruitless meditation in the tranquility of the ramshackle church, I begin my late-afternoon solo tour of the settlement. Warm hues of red and orange soak the exposed west side of each building, standing in sharp contrast to the increasingly nippy air. Each crunching step casts a spell of silence over the nearby crickets, but those in the distance continue their soft chirping in a soothing evening symphony. Carver may not offer the total solitude of the farm, but there's a certain sense of comfort in knowing that friendly Nephilim are just a shout away.

Thankfully, now that I've met with Reb I'm no longer under Drake's watchful eye. He wasn't waiting for me when I exited the church and I'm not wasting any time looking for him. A complicated man, he's not what I would've expected from a human who has willingly embraced a role as a Nephilim assistant. His confident, standoffish bravado suggests a naivety about the power we wield, but he's fully aware of our might and still fancies himself an equal. Even my transition from potential enemy to neophyte ally has only peeled back his arrogant hostility enough to reveal his tangy good nature and irreverent sense of humor. If it's true that most Nephilim are like Jan, it's easy to understand his hostile feelings toward us. It wouldn't even be a stretch to say that I empathize. Still, I suspect there's more to his story.

The knowledge that my race is not only more corrupt than human beings, but is also the primary source of creation's dissonance still hovers over my consciousness. It follows in the shadows but has yet to land, take root in my heart, and sew itself into my worldview. Accepting a world in which humans are more noble than Nephilim and are victims in need of deliverance will take time.

My stroll along the sidewalks of Carver proves more therapeutic than my time in the church. The brisk atmosphere invigorates my mind and senses, and in that alertness, I feel awake to the truth around me. No matter what I choose to do next, the facts of this decaying world will not change: the Nephilim as a whole have lost their way and I will be powerless to change that as a lone operative. My decision is not between joining the alliance or fighting alone, it is between joining the alliance or giving up the fight altogether.

That perspective makes the decision rather simple because no matter what lies have led me to this point, I could never stand by idly as the world is ravaged. There is, however, a complicating factor, because I also can't imagine being relegated to the level of an errand boy like Drake. As admirable as his commitment to the alliance is, such a role is unfitting for a Nephilim. I may not have the strength and potency of Mel or some of the others, but I still have too much to offer to be anyone's sidekick. The blood test will tell me where I stand amongst the others and make my decision obvious.

My mental train derails with an *oompff* as I bump into a stranger rounding the corner. Forgettable brown hair sweeps across the top of his head, which is all I can see until he steps back and looks up to my face. The young male looks barely twenty and entirely human. His doughy cheeks, round face, and youthful eyes don't match his lean muscular frame or his rugged scruff.

"Sorry, man. I was cruisin' and didn't see you. You must be Ted," he guesses with a voice that matches his scruff better than it matches his eyes.

"I am. And you are?"

"Call me Doc. So how are you liking it so far?"

"I like it. I've never seen anything like it, actually, and I mean that in the best way. Although, I'm not exactly sure where I fit in or what I have to offer," I admit.

"Well, if a dimer like myself can find a place taking down evil Nephilim monsters, then there's definitely room for whatever you're bringing to the table."

"Dimer?"

"Oh, sorry," he says with a chuckle. "It means I'm only ten percent Nephilim. Don't worry though, I made up that nickname myself. Everyone here respects each other regardless of blood purity. By the looks of it, you don't have anything to worry about. Hey, it was nice meeting you, Ted, but I gotta run."

"Nice to meet you too, Doc."

"Oh, I almost forgot. A group of us are doing a campfire tonight at seven; just a chance to hang out and tell old war stories. It would be great to have you join us."

"I don't know. I appreciate the invitation, but I've got a lot on my mind."

"Well, just know that you don't have to go through this alone. All of us were loners before we joined the alliance. It can be a big adjustment, but we all know what you're going through. We're glad to have you here, Ted. Hopefully I'll see you tonight!"

Doc hustles away and I zone out as I imagine myself at the campfire, a stranger amongst a group of old friends; the awkward outsider cramping their camaraderie. The image is far from appealing—awkward for them and even more so for me.

Unfortunately, the alternative is an early night in a foreign room with only my demons to keep me company. Perhaps the campfire is worth considering.

As I return to reality, a gaseous, fluttering mirage, a visible disturbance of the air, shifts at the rear of the old hardware store, catching my attention. Curious, I investigate what strange Nephilim abilities are in use this time. As I stroll in its direction, the seven-foot-tall amorphous disturbance moves smoothly through the closed back door of the store. I try to follow, but the flimsy excuse for a door is locked. With just a couple of steps for momentum, I ram my shoulder into the brittle wood that crunches and gives way, nearly falling from its hinges.

Dust floats, glowing in an errant ray of sunlight against the darkened hallway. I walk the cluttered hall that runs between the offices on the left and the restroom on the right on its way to the front of the store. The old floorboards let out a creak and pop that travels up my spine. An ear-piercing shriek assaults my frayed nerves as I push through the swinging door and enter the main sales floor.

Rows of shelves sit well stocked with abandoned products, all caked under a thick layer of dust. I stand and survey the eerie sight. The scene is a snapshot of someone's personal apocalypse. Whether through disaster or the rapture, it's as if they simply vanished, leaving their unfinished business right here on these shelves. According to Drake's version of events, people migrated away as the wells dried up, but the visual is far more unsettling than the story and it's easy to see why the town has a ghostly reputation.

The mirage's slithering, rippling motion enters my peripheral vision. Despite being transparent, it bends the ambient light and makes the tools hanging behind it appear as though they're under shallow, turbulent water. Shifting, wiggling, the dirty axe dances through the wondrous illusion.

A sickly whisper calls to me from the mirage. Uneasy, but more curious than ever, I take several steps toward the mirage before *thump*, *thump*, *thump*, *SHRIEK*—the swinging door to my right flies open, nearly scaring me airborne. Having noticed my startle, Mel stops in her tracks with an apologetic grimace. I look back to the mirage but it's gone, and a quick three-sixty confirms it's nowhere in sight.

"Oh my gosh, I'm sorry, Ted. I didn't mean to scare you," Mel says sweetly with a sheepish grin.

To avoid admitting I was scared I ignore her apology, instead asking, "Were you doing that just now? The…shimmering mirage thing?"

"Mirage? No," she replies, concerned. "What did you see?"

"I don't know. I thought I saw something like a heat mirage by that wall over there," I answer. "I thought I heard a whisper too." I give her the whole truth and nothing but the truth.

"Could it have been a sunset reflection off a store window? What did the whisper say?"

"No, it definitely wasn't a reflection. It moved from the alley into the store and I could *feel* it. It had a presence. I couldn't make out the words it whispered."

Mel ponders with a furrowed brow. She looks around the room before closing her eyes as if to meditate. Fifteen seconds pass, and I take the opportunity to appreciate Mel's knee-buckling beauty while I wait. Her eyelids slide open and intercept my gaze, which I avert, but not swiftly enough. I examine my tan work boots and scratch the back of my neck as she speaks.

"Hmm, I don't feel anything, and I know that no one here has discovered an ability that presents as a heat mirage. Honestly, Ted, I'm a little bothered by it, but that doesn't mean it's something to worry about. Keep a watchful eye and let me know if you see it again, okay?"

"Okay."

"Anyway, I'm glad I finally found you. Doc said he saw you around here, and I heard that door shriek from a block away. I wanted to welcome you and have a normal conversation for a change, but if it's alright with you, I want to get out of here. These old abandoned stores aren't the atmosphere I was going for…especially in the dark," she says with a chuckle.

"I can see why the local teens think they're haunted."

"You think this one's bad, you should see the clothing store with all the mannequins!" She laughs with a wide-eyed expression of faux fear and puts a hand on my shoulder. "Let's go for a walk."

"Yeah, let's do that," I reply, trying my hardest to swallow the lump of excitement in my throat. She pulls an about-face, heads for the exit, and I gladly follow.

Back outside, we amble the remarkably quiet sidewalks of the settlement at Carver. Soft lights glow through drawn curtains at several nearby houses. It's hard to get used to the fact that behind those windows are Nephilim families. Regardless of their number, being immersed in a community of Nephilim really is my personal utopia and was only a pipe dream until a couple of days ago.

"So, how are you liking it here so far?" she starts.

"Well, I haven't decided about my future here yet and, honestly, I haven't really spent any time processing this whole thing. My short conversation with Reb pretty much burned my world to ash. I don't really feel like I can assess my potential future with the alliance until I first deal with my personal issues."

"I'm sure that was a lot all at once, Ted. Reb is a wise leader, though. He wouldn't have shared all that in one short conversation with just any ol' Nephilim. He knew you could handle it and wouldn't appreciate us holding back that info to dump on you later. I helped with Reb and Julius's research, so I know what you're dealing with right now. I'm just saying that because I want you to know that I'm here if you need to talk. I can't say that I understand your exact situation, but we've all had our struggles. My mother was Nephilim. She was compassionate, nurturing, and loving while still being strong as steel, but I never even met my father." Mel stops and changes subjects with a gesture to the stonemasoned building across the street. "Here we are."

The words above the missing front doors read *Carver Town Hall,* which is only legible now thanks to the rich, early nightfall moonlight. The stonework makes the building look strangely out of place in a town of mostly wood siding and stucco. Clearly it was meant to be a focal point, a source of pride for the mayor and the townsfolk. Now, it's just another ruin.

"What's at the town hall?" I ask.

"We are," she notes with a playful smirk. "Follow me. I want to show you something."

With no observable interest in my agreement, she trots across the empty street and up the stairs. I play catch up, following her into the dark structure. Through the hollow doorway and at the far end of the grand hall is a stairwell that climbs all the way to the roof. Mel wastes no time getting there and bounds up the steps with more confidence in their structural integrity than seems wise. I follow at a more prudent pace, and when I arrive at the rooftop landing, Mel is already trying to light the first of four tiki torches that mark the corners of a cozy seating area. The patio furniture is arranged around a low, glass-top table and as the first flame ignites, the glass reflects the mellow, citrusy ambiance. After lighting the remaining torches, she invites me to sit. Despite the inviting arrangement, I can't help my discomfort while perched above a thirty-foot void with a roof of questionable stability as my only protection against a fall to my death, or worse, a broken spine.

"You don't have to worry, Ted, this is the strongest building in town," she assures. "It's one of the only ones that they actually took their time with and used quality materials. We've been coming up here for years to relax and enjoy the view."

Replying would force me to confirm my nervousness about the roof, so I just nod and try to release the tension in my body, with little success. These moments, though they seem insignificant, could form a lasting first impression with Mel. I don't want to be seen as the frightened Nephilim who's scared of the dark, scared of abandoned buildings, scared of heights, and probably scared of my own shadow. And it's not just about wanting Mel to like me. If I decide to stay, I don't want everyone here to see the weakness in me. I can't show them my humanity.

The view to my left overlooks two thirds of Carver, which is still and peaceful. With the sun long gone, the moon and stars are vivid against the backdrop of limitless space. I can now see that there are eight small houses with lights on, all a safe distance from the main roads. Two columns of gray, swirling exhaust, only visible in the spillover of the house lights, spiral their way from the generators toward the heavens. It won't be long before similar plumes ascend from nearby chimneys and the campfire pit, wherever that is.

I break the silence, saying, "You're right, the view is serene. Reminds me of a painting."

"It's a small community, but it's very special to me and everyone here," Mel responds.

"So, I asked Reb earlier and he dodged the question, but I'm really curious how many Nephilim live here. I've spent my whole life alone since my parents—my adoptive parents—died. I've never even seen this many of our kind in one place," I admit.

"Right now the number is eighteen, not including you. There's a couple with two kids, a couple with one child, we have an orphan, and also a single dad with two kids. His wife died a couple years ago. Then there's a handful of singles like Reb, Doc, me, and a couple others. We've had others come and go. They've trained with us, then moved on to new areas to recruit and expand our reach. I know it doesn't seem like much, but it's a pretty high concentration of Nephilim for one region. We're not exactly an army, but when three or four of us tackle a mission, we almost always have numbers against the corrupt Nephilim out there. Every new Nephilim that joins our ranks is really an exponential increase in firepower. Just like how many of us started life as loners sowing human targets, many of the evil Nephilim still function as loners taking advantage of the human system."

"Did you start off living alone and sowing individual human targets?" I ask.

"Yes. It really is a special calling that we have as Nephilim, but until we deal with our own evil, manipulative ranks, it's unfair to keep sowing human beings. If they're acting based on the lies of our kind, I'm not sure how much blame we can really place on their shoulders."

"You sound like Drake."

"Julius and I have spent a lot of time together. He really gets it. He is one of the only humans I've ever fully trusted, and I honestly can't imagine doing this without him," she gushes.

"Drake? The same guy who calls me 'Sunshine' and gives me flack every chance he gets? I realize there's a history there but, from my experience, it's hard to imagine thinking so highly of him or any human for that matter. He's a nuisance."

Silence ensues. With each second I feel more uneasy about my choice of words. Clearly Mel and Drake, Julius as she calls him, share a special bond. Just thinking about it makes me feel like even more of an outsider. But if I'm going to stay, I can't sabotage these bridges before they're ever built.

Trying to patch the damage, I say, "Sorry, Mel. I don't mean to bash your frie—"

"I understand why you feel the way you do, but Julius has been through a lot. We all have a past that shapes our outlook and sometimes leaves scars. He may be prickly, but if that's the worst thing you can find to say after what he's been through, it's a minor miracle. His entire life has been a series of tragedies and offenses that would have destroyed anyone else.

"First, his mother, a true saint if there ever was one, died unexpectedly when he was only eight from a brain aneurysm. One night she was tucking him in with a lullaby and a kiss, the next morning she was gone forever. Seven years later, he and his father, a high school principal, had mostly healed from her sudden passing and established a new normal. On the way home from a school basketball game, the two of them stopped at a gas station. When his father went inside to pay, he found himself in the middle of an armed robbery, a situation he may have survived if he hadn't recognized one of the perps as a student. He called the young man by name and pleaded with him to put down the gun and choose a better way. The other perp, the student's uncle, shot Julius's dad three times in the chest and abdomen. When he heard the shots, Julius raced inside, fearing the worst. The robbers beat him unconscious and when he awoke with several broken ribs and a traumatic brain injury, his dad had already finished his slow, painful passage into the afterlife…alone."

"Oh my God," I react in breathy horror.

"Oh, I'm not done. Julius spent the next three years bouncing around the foster care system until he turned eighteen, at which time he eagerly joined the Ridge City police force. He had his dad's bravery and a neurotic motivation to fight crime after how it had affected his life. Police work came naturally and he graduated the academy with honors. After six months on the force, he had already earned two commendations and was on the fast track to sergeant. He had once again overcome a world bent on his destruction.

"The final phase of his rebirth was love, and that came when he met Vivian at his twentieth birthday party. They dated for a little over a year before they got engaged and married on the same day at the Dillman County Courthouse. The next year was the happiest year of his life, hands down. At the end of that first year of marriage, he and Vivian conceived, and thirty-eight weeks later she gave birth to a beautiful baby girl that they named Holly, his mother's name. Unfortunately, as drunks go, life is an angry drunk and its sobriety short-lived. After seven blissful weeks, Holly passed away in the stillness of the night, much like her grandmother before her. Sudden infant death syndrome."

I cover my mouth and swallow the stone in my throat.

"You've got to be kidding."

She shakes her head solemnly and continues. "It took two years and intense therapy before either of them arrived at the threshold of healing. Their therapist suggested that if they were ready, a dog may help them recover, so they rescued a mutt that looked something like a Scottie. It worked. They were a family again, full of love, and things seemed to be settling into another new normal until one day, as part of another investigation, Julius stumbled into a hornet's nest. He discovered that at least two of his fellow officers were corrupt and deeply involved as a protective buffer for several criminal outfits including an illegal gambling ring and a drug smuggling and dealing operation. Julius being Julius, he confronted them and tried to set them straight. Spooked, they took drastic action. He arrived home from his shift the next night to find his wife held hostage, duct-taped to a chair, and their sweet dog Howard, tail wagging obliviously, in the clutches of Officer Timson. Brantley and Timson warned Julius what would happen to Vivian if he didn't back down, then Timson proceeded to drive the point home by snapping Howard's neck. Julius lost it, drew his service weapon, and plugged each of them between the eyes with blazing precision. The horrific situation was recorded as self-defense, but it was the end of his career with the Ridge City Police. Unfortunately for Julius, it was also the end of his marriage. Vivian had had enough of the turmoil. She divorced him before their fifth anniversary and they've never spoken since.

"At first, he stayed in Ridge City and spent three years in an existential vacuum working dead-end jobs, hoping that his self-imposed futility would satisfy life's drunken wrath. Eventually, however, he accepted that the only thing that made life worth living was hunting down bad guys and, since it was just him now, he had nothing left to lose. He moved from Central California up to Port Ellis and got a fresh start. I met him several years ago while working a story and immediately sensed his integrity. I recruited him and here we are."

"How is it possible for all of that to happen to one man? I think that's the saddest story I've ever heard. And he somehow still believes humans are unfairly judged and that Nephilim are the real problem?"

Her face goes flat and she studies me the way she might study a boulder or some other impossibly dense object.

"Ted, I'm not telling you all this to gossip. Julius gave me the go ahead to tell you his story because we thought it might help you better understand the human condition. And, before you try, he doesn't ever want to talk to you about it. We looked into the corrupt officers, Brantley and Timson. The criminal organizations they worked for were managed by a small network of low-level Nephilim. They weren't powerful enough to achieve a station like the Jans of the world, but they were devious and brazen enough to forge their own path to wealth and power. We also tried to look further back into the robbery-gone-wrong that killed his father, but we couldn't confirm any Nephilim connection there. Either way, the point is this: humans may be more fragile than us, more vulnerable, but life doesn't pull any punches and they are not weak and useless. There are plenty more like Julius out there—trustworthy, honorable, resilient, and courageous."

I sigh and ponder the moral of the story. "You're right. I was wrong about Julius. I still have no idea how to relate to him, but he is everything you say. That being said, I think he's the exception to the rule. Like you, I detected his goodness and strength when I first met him, but I've never met another human like him."

"You've never met a human who you trusted or respected?"

"Until I got to Pentastar, I had never given a human the time of day. They were always just targets, nothing more. My time at Pentastar had me even more convinced of their depravity until I prepared to sow Dave. By pure happenstance, I met his wife and nephews, who exposed me to another facet of his character. Ever since then, I've been struggling with doubts about the true malignancy of human behavior. Obviously, Jan amplified those doubts by showing me the ugly truth about our kind."

I sigh, stare at the wobbling flame of a tiki torch, and contemplate her question. She waits patiently and watches me intently. I can feel her empathy, her compassion. She's not bothered by my feelings about humanity; she understands them, and the only reason she's challenging me is because she wants what's best for me. To be fair, I *can* think of several recent examples of virtuous human actions and, despite my persistent reservations, I offer them to Mel as tokens of my good faith efforts to grow and be open-minded.

"I have witnessed a few respectable human behaviors lately. Tyson is a positive, kind, and helpful individual. Drake, as much as we butt heads, is brave, noble, and loyal. Dave's willingness to step up for his nephews was selfless and honorable. Even so, a few good deeds over a lifetime of deceit doesn't make them admirable creatures. I'm just not ready to embrace humanity as a whole the way that you have."

"I don't think I know Tyson. Regardless, you're right and that's just a small sample of the good that they're capable of. I've seen things that would inspire you and bring you to tears, Ted. Of course there are bad eggs and there always will be, that's when we intervene with sowings, but on the whole, as a matter of percentage, I think they're doing a lot better than us Nephilim."

"I believe you, but I haven't seen the things you have. I've never seen people act in a way that inspired me. My mind is slowly changing about humanity, but it may take some time before my heart comes around."

"Fair enough. I can respect that." Mel pauses, still studying my face, then pans around to survey the town below and speaks without making eye contact. "Just so you know, your beliefs about humanity aren't a deal breaker with the alliance. As long as we agree about taking the fight to the corrupt Nephilim, your views about humanity are yours to hold. No one here can change your heart and we aren't going to waste our breath trying, but I want you to remember what I'm about to say. There will come a moment when you discover the strength in your own humanity. Only you can change your heart, but in that moment, you will. We all have."

Her confident predictions about my future are almost as reassuring as they are presumptuous. In a time when I don't even know myself, it's a strange relief to be with someone who so boldly claims to know something about me. In fact, everyone here seems to know as much about me as I know about myself, a fact that should be unnerving but is oddly comforting. My inborn resistance to vulnerability, to openness, doesn't matter here. Jan's betrayal of my vulnerability has only increased the sturdiness of my walls, but this place and these Nephilim have made those barriers transparent. They conceal nothing, leaving no point in even trying to hold back. My book is open, my pages have been read, and there's nothing left to hide. I'm free.

Considering the alternatives, there is no better place for me to be right now than surrounded by those who know of my shame but embrace me anyway. Nowhere will my struggle be better understood, and there is no one outside of this camp who can help me become who I *want* to become—who I *choose* to be.

I look at the breathtaking Mel, bracing for and tempering the rush of premature fondness that always follows. "Thanks for bringing me here, to Carver I mean. As much as I'm leaning toward joining your efforts, I still need to take the night to think it over. I've been hit with some devastating information today and I want to make sure I'm thinking clearly."

"Of course. Take your time. I don't know if Doc mentioned it, but there's a campfire tonight—actually, they're probably getting it started now. Please come. You don't have to say much beyond a simple introduction to those you haven't met yet. Just be a fly on the wall, enjoy the distraction, and embrace the community of it. It'll help you make the right decision if you get to experience the camaraderie of this group. They've become my family. It's a powerful bond."

"Thanks, Mel. Doc mentioned it when we bumped into each other and I was on the fence about it then, but I think I'd like to join you all. If nothing else, I could use the distraction from my thoughts, and it would be great to meet more Nephilim."

"Great, let's go now," she says as she stands. "We can continue our talk along the way and at the campfire if you want, or you can just relax and take it all in."

I stand and we make our way down the stairs and through the nearby neighborhood. Out past the muffled rumbling of the generators, on the border between Carver and the middle of nowhere, lies a gully that dances with the campfire's frolicking radiance as we approach. A jagged orange cleft in the ashen prairie, it looks like a gash straight to the Earth's molten core, glowing heat rising from the chasm. Cheerful voices echo up from the torn earth, and as we clear the gully's edge, I see the familiar faces of Reb, Doc, and Drake along with a couple of new ones.

After brief introductions, I spend over an hour just passively observing the group, tossing small twigs into the flames and listening to the crackle as they're swallowed. As a lump on a stump, I get to know Reb and Doc quite well, learn a little about Pam and Vic, tolerate Drake, and pine for Mel. Unsure whether to credit the heat of the burning logs or the warmth of this newfound companionship, I can feel my guarded heart soften and even discover the value in their playfulness, jumping into the fray during my second and third hours by the fire. I marvel at their tales of hard-fought victory, laugh at their embarrassing stories of personal failure, and genuinely relish the frivolous, quick-witted banter of the alliance members. Their play solidifies the bonds that fortify the alliance. They play together, they fight together, and they may even die together, but there's no one they'd rather spend those final moments with than their alliance family. Despite the devastating revelations of the day, it's around that campfire that I find the camaraderie I've come to admire, the community I've been longing for, and the family I've always needed. It may be dysfunctional, but it's nevertheless fulfilling.

It's nearly ten thirty by the time Mel drops me off at the small, two-bedroom house where my day started. We reach the stoop and hold at the unlocked door. For the briefest of moments, we lock eyes and the beating in my chest halts. Both exhilarated and terrified, I keep my distance for fear of humiliation. Mel makes the first move as she leans in. Her arms wrap around my shoulders in what is one of the most platonic hugs imaginable. Disappointed but not surprised, I hug back and savor the moment.

"I'm really glad you're here, Ted," she speaks quietly into my ear. "I know this is where you belong and that you bring something special to this group. I hope you decide to stay. If you do, I think you should do the blood test Reb mentioned. It may shed some light on your past, but it will also help you set realistic expectations for yourself. Just remember, no matter how it turns out, we want you to stay."

I nod as we separate, but don't speak a reply. She looks at me with her eyes of pure, icy light and takes a step backward.

"If you do stay, we can start your training tomorrow!" she says with an excited smile.

I allow a subdued grin as I respond, "That sounds excellent."

"Okay. Goodnight, Ted," she says as she turns and descends the couple of steps to the ground.

As she strolls away, I call out, "When do I get to hear your story?"

She stops and turns back. "What was that?"

"I heard all about Drake, Doc, Reb, and even a little about the others. When do I get to hear your story?"

Her coy smile says, *You caught me*, but her tired voice says, "Not tonight. I'll see you in the morning."

"Goodnight, Mel," I say as I turn and enter the house.

Once inside, I head straight to the shower to clean up and wash the campfire smoke from my itchy eyes. I don the neatly folded dark-green cotton robe that was placed on the vanity counter and head back to my room. As I pass the dining table, I notice a handwritten slip of paper that details the old-fashioned laundry process using the tub and a washboard along with the following statement: *The generators provide just enough power for refrigeration, basic lighting, and incidental use (charging cell phones, radios, tools, etc.). They cannot sustain prolonged high amperage usage. Think of it as a very limited resource to be used sparingly. Thanks.*

I scrub my outfit accordingly, hang it outside to dry overnight, and finally climb into bed more exhausted than I should be given my recent day-and-a-half of sleep. Just minutes after falling asleep, my eyes burst open to find that I'm not alone in my room, only it's not exactly my room. Through the black mist that gets thicker as I pan toward the ceiling, an immense, dark figure towers near the windows. Even in this murky atmosphere I can make out his gray flesh and inky eyes. My jarring pulse travels through my bones to my eardrums and out to my fingertips. My whole body tingles and my mind races. His dead eyes glare directly at me, and he speaks.

CHAPTER NINETEEN

With a husky, melodic, almost choral voice, the intruder utters, "Theodonis, it's time to have a talk." Despite his elysian features, he seems almost personable. He has familiar Nephilim qualities and, unlike the dark hooded attire from his break-in at my old apartment, his garb looks like breezy linen, albeit black or dark gray in color. It flaps gently in a nonexistent wind that moves the dark mist, like visible black spores, in swirls and billows. I reach for the bedside lamp and twist the knob, which clicks but provides no light. It could be the generators, or this could be a dream; I'd prefer the latter.

Threatened by his presence and emboldened by my newly minted friendships, I rudely address my uninvited, possibly imaginary guest. "You're the same slug who broke into my apartment. Whatever this little game of yours is, I'm not interested. It's been a long week and I'd really like some sleep, so get lost and take your talk with you."

He appears frozen for several seconds, a glitch in what is nothing more than a nightmare, I hope. A quiet snapping sound reaches my ears, maybe a memory from breaking twigs at the campfire, and almost instantly the man darts from the windows to the side of my bed in a blur. He stands over me like an undertaker, the dark lines of his silhouette blending against the murky spores. I swallow hard, reminding myself he's not real.

"That's some tough talk, Ted. I didn't think a broken little boy like you could muster such courage. Too bad you'll never know whether you got that from your mommy's side or your daddy's. I can't even imagine what it feels like to be abandoned by your own parents. If they found you so unlovable, just imagine how easily your new friends here will toss you aside."

That hurts: a finger plunged deep into my fresh wound and a reminder of my overwhelming fear of rejection. My fight deflated, I glare hatefully at his looming shadow. He knows exactly what buttons to push and has no restraint. The longer this goes, the more my spirit will be crushed, my will broken, and my trust for Mel and the gang lost.

"I don't know how you're doing this, but if you're going to kill me, just get it over with so I can wake up from this pointless nightmare. Just know that if you try anything in the real world, it'll be the last thing you ever do. You've never seen Nephilim numbers like those that will slam down on you before you make it out of this camp."

He snickers condescendingly and says, "I know about this little camp of do-gooders and I'm not worried. They and their ancestors have been around for centuries trying to redefine what's written in the genetic code of the Nephilim. At first, we tried to fight back and destroy them, but they kept resurfacing. Eventually it was clear that they'd never even make a meaningful dent in my horde. We may not be a cute little team, but we outnumber them fifty-to-one, which is why I have always won and will always win."

The figure withdraws from his aggressive position over my bed and walks back to the windows, where he looks out at the Carver Public School building. Something about him looking at that playground where those innocent Nephilim children played just hours ago feels vulgar, menacing. It almost feels like a threat. *No one is off limits, not even them.* With his back still turned to me, he continues.

"My goal is not to destroy you or any other Nephilim for that matter; it is to give your existence greater meaning than any of you ever imagined! I want you to fulfill your birthright, your ultimate purpose as the pinnacle of creation to reign over this earth. It is ours to command, but more than that, to *enjoy*. Why endure a life of loneliness, hardship, and rejection when you could live in unimaginable luxury. Food, travel, women, wealth, power, pleasure—they can all be yours, and it's so easy.

"You've seen the way that Jan lives. Her power and authority will be laughable in comparison to what you can achieve. She will live in the shadow of your throne, your underling to command; a city, a state, and eventually a nation yours to rule. We control, through occupation or influence, almost every seat of significant power on this planet. Nearly all of the world's presidents, prime ministers, chancellors, and judges are either Nephilim or are beholden to us. If you don't join us, you will be dominated by us and will be just another cog in the machine that makes us rich and powerful.

"I'm not your enemy. In fact, I'm your only true friend. I'm the only one who's honest enough to tell you that this whole alliance thing is a waste of time. You're just going to get hurt in more ways than one. Rejection, betrayal, broken spine, death—that's what you're signing up for."

I can tell he's not done, but I've heard enough of his sordid sales pitch. With impressive swiftness of my own, I throw off my covers and hurdle across the room, trying to take Nephilim form as I do, but something is wrong. My spine is locked, my veins lifeless, as he turns back from the windows. Just before the point of no return, I manage to halt my movement a couple of inches from the nine-foot-tall monster. Craning my neck up painfully, I look into his soulless eyes. He seems amused by my close proximity and cracks an ugly smile.

Furious, I spit and bark, "That's enough out of you! Your fear that I'll join the alliance is pathetic. You're embarrassing yourself. Think of me shutting you up as a favor, and there's no need to thank me. But before you go on your way, I would like to thank you for helping me make my decision. I will join the alliance, we will take you and your 'horde' down, and you'll regret ever showing your face!"

The figure, frozen again for a couple seconds, seems to tremble with rage. I take a step backward, but not quickly enough as the behemoth grabs a fistful of my hair and lifts me from the ground. In my helpless human form I dangle, grabbing at his arm to relieve the searing pain in my follicles. He effortlessly raises me with one arm to meet him at eye level. Immersed in the smoky mist, my scalp feels like it's peeling away from my skull. His black eyes swallow goodness, hope, and joy as he leans forward and pulls my head alongside his.

Calmly and quietly, he whispers in my ear, "We'll see."

I feel my body begin to sway, bringing an eye-juicing, tooth-crushing grimace to my already pained face. The sway rapidly and violently accelerates as he slings me across the room and against the wall. I hit it with a crunch and drop like a lump onto the bed.

The instant I flop against the mattress, the jangling bell of the mechanical alarm clock screams. I lie face down with my aching head at the foot of the bed and as I open my eyes, the darkness is gone—no fog, no threatening intruder. In fact, the room is unexpectedly bright. I set my alarm for 5:30 a.m.—a couple hours before sunrise this time of year—and yet the room is vividly aglow. Delirious after what feels like zero sleep, I stretch the grogginess from my body and rub the sleep from my eyes before discovering the light source: the bedside lamp. I'm positive I turned it off before I went to sleep. I *did* turn it on during my nightmare, but it yielded no light. I'm also positive that I laid down with my head on the pillow, but here I am in the exact position from my dream, a lump with my head at the foot of the bed and a throbbing scalp.

Nausea sets in with the impossible notion that my nightmare was somehow more than just a figment of my sleeping subconscious. The more I think about it, the more the evidence fits despite its impossibility. Just because I lack an understanding of how a real being could appear and interact with me in a dreamlike state doesn't mean that it didn't happen. If it did, however, I'm gravely concerned about the implications of that interaction for my safety and that of the alliance. Maybe I should have responded differently.

I give my small residence a once-over, checking every room, every closet, and every cabinet just to put my mind at ease. By the time I finish, the sun has broken the horizon and beams through the kitchen windows. There's a knock at my door and I rewrap my robe before I answer. Pam, blonde and rather plain looking by Nephilim standards, awaits with a pleasant smile and a plate of fresh fruit.

"Mornin', Ted," she greets with a slight Texas drawl. "Figured you'd need somethin' for breakfast."

"Good morning, Pam. You figured right. Thank you!"

She smiles shyly and hands the plate over to me before asking, "So will we see you at training today?"

I pause in thought even though I don't need to. Last night's nightmare, vision, experience—whatever it was—made the stakes very real, and even if the alliance is doomed to fail, I can't sit back and let that monster have his way.

"Yeah! I'll be there," I reply, surprised by my own excited grin.

"Good! I'll see you later then. We usually start at ten in the mornin' at the school gym. I'll see you there!"

She strolls off in the crisp golden air and I devour the entire plate of fruit without setting it down. A bland hour passes during which I complete my usual morning hygiene, retrieve my chilled but dry clothing, tidy up my room, and wash the only dirty dish in the house. Afterward I dress and take a seat on the small landing outside the front door to think and take in the beautiful, steadily warming day.

Fifteen minutes before my nine o'clock blood test appointment, I make my way to the school building next door in an effort to impress my future leadership with my punctuality. As I stroll the short stretch of sidewalk between my cottage and the school, fast, measured steps suddenly approach from behind until Vic jogs past with a hand-flip wave and a breathy "Hey, Ted."

"Morning, Vic," I greet as he runs along without looking back.

Vic is black, a little taller than me, and lanky. He's quieter than some of the others, but equally friendly. Despite knowing him the least out of any of the campfire attendees, I know that he and I will get along. Simply based off of his demeanor around the others and the few comments that he made, I can tell that he's the Nephilim I have the most in common with personality-wise in Carver.

I reach the school entrance and pull open the door with renewed determination. It appears no one is here yet, so I indulge my curiosity with a private walkthrough. The hallway of the school is a pleasant surprise. It's a little dark. The only light inside is whatever the sun can manage to force through the discolored skylights and the dusty windows, but it's clean and organized, unlike any of the other businesses or public structures in town. If the lights were on, I'd say the school is ready to pick up right where it left off fifty years ago. The floors are swept, the ceiling tiles are all in place and accounted for, and the desks and chairs are still neatly arranged in each room. Upon my perfunctory survey I don't see any notable disrepair or decay. The only thing missing from this still frame of historic Carver life is the kids' prized artwork and assignments hanging on the lockers and bulletin bar strips.

Such a small town had no need for multiple schools, and they managed to comfortably fit first through twelfth grade down one central corridor. Six classrooms flank each side of the hall, with several offices and additional classrooms down another, shorter wing of the building. At the end of that shorter wing is a small gymnasium with just enough room for a basketball court and a couple rows of bleachers on one side. As I made the short walk over here, I noticed a large house across from the school that had been repurposed as a preschool and kindergarten, accounting for the remaining educational needs of the once-promising little town.

My nosiness satisfied, I walk back toward the entrance and front office to await Reb's arrival. I reach the doors and glance out the front windows. Across the street, a row of buildings basks in the heat of the morning sun, and in front of them, as if standing on the sidewalk, is another wobbling, transparent mirage. Perhaps it's the same one, I don't know.

I lean closer to the window and squint to focus my vision. It's just standing there on the sidewalk. The feeling of being watched presses in heavily around me. Just as I place my hands on the door's handlebar and push it open, Reb, Mel, and Doc round the corner of the entryway. Mel immediately spots my strange fixation across the street and looks over her shoulder, then back to me without seeming to see anything. For me, the mirage is still there.

As Mel steps into the foyer, she eagerly asks, "What were you looking at? Did you see it again?" Her furrowed brow and higher-than-usual pitch implies a raised level of concern compared to last time.

"Yes, and I'm still seeing it," I answer without releasing the mirage from my gaze.

She quickly slides in next to me and asks, "Where do you see it?"

Reb, moving gingerly, takes a touch longer to reach my left flank, while Doc just turns and looks from where he stands.

"Do you see the tan brick building with the red trim?"

"Yes," Reb and Mel reply simultaneously.

"Look about eight feet to the left of the door on the other side of the big window. It looks like a heat mirage. It's just squiggly, bending light, probably seven or eight feet tall. Do any of you see it?" I ask.

Silence.

An answer in itself. Between these mirages and my repeat visits from the rogue Nephilim, I'm beginning to doubt my own sanity. Maybe these things are manifestations of the psychological and emotional strain of the past few days. Either way, I'm now embarrassing myself and I decide against mentioning my nightmare.

"Sorry, Ted. I don't see anything," responds Reb.

"Nothing here either," says Mel.

"I don't understand. I can *still* see it. It's just standing there," I add, deflated. I continue watching the mirage, preferring its taunting glimmer to the judgment I assume is written on their faces.

Reb, unfazed by my hallucinations, supportively offers, "Well, we can go with you if you want to investigate or we can head to the science room to do the test. It's your call."

As nice as it is for him to humor what he probably sees as delusions, it's unlikely anything beneficial will come of investigation, and the potential danger seems untenable. Of course, that's only if there actually *is* something there to investigate and it's not just in my head. In that case, it would only further whatever doubts they have about my membership in the alliance.

"Let's just do the test. I don't know what's going on with me. Maybe I just need glasses, maybe it's in my head, but I don't want to waste everyone's time," I concede.

"Sure thing, man. Right this way," Doc says without wasting a second.

He crosses behind us and we peel away from the windows to follow. Partway down the shorter wing of the building he makes a left and takes us into the school's science lab. Even darker than the hallway, I reflexively reach for the light switch and give it a flick as I enter. The fluorescent bulbs tick sporadically as they try to ignite, but before they succeed, Mel flips the switch back off and says, "We don't use the school lights unless we have to."

As Doc opens the window blinds on the far wall, Reb says, "We only left a bulb in each fixture, but there are still enough lights in this building alone to overwhelm both generators. About the test, do you have a vial of blood for the test or do we need to draw some?"

Doc moves to the other side of a lab table where a relatively simple contraption sits. He takes the lid off of the central container and twists the dial on a meter. He touches two probes together, gets the indication he's looking for, shuts the meter off, and then attaches the probes with clamps onto each side of the container. I slip my hand into the pocket of my overalls to grab the vial that I just can't quite break the habit of carrying.

"I've got a vial with me, but I'm guessing you suspected as much," I respond.

"Yep, we did. You're old school, Ted. Traditional Nephilim always have a vial," Doc says before he extends an open hand.

I give the vial over to Doc and watch with uneasy anticipation as he pours my precious blood into the clear glass container. He replaces the container's lid and locks it in place with a quick twist.

Mel steps alongside me and asks, "Nervous?"

"A little."

"Thankfully, you won't have to wait long," Doc notes. "The test is quick and easy. Blood goes in, I turn on the modified multimeter, blood enjoys some good vibrations, and I read the resistance. We discovered during some early experiments that the organism in Nephilim blood—we call it the scintilla—creates electromagnetic fields through its movement and interaction with itself and with the body's nervous system. Its movement creates friction, and the friction yields an electric charge which excites the scintilla, causing a discharge of electromagnetic energy. Basically, the more of the scintilla you have, the higher your angelic blood purity and the better your blood conducts electricity—the lower its electrical resistance. Oh, and just FYI, there's no putting this blood back in the vial. Your scintilla's gonna be a little toasted."

"And remember, there's nothing to fret. You're welcome here no matter the outcome," Reb adds.

Doc, his hand on the dial of the meter, looks across the lab table and asks, "Ready?"

I nod and Doc clicks the meter's dial into position. The blood instantly reacts to the electric current with flares of light like fireflies. At first, they float slowly through the red, viscous liquid, then faster and faster. The others' faces deform first with confusion, then concern as pea-sized lights zip around the container, radiating an intensifying light before appearing to burst and diffuse. The blood begins to surge as if boiling. Rolling mounds of red precede frenetic oscillations, captivating the wonder of the group.

At this point it's clear that the test isn't going as planned, but the sight is so mesmerizing that it draws the four of us toward the cylinder. The blood continues to churn with racing, flashing lights, a submerged thunderstorm of yellow, red, and occasional, brilliant white. We lean over the table and study the cosmic sight, but our collective awe is shattered when the lid of the container launches upward with enough force to hit the ceiling. Tiny yellow lightning bolts reach for the top of the cylinder as we all stumble back from the device.

Reb shouts, "Shut it off! Now!"

Doc lunges for the device and twists the dial, shutting off the meter and the flow of electricity. The contents of the container settle quickly. Steam trails upward and a quiet sizzling vibrates the glass.

"What was that?" Mel cries to Doc. "Did the tester malfunction?"

"No, the device is fine, but I've never seen blood do that," replies Doc.

"Did you get the resistance reading?" Reb asks.

Doc nods to himself and says, "Yeah, but with that reaction I'm not sure if it's accurate."

"Well, what was the result? What's my percentage?" I anxiously ask.

Doc grabs a notepad and pencil. "Hold on, I have to do the calculation. The resistance measurement in ohms has to be converted to a percentage."

"But you said that the lower the resistance, the higher the purity of my blood, right? So, you could just compare resistance measurements with the other Nephilim to have an idea."

Doc stops writing and says, "Yes, but we figured out a formula that factors in the total range of realistic measurements. If you don't account for the range, there's no way of knowing if a one-ohm difference is a change of one percent or fifty percent. Just let me do this calculation and I'll tell you."

"Okay, I'm sorry. I'm just anxious and confused. Why did my blood do that? That's not normal, right?"

Reb fields my question, saying, "I don't know, Ted. In all my years, this is a new one."

My mind races as I ask, "What does it mean? Is there something wrong with me?"

"None of us know," Mel states calmly, soothingly, "but we will do our best to find answers. Do you have more vials of blood?"

"No. I had some in my briefcase, but I left Milburn Tower in such a hurry that they're still locked in the safe in my office, hopefully."

She places a soft hand on my shoulder. "Let's draw some more for them to test while we're training, and they'll let you know what they find. Sound good?"

"Sure, that's fine," I answer, still eagerly awaiting Doc's calculation.

Just then, Doc finally pipes up, "Got it! Ready, Teddy?" He raises an eyebrow in a goofy inquisitive look. When he sees the lack of amusement on all of our faces he says, "Sorry. Never had good comedic timing."

"We're ready," Reb answers for all of us.

"Thirty-eight percent. Not bad, Ted. I told you, you had nothing to worry about!"

His positivity only increases my edge. Thirty-eight percent is disappointing despite knowing it was unlikely to be much higher. My mistake was allowing a part of my heart to be so naively optimistic as to hope for at least fifty percent. I make no effort to hide my disappointment, which the others easily notice.

Reb combats my chagrin, saying, "Ted, thirty-eight percent is really high. Actually, that puts you in the five highest here. Fifty percent is quite uncommon. Realistically, you would have to be first generation Nephilim or the child of generations of fifty percenters to maintain that number." He puts a hand on my other shoulder and says peacefully, "You should be happy, Ted. This is good news."

I nod, hoping that the physical act of affirmation will influence my attitude. Mathematically speaking, he's right, I couldn't have hoped for much better. Coming into this I felt like a Nephilim joke, but thirty-eight percent is respectable, and I'm actually feeling somewhat validated. Everyone else's positivity is also helping to encourage my acceptance and hasten my embrace of this outcome.

"So, what happens next?" I inquire.

Mel wraps her arm completely around my shoulders and replies, "Let's get your blood drawn and then I'll take you to the gym to start training. We'll start with physical combat in various styles and mix in sessions of Nephilim abilities along the way. Everyone's always eager to hit the Nephilim stuff so let me just get ahead of you on that. Nephilim abilities have their place in this war, but they're not particularly useful as offensive or even defensive skills. Hand-to-hand combat is where this war has always been won and lost."

I'd ask why hand-to-hand combat is the preferred method of engagement, but I already know. All Nephilim, good, evil, or somewhere in the middle, are better off keeping a low profile.

Weapons of any kind increase the chance of dead Nephilim, police, autopsies, media attention, and the worldwide exposure of our existence. The world isn't (and will probably never be) ready for that. Corrupt Nephilim could no longer hide in plain sight making themselves rich and powerful. Every suicide would be first investigated as a Nephilim sowing. We would be hunted, imprisoned, and killed by humanity.

Fistfights, even those including blunt objects and knives, won't make the small-town evening news. We are strong enough to inflict mortal wounds on humans and against each other, but killing Nephilim leaves a body that must be disposed of quietly. Guns leave witnesses and attract police like flies to dung, especially in an era of mass casualty active shooter violence. Using our hands keeps things quiet and allows us more control over the level of damage we inflict.

Reb draws a few vials of blood and tapes me up, then I follow Mel to the gym where we start my training. As we cover the basics of grappling and kickboxing, she is a rough but patient teacher. Despite our repeatedly intertwined bodies, I remain surprisingly focused, which is more likely a result of my intense desire to impress her than of a lack of romantic interest. My chest spasms as we tangle and brawl in Nephilim form. The foreignness of taking my true form in the light of day with witnesses is exhilarating and liberating, but to do so with Mel by my side, also in Nephilim form and without the whispers of my guilty conscience, is downright euphoric.

We zip through the basics and by lunch are ready to move into some intermediate combat. Though I've never had any formal hand-to-hand combat training, the skills are coming naturally and fighting already feels second nature. I know Mel is still holding back, but I'm seeing the fight clearly in my mind, and once my technical skills catch up to my understanding, I'll be formidable. If only I had this training before I faced Jan.

Lunch break comes and goes, and we're back on the mats before our food settles. Several others join in for the afternoon session, making the experience ever more surreal. Surrounded by my own kind—giants of the earth—we train and spar, sharpening our bodily weapons while others hone their Nephilim abilities in the other half of the basketball court. When I'm not distracted, staring at the other side of the court in the hope of seeing something spectacular, I'm holding my own against everyone but Vic and Mel. They're taller than me, stronger than me, and are far more experienced fighters.

Still, Mel seems pleased with my technical progress and tactical acumen as I practice the physical techniques and learn how to best employ them. At four in the afternoon, after almost six hours of combat training, Mel decides that's enough fighting for the day and that it's time for an introduction to Nephilim abilities. I slam a couple of water bottles and trot to meet Mel on the other side of the gym when I hear my name being called from the gym entrance.

"Ted," shouts Doc, "Reb and I finished our tests. Come talk to us."

I look to Mel, who is already moving my direction, and we make our way back to the science lab. Her presence is comforting and settles my nerves as we round the corner and look upon Reb and Doc's troubled expressions.

"What did you find?" I ask impatiently, still a few steps from the table.

Doc fields my question, saying, "So, man, we tested a fresh vial of your blood and it had the exact same crazy reaction. Oh, and just FYI, the resistance readings were identical to the results from our first test. Then we tested a vial of Reb's blood to confirm the device's proper operation and it worked like normal, so there's nothing wrong with the device. Finally, we took a look at the scintilla in your blood under a microscope." He inserts a pregnant pause before finishing, "We found some anomalies, man."

"Anomalies? What kind of anomalies?" Mel asks, beating me to the punch.

Reb sighs and answers for Doc, saying, "We don't know."

"Well, can you at least say if it's a good thing or something I should be worried about?" I ask, desperate for some emotional direction.

"We really don't know, Ted. I'm sorry, but none of us are biologists and even if we were, there isn't exactly a library of literature published about Nephilim biology and the anatomy of the scintilla," Doc responds.

"Seriously?" I ask incredulously. Their lack of reply speaks for itself. "Okay then. This just keeps getting better."

Reb speaks up again. "We really don't think it's anything to worry about. You've made it this long without any harmful effects from the muta—from the differences. You've even sown people with normal results, correct?"

I say, "Yes," but with the inflection of a question.

"Here, see for yourself," Doc interjects, motioning to the microscope.

I move into position and lean down to the eyepiece.

"This first one is Reb's sample. See the two antenna-like growths on the left of the seed?"

"Yes, I see them."

"Okay, that's what it's supposed to look like. This next sample is your blood," he says, swapping out the slides. "Look to the right. Do you see the seed?"

"Yes. At least, I assume what I'm looking at is the seed. Mine looks like a squid."

"Exactly. Now," he says as he pulls the slide to the right, "take a gander at the seed over here."

Unable to make any sense of the sight before me, I simply observe. The tentacles of two of my squid-like seed are interlocked and new antennae are growing out of the sides opposite their union. I wish I knew whether to celebrate or start praying. A part of me is excited about my uniqueness while the rest of me is horrified by it.

"They're connected, merged like the beginnings of some kind of network," I finally say.

"Let me see," Mel says, tapping my shoulder then bending over the microscope.

"Ted," says Reb, "we don't know exactly what any of this means at this point, but my gut tells me it's something astonishing; something that this alliance and this world needs, whether or not any of us knew it before this moment. You may not have the highest blood purity, but something about you, about your past, about who you are is quite possibly the greatest advancement our kind has ever seen and I, for one, can't wait to see what you're capable of."

He turns to face Mel before delivering new orders. "I want to shift the focus of Ted's training. I don't think the uniqueness of his scintilla is going to make him any stronger as a physical fighter. What do you think about going eighty-twenty in favor of training Nephilim abilities?"

"I think that's a good idea, Reb. He's a natural fighter. He needs a little more technical training and then plenty of repetition, but he can already hold his own against most of us."

"Good," he says, turning toward me. "Take the rest of the day off and get plenty of sleep tonight." Then back to Mel, he says with deep eye contact and fiery intensity, "I want you to make it your personal mission to unlock Ted's potential. If I'm right about the seed in his veins, he may be capable of things well beyond the limitations of his blood purity. He may be capable of things well beyond what we even understand at this point. If he is, I want to unleash Verity on the wicked ones and set creation straight."

CHAPTER TWENTY

Learning Nephilim abilities is not as easy as I expected it to be. According to Mel, the key is learning to command the scintilla. That is the greatest oversimplification I've heard in my entire life. The unwrapped version of that statement is that I must somehow learn to influence the electrical output from my brain in order to communicate on the proper frequency or channel with the seed while still maintaining normal electrical communication throughout my body.

Apparently, like humanity, Nephilim don't normally utilize much of our total brain capacity either. Our usage is between twenty and thirty-five percent, depending on blood purity. This is higher than the estimated ten percent workload of human beings, but still leaves some parts of the brain quite infrequently used. As I've been told by Mel and seen demonstrated by her and the others, there is a small part of the Nephilim brain, no bigger than a black bean, that serves as the command center of the scintilla but must be "activated" before it's functional. The only way they have discovered to accomplish this is a regiment of meditation, pressure point therapy to divert blood flow, thought exercises designed to stimulate that segment of the brain, and sheer willpower. It's as ridiculous as it sounds, and if it wasn't for my firsthand experience with the alliance's use of their Nephilim abilities, I might think I was being pranked.

Pair this seemingly impossible task with the pressure of Reb's loudly professed and widely disseminated belief that I'm going to become some kind of super weapon, and I'm getting frustrated with myself and these expectations. It's been three long days of training since the blood test and I've made almost no progress in my attempts to harness the power of the scintilla. Despite the others' support and understanding, I can't help but sense their growing impatience and furtive disappointment.

There have been a couple of short-lived, hopeful moments: one where I created enough of an electrical disturbance to make my own arm hair stand on end, and one where I altered the blood flow to my brain enough to briefly lose consciousness. Strange for either of those to bring hope, but learning to intentionally influence my own body's processes using nothing but my body is just the type of paradox that could drive a man crazy. Any alterations, even those with counterproductive results, still show progress and prove that my mind is capable of such feats.

Each day has included at least six hours of intense, focused sessions during which I try to access parts of my body that I didn't know existed until a few days ago. I've continued to see mirages here and there, but whenever I approach they flee or dissipate before I reach them. My nights are continually afflicted by the rogue Nephilim's plague. If I don't awake in the darkness to find him standing in the corner of my room, I toss and turn with ghoulish nightmares of serpents, insects, and putrid deterioration. But in spite of this nightly onslaught, I persevere to unlock the potential within my veins.

Throughout the last few days, I have forged ironclad bonds with Vic and Mel as they train me. I've even found a spring of playfulness buried under the many years of repression and sobriety. It's these moments of lightheartedness that have helped me survive the burdensome, hopeful anticipation that afflicts me and the rest of the alliance. When Reb speaks they listen, and what they've heard is that I am a legend in the making. It's a role I relish, but also one that I have yet to earn in any way.

Mel's patience is supernatural. With days of failure under our belts, she continues to invest in my training as if each minute is the first we've shared. She brings fresh hope every morning that it will be the day of my breakthrough, and if it weren't for her peaceful strength, I'm not sure I could sustain this pace. Simultaneously my harshest critic and my most sincere advocate, she has read me like a book from the beginning, providing rest when I reach my breaking point and pushing me back to my breaking point when I'm sandbagging.

It isn't until late afternoon of the fourth day that everyone's hard work receives a well-deserved pat on the back. Mel and I are performing an exercise aimed at focusing my brain's electrical energy on the scintilla command center. At this stage I've felt only momentarily the sensation of a deeply embedded brain spasm, the tension and pressure of a foreign object within the brain tissue near the back of my skull that accompanies the command center's activation. I have yet to be able to sustain it, much less control its output.

We enter a time of meditative silence, but I can't quiet my mind. A kaleidoscope of the last couple of weeks spins before my mind's eye: the revelations of truth that rocked my foundation, the ass whoopings I've received, the intrusions of that dead-eyed Nephilim, the sight of my mutant scintilla, the slimy bits of Dave's brain and bone, Jan's betrayal, and the incendiary agony of being tased. I refuse to dwell on those memories, and I will not be defined by them. If Reb is right, my future will outshine all of this darkness. I am Theodonis Verity. I am a divine being of truth and I will remain loyal to my nature even if it means my death!

Somewhere beneath the wrinkled recesses of my brain's surface and near the back of my skull, a twinge and a spasm seizes and holds like a tightly balled muscle. My eyes snap open.

Around the gymnasium, the others are still hard at work, oblivious to the change in my body and for good reason. Nothing has changed externally. The lights aren't flickering, no little yellow lightning bolts are stretching from my fingertips, and I'm not being bombarded with signals from the others, but I know that this is the breakthrough I've been working toward.

I lift my arms to investigate the prickling ripples that continually flow over my skin, massaging me from the neck down. With my sleeves already pulled up to my elbows, I can see every last hair standing rigidly with the passing of each wave. Mel must have heard my movement because I watch her eyes sneak open in the blurry background of my arm hair. Looking through the hair, Mel and I make eye contact, brimming with joy and excitement.

Without alerting the others she leans in next to my ear and says quietly, "Let's try something before we get everyone's hopes up."

I nod in agreement and whisper, "Okay. What did you have in mind?"

She pops up from the mat and hurries to the side of the gym opposite the bleachers where a table stands bearing a selection of random objects. From the various options (a silver flip phone, a battery-powered radio, a table lamp, another multimeter, a tube TV with rabbit ears on top, and more) she selects the badly outdated table lamp. Returning to her position off the corner of my crossed legs, she sets the lamp on the ground about one foot in front of me. Leaning so close to me I nearly expect a peck, her cheek rests softly against mine, intensifying the electric atmosphere as she whispers, "This old table lamp. See if you can turn it on, light it up. Be careful not to burn out the bulb though. Control it."

"I don't know how to do that. I don't know how to make it do anything. I can tell I'm connected to the control center though. I can feel the scintilla's movement through my entire body."

"Getting connected is the hard part, Ted," she says. I can feel the warmth of her breath against my ear as she tries to hush her excitement. "All you need to do now is think the command in the same way that you would tell any part of your body what to do. Look at the fixture and visualize the scintilla energy field reaching out and engulfing the light. The field allows us to induce a voltage into some simple electronics and disrupt the operation of others."

"Okay, here goes nothing," I say with hesitant expectancy.

"Just focus. You can do this."

I look at the light fixture with its lifeless bulb and imagine it firing up to a glowing yellow. Nothing. Willing it even harder, I again imagine the bulb's filament warming to a white-hot glow. Again nothing. Without success, I adjust my approach, thinking instead about the invisible electromagnetic field as some snaking vaporous extension of my body that wraps around the bulb like a fist, bringing it to life. It remains lifeless.

"It's not working," I whisper to Mel.

"I wish I could tell you exactly what to think or visualize, but everyone is different. Everyone's scintilla is unique, yours more than most. You have to find what works for you. Try it again but do what comes naturally. Only you know how your brain processes information. Do it your way."

I look ahead and examine the old light fixture, taking note of every detail: the glossy porcelain housing with its avocado finish and wavy form resembling that of a curvy female's figure, the standard incandescent bulb with its loosely coiled filament, the translucent, discolored power cable with its braided copper conductor terminating at the fixture's base, and the small two-pronged plug resting on the gym mat. Armed with fresh mental snapshots of the lamp, I close my eyes and imagine the cool, twisted copper. I picture the electrons flowing through its lattice, across the terminals of the fixture, through the socket, into the bulb, and along the filament. I dwell on this thought, investing my will, my emotional energy, my desire. The muddy drubbing of my racing heart floods my eardrums, nearly drowning out Mel's quiet gasp.

Through my sealed eyelids, I detect the glow of the burning bulb. Slowly, to preserve my focus, I retract the thin flaps of protective skin shielding my eyes from the lamp's direct beams. Actually, the light is rather weak, but, sure enough, it's glowing a faint red orange that reminds me of a lipstick shade that my adoptive mother used to wear—a versatile color, dramatic enough for a winter gala, but light and refreshing enough for a summer date. I stare more deeply than I should into the bulb's dim ambiance and strain my mind to increase its output.

At first there's no change, but slowly, methodically, I find my stride, moving the electrons at an even higher rate and with greater force. The filament burns hotly, slinging heat against our awestruck faces.

"Careful, you don't want the bulb to burst, Ted," Mel warns.

I turn the lamp off and back on with ease, then again, and once more, each attempt bringing its own unique hue of orange and fading off at its own leisure. Rather than bring the bulb to life with a swelling wave of electrons, I decide to hit it with a surge of juice like the flip of a switch. My eyes again closed, my mind focused, I wipe my thoughts away and with them the electric current. Behind a mental dam I build a cache of voltaic thought, again envisioning not just the result, but the path to it. When the dam bows under the mounting pressure, I let loose, unleashing a reservoir of energy into the lamp which radiates gloriously through my eyelids. But it's not just the lamp. The entire gym is lit up like an operating room! A DJ's garbled banter squawks from the portable radio's two-inch speaker. Scrolling, checkerboard static paints the TV screen's pixels white, gray, and black. Every bulb burns brilliantly, casting shadowy spokes around each upright body. A clamor builds as the others take notice and close in around me.

"Ted, how are you doing that?!" Mel cries ecstatically, but I'm locked in and offer no reply.

In a sporadic staccato pattern, I pulsate the power to the entire array of overhead fixtures and nearby electronics, eventually learning to exclude the TV, radio, and flip phone from the grouping. The lights flash and dim repeatedly until I start varying the timing, staggering the flashing amongst the numerous rows of lighting. Mel's expression of amazement is pasted on every face in the room.

I'm feeling it now, so I decide to push the limit. I raise my arms like a conductor, extended outward and upward to dial up the drama and give physical manifestation to my state of mind. The frequency of the flashing and the intensity of the bulbs' output increases suddenly. The collective breath of the alliance escapes their lungs, everyone standing in stunned suffocation while they behold the demonstration of my newfound power.

Their eyes squint narrowly at the intensifying flares of light I create until eventually, and to my embarrassment, several bulbs burst with the surprising pop of an exploding balloon. A cascade of glass peppers everyone in the room and taps against the floor like crystal rain. Mel is speechless, and no one else seems to mind my costly mistake that serves to finally satisfy their expectations for my potential. Reb, Doc, Pam, Vic, and the others look at me with wide-eyed admiration and Drake, who has been spectating from the bleachers, initiates a slow-clapping round of applause that is straight out of an eighties flick.

"Well done, Sunny," he hoots.

I can't help beaming at the applause and cheers, but at the same time it seems unnecessary. Like a parent who gushes over their mediocre child simply doing what was expected of them, the entire alliance is coddling me for taking my first baby steps.

Congratulations for overcoming your total ineptitude, Ted. We're so proud of you for not being a waste of time.

"Ted," Mel's voice interrupts the ones inside my head, "how did you do that?"

"What do you mean? I just did what you told me to do."

She steps on my next thought, saying, "No, Ted. I told you to turn on the lamp. Several of us can do that. Nobody can do what you just did." She lets out a breathy laugh of disbelief. "Those lights are at least twenty feet away. Lighting up one would've been unprecedented, but what you did is unfathomable!"

There's a tinge of insignificance in her otherwise exuberant tone. It's the smallness she might experience in the presence of her father, or perhaps at the sight of a powerful predator, or while watching a cyclone sweep across the plains—fear born from respect. Reb carefully hobbles around the minefield of glass between us. With a big, toothy, slightly self-satisfied grin, he lowers himself delicately onto the mat, completing an intimate triangle powwow.

"She's right. That was exceptional, Ted. I knew you were special, but that was beyond my wildest hopes, and you're just getting started. Who knows what your top end looks like."

I beam again, this time bashfully. "Thanks, Reb. I'm sorry about the lights. I didn't mean to; I was just experimenting."

"Don't apologize, they're just lights. You have carte blanche to experiment and explore your abilities. I don't care how many lights we have to replace!" He puts a firm hand on my shoulder. "How do you feel?"

"I've never felt better."

"Do you want to continue training or call it a day? It's nearly quitting time and it's been a long wee—"

"Oh, I'm not done yet," I blurt, cutting off Reb mid-sentence. "Sorry, but I'm just getting the hang of this and I don't want to quit now."

"I'll stay and keep working with him," Mel volunteers—more palpitations.

"All right, then. Anyone else want to stick around to help clean up this glass?" Reb asks the others, their response a unanimous yes with the exception of Pam who is slated to babysit for one of the families. My confidence building, it emboldens me to know that they're likely only volunteering to clean so they can see what I do next, though I'm not accustomed to an audience. Mel takes my hand and leads me to a back-to-back set of chairs underneath the basketball hoop's netless orange rim. We shake the jagged debris from the seats and turn the chairs to face each other.

Phase two of Nephilim ability training covers the gamut of basic skills like those Reb and Mel have already used around me. Mel's lie detector trick comes pretty easily and utilizes, at least in my case, an oddly similar thought process to manipulating the lights. I picture my electromagnetic field like porcupine needles probing through her skull, sensing the signals of her brain. A more nuanced form of this ability involves creating a small electromagnetic field to detect the heart rate of anyone standing close enough to me, providing useful information about their health and stress levels. Surprisingly, the most challenging of the basic skills is Reb's "open book" ability. I'm told by Mel that the key to this skill lies in achieving an exceptional level of emotional vulnerability and cannot be achieved by any amount of brute force or intellectual prowess. Therein lies the problem.

Emotional vulnerability is the language of the weak, the language of humans. *Follow your heart*, they say. *If it feels good then it must be right.* Such sayings have steered far more people to ruin than fulfillment and contentment. That's not to say that I have no emotions. Obviously I do. I felt frustration that led me to haphazardly sow Dave. I felt loneliness that led me to join forces with Jan. I felt rage that led me to goad and attack a dangerous enemy. I can encounter the full spectrum of human emotion, but these experiences have shown me that they're better employed as a device for understanding myself, not for making decisions and definitely not for sharing with anyone else. Allowing the free flow of my emotions has always led me astray. Vulnerability at the level this skill requires will not come so easily for me and could even be dangerous.

At the moment, my turbulent reservoir of feelings is held at bay by a dangerously eroded levee. Waves have sloshed and thrashed with each of the devastating revelations of the last couple of weeks and, if I'm not careful, I fear a lifetime of bottled emotion may break loose. Such a day I would gladly delay until I'm a pile of ash, but it's about more than saving face. I've already seen how quickly these Nephilim abilities can get out of control, and the others have admitted that they don't know the limits of Nephilim power. If that dam crumbles and I lose control, it could mean the end of me, or worse, the end of everyone here.

I spend two hours trying with vigor to allow my emotions to flow through my body and, by extension, through the scintilla, but I'm forcing Play-Doh through a pinhole. If I allow myself a moment of transparency, I can admit that fear is holding me back. I function very well with my thoughts and emotions neatly compartmentalized like the food on a picky child's dinner plate, but what they're asking me to do is dump that plate into a bag and shake it around, allowing my feelings to permeate my being.

Finally, at the end of those two hours, I'm hungry and eager to escape the pressure to peel open the chambers of my heart. I'm congratulated by everyone about my progress and "truly remarkable ability," and yet I can't help but feel like a failure for not following through on that final skill. Still, the group sets up another campfire to celebrate and officially welcome their newest ally, both friend and secret weapon. I welcome the distraction from my nagging failure. While I genuinely felt unable to attain the vulnerability required, I also know that I resisted the process, unable to trust myself enough to let go. I resisted and I failed, but with full commitment I know it's within reach.

I've already learned most of the basic skills and imagined how I might apply them in my pursuit of Jan and targets like her, which we discuss openly around the campfire. I should be able to scramble security cameras and shut off lights to conceal my presence and identity. Vic has uniquely adapted the ability that I used to influence the lights so that he can jam nearby cell phones and radios. He's going to work with me on that in the morning. As an added bonus, my ability to read the honesty of humans and Nephilim alike has never been more astute or effortless. My mastery of these skills is a fair consolation for my failure to open up emotionally, but I can't allow myself to settle for mediocrity. Reb promises to pursue Jan as soon as I'm ready, further bolstering my motivation, so tomorrow I will rupture the levee no matter the dangers that lurk within. If ever I'm going to do it, it should be in this place and surrounded by these Nephilim.

I sleep hard after a long, exhausting day of training. During the night, as with most of the nights since I arrived at Carver, the rogue Nephilim visits me in the darkness. We don't interact or exchange words. I stir, open my eyes to the sight of him standing by the window, close my eyes, and go back to sleep. His silent presence carries a significance that I don't understand. If not for his obvious opposition to the alliance, he could very well be my personal sentry. But he is evil, a well-established fact, and apparently has a vested interest in turning me to his wicked ways rather than killing me. He looms and stalks me hungrily, bitterly, angrily, but also nervously as if he frets the moment he'll have to do more than simply watch and intimidate.

I work with Vic the next morning and within an hour or so have a basic grasp on jamming electronics. Where Vic can isolate a specific device in a room full of tech, I can only jam whatever devices are within a pretty tight radius of myself. It's not particularly useful at the moment, but with practice it could be.

Reb is chomping at the bit to pick up where we left off yesterday, but I'm not. I go through the motions and promise myself I'll make a concentrated effort to truly open up during the afternoon session. Guilt from procrastinating while everyone has been working so hard to help me dampens my appetite, but I still munch on vegetables and a few strips of peppered venison jerky. As Reb, Mel, and I head to the metal folding chairs in the middle of the gymnasium, my stomach is wrapped in a tight knot.

It's time to dig into the scarred chambers of my heart and connect its contents to the network of excited scintilla that await their next command. Reb, seated across from me, asks me to close my eyes and relax my whole body, and I do so with the exception of my knotted stomach. I lean against the chair back with my arms hanging loosely at my sides and my legs stretching outward. The tension melts through my skin with each deep breath and slow, silent release.

"Now," says Reb, "I want you to imagine a time as a child when you were safe and truly vulnerable. Think of how comfortable you were with your feelings and dwell on that comfort."

Mel adds, "When I learned this skill, I thought about a time when I was seven years old. I cried bitterly and angrily about my father not being a part of my life. I couldn't understand why he didn't want to know me, and I gave all that darkness over to my mom. She held me so gently, absorbing all of my anger, pain, and worthlessness before responding that my father's absence was entirely a reflection on him, not me. She said that whatever his reasons for not being with us, she liked it better that way because it meant she had me all to herself and assured me that it was a privilege to have known me at all, much less as a daughter and best friend."

She wipes a glistening tear from her lower eyelid, sniffles, and swallows the frog in her throat.

Continuing, she says, "Think back to a time that you felt so small and free to feel. Grab that feeling and wear it like a comfy sweater."

Her choice of analogies strikes me as a little cute, but it's a perfectly tactile description of the emotional state I need to attain. That soft, warm, coziness that heats the skin and thaws the heart is a feeling I can relate to, but finding a memory where it was something more than a sweater will still be a challenge. Nevertheless, I dig for it, sifting through my childhood days; days spent working, training, and learning. Happy moments are sprinkled around, marked with smiles and laughter, but the free flow of primal emotions at the depth and breadth that Mel is describing rarely, if ever, happened.

At once, my mind is consumed with a living image. A young toddler, disturbed, squirms in the lap of a crying woman. His face is streaked with the venous trails of the Nephilim and he is angry, but more than that he is sad and scared. The child knows no words to express his anguish, so he screams and he squirms and he hides his pain under a boulder and hedges the boulder behind a palisade of anger. The woman's soft arms surround the boy and pull him close, holding him tightly against her bosom. In the comforting warmth of her embrace, the trails that marked his skin fade away and the anger that surged through the vein on his forehead smooths to a somber, aching grief. The two weep together: the boy from his profound pain and the woman from her profound empathy.

A tear falls from her chin and splashes against the blue plastic name tag pinned to her blouse. *Nancy.* More words are stamped neatly beneath her name. *Burkwood Orphanage.* The woman strokes the child's head, gently running her fingers through his fine blonde hair, and sings softly with a sweet, quivering voice. Until this moment I didn't remember her, but in this moment I love her. This woman, a human, is treating me, a discarded freak, with more love than my own parents could muster. An overwhelming tsunami of emotion smacks into my levee, hurdling over and through. As another tear descends the woman's cheek and falls onto the boy's hand, I feel a cold, wet pat on my own; the first drop of the greatest emotional purge of my life.

Ready or not, my pent-up emotions flow unrestricted in a great and undignified catharsis. I lean forward in my chair, doubled over with convulsions of joyful release and spiritual lament, an indivisible potpourri of my emotional spectrum. Love for the caring woman from my memory gives way to anger at my birth parents, then gratitude toward Reb and the alliance, then resentment at my adoptive parents for lying to me, then admiration and fondness for Mel, then rage toward Jan, Harvey, and the rogue Nephilim. The flow widens and folds over itself and explodes from every cell in my body and leaves me reeling in its wake.

With my soggy, burning eyes still clenched firmly with the seizure of my entire body, I enjoy the added perk of avoiding my peers' inevitable revulsion. There's nothing more awkward than a proud, grown man wailing and slobbering all over himself because he has finally acknowledged his feelings. Still, other than my blubbering it's quieter than I would have expected. Surely Mel, at least, should have offered a comforting word or touch. I snort a faucet-full of snot and wipe away the remaining face fluids with my sleeves then dare to look upon my audience.

What a consolation to my weary soul it is to find that none of them are looking at me at all. In fact, it seems they're looking *for* me. I rub my eyes roughly enough to checker my vision with black spots, but when they clear, the hazy film that I see is no longer a product of my tearstained eyes. With a little concentration I detect their faint, muffled voices calling out for me and I try to respond, but my voice sounds different, bland and lifeless. It's missing the usual rebound back to my ears, as if the sound is being absorbed or finding nothing solid off which to bounce back, but I can still make out its vibrations through my bones. The gymnasium is bright with the afternoon sunlight, but the temperature has dropped and the air is thick with a fine mist that tingles as it floods my lungs. Then, with shock and wonder, I realize where I am and what I've done.

In the throes of my emotional eruption I lost control, whipping my scintilla into a frenzy and yielding an almost supernatural surge of energy. Inadvertently, I truly have done something remarkable, something impossible, something complicated, something dangerous. I have bridged the Pneuma Rigma and, with no discernable pathway home, I might be trapped in the spirit rift.

I call out again, louder this time, hollering for Mel or Reb or Vic, hoping that their ears perk up. Even if they did, what good would it do? This is uncharted territory. Only the ancient tales of Verdonos document anything about this eerie dimension. No one in that gym can help me find my way home.

"MEL!" I bellow desperately, but she doesn't flinch.

Horribly, something else does. From the gym entrance, a rustling and series of hyena-like woops. My heart pummels quarter notes against my chest and my breathing reflexively halts. A hideous shadow emerges from the doorway—then two more. The snarling, hairy creatures walk upright like a human then leap acrobatically onto the bleachers and walls, latching onto the windowsill before launching toward and around me, boxing me in. As they close in, I'm able to make out their revolting features. Thick, wiry hairs protrude from their dark gray flesh, their appearance a terrible blend of baboon and vampire bat. The stench of sweet rot swirls in my nostrils. Several more enter before the dead-eyed Nephilim monster glides into the gym towing a shroud of dark spores that absorb the light from the room and bleed into the white haze, generating a black cloud below and above, the same as in my nightmares.

"You aren't supposed to be here, Theodonis," the monster growls in a fizzing chorus. "I tasted the difference in your blood when I broke into your apartment. I knew of your potential to empower our kind. I gave you a chance to make the right choice for yourself and the rest of the alliance, but you were too self-righteous and now you've changed things. Thanks to you, the alliance is no longer merely an annoyance, it's a threat. It's too late for them now; they will all die. They've seen too much and won't stop working to replicate what you've done, what you are. But it's not too late for you to save yourself. This is your final chance: join me in my mission to restore the Nephilim to their rightful dominance or die with your friends."

I take a half second to steel myself for a painful death, then look directly into his obsidian eyes and deliver my reply.

"Go to hell."

CHAPTER TWENTY-ONE

A queasy stillness arrests the passage of time and constricts space, injecting numbed silence into the atmosphere. The twelve eyes of the six beasts look to their leader in anticipation of the order they so long to hear: the order to kill. Without having seen them before, it's dreadfully obvious that they are creatures of pure, reckless hatred that thirst for flesh and feed on agony. With teeth stained brown from the dried blood of their innumerable victims and sickly, jaundiced eyes, their outer appearance matches their inner complexion. The only thing more satisfying to them than the shredding of my sinew and crunching of my bones would be the aroma of my spiritual anguish at the realization that I'm being killed. Perhaps one-on-one I could take out a few of them before relenting in total exhaustion, but they're not looking for a fair fight. This is an extermination.

As capable as I've grown in my combat and Nephilim abilities, the only skill that can save me now is the same one that got me into this mess. I need to bridge my way back to the human plane, if only I knew exactly how. If nothing else, I need to get back to warn the others. Every second stuck here could mean the difference between them getting caught completely by surprise or having a chance to evacuate the families to safety and prepare a defense against Carver's approaching apocalypse.

The dead-eyed, rogue Nephilim interrupts my plotting. "Go to hell?" he asks with a cocky chuckle. "Not yet, but maybe I'll see you there." With a calm and crooked smile, he shakes his head in disbelief. Surveying his pack of seething beasts, he gives a magnanimous nod of blessing over the feast before them.

Certain that they'll swarm me all at once like a pack of rabid dogs, I strike first, opting for brutish aggression. I lunge into a crouching leg sweep of the beast farthest from the dead-eyed Nephilim, then launch into an explosive uppercut of the next creature to my left. Its jaw pops against my fist, and with its pained shriek, broken bits of nasty teeth drop onto my arm. My body on autopilot, I'm already moving to strike the beast to its right with a spinning back fist that lands squarely across the creature's throat with a crunch. It buckles then collapses onto its back, gasping and scratching for air. Before it has a chance to recover, I flatten its larynx with a firm stomp to the neck that produces a terrible hissing gurgle.

I hurdle the dying creature to escape their ring of death and turn to face the pack, keeping them in front of me. I'm proud to have held my own, severely wounding one and likely killing another, but after only a week of training I'm already feeling winded, and I'd still have to incapacitate four or five more just to earn a death at the hands of the rogue Nephilim. He looks unimpressed by my display of violence and joins his gaggle of hellish baboons as they move toward me faster than I can backpedal.

"It really is a shame to waste your abilities this way, Theodonis. You really are something special. What a god you could have become." He pauses, quite satisfied with his own voice. "On second thought, it won't be a complete waste. You're going to feed the hungry. You'll live on in the bellies of my hellions. At least, that is, until they shit you out."

The hellions, as he called them, whoop and bawl as one bounds onto the bleachers to my left and behind me, then leaps onto the wall and hangs like a wrestler poised to strike from the top rope. At the same time, another one moves to my right and vaults from the bleachers to the rafters, where it swings overhead from light fixture to steel girder and steel girder back to light fixture. Their next attack will add a third dimension with enemies coming from every direction except under my feet. Even if I find a second wind and survive them, the monster will finish me.

I close my eyes, intending for it to only be a second's meditation, but it feels like minutes. With no thought to the fast approaching beasts, I indulge in a remembrance, a visitation of the warmest memories of my past but also a reverie of the beautiful future I'll probably never get to experience. Despite not knowing if any of it will come true, I see decades spent fighting alongside Mel, my best friend and only love, against the tyranny of deceit. I see a gathering of my own family, including two children that look just like their mother, and the many members of my extended alliance family that is growing and thriving. I see a world of free human beings, released from the bondage of lies and living a fulfilling life in true community.

Then, as a counterpoint to the first images, my mind offers another series of realities: love lost before it begins, thousands of Nephilim left hopelessly outmatched by such maleficent forces, a world of seven billion humans deceived into forfeiting their free will to Nephilim slave masters, and countless dead being bulldozed into mass graves like rubbish. Basically, a continuation of creation's destructive trajectory leading to a holocaust of all who would oppose their Nephilim oppressors.

For the second time in the last hour, my eyes begin to flood. A tear squeezes through my eyelids and follows a salt-glazed trail down my cheek, a trail formed less than an hour ago when I believed I had an entire lifetime of magnificent possibilities ahead. I'm not ready to give up on that future. I'm not ready to give up hope. Through my contemplative cone of silence I can hear the beasts' noises all around and closing fast. I want to go *home*, to Carver, to be with Mel and the rest of my alliance family. I want it from the depths of my soul, stirring a fluttering pulsation, one not produced by my heart and felt in my chest, but one that pervades my skin, building to an eruptive crescendo at the same time that the first beast lands on my shoulders. As it digs its gnarly claws into my flesh, I snap.

Both arms reach for the hellion in a blur and, as soon as my hands find something to grab, I rip it from my back, the creature taking out several chunks of skin within its clutches. With every scintilla-infused muscle fiber answering the call, I slam the creature against the gym floor with a resounding thud. The sight of dark blood already oozing from the motionless beast's ears does nothing to dissuade my savagery. I must make an example of this fiendish creature. I step firmly on its neck, wrap one hand under its jaw and the other around the base of its skull, and pull. I pull with my arms and with my back. I pull with my legs. I pull with a guttural growl of madness until something snaps, the greasy skin and muscles stretch to their breaking point, and the hellion's baboon-like head rips free from its body. When I look up to invite my next challenger, painted with my blood and that of the creature, I see the flabbergasted faces of Mel, Reb, Vic, Doc, Drake, Pam, and several others staring on in disbelief.

That peculiar fluttering sensation must've marked the moment I bridged my way back home, meaning that I just decimated that beast in front of everyone. It takes a couple seconds before I notice the rippling mirages standing in the exact positions of the creatures in the Pneuma Rigma and realize that I've been seeing their stalking presence through the dimensional divide ever since I arrived at Carver, maybe longer. They've been following, watching, and slipping away before I could confront them. The realization brings new questions to mind like why the others can't see them, how they could simply dissipate as I approached, and what they were able to see and hear during their observation, but now is not the time to flesh these out.

"Ted?" asks Mel, unsure if it's even me. "What happened? What was that thing?"

I drop the hellion's head and march past her, straight for Reb.

Vic asks, "Where'd you go?"

"I bridged the Pneuma Rigma," I answer in the manner I might tell someone that I took out the trash. I reach Reb and grab him by the shoulders, leaving bloody handprints. With mania in my eyes and urgency on my breath, I nearly shout, "Send a runner. Send one now. We have to warn the others and get the families out of here."

Calmly, despite his obvious confusion, he asks, "Why, Ted? What's going on?"

"They're coming. He's coming! The Nephilim monster from my visions, the same one who broke into my apartment in Port Ellis. He's coming to kill all of us!" I warn frantically.

Reb leans to his left and looks past me to scrutinize the dark gray carcass. He then trains an unnerving gaze on Vic and orders purposefully, "Go, Vic, warn the others. Tell them to get in their vehicles and drive straight to the rally point alpha." Vic starts to jog away as Reb yells, "Tell them to leave everything behind. Time is of the essence!"

A racket builds as the others inspect the creature's corpse and react to Reb's validation of my warnings. Drake is crouched low near the beast, craning his neck and using a pen to lift and examine its hand. He pops up and walks to the severed head then crouches again, shoving the pen into a nostril in order to turn it for a better look. To him the scene is just another day on the job, although probably his first with a demonic humanoid victim.

"Kinda looks like an evil baboon except that it would be at least seven feet tall with its head attached and it smells like death and sweet shit. How many of these were there?" Drake inquires.

"There were six. I killed two, but he may come through with more, and those things are only part of the problem. I don't know who this Nephilim is, but he's enormous and powerful like I've never seen before. He tried to seduce me to the ways of the wicked Nephilim, but I told him to go to hell."

Drake looks at me with eyebrows raised in amusement. "You said that, Teddy boy?" he asks with a laughing snort. "Look at the stones on you!"

The atmosphere stirs with a musky breath that slides across my neck. Building gradually in intensity, the disturbance swells to become a steady breeze that whirls throughout the gymnasium. I look to Mel, who predicts my thoughts and responds.

"This is similar to what happened when you vanished and again when you reappeared. Although, this is a little more…"

The lamp topples from the table and I snap around, expecting the worst, but it was just the growing wind. Unfortunately, the relief is short lived, fractured by the appearance of dozens of mirages racing in through the gym door, flooding through like a firehose, then leaping around the gym. Hell has arrived, and it's only a matter of seconds until they breach the divide.

"Are any of you seeing this?" I ask desperately.

None of them answer aloud, but their panicked faces search the empty gym for something, anything.

"Seeing what, Ted?" asks Reb.

"They're everywhere. The mirages. I'm seeing their presence on the other side of the divide, in the Pneuma Rigma. There are dozens of those beasts."

Without hesitation, Drake unholsters his service pistol and releases the magazine. Satisfied with his ammo count, he reinserts the mag and racks the slide, chambering a round. Doc approaches Drake, who hands the firearm over then reaches down and hikes up his right pant leg, revealing a five-round .38 Special revolver. He unstraps the holster and withdraws the pistol. Thumbing the cylinder release and flicking his wrist, he opens the cylinder to confirm its ammo count, then slaps it shut and reaches to his right where Pam retrieves the gun.

"Wish I had time to get the ARs, but we'll have to make do with these," he says to the two of them.

His hand slides down the small of his back and lifts his shirt to retrieve yet another handgun; this one for himself. The ammo-check routine is repeated, and he chambers the first round in the magazine before he begins a short tactical briefing.

"Okay, remember your training. Keep your finger outside of the trigger guard until you're ready to shoot. Never point the muzzle at anything you don't want to kill. Pam, if you have a misfire, just keep squeezing the trigger. Doc, if you have one you have to drop the mag, rack the slide, clear the brass, reinsert the mag, and release the slide just like we practiced. Let's move to the corner with the emergency exit and keep everything in front of us. I want overlapping fields of fire outward from this point. If you run out of ammo, turn and bolt through the exit unless we've reduced their numbers enough to have a fighting chance."

"What are we supposed to do while you're slinging lead all over the room? And what happened to not using guns?" I question.

Reb interjects, "You know why we don't use guns, but out here in the middle of nowhere, facing enemy numbers like what you're describing, we need the firepower, and there's no one around to hear it. As for what you're going to do while they unleash a storm of bullets, you're coming with us."

Mel wraps her arm through Reb's, and with her help he moves faster than I thought possible. I start to follow before I turn back, irked by the kid-glove treatment.

"Wait. Why am I being sidelined? I killed two of those things by myself—alone and unarmed—and I'm not even our best fighter. If we get the families to safety then stand together, we should be strong enough to win."

"*Should* isn't a risk I can accept," replies Reb, somehow still calm. "If there are that many of those beasts and possibly more demonic Nephilim like him that are about to breach the Pneuma Rigma bent on our destruction, the odds are not in our favor. What you did here today will bring immeasurable hope to the alliance, and not just here at Carver but the *global* alliance. The ability you gained to enter the Pneuma Rigma has the enemy scared—and they should be—because they can't win against an alliance that can move to and fro without a trace, snatching up their converts and minions, tearing apart their network of control over humanity. But none of that happens if you die today. You are a living Verdonos. Do you remember how those stories inspired you, how they made you feel?"

"Yes. They gave me something concrete to aspire to, even if a part of me never believed it was possible."

"Can you imagine how you would have felt if you knew unequivocally that bridging the Pneuma Rigma was not only possible but that your hero was real, alive and well, and available to teach you how to be a hero too?"

"I would've wished for it every birthday and dreamt of it every night. I wouldn't have accepted anything less than becoming as great a hero as him."

"Then you see why we have to go?"

"Yes. But, Reb, it's a suicide mission. Pam, Doc, Drake…they won't survive."

"You don't know that, Ted. Regardless, the choice is theirs to make and they've made their choice. They've been training hard for a moment like this for years, and I know that they are honored to finally have an opportunity to fight for the families of Carver and for *you,*" Reb asserts as I note their nods of agreement. "Say your goodbyes, Ted. We need to go."

Doc is already stepping in my direction and throws his arms around me in a hearty man-hug complete with back patting.

"Make us proud, bro. Don't ever doubt yourself; you're a living legend. I'm glad to have known ya!" he says in his congenitally chipper tone that feels, for once, artificial given the circumstances.

Pam waits a step behind Doc and offers a warm, cheek-to-cheek Southern hug.

"We're all blessed to have shared this week with you, Ted," she says sniffling. "Take care of Reb. He's the closest thing to a father I've ever had. And take care of yourself, ya hear? We love you, Ted."

She gives me a peck on the cheek that intercepts the tear streaming toward my jaw. I hold her tight and fully appreciate how much each of these relationships has come to mean over such a short time. We separate, and as she steps aside I see Drake behind her, surveying the room. However adversarial our interactions have been, it's always been clear that Sergeant Julius Drake is a selfless man of honor, the most admirable human being I've met in my lifetime. This is exactly how such a courageous man deserves to die: in a heroic last stand to preserve the promising future of the alliance.

In what are most likely the waning moments of his existence, offering me a heartfelt goodbye is understandably not his highest priority. I swallow whatever pride still loiters within the recesses of my skull and approach him for a loaded handshake, one overflowing with a subtext of gratitude, admiration, apology, and solace. He pauses his survey of the room that's still empty in his eyes and locks pupils with me.

"You don't have to do this, Drake. We can all make a break for it, go in different directions."

"You're wrong about that, Tedarina. I do have to do this. Even if every single one of us runs separately, we have to assume that there's more than enough of them to pursue each of us to our first stop and slaughter us there. Someone has to stay here and slow them down so the rest of you can escape."

The wind howls through the rafters as a perfectly round void not much bigger than a basketball appears in the middle of the room. Ambient light arcs in refracted waves around the object, preserving but distorting the space behind it. Paper thin and black with the absence of matter, this void is something beyond what I used to breach the Pneuma Rigma; it's a gateway for an army. My ability allowed me to pass between planes and, by extension, the ghoul that was on my back, but I haven't even begun to approach such power. It's a manipulation of creation itself, a fusing of two separate dimensional planes never meant to be conjoined for free passage. I look back into Drake's eyes, now seasoned with a dash of fear by the appearance of the gateway.

"It's game time, Ted. You need to get the hell out of here. Do right by Reb and Mel, brother."

Brother.

It's hard to imagine such an unrelatable word feeling like such a perfect fit. I've never had much of a family, no real brothers or sisters (that I know of), so I can only guess what it's like to have a brother. Either way, the bickering, competition, and rivalry between us was destined to give way to loyalty to each other and to our cause, and a mutual, unspoken admiration. All of that sounds very brotherly.

I put on my bravest face and respond, "I will, brother. You have my word. Give 'em hell, Julius."

"You know I will. Oh, and Ted, make sure they write songs about us."

He withdraws his hand with a cocky smirk and turns back toward the swelling void in the center of the room. His weapon at the ready, bravely facing down a supernatural threat against all odds, he is something more than human and I don't just respect him, I want to be like him. Then a thought arrives as if delivered from outside of my body: perhaps human is exactly what he is and nothing more. Perhaps this is the moment Mel predicted when I would see that the source of my own strength and courage stems from my humanity. I've known plenty of Nephilim that wouldn't have the courage to so boldly embrace their death for the sake of others. This is his legacy. Rallying the troops for a glorious last stand that will save the lives of many; who could hope for a more meaningful death?

Like a giant, unstable pupil, it dilates to the size of a beach ball, then shrinks to a baseball; inflates as large as a train tunnel, then rapidly constricts back to a basketball. Drake takes aim and orders the others to form up. They take their positions shoulder to shoulder, backs to the emergency exit, covering all angles of the gymnasium. From the exit, Mel clutches my arm and pulls me vigorously away from the battle I started but am powerless to finish. In my silent sorrow I vow that it will never happen again. Next time, I finish my own fight or die trying.

"Come on, Ted. We're running out of time to get ahead of this. We need to go now!"

We make it one step outside the emergency exit and toward the awaiting car when Doc's voice cries out, "Oh my God," with more fear than I've ever heard from a grown man. I glance back over my shoulder and witness through the waning sliver of the closing door a funnel cloud of scurrying black hellions rocketing through the wide-open, now stabilized gateway. Sporadic gunshots crack like popcorn within the gym's block walls, their report only slightly muted by the mortar and stone. In the driver's seat of the same battered Crown Victoria that brought me to Carver, Vic impatiently fidgets as Mel and I approach, fling open the door, and dive into the back seat. Reb pats Vic from the front passenger seat, saying, "They're in. Let's go!"

Before he can floor it, something slams against the gym's exit doors, shocking everyone in the car, then falls through onto the concrete outside. Our heads snap left in unison and our faces distort with horror and sadness as we recognize what remains of Doc's face. Unrelenting, the horde allows only a glimpse of our dying brother before dragging him back into the gym, arms dangling in tow, limp as noodles.

"Drive, Vic," Reb orders sternly.

The wheels yelp as he stomps on the gas, then yowl through his high-speed left turn onto the county road, then silently endure the abuse as he slams the gas pedal again. Its engine growling and transmission thrashing, the vehicle drags us farther and farther from Carver until the steadily shrinking town is absorbed into the horizon, taking with it at least three of our beloved family members. While Vic focuses on the road ahead, the rest of us stare aimlessly into the past, far more worried about Doc, Pam, and Drake than whether or not we're being followed. It's hard to accept that they're gone, and with no confirmation of that fate, it may always feel like a bad dream. While the others undoubtedly hope against all odds that they're still alive, I'm not so optimistic. They haven't met that dead-eyed Nephilim bastard or seen his sadistic beasts alive and virulent.

I quietly hope it was a quick death, one as painless and honorable as possible, but if I'm honest with myself I'm not sure that even matters. The dead are gone, and whatever horrors escorted them to the blissful numbness of the afterlife makes no difference to them once it's over. Free from the burdens and limitations of this life, they float amidst a tranquil, healing sea. I don't envy them, but they have made it through the woods. They have crested the summit and now have gravity on their side. They will never again face the struggles of this earthly existence. As for me, my struggle is just beginning, and I know just where to find my next fight.

"Reb, I don't mean to be insensitive, but this fight isn't over and we need to know more about our enemy," I boldly assert, confident that my abilities have earned me some clout with the alliance leadership.

"I agree. Do you have something in mind?" he replies.

"Yes. During my vision he mentioned Jan's name. I think he converted her to her wicked ways, and I think Jan may know who he is."

Reb considers this briefly. "She isn't going to freely answer your questions, Ted. Especially if that monster will be bringing harsh retribution if she talks. How will you get her to cooperate?"

"I don't think there's anything I could do to get her to cooperate, but I have a plan to get the information we need. With that dead-eyed freak and his army back at Carver, we have the perfect opportunity to make a move on her without his interference. It's the immediate counterpunch we need to throw, but I'm going to need you to trust me, and I'm going to need to bring Mel with me."

A quick glance to my right confirms that she's on board with whatever plan I've concocted. Reb deliberates, but not for very long before he agrees.

"Okay. Vic and I will stay at the rally point and await the survivors while you and Mel pursue this lead. Ted, I shouldn't need to remind you what's at stake here. The two of you mean everything to the alliance and to me. Do what you have to do, but if it goes south, don't hesitate to get out of Dodge. Living to fight another day is always a better choice than dying for no gain. Be dangerous, but be smart."

"I got him, Reb," Mel replies, patting my hand then letting hers settle softly onto mine. "Whatever we do, we'll put the alliance first. This Nephilim monster isn't going to stop until we're dead. We have to find out more about him if we want any hope of stopping him. That's our primary mission: information."

I nod in agreement, though I don't really feel equipped to determine what's in the best interest of the alliance. Thankfully Mel is, and I have no problem following her lead. In a fortuitous convergence of fate, my plan to save the alliance will require tuning up Jan in the process. Two birds, one stone.

We spend a couple hours chasing the setting sun through the winding hills of US Highway 2, craggy and punctuated with dense tufts of rigid hemlock trees. We finally break through the stifling landscape, and Vic slows to within a few miles per hour of the speed limit. After another mile or two, he pulls off to the side of the highway and waits as the car behind passes and one in front approaches from the other direction. Once it passes and rounds the bend, he makes a quick right turn onto a narrow driveway, overgrown with brush and sagging branches. It's a path I never would have noticed on my own. Branches scrape and scuff the panels and mirrors as the car bumbles through the woods to a clearing with an old cabin. Rally point alpha.

Without stopping the engine, we all unload and exchange handshakes and hugs in the light of the Crown Vic's low beams. Vic helps Reb to the front porch of the cabin as Mel climbs into the driver's seat and I plop down next to her. She throws it into drive, pulls a U-turn, and follows the narrow chute through the trees back to the highway. A westward turn puts the distant Port Ellis skyline in sight, blackened by a small slice of blazing sun that has yet to sink into the Pacific. Its beams clip the tops of the waves, graze the bottom of the angry, gloomy clouds, and ignite the edges of each building. It's the ideal setting, an atmosphere smoldering and convulsing in anticipation of our collision with Jan.

CHAPTER TWENTY-TWO

When I was sixteen years of age, my parents (adoptive parents) died before my eyes. We were returning from a run to the nearest hardware store and pharmacy and were only a few miles from home. I was riding in the roomy back seat of our weary family sedan when a human, high on drugs and driving a low-riding pickup, crossed the center line and plowed into us head-on. The human died instantly, likely before the drug paraphernalia even finished bouncing around the floor of the truck. My dad was driving and took the brunt of the impact, also dying immediately, but my mom survived the initial crash. She didn't pass away until a few minutes later (from internal hemorrhaging if I had to guess) after repeating a phrase that until a week ago I always attributed to her traumatic brain injury. Her head bobbed weakly atop her broken body, her eyes half-shut, as she said over and over, "You are my son. You *are* my son. My son." It's apparent now that in her moribund stupor she knew I would someday learn that I was adopted and wanted me to always know who I am. I am her son.

That was the second time I became an orphan.

My reward for surviving: I got to lug my parents' dead bodies three miles back to the farm where I cremated them myself. The accident would eventually be filed away as an unsolved hit and run by the sheriff's office. The vehicle couldn't be traced back to us, and though some Nephilim are born in human hospitals and documented by their respective governments, my parents were not. With no records or previous run-ins with the law, whatever fingerprints and DNA that were recovered from the vehicle were dead ends.

Such memories tend to surface at the most inconvenient and irrelevant times, often while driving or riding somewhere. Every memory of my upbringing conjures a complex brew of emotions, even more so since the revelations of my adoption and my parents' lies about the Nephilim. If I'm able to overlook my disgust about their dishonesty, it's not difficult to believe that they lied because they thought it would set me up for the best possible future. Dan and Val weren't perfect parents, but I know they cared about me and my well-being.

They didn't always show me the warmest love and they never coddled me, but after learning from Reb that they weren't my biological parents, that makes perfect sense. There are two different kinds of love that a decent parent can offer to a child. One is the instinctive love of a birth parent. It's an involuntary and primal kind of love that requires little effort to maintain, wherein the very sight of their child brings a fresh spring of pride and joy. Even in the face of defiance and disappointment, this type of love cannot be squashed. This is not the kind of love that Dan and Val had for me. They demonstrated the second kind of love: elective love.

It's possible that there are adoptive parents, aunts and uncles, grandparents, or others who are capable of offering a child instinctive love, but Dan and Val were not those Nephilim. They *chose* to love me as their own, but it's a choice that had to be made and remade every day, and there were days that they made that choice reluctantly, and there were days they didn't make that choice at all. On those days, I didn't feel like a blessing to be cherished, I felt like an inconvenience to be tolerated. Perhaps all children feel like that sometimes. I would survive those days, go to bed, and wait expectantly at breakfast the next morning to see whether or not my parents had made the choice that day to love me as their own. More often than not, they had.

As a kid, I didn't know any better and loved them like any child loves their birth parents, but having spent years observing human beings in all kinds of environments, I've learned to discern the difference between the two types of love. Both types of love have a common goal—to nurture and mold a young being into a capable and caring adult—and both types are represented inside this Crown Victoria. From Mel's description, her mother was one of those instinctive lovers, and based on my experience with Mel, I'd say that much is obvious.

She seems far more complete and confident in her identity than I am. As she focuses on the increasingly congested road, my eyes are caught in her gravity once again. I can't understand her bewitching affect. Her hair so black that in the darkness of night it's nearly invisible. Her eyes bluer than the shallows of Belize. Her skin the perfect paleness to hide the minor scars on her forehead, neck, and left cheekbone. But these things alone don't explain why I'm so hopelessly enthralled with this woman. There are millions of beautiful women in the world, both Nephilim and human, but she's the only one I've seen who produces something more than an intellectual acknowledgment of her beauty. She's the only one who ties my chest in knots.

"Mel, what was it like to grow up with such a loving mother?"

Her head turns just enough to shoot me a look from the corner of her eye, then she turns back to the road ahead. "I'm not sure this is the right time to have that conversation. We need to go over your plan so we have time to work out any potential flaws—no offense—before we get to Milburn Tower."

"We have plenty of time. It'll take another forty-five minutes from here with the usual evening traffic. If there's a football game or concert of some kind, it'll take even longer." Her demeanor unaffected by my reasoning, I add, "Besides, my plan is pretty simple. There's not much to discuss."

"Then let's go over it now, and if there's time when we're done we can talk about my childhood. Deal?"

She's right. I'm distracted and drifting, but after what just happened at Carver and what may happen at Milburn, I can't help but ponder my life and love, that thing I've heard so much about but have yet to truly experience. It doesn't help that I'm sitting in a car alone with her. She may be right to redirect my attention to the operation at hand, but her motives are also blatantly self-serving. The nervous dancing of her eyes, the flex of her jaw muscle, and the tension in her grasp of the steering wheel all make it clear that she doesn't want to have that conversation.

I raise an accusatory eyebrow that she notices but ignores. "Okay, plan first," I agree, "but then we talk about you," I add. Her palpable cringe confirms my suspicions.

"Mm-hmm," she mumbles. "So, what do you have in mind for Jan?"

"We have to catch her off guard and force the issue here and now. Who knows how much time we have before our next run-in with that rogue Nephilim. We can't risk her declining to engage us or risk arranging a meet-up elsewhere where she can just send the police to intercept us. Unfortunately, I can't just walk into that building. Someone will recognize me, and it'll be a miracle if I make it out of Milburn without handcuffs."

"Right, agreed, so what then?"

"I'm going to use the Pneuma Rigma to enter the tower and gain access to Jan's office undetected. No one is looking for you, so you can simply walk in and take the elevator to Pentastar. Once you're at her office, ask the secretary for a meeting. If she denies you the meeting, or if the secretary isn't there since it's closing time, just let yourself into Jan's office and tell her you're with me and that you need to speak privately. I'm confident she'll be intrigued and give you the privacy we need."

"What if Jan's not there? Like you said, it *is* closing time."

"She'll be there. During my entire time at Pentastar, she never once left before seven thirty. Once we're in her office with the door closed and privacy glass activated, I'll bridge back from the spirit rift and we grab Jan together. Then I take all of us back into the Pneuma Rigma so we can get out of Milburn."

"I don't mean to keep doubting your abilities, Ted, but are you sure you can bridge with all three of us?"

After a moment's thought, I respond, "When I bridged into the gym with that creature on my back I didn't even mean to bring it with me. It just happened to be touching me when I came through. I don't know why it would work any differently with the three of us."

"Okay. Hopefully you're right. So, we've got Jan, now where do we go?"

"I still have my apartment in Port Ellis, and the building is mostly empty. We'll drag her back down to the car, bridge back from the Pneuma Rigma, and drive to the apartment where we ask her our questions."

"I can tell you've put some thought into this, but I see one big problem: Jan isn't just going to cooperate with all this. How do you plan to get her out of Milburn Tower against her will, and what's the plan for getting her to talk?"

I smile deviously and pop up the center console armrest. From inside the small compartment I produce a stun gun, the same one Drake used on me in the farmhouse. I lift it between our faces and give the button a squeeze. Blue lightning appears between the small metal posts, snapping and flickering brightly into our yawning pupils.

"Drake told me that he left it and a set of handcuffs in the car. I'm going to zap her into a mini coma as soon as I bridge through into her office. We'll carry her out to the car together and zap her as many times as necessary to soften her up some more before we ask our questions. When she comes around, she'll be too weak to resist. Trust me, I was Jell-O when I came around after Drake tased me."

"Oh, I remember," Mel says with a giggle. "Then we ask her about the Nephilim monster while I read her responses," she adds with a satisfied nod.

"Exactly."

She smiles and glances my way a couple of times while keeping watch on the road. *What a smile!* And she likes my plan. I stifle a smile of my own as I set up the next phase of the conversation.

"What do you think? Any concerns?" I ask.

Her head tilts slightly as she gives thought to my question. "Nothing major that I can think of at the moment. The plan includes some assumptions, like Jan being alone or even being there to begin with, and you being able to bridge with all three of us. There are some things that only you would know about Jan and Milburn Tower, and I'm taking it on faith that you know what you're doing. Also, that Nephilim monster knows about your apartment too, so we can't linger there too long, but I agree that it's the best nearby location. Either way, we can't cover every possible contingency, so we have to be willing to adapt or abort the mission as required. Other than that, it seems solid."

"Good points, Mel, you're right. So, that's the plan…" I conclude, my tone prompting her to uphold her end of our bargain.

The awkward silence in the air is briefly broken by gargling road noise as we hit a pitted patch of highway. With about thirty minutes left to our destination, my window of opportunity to learn something meaningful about Mel is closing. I understand her desire for privacy. I lived a very reclusive life until I landed at Carver, but I haven't had that luxury since I arrived there and I think it's time for some reciprocation. It's an uncomfortable feeling to be the only bare soul in the room—a powerless and vulnerable position.

Mel, eyes fixed on the road, draws a deep breath. "Listen, Ted, I know I agreed to talk about me, but I don't know if I can. There are things about my past that will change the way you think of me. You've always walked the straight and narrow, you have strong opinions, and you can be a little judgmental. I haven't always been the Mel you've come to know, and I'm not sure you can accept who I was. It's taken me a long time to even forgive myself, and some people who are very important to me never have."

"That's hard to believe. I've noticed a light in you from the first time I saw you, and it's more than just your good behavior. It's *you.* I asked about your mom because I've never been loved that way and I think that it might have something to do with your wholeness."

A short silence follows while Mel takes several long blinks, searching the inside of her eyelids for peace or strength or anything to help her through what comes next.

"Ted," she starts, emitting a frustrated grunt. "Yes, my mom loved me in a very special way, but not having a dad in my life crushed me every single day. Every time I saw a little girl holding her daddy's hand, or riding on his shoulders, or him pushing her on the swings it was a reminder of that debilitating rejection. It was the only thing I could think about. When I was maybe six or seven, I was at the city playground with a friend. I was on the swing set that stood off a little ways from the other playground equipment and watched as a dad told his daughter it was time to go home. She protested at first, but after he said her name sternly—Abigail, if I remember—and it was clear that he meant business, she zoomed down the slide and ran into her daddy's open arms. He scooped her up and carried her away, giggling. A few minutes later, a man was standing at the edge of the playground watching his son climb on the jungle gym. I approached him slowly, cautiously from behind, eyeing the empty left hand hanging at his side. I got within reach and slid my hand carefully into his, holding it tightly just to see what it would feel like to have a dad who held my hand. Of course…he yanked his hand away in reflex and looked at me like a leech that had tried to latch on. It was that bad for me, Ted. His reaction didn't make things any better. I didn't even realize how good of a mom I had until later in life. She was an extraordinarily loving woman, and strong, but I had no real leader, and so I drifted.

"You don't get it. You don't understand what it's like out there. You were so lucky to have Dan and Val as parents. Yes, they lied to you about some things, but they did it to set you on the right path and protect you. They cared enough to be there for you and they never gave up, even on the days that they woke up, stared at the ceiling, and second-guessed everything.

"I would've done anything to have parents like that. I felt cheated and angry. I rejected my Nephilim nature and my angelic roots. I hated angels and I hated people. Having an angel for a father may sound neat, but it's not. Nephilim with high blood purity are far more likely to fall into corruption because the only way such potency happens is with an angelic parent, but angels don't stick around to be parents to their kids. That's also why this war is so lopsided. The ranks of the wicked Nephilim have a much higher average blood purity than the alliance. They're typically stronger and more powerful than our alliance members.

"Ted, I started down that wicked path. I lied, used people, acquired wealth and power at the expense of human lives and freedom. The worst part is that I liked it. As far as my loving mother is concerned, we haven't spoken in a very long time. She hated who I became back then and has never been able to forgive me.

"Reb saved me from myself. He and a couple other alliance members abducted me from my own home eight years ago and pulled me away from that life. If not for their intervention, I'd be worse than Jan. He is the dad I never had; the one I needed as a child more than anything," she recounts tearfully. Her lip quivers as she fights to keep it together.

Always a warrior.

She wipes her eyes with her shirt sleeve then, after a series of sniffles, she adds, "You're the good one, Ted—the one with the light inside of you—and you have Dan and Val to thank for that."

Once again, she's right. I do think of her differently, but I don't think less of her. Knowing the struggles she faced and overcame only makes her stronger in my eyes.

"Mel, you're right about a lot of things. I have been taking Dan and Val for granted and didn't appreciate how great they were or how bad it would've been without them. I've also been unfairly judgmental toward people and Nephilim that I know little or nothing about. But you're dead wrong about one thing: your past isn't something to be ashamed of. I didn't realize how rough you had it as a young girl, but being fatherless isn't something any of us can control, and no one should judge you for making the choices that you did. What matters is that you triumphed over all of that. When confronted about your error, you came back from that place of despair and deceit, Mel. How many Nephilim can say that? How many, even when confronted by the alliance, choose to give it all away for this life?"

Her gaze drops to the dashboard, then back out the windshield. She answers quietly and humbly, "None. I'm the only one that I know of."

The dejection fades from her eyes, washed away by her reluctant acceptance of my argument. She's thankful for my kind words but not fully convinced that my opinion is objectively true. She also knows that I couldn't say it if I didn't truly believe it. She grins a little and turns the steering wheel slightly, pulling off the interstate loop and onto the city streets of downtown Port Ellis.

"Thanks for saying that, Ted."

"Well…it's true," I reply with a smirk.

"I'm actually kinda glad we talked, and I want to talk more, but it's going to have to wait." Mel gestures to the familiar sight of Milburn Tower several blocks ahead. "Where are you wanting me to park?"

"There's a dead-end alley a block behind Milburn. You can let me out there so I can bridge without being seen, then you can park in the public parking that's at the corner of the block."

Mel's head bobs in agreement. "Okay. It *is* a pretty simple plan, but if something goes wrong, let's not force it. Let's just meet back at the car and regroup. Agreed? I promised Reb I'd take care of you."

"I agree."

We approach the sidewalk near the alley and gently slow to a stop. I casually exit and do a quick scan before I saunter into the desolate alleyway. Crumpled food wrappers, glass bottles, and rotting produce spill from a disemboweled garbage bag that leans against an overflowing, graffiti-tagged dumpster. As my left foot strikes the sticky asphalt, a small swarm of flies erupts from a brown, fudgy mound near the wall, zipping around in a tangled flurry of spirals before settling back onto their meal. *Charming.* It's amazing the things humans get up to when they think nobody is watching. I take my next step a little more cautiously to avoid stepping on any used needles, piles of human waste, or other biohazards.

As much as I'd love to avoid the fringe of filth around the edges of the alley, I can't risk standing in the middle where someone could drive by and see me vanish into thin air, so I crouch and lean against the wall behind the dumpster. The last thing I need is to be the star of a viral video or come back down from Pentastar to find a curious crowd gathering in the alley. I close my eyes and try to flush my surroundings from my consciousness.

Focusing on my intense emotional connection with the scintilla, I yearn deeply for the Pneuma Rigma and take Nephilim form, my back scraping up the wall. The scintilla begin their vigorous interdimensional dance, intensifying gradually until they plateau at a pace that rivals a hummingbird's flapping wings. I open my eyes and watch as a wind emanates outward from my position, stirring the wrappers and debris around me. The color fades from my surroundings in a dizzying swirl to a momentary blackness that then gives way to the ethereal spirit rift. I hop up quickly and jog out of that dank alleyway toward the back entrance of Milburn Tower.

The Pneuma Rigma is difficult to describe, especially on account of my inexperience. It's not like wading through an empty mist on a bare and infinite plane. In actuality, it's very much the same as the human plane. Each structure stands exactly where it was built, each tree planted by humans spreads its roots here too, and even that lovely fly-covered, fecal biohazard lies exactly where it was deposited by its creator. People mill about, chatting with each other, paying ungodly amounts of attention to their phones, hailing cabs, and driving them. And yet, it all strikes me as a hologram, some virtual reality that I could just wave my hand through, scattering pixels that some advanced projector would reassemble in seconds. Once again my own sounds (footsteps, breathing, rustling) project into a void, failing to return to my ears, and the voices of the human beings around me are muted and tinny. The colors and smells of the spirit realm are also subdued, lacking the saturation and intensity of the other side.

Walking the earth as a phantom is equal parts empowerment and limitation. In this place, I can manipulate the real world and move around entirely unseen like a force of nature. I am everywhere and I am nowhere, but I am also no one. Despite being so close to the beings around me, I'm cutoff and more alone than ever. I'm surrounded by people who are within reach, close enough for me to hear, but who cannot see me or hear me back. Sadly, I have sensed in many humans the same melancholy of irrelevance that I now feel.

I have half a mind to tap someone on the shoulder right now or stand in front of traffic to satisfy some of my many curiosities about this place, but now's not the time for such experiments. Thirteen floors above, Jan sits in her supple, leather desk chair, hunched over a stack of lies that await her signature in order to become truth. She's oblivious to the approaching assault, likely thinking her prosperity will last forever. Like many others who have made that same assumption, she's in for a rude awakening.

Up the stairs at the back entrance of Milburn Tower, I reach the door and quickly discover that unlike the mirage at the hardware store, I can't walk through walls. Narrowly, I open the door, hoping any witnesses will assume an outflow of air is responsible. I make my way to the stairwell, keeping an eye on the security booth. I see Barry but no Tyson, and in his place is a stranger, some boyish type with a surfer's haircut and an obvious attitude problem. It's possible they've simply rearranged the shift schedule, but Barry and Tyson have always worked together, and my gut tells me he's gone, probably locked away in a holding cell for helping me escape.

A quick glance confirms the stairwell is empty before I enter, again opening the door as little as possible. I soar up the stairs, my footsteps eerily silent in the two-hundred-foot-tall resonant chamber. Scaling three or four stairs with each lunge, I make it to the tenth-floor landing in less than a minute, but as my foot meets the floor, the stairwell door swings open.

Somehow, I manage to redirect my momentum, narrowly avoiding a violent collision with a middle-aged woman in a cleaning uniform. Instead, I slam into the stairwell door that closes with a shockingly loud whump, rattling the glass on the fire extinguisher's case. The woman jumps and screams in terror, staggering backward toward the stairs. She reaches for a lifeline as her heels eclipse the edge of the top step and her weight begins to teeter. In Nephilim form, I reflexively panic before it dawns on me that I'm invisible to her. I lunge forward and grab her wrist with a quick yank that brings her stumbling back onto the landing. Momentarily frozen, I watch anxiously as she looks at her wrist and begins to search the air, first with her eyes, then with her hands, feeling around for her invisible savior. I slide slowly along the wall and out of her field of view, trying for absolute silence with every movement. After a long ten seconds, she shakes her head and curses as she continues her original trek downstairs.

I charge up the remaining flights of stairs and peer down the main hall of Pentastar Pharmaceuticals' headquarters. Empty. I slip through the door and stride purposefully straight to Jan's corner office. A small relief washes over me as I pass the empty receptionist's desk, but I stop in my tracks when I notice Jan's closed door and frosted privacy glass. Opening that door and walking into her office without knowing what lies on the other side isn't something I had fleshed out in my plan. I suppose a part of me thought I might be able to pass through walls like a cartoon ghost, but it seems I'm still subject to at least some of the physics of the human plane. A bolt of fear strikes my spine as I consider the possibility that the Nephilim monster is waiting on the other side of that glass.

The eerie stillness of the thirteenth floor takes center stage. Even at this hour, there should be stragglers still chipping away at their mountain of reports, research, spreadsheets, slideshow presentations, and more. If not them, then at the very least the cleaning service should be scurrying around, running vacuums, and rolling mop buckets around. Yet, none of them are here. If I hadn't seen so many people since entering the Pneuma Rigma, I'd guess that being in the spirit realm had something to do with it. But even in the gymnasium at Carver I could still see everyone who was on the other side.

A warning that I'm entering a trap groans within my gut, then the elevator dings.

Mel steps out onto the tile floor, moving swiftly toward Jan's office. I yell in a desperate attempt to get her attention before she barges through the frosted glass, but my sounds can't transcend the void. Bridging back is too risky. If there is no trap and I reveal myself, it could blow the whole operation, but allowing Mel to walk through that door blind isn't an option.

I make a rash decision, but the only one that makes sense in the moment, and sprint to Jan's door. Better for me to walk into a trap as an invisible man than Mel in the flesh, and if I move quickly enough, I may be able to save us both. I swing the door open and step inside, expecting to discover the black mist and nauseating presence of that diabolical creature. Instead, I see a peaceful room, empty and softly lit by the glow of Jan's desk lamp. The white haze floats gently throughout the space, transmitting the lamp's light drop by drop.

Mel rushes through the doorway and rams into my back with a grunt. She calls out to me, "Ted? Is that you?"

I focus on Mel and bridge back from the Pneuma Rigma, bringing a swirling gust of wind that surges from my position and dissipates outward. A slip of paper rustles as it slides across Jan's desk then spills off the edge, rocking leisurely on its way to the ground. We round the desk and retrieve the note that reads:

Hello, Ted and Company,

A little birdy told me you were headed my way. I know you probably had your own plans for how this would go down, but we're going to do this my way. Harvey and I are anxiously awaiting your arrival on the roof. Would you and your companion(s) grant us the honor of your company? Truly, I'm only asking out of courtesy, it's not exactly optional if you want any hope of saving your friend. Our scary Nephilim associate will be bringing him along shortly.

P.S.—If you elect to do anything other than join us, your friend will be executed and you two will be lucky if you end up in jail. I've already alerted security to the possibility of your presence. You'll never make it out.

Mel and I exchange looks of desperation, and I can tell we're both thinking of Drake. We saw Doc killed at the gym and Pam wasn't the strongest fighter—they're also both Nephilim. While the intruder said he had no interest in killing Nephilim, our reclusive nature makes it easy. Killing a human usually leaves a grieving family. Even estranged aunts or uncles, cousins, or grandparents will come out of the woodwork to seek justice for their dead or missing kin. Nephilim are different. We may seek justice, but we do it quietly—no press conferences, no prayer vigils, no news articles—and that's only when there's actually kin who care.

"What do we do?" I ask Mel, who mirrors my deep vexation.

"I don't see what choice we have. It was hard enough to walk away while he sacrificed himself once. If he survived, I can't abandon him to be executed."

"I agree, but we don't know for sure that it's him or that they have anyone at all. She could be bluffing about the whole thing, just trying to lure us up to our deaths," I counter.

"No, think about it, Ted. She knew we were coming, she knew to mention that rogue Nephilim, and she knew that he had access to our friends. Somehow, he reached out to her and set this up. I really don't think she's bluffing."

My lips purse and my head bounces as I consider her point. "Okay, you're right. We have to take it seriously. Come with me through the Pneuma Rigma, though, just in case. If Jan wants a rooftop showdown, we'll give her one she never sees coming."

CHAPTER TWENTY-THREE

Mel's hands slide gently into mine as we stand face-to-face in Jan's office. The lamp's candle-like ambiance would probably be cozy, even romantic, if we weren't minutes from a fight for our lives. Her worried expression is justified several times over. Our upcoming fight with Jan and her gun-wielding juggernaut. Drake being held hostage. The foreboding approach of a Nephilim warlord. Mel's first time entering the Pneuma Rigma. Each would be panic inducing in its own right, but all of them converging in this moment is enough to instill fear in even the bravest of warriors. I feel it too, and I'm sure it's plain to see.

I give her hands a squeeze. "Are you ready?"

"Doesn't matter, we're bleeding time," she answers. "Do I need to do anything or—"

"Not that I know of. That creature was attacking me when I brought it through the bridge, but I'm really hoping we can just hold hands. I guess if it doesn't work you can smack me around a little."

Mel's short-lived chortle vents some of the pressure from her eyes and I smile pridefully at my successful joke—well-timed too. I've never known the value of comedic relief, but even I feel slightly more relaxed and confident. The endorphins whisper into our minds a baseless reassurance that everything will be okay, and for now we believe.

"Okay, let's give this a try. You can close your eyes if you want, but you don't have to. You should just know that watching the transition can be a little dizzying," I warn.

"Okay, let's go," she says with a thin confidence.

I hold her hands tightly, close my eyes, and concentrate on the Pneuma Rigma. The lamp flashes as my scintilla begin their dance while streams of warped atmosphere whirl around us. I open a slit in my eyelids and see the light bending and wrinkling as the vibration in my blood intensifies.

"Ted, I've never felt anything like this before," Mel exclaims.

"You can feel it too?"

"Yeah. It's jittering every cell of my body! It's…extreme!"

After a blink, the darkness weeps into the Pneuma Rigma and I see Mel, eyes clamped shut, waiting for my cue. I give her hands a subtle shake and tell her that we're in. She nods and says she could feel the scintilla stabilizing. In no particular hurry she opens her eyes, her blank expression shifting to pleasure as she calmly absorbs her new surroundings.

"Ted, it's exactly what I expected from the stories," she notes in wonder. "Whoa, I wasn't expecting things to sound so different. It's like my voice just flows out into the ocean."

"That caught me by surprise too. The fog is different than what I pictured; it's more like a smoky filter over everything than a literal mist," I add.

Mel scans the room from floor to ceiling and says, "So give me a crash course. What do I need to know about the Pneuma Rigma?"

"Well, I don't know that much yet, but it seems the same rules of nature apply to us here as in the human plane. We can't walk through walls or defy gravity. On the fun side, we are completely invisible to those on the other side. It's possible there are others like me who can see a mirage, but they won't know what they're looking at. As for sound and communication, I yelled your name when you came out of the elevator, but you didn't react."

"Oh, I didn't hear anything."

"I figured. I don't think sound can travel across the divide. Besides that, it's all uncharted territory," I conclude.

"Okay. Sounds pretty straightforward," says Mel as she turns toward Jan's office door and releases my hands.

Instantly she's vaporized in a chalky billow and sucked into a vacuum, gone for a fraction of a second before being spit out in the human plane. She lets out a pained groan as she doubles over and dry heaves toward the floor. Panting, she props herself upright and finds her composure before she turns back toward where she expects to see me, but I'm invisible, still watching from the spirit rift.

"What the heck was that, Ted?" she asks.

"I don't know. As soon as you let go, you got shot out of the Pneuma Rigma," I observe before remembering that she can't hear me.

"I know I can't hear you through there…but you can hear me," she recalls, perking up in the process. "Before you come back to get me, I want to try something." She stretches her left arm toward me. "Take my hand. Let's find out how much influence you have from that side."

Brilliant. I reach out and grab her hand, squeezing it tightly. The tiny film of air in between the grooves of our skin erupts with a sizzling tingle.

"I can feel my scintilla surging again, Ted! You know what this means?"

Before either of us can deliver an answer, the light of the human plane warps around her silhouette and she emerges in the Pneuma Rigma with a cyclonic burst. She holds my hand firmly then twists and interlocks our fingers. Her breathing steadies and she looks into my face.

"You can pull me through from the other side!" she exclaims.

I smile gleefully and remark, "That's amazing! I never would have thought to try that."

"Okay, so my scintilla won't open a bridge to the Pneuma Rigma on their own, but when we touch it's like they become an extension of yours. Like I'm a conduit for your scintilla's energy. Interesting," she notes. "We also learned that you can attack Jan and Harvey from inside the spirit rift."

"That's a crucial discovery, especially since we need to get up there and make our move before that abomination arrives. We're running out of time to get any answers from her, Mel. Once he gets here, it'll be too late."

"Right. I'm just making sure we don't go up there all half-cocked and clueless about the way this works. It's my job to protect you, and I refuse to abandon Drake, or whoever his hostage is. But this discovery is just what we need to make quick work of Jan."

"You mean being able to fight her while we're invisible?"

"No, not *we*. We'd have to fight while holding hands. I'm not sure that would even be an advantage at that point. But you being invisible while their focus is on me is the perfect advantage. You can flank, disarm, and attack from the Pneuma Rigma while I have their attention. And you can pull me in with you if we need to disappear."

"I don't know, Mel. It's safer if you're in here with me the whole time." I say, tightening my grip.

She sinks her fingers deeply into the notches between mine and says, "Ted, I know you mean well, but I think you're forgetting which of us is the best fighter in the alliance. I don't need your protection. Now, let go of my hand and let's do this."

Her grip goes limp and she pulls her hand forcefully from mine. After a slightly longer delay than the first time, she's vaulted through the void and back to the other side. She relaxes her spine back to human form and opens the office door.

"Come on. Coast is clear," she says.

Mel leads the way from the other side and I follow through the rising, shifting mist of the spirit rift, careful to avoid contact with passersby and always keeping an eye on our six o'clock. It's impossible to predict when the warlord might arrive with his beast army. For all I know that Nephilim monster can fly through the Pneuma Rigma like a bird. Our own swiftness in dealing with Jan and Harvey is the only insurance we have against being blindsided. Of course, he could already be waiting on the roof.

Like the hallways and offices of Pentastar, the remaining flights of stairs are more desolate than usual for the time of night. This would normally be a busy hour for Orchid Song. Its kitchen shares a wall with the stairwell, and at all hours of the day it's normal to hear the muted clanging of plates and gonging of pots and pans when passing the sixty-fifth floor, but tonight it's chillingly silent. It's late, but not so late that everyone should be gone. In retrospect, I wonder if the cleaning woman I passed in the stairwell was on her way out of the building. Does Jan have enough power to evacuate Milburn Tower? It's possible. The right lie can make anyone powerful. Maybe she just had Harvey call in a bomb threat, although I doubt they want police combing the building.

After five tiring minutes, Mel and I reach the rooftop door, which Jan was smart enough to close. She would know we've arrived as soon as the door swings open whether or not we're visible. Mel looks back so I give her shoulder a quick squeeze, knowing she can't actually see me. She offers a brief smile and nod before her face hardens with taut lips and an intense brow. Fire flashes through her eyes as she turns and plows through the door.

Against the backdrop of a cool, overcast sky, Jan sits patiently atop the far concrete ledge while Harvey paces wolfishly in front of her. The radio equipment to the right and industrial air-conditioning units to the left form a wide corridor in which we'll make our stand. Slow-burning city lights reflect off the wet troposphere, leaving the rooftop aglow in a pale, sickly orange. Mel steps slowly but confidently in Jan and Harvey's direction, and I follow in her wake.

Jan stands from the ledge, saying, "Melodia Galanis, our mutual acquaintance told me that you're an alliance fighter, but it wasn't always that way, was it?" She looks at Mel with an accusatory sneer. "I remember our interview after Ted killed Joel. You guarded your secret well. I bet you were a terrific liar. You must've been good at it to build the small empire you abandoned to live as an impotent beggar. Is it true that you were the sweetheart shoo-in for mayor of Corellia Falls?"

Mel stands firm and says nothing, unfazed by Jan's attempts to worm into her head.

Walking slowly toward Mel, Jan continues. "I mean, Corellia Falls is no Port Ellis, but it's a city of what, two hundred thousand? How did it *feel* to stand on their backs? I bet it was like a plush, memory foam rug. You made a lot of money off of those desperate young ladies, didn't you?"

"Shut up, Jan!" Mel barks fearfully.

Harvey continues pacing, head on a swivel. The massive air-conditioning units come to life with the click of a relay, drowning out the honking and grumbling that climbs weakly from the street hundreds of feet below. It's the perfect opportunity for me to move around with impunity, both invisible and silent. I move swiftly into the grid of air conditioners, ducking and sliding between the units to flank Harvey. Once inside, the giant fan blades cut through the air, creating waves of turbulence that are nearly visible in the Pneuma Rigma, yet their volume is somehow lower than that of the vocal range.

Jan keeps talking, clearly stalling and trying to divide our ranks. "How did it go? A scared, pregnant girl would walk into your nonprofit looking for advice and you'd listen for all of two minutes before directing her to the abortion clinic one block over? The clinic where you were a silent partner; the one where the doctors paid you a hefty percentage of each operation, like a finder's fee. You were such a powerful god of deceit that the humans actually celebrated your genocide, calling you a champion of women's rights."

"It doesn't matter what you say, I'm not that Nephilim anymore," Mel says with deflated conviction.

"Oh, but I'm just getting started. That nonprofit was just a pet project, wasn't it? It's not what made you a frontrunner in the race for mayor. But first, to set the record straight, you *are* that Nephilim. You will always be *that* Nephilim. We're all *that* Nephilim. You think I really care what you did to those humans? I don't give a shit! They're humans. Do humans care what horrors befall the chickens in a poultry plant? As long as they get their legs, thighs, wings, and breasts, they couldn't care less. But you know who will care what you did, Mel?" She pauses with raised eyebrows and no intention of waiting for a reply. "Ted. Ted will care about what you did and who you are. Does he know who you really are?"

Again, she stops for a moment and looks around the roof, leaning from side to side as if to peer around the trees. "Speaking of Ted, where is that little bitch?"

Now a little rattled, Mel replies, "You don't know me. That was a long time ago." A heavy pause ensues while she regroups, "As for Ted, he's getting closer as we speak. You'll see him soon enough."

"Well, I also heard Ted learned a new trick. How should I know he's not already up here with us, lurking in the spirit rift like a coward?" she asks pompously, continuing to goad us into a fight.

Having regrouped, Mel pushes back. "From the note you left in your office I got the impression that we're supposed to wait for your boss to arrive, but it really sounds to me like you want to take your shot now."

"You're right. He wants you delivered alive, but I don't think he'll mind if we soften you up before he gets here."

Harvey speaks up, still scanning every inch of the roof, "Ma'am, Ted's here. Don't know where, but I'm certain."

"Of course he is, Harvey. They think they're being clever. I wouldn't have wasted my breath on Mel's past if I didn't think Ted was here to hear it. Take care of it," she orders. "I've got Mel."

Jan walks toward Mel, taking Nephilim form, as Harvey finally stops pacing and draws the same revolver that made him so bold in that conference room. I wonder if he'd be half as tough without it. I step around the final air-conditioning unit to gain a straight shot at Harvey's right side and start my charge still shrouded by the groaning machines. He raises his gun and pans around calmly, looking for any hint of my position but focusing mainly in Mel's direction. In Nephilim form I gain incredible speed, enough to break human bones on impact. A rocketing specter, I close the distance between us in a flash. But only five steps away, the blowers shut off.

In the milliseconds of stark silence that follow, Harvey hears something. A footstep. A scrape. A speck of loose concrete grinding. Whatever it is, he turns straight toward me as I lower my shoulder for impact, and he squeezes the trigger.

Crack!

Pain travels down my spine to the tips of my toes as my body crashes into his. Over the ringing in my ears I detect the distinct pop of broken ribs as my momentum transfers to his body, launching him across the roof and against the nearby radio tower. The impact vibrates the tower pole like a ringing bell and I tumble onto the ground, delirious.

Through the floating black dots in my vision, I see Nephilim Mel and Jan locked in combat. Jan, clearly outmatched, is still holding her own with scrappy ingenuity and no regard for fair play. She slashes across Mel's abdomen with a blade, but Mel jumps back, parrying the attack and grabbing Jan's arm at the end of her follow-through. She wraps Jan's arm in her armpit and twists forcefully against her elbow. Jan shrieks and drops the knife, which Mel kicks safely away.

As my eyes find clarity, I notice two things: I've returned to the human plane, and I'm bleeding from somewhere. Pushing up from my prone position, a pain—searing, stabbing, and throbbing—swells from the lower right side of my neck. I touch my neck and withdraw gleaming red fingers. I've been shot.

At the base of the antenna tower, Harvey stirs and whimpers in pain. My bleeding neck suddenly takes a back seat to finishing what I started. The blood isn't spurting, so he must've missed the artery, but he has at least four more attempts loaded in that revolver and I can't give him another chance. I stagger his direction, gaining more agility with each step in spite of a growing numbness in my right arm. I stride past the revolver, sweeping it up from the ground and popping its cylinder open.

One, two, three, four, I drop the remaining rounds to the ground then toss the handgun away, eager to level the playing field. Harvey sees me drawing near and stands slowly, babying his ribs with his left hand and pulling a switchblade with his right. *So much for a fair fight.* He notices the stun gun that must've flown from my pocket during our collision and stomps it to pieces as he tramps my way. As soon as I get within reach, he lunges with an agonized growl. I strike his arm aside and land a right cross to his healthy ribs, lackluster on account of the tingling weakness in my arm. He cries out and stumbles around me, flailing haphazardly with the blade that finds the back of my left shoulder and sinks a couple inches deep.

He leaves the knife in my shoulder as he buckles and gasps, arms wrapped around his torso. Fighting for air and in serious pain, Harvey drops to his knees.

"Shit!" he barks angrily as he takes frantic, shallow breaths.

Looking over at Mel, I see blood trickling from her brow, and she's looking more fatigued than I would've expected. My only reassurance is the sight of Jan, whose right eye is swollen nearly shut, and who is clearly favoring her left leg. No matter which of them is winning at the moment, I need to finish this with Harvey and help Mel, not because she needs it but because without a stiff electric jolt, Jan will fight to the death before she talks. If that happens, we'll be no closer to answers about the Nephilim warlord. Now, with the stun gun trashed, I'll have to find a new way to loosen her lips.

With his knife still stuck in my back, I stride toward the folded-over Harvey and line up for a finishing kick to the head, but as my leg swings through, he pulls up, blocks my kick with both hands, and grabs my ankle. Holding it tightly, he sweeps around, taking out my planted leg and sending me into an uncontrolled fall. The wind quits my lungs as I thud flat onto my back, driving Harvey's knife even deeper into my flesh and bone.

A resurgent Harvey finds his feet and moves under the power of his second wind. Meanwhile, I struggle to find any air at all as I wheeze in anguish and watch helplessly while he targets my ribs with a simple but effective soccer-style kick. Then another. Then a stomp on my abdomen. I try to fend off his attacks with my right arm, but it's like blocking a baseball bat with a pool noodle. He continues his flurry of kicks and stomps, softening my right arm and ribs to the point of breaking. He's so fixated on my ribs that he fails to notice me reaching over my shoulder for the handle that protrudes from my back. He draws his leg back for another blow and I roll toward him, yanking the knife from the notch in my bone and slamming it through his foot with enough force to chip the concrete beneath.

He howls in pain and tries to remove the knife, but it's too late. My scintilla are already raiding his blood stream, flowing from his foot to his heart, and then to his brain. Harvey crumples limply to the ground and I roll away, wincing and gritting my teeth. I sit upright and watch the human lump, cautiously at first, then confidently, because it's clear that his sowing has begun. My work here is done. Live or die, the outcome is up to him.

I gingerly rise and make my way toward Mel and Jan, who trade a series of blows as I approach. Mel lands a glancing left hook, then a right jab that Jan absorbs and turns into a grapple and headbutt. Their brawling isn't pretty. It's as savage as one would expect from a street fight to the death. They're bloodied and swollen, Jan far more than Mel, and each blow is a little weaker than the one before, but Jan refuses to relent. Of course, I've been shot in the neck and stabbed in the shoulder, so I don't have much room to talk. The right half of my shirt down into my pant leg is soaked red, and my lightheadedness has me worried that the gunshot wound is more serious than I originally thought. If I could fully feel my right arm, I'm sure I'd be in agony, but its partial paralysis and my stiff slug of adrenaline have dulled nearly all sensation.

Still locked in a grapple, Jan and Mel each try to kick the others' legs out and throw the other down with no success. Mel quickly pulls Jan close and launches her right knee into Jan's stomach, causing her to release Mel, double over, and puke. Mel takes the opportunity to wipe the blood that's running into her eye from her brow and notices my approach. I vanish into the Pneuma Rigma and beeline to her, pulling her into the rift with me just as Jan brandishes a firearm of her own and takes aim at Mel. Jan pulls the trigger repeatedly, expending several rounds of hot lead where Mel stood only an instant ago. The bullets perforate an HVAC unit with a wallop and hiss that rival Jan's enraged growl.

Inside the Pneuma Rigma, I relay a quick plan of attack to Mel, explaining the broken stun gun and pointing out the radio equipment behind Jan. Releasing Mel's hands, I send her back to the human plane, now at Jan's flank and in the perfect position to disarm her. Mel clamps down on Jan's gun, staying clear of the muzzle, then twists and throws an elbow into Jan's diaphragm. Hands on her knees, overwhelmed and reeling, Jan glances across the roof at Harvey's still body.

"Harvey!" she snarls as I pass behind her on my way to the stairwell door.

He doesn't answer.

"Harvey, get your ass up!"

Still nothing. She huffs in pride-fueled rage and grunts in pain.

"Really? You lost to Ted? TED?!" she harasses, but Harvey's not home.

I bridge back from the Pneuma Rigma near the stairwell. "Shh, he's sleeping," I taunt. "He may be back soon, but he won't be the same. Whenever he does wake, it's going to be too late for you anyway."

"Just give up, Jan," Mel offers. "Tell us who that Nephilim warlord is; tell us everything you know. It doesn't have to go down like this."

Jan shakes her head in disgust. "How did you two fools find each other? Please, do our kind a favor and sterilize yourselves." she scoffs with a snort. Then, angrily, she continues, "Why would I give in to you? I don't *fear* you. You're not going to kill me. You need me alive or you get nothing. But him, the Nephilim 'warlord' as you put it, he'll skin me alive if I tell you anything. He'll feed my pelt to his devil dogs and remove my eyelids so I have no choice but to watch as they gnaw me to death from the legs up. Unless you have something worse than that in store for me, you're wasting your time."

"At the risk of sounding ominous, Jan, I think you've underestimated Ted and me. While you were mastering the art of deceit and building your fortune, we've been mastering our Nephilim abilities and plotting your end. You have no idea what we're capable of."

I slink around in the background during their dialogue, searching for a new weapon against Jan until I find exactly what I need to loosen Jan's lips. Attached to the outside of the stairwell shaft wall is a fire hose coiled around a reel, a halon extinguisher, and a fire axe. I snatch the axe from the wall and slide enough into view for Mel to see me nod.

"We're not stopping until we have what we came for. You'll talk," Mel predicts.

Jan smirks tiredly and quips, "Better get to it, then. You're running out of time."

Mel immediately pulls up her fists and closes the distance. Jan backpedals, hastily raising her defenses, but it's too late as Mel lands a couple of jabs to her face. She sends several body shots, right and left, that Jan mostly blocks before landing a kick against Jan's weak leg. Jan yelps and drops down to a kneel then rebounds, barely avoiding Mel's incoming knee. But as she throws herself away from Mel's attack, she loses her balance, stumbling back several steps. I raise the axe high, preparing for my moment.

The spacing between them is perfect, so Mel unleashes a powerful front kick that sends Jan careening toward the intended path of my axe. I muster every ounce of strength that remains in my wounded arms and swing. Jan's staggering feet snag on the radio equipment's low concrete platform, felling her like a tree. With my window closing rapidly, I aggressively accelerate the axe to my target. My timing impeccable, the sharpened edge cuts through the air only a few millimeters from the back of Jan's descending head, and as I strike my target squarely—the high voltage power and ground cables coming out of the radio tower's base unit—the bit of the axe embeds into the metal conductors, creating a short circuit through its head. Sparks fly as Jan's neck bounces off the butt of the axe and a loud pop resonates from inside one of the nearby radio cabinets. As Jan's limp body settles next to the cables, the red strobe at the top of the tower fades out.

Mel and I stare, frozen, wondering if Jan got the proper dosage of electric anesthesia. She's not moving yet, which is promising, but if that pop of the circuit breaker came too soon, she may not be out for long. Of course, if it came too late, she could be out for good. We share a look and Mel dashes over as

I crouch to feel Jan's neck for a pulse. Her artery taps a sinus rhythm against my fingers, and her warm breath condenses in the cool evening air. Somehow, we've managed to arrive at the desired result. Now we just need to get Jan back to my apartment to ask our questions.

"Mel, help me carry her and I'll get us into the Pneuma Rigma," I direct as I squat near Jan's head and scoop my arms through her armpits.

Mel steps between Jan's legs and crouches to wrap them up when a sudden puff of wind brings a rush of dread. One puff becomes two, then three, then a steady zephyr that builds abruptly to a gale. I search the sky, hoping to discover an approaching storm. Even a hurricane would be better than what I fear has arrived. But as I scan the endless reaches above, there is no lightning to comfort my woe, no thunderheads to soothe my dread; in fact, only a few clouds blot out the speckled night sky. I pan down and across the roof to discover the pulsating pupil of the Nephilim monster's gateway above Harvey's motionless body. Each time the gateway swells, it swallows the heavenly lights before contracting to reveal them again. I can feel the color drain from my face with the noose tightening around my neck. It's too late. He's here.

CHAPTER TWENTY-FOUR

Snapping over her shoulder, Mel sights the gateway and hurriedly tries to lift Jan from the ground. "No, no, no," she cries, "we have to get her out of here! Get us into the Pneuma Rigma, Ted!" As Mel lifts Jan's legs, I slide my arms out from under her armpits and step away.

"It's too late, Mel. He's coming *from* the Pneuma Rigma. If we bridge through now, we'll just end up face-to-face on his turf. Maybe we can trade her for Drake, you know, a hostage exchange." I shrug my shoulders, disappointed with my own suggestion but at a loss for a better one.

The gateway stabilizes and the Nephilim abomination steps through with the officious swagger of royalty. His flowing black garments ripple in the wind and lick the charcoal vapor that spills out from the portal to the spirit rift. He says nothing at first, taking his time as he surveys the state of affairs on the roof of Milburn Tower. His black, dead eyes roll to the back of his skull and he holds a deliberately long and incensed blink.

"This is not the scene that I hoped would greet me," he asserts with his haunting, choral timbre. "What has she told you?"

"She hasn't said anything…yet," Mel states.

"And she won't. I'm certain of it," he says calmly.

"I wouldn't be so certain," Mel rebuts. "We have our methods for extracting the truth."

"And I have my methods for burying it," he rumbles. "Hand over Jan and I'll give you my hostage."

"I don't see any hostage. How do we know you're not lying?" I question.

He tilts his head and shoots an irked glare through his bald brow. "Don't push your luck. I'm already being far more generous than necessary. I could call my horde through that gateway to destroy you both and take Jan for myself, but this isn't Carver and I'd rather not risk some human witnessing my beasts."

I sneer at him and goad, "Then why don't you do it yourself?"

"You petulant fool! You're squandering your hand. I'm offering you the only way out that gives you any hope of saving your friends and yourself. Even if I fought you and lost, which is impossible, my beasts have orders to eviscerate the hostage. Take the deal, give me Jan, save his life, and survive this, you imbeciles."

His shoulders rise and fall heavily, tensely with each raging huff. We truly don't have a leg to stand on, but we can't risk forfeiting Jan for no gain. What's to stop him from taking Jan and disappearing into the spirit rift without even giving us Drake? Although, if he's bluffing about even having a hostage, that wouldn't be such a bad outcome. We'd lose Jan, but we'd still walk away with our lives.

Live to fight another day.

"Okay. We'll give you Jan, but we need proof that you have Drake and that he's still alive," I barter.

His lips curl with sinister pleasure and a slight laugh escapes his nostrils. Looking down his nose with condescension, he says, "Right…*Drake*," then casts his gaze on the bare concrete to his right. His gray fingers extend from the bottom of his sleeve, thumb pressed to middle finger, and snap. A body is heaved through the gateway, landing at the warlord's feet and exactly where his eyes are fixed.

He maintains his gaze on the broken body that lies in a crumpled pile on the rooftop. It's a wounded form, bleeding inside and out, tender and swollen. Its coloration is that of an overripe avocado, browns seeping into pale yellows, wrapped in deep purple and green. From this angle, he's barely recognizable as human, much less anyone I know, but it's clear that this unfortunate creature is not Julius Drake. Unfortunately, this brings little comfort. It was crudely uplifting to think that Drake could still be alive even if he was this monster's captive. Now, the hope that Drake survived the gymnasium is gone, and it seems that another of our alliance family has fallen prey to this onslaught. The question is who.

I move slowly toward the hostage, keeping my eyes on the warlord who silently consents to my approach. He watches in amusement as I stoop over my fallen comrade who's still breathing, albeit weakly. Even with his face angled away, I can tell his eyes are swollen shut and his skin is lacerated beyond any hope of healing. His hair is wet, matted with blood, so I carefully cradle his shoulders and turn him just enough to look upon his face. At first, the bloated features, torn, discolored skin, and smeared plasma effectively veil his identity; even his overall face shape is altered and unusual. But after a minute of examination it dawns on me that this pitiful mess is Reb.

I drop to my knees and begin weeping bitterly. "Oh my god, it's Reb! Oh my god," I wail.

Mel races over and slides in next to me, already emotional without having seen for herself. She recognizes Reb immediately and pulls him up onto her lap. Rocking gently and shaking violently with each devastated sob, Mel holds him and I wrap my arms around them both, forgetting for a moment where we are and who is looking down on us with his sordid smile.

He interrupts our grief, his tone betraying his measurable enjoyment of our pain. "This is all very touching, but you still need to uphold your end of the bargain. I gave you your friend, now you give me Jan. Bring her here, though. I won't risk stepping in some trap you've set." I stand and face the monster, fighting every red-hot cell in my body to keep from picking a fight that would undoubtedly get us all killed. I swallow the venom in my throat and walk to Jan, then grab her ankles and drag her across the roof, her head bouncing along the way. Once in front of him, I drop her legs and take a step back, staring defiantly into his dead eyes. He reaches down and lifts her by the neck, dangling her like a piñata.

Out of nowhere, he produces a short sword, barely longer than twelve inches, that he plunges into Jan's back and through her torso, piercing her heart. Her eyes burst open and bulge as she looks down at the blade protruding from her chest. In a tight, cartoony voice she rambles with panicked utterances as a red inkblot rapidly blooms and weeps down the front of her shirt. He extracts the sword and drops her alongside Harvey's yet motionless body, where she twitches and whimpers for a few seconds before lying still.

Mel has shifted her position to better watch the monster's actions and scooted several feet back toward the stairwell with Reb still in her lap. "What the hell is wrong with you?" she screams. "We already told you she didn't tell us anything. What do you get out of all this suffering?"

"I told you. I have my ways of keeping the truth buried. Besides, she failed to deliver you to me as I ordered. There's no place for such weakness in my ranks."

He wipes the blade on Jan's back before replacing it in its sheath. He purses his lips and whistles a brief, wavering tone that summons his hellions' attention. Dozens of their black arms protrude from the gateway's void, stirring and reaching and grabbing frantically and ravenously for anything they can touch—a true vision of the gates of hell. The warlord grabs Jan's wrist and drags her within reach of the horde, who latch on and pull her through with voracious intent. Next, he grabs Harvey by the wrist and drags him to the gateway. Again, the hellions grab on and snatch him into the Pneuma Rigma to be devoured.

The Nephilim monster dusts off his hands and sighs. "Now that that's done, my business here is nearly concluded. Theodonis, let's go. You're coming with me."

Mel, soggy-eyed and quivering, shouts, "What did you say?"

My stomach churns as he waves his arm like a traffic cop, directing me toward the gateway that teems with the devilish beasts who are only momentarily out of sight to eviscerate their appetizers. I won't be their entree.

"That wasn't the deal!" I snarl. "You've made your damn point! Who do you think you are that we should just bow in fear at your every whim?"

"Given the fear that warps your face every time I appear, you seem to already know all you need to know. But it's not just me you should fear, and the command I give is not my own. The dark ones to which I answer have demanded your presence. I'm only the messenger. Deny me and you may very well invite them to your doorstep, and they won't be denied."

"So, you're nothing more than their errand boy?" I provoke as I turn to grin at Mel.

Black veins surge through his gray flesh as he grabs my neck in one hand and withdraws his sword with the other. His giant grip sends a web of pain in all directions from my gunshot wound.

He pulls me close enough that I can feel the tiny drops of spit fly from his lips as he quietly roars, "I will not be goaded into a fight with an ant. I will not be goaded into telling you what you want to know. I will not be goaded into allowing you a quick and painless death. You will do as you're told—"

"Ver…" Reb grunts hoarsely and frailly from Mel's lap. A coughing fit ensues, producing blood from his lungs that trickles down his chin. When the fit settles, he makes another attempt. "He's ver…," he tries again, quickly running out of breath. The rooftop is frozen, and the warlord grows uneasy with each silent tick. With a third determined heave, he groans hauntingly, "He's Verdonos!"

It's not possible, and yet it makes perfect sense. He's the only Nephilim that was ever recorded bridging the Pneuma Rigma, but if there's any truth to the legends, Verdonos lived millennia ago and was killed by a demon horde. Reb collapses back into Mel's arms and, given the amount of trauma he's experienced, it would be reasonable to blame delirium for his outburst. Like waking from a nightmare, he snapped up from his rest and blurted out the unprocessed content of his subconscious, nothing more. Except the monster's grip on my throat is tightening and his teeth are clenched together. My airway compresses under the weight of his ire, and the blackness of his eyes deepens to the point of pure emptiness.

Then, slowly, his grip loosens until it releases me altogether and an eerie relaxation melts away his tension. His eyelids slide shut, and he takes a cleansing breath.

Setting his sights on Mel and Reb, he sighs woefully. "Oh, Reb. With that little outburst you have sealed everyone's fate. Now I *have* to kill all of you, except maybe Ted." He turns to me and speaks. "You can still survive this if you agree to come peaceably with me."

I shake my head, bewildered by his implied confirmation of Reb's claim but nevertheless convinced that I want nothing to do with him. I don't understand how he could be Verdonos, my childhood idol, the hero of Nephilim lore, but it makes no difference what he was. He is abominably evil now.

"Never. I'll die first," I declare, fully realizing that is the likeliest of outcomes.

"So be it."

His body snaps into action like a striking cobra, the moonlight glinting off his sword as he slashes back and forth. I dodge once, twice, but each pass of the blade gets closer than the last and my injuries make fighting back all but impossible. Swelling, soreness, and limited mobility are setting in, and even if they weren't, I've lost even more feeling and control in my right arm.

Backpedaling and quickly running out of room, I block his arm during his next slash, but it sends a debilitating jolt across my shoulders and down my spine. My left arm joins my right in hanging loosely at my sides, capable of movement but not that of the spry variety necessary for any hope of fending him off. He recoils and winds up for what I fully expect to be a deadly blow, bringing a surge of dread, sorrow, anger, and denial that stretches my nerves like taffy and sickens my spirit.

But the instant that his arm starts downward, his forearm is met with the axe blade moving in the opposite direction. A revolting, fleshy *thunk* peals across the roof as the axe cuts to the bone. He releases an agonized bawl from the pit of his stomach and stares, bewildered, at the axe. His arm, still attached but clearly broken and a bit floppy, drops the sword, and for a moment no one moves. Mel released the axe handle on impact and it now hangs like another appendage from his body. Verdonos grabs the handle in his left hand and yanks the axe free with a yowl. Bottling the surge of pain, he stands like a vibrating statue, as if imitating stone will limit his feeling.

Globs of black mud that can only be his ancient, spoiled blood fall from the axe head to the concrete roof as Mel and I take positions at his flanks. She lunges to scoop the sword from the ground but he comes to life once again, stomping on and bending the blade before she can pull it clear. He whips the axe, striking me in the jaw with its butt during the back swing of a hack that's headed straight for Mel. The tool's heavy head plunges like a guillotine toward her as she's still off balance and unprepared due to her failed attempt for the sword.

A zip and snap pierce the air almost simultaneously followed by the staccato clap of handgun fire. More zips and claps follow, the impact of each bullet producing a palpable thump against Verdonos's torso. The axe halts its trajectory of death and falls aimlessly to the ground as he lurches with each successive bullet wound. Tiny droplets of that motor oil blood burst like solar flares from his back as several jacketed rounds rip cleanly through his thick abdomen.

Backlit by the stairwell lights, a figure moves tactically toward Verdonos with his weapon trained steadily on his target. He empties the first magazine and ejects it straight to the ground without lowering the sights. Verdonos staggers back toward the gateway that is once again swarming with his rabid beasts. Their dark arms flap frantically like tall grass whipping in a howling wind, and their shrieks make the sound to match. In a well-rehearsed choreography, the shooter pulls the next magazine from his belt, slips it into the grip, and racks the slide to chamber the next bullet.

As his finger rests heavily on the trigger, Verdonos's baboons scuttle through the increasingly unstable gateway and drag their severely wounded master into the Pneuma Rigma in a repulsive sight like a loosely packed wad of black hair being sucked into a drain. The gateway collapses, sending ripples of light in all directions and a blast of cold wind that stuns my lungs and stings my eyes. My lids clamp shut until the air settles and then, upon opening my eyes, I look to the one who saved us.

CHAPTER TWENTY-FIVE

Once again, Mel is quick to recognize the figure even in the dim moonlight and enthusiastically finds her feet. Like a honking flock of geese, approaching sirens wail distantly, growing louder moment by moment. He walks toward us, holstering his weapon as he passes through the dark beams of the radio tower's shadow.

"JULIUS!" she cries in gleeful disbelief as she wraps him up in a giant hug. Then through a beaming smile she asks, "How are you here?"

He doesn't return her delight, instead asking solemnly, "Where's Reb? Vic told me that monster took him."

Mel snags Drake's hand as we both move swiftly past him to Reb, who has scooted himself back to rest against the stairwell wall. His arduous breathing is dangerously shallow, each breath struggling to keep the previous one from being his last. It's difficult to tell if he's wide awake, unconscious, or even still alive through the tiny openings between his bulging eyelids. If it weren't for the weak fluttering of his diaphragm, weighed down by some invisible boulder, I would say maybe he's already gone.

She kneels by his side and, noticing the frothy puncture wounds in his left rib cage, lays him on that side, hoping to prevent his other lung from collapsing. Reb groans softly and Mel freezes to listen, but it was nothing more than an involuntary vibration as air escaped over his vocal cords. Tipped aside, he lies with his face smooshed to the concrete, blood spilling from between his ribs, and dust stirring near his mouth and nose less with each breath until it stops altogether. Mel sticks her hand in front of Reb's face to feel for breathing, but his body is still and the only moving air she feels is whatever gravity squeezes from his halted lungs. She lays him flat on his back and starts with chest compressions and weeping, but after three minutes neither has brought any recovery.

"No…" she mourns. "No…no…he can't be gone. He can't be gone. He's not gone."

Her head wags in disbelief and her tears flow freely. Drake takes Reb's other flank and begins his own attempt at first aid as I crouch next to Mel and wrap my arms around her. Drake moves with the systematic composure of an experienced first responder. Carefully but urgently, he checks Reb's airway, breathing, and circulation before starting another set of chest compressions. A minute later, I ask him to stop. With each press of Reb's sternum, blood is oozing from the holes in his side. He has bled out into his chest cavity and no amount of CPR is going to bring him back. Reb is dead.

After several anguished minutes that stretch well beyond the constructs of time, minutes burned forever into our amygdalae to be remembered in our quietest and loneliest of moments, I remind the others that we still need to leave this place and link up with the alliance survivors. They deserve to know of Reb's fate and be given the opportunity to hail him into the afterlife. It's what Reb would want. It's what he deserves.

We head back down to the car in a somber funeral procession through the netherworld, Mel and me carrying Reb's body and Drake leading the way from the other side. A heavy police presence has accumulated around the city, squad cars posted at street corners and officers responding to reports of an active shooter at various locations in the vicinity of Milburn Tower. It strikes me that the conflicting reports could be Jan's doing, a concerted effort by her minions to keep the police chasing wild geese around and away from Milburn Tower. Then again, it could just be the fact that Milburn stands several stories taller than the next building, so no one could isolate the exact location of the gunshots. Drake, dressed in his Port Ellis Police Department uniform, blends in with the other officers and moves through the streets unnoticed as we follow through the haze of the spirit realm.

The next hour is a nightmarish blur of grief and hopelessness. Trapped in the silent car, there's no song on the radio, no chitchat, nothing but grating road noise that only serves to highlight the millstone of despair grinding our spirits to fine powder. From the passenger seat, I periodically break my thousand-yard stare out the window to check on Drake, who is alert at the wheel but clearly fighting to preserve his steeled countenance. Mel, on the other hand, repeatedly breaks out in quiet sobs that are painful to listen to, but a welcome break from the grinding millstone. At least one of us is releasing the heartache. Then again, she's sitting in the back seat with Reb's head on her lap, with every downward glance bombarded by the stark reality of his passing. With the failing of his bodily functions, Reb's swelling has subsided and he's once again recognizable, at least in a vulgar sense, like a macabre caricature.

We arrive at a warehouse in an old industrial complex, headlights sweeping across its rusted and peeling walls. What used to be white has yellowed with age, and the black letters painted across the building's side look more like an abstract checkerboard. Enough fragments remain to make out its history as a Yuzumi Iron Works factory, meaning it will have a furnace hot enough to cremate a body, which I'm guessing is the reason we're here. At a stop along the way, Drake sent a text message to Vic from a burner phone, so if the alliance survivors aren't already here, they will be shortly. We park and exit the retired squad car, heading straight back to help Mel as the warehouse door grinds open with an offensive screech.

Out steps Vic and all of the surviving families from Carver. Instead of helping us, Drake peels off straight to Vic with a crazed look in his eyes. He starts shoving Vic and shouting, "How could you leave him!" The children cling to their parents, seeking shelter from the unexpected angry outburst. Then, grabbing Vic's shirt, he pulls him toward the car and points to us as we unload Reb's body. "Look what you did! Look!"

Stunned and defensive, Vic shouts, "Reb told me to go! He said he'd received a message, a warning from his angel friend that the Nephilim monster was headed to the cabin! He ordered me to warn the others and to lead them here instead."

"But why did you *leave* him!" Drake questions.

"I didn't *want* to leave him! I tried talking him into coming with me, but he said it was the only way to save those two," Vic says, gesturing to Mel and me as we ease Reb's body from the back seat. "He said if the monster got to Milburn Tower with no one that they were willing to trade for Jan, he'd have to kill them before they'd hand her over."

Yanking Vic around by his shirt collar, Drake snaps back, "Then *you* should've stayed at the cabin and sent Reb here!"

"Guys…" I say, trying to intervene, but it's no use as Vic explodes.

"You know he wouldn't have let that happen! But, if he had, then we'd all be dead! Children included!" shouts Vic, swinging his arm in the direction of the little ones who recoil in fear. "He knew he was the only one besides these kids that Mel would give up Jan in order to save. What about you, Drake? How did you escape death back at the gym? Did you make a deal with the devil, or did you just shoot Pam in the leg and make a run for it?"

"THAT'S ENOUGH!" barks Mel, sending a shockwave through the small crowd. She props Reb's shoulders on her thighs as she repositions her grip under his armpits. "Reb was wiser than all of us, wiser than anyone I ever met! He did what he did because he knew it was the only way to be certain that we would all live to fight another day. He would be heartbroken to see you acting this way, and you both know that's true.

"Julius, you tried to get to the tower in time and you didn't, but this is not your fault. I know you're in pain and you don't know how to handle it, but even though anger is easier, it only masks the pain. Allow yourself to grieve. Vic, you followed your leader's orders and he died, but this is not your fault. You need to absolve yourself and grieve." She looks past them to address the group. "We all need to grieve. We need to celebrate what Reb meant to all of us, to commemorate what a great leader he was, and we need to let the pain flow from our tear ducts and seep through our pores. And then we need to move on. Now, please, clear a path. He's not getting any lighter and we need to get him to the furnace."

The group disperses randomly to either side, leaving a clear channel through the factory doors as we carry Reb inside. In our wake, and face by face, a wave of despair moves through the onlookers. Despite hearing Mel say that their beloved leader is dead, they aren't met with its reality until they see his battered corpse for themselves. Sniffles like the distant rumbles of an approaching storm serenade our otherwise silent march toward Reb's final resting place.

When Zia, a four-year-old Nephilim girl, asks, "Momma, is Papa Reb gonna be okay?" the storm lets loose. Tears cascade down the cheeks and drip from the chins of nearly everyone in the room, making tiny mud craters on the dusty factory floor and wetting the weeds that have inexplicably forced their way through the concrete foundation. Through the cacophony of sobs, mine included, I can barely make out her mother's answer.

"No, darling, Papa Reb is gone. He died to keep us safe."

"Like a hero?" asks Zia.

"Yes, just like that," her mom says with a forced smile that momentarily settles her quivering lips.

We load Reb onto a large concrete slab, empty his pockets, and remove all the metal from his body as Vic works on starting the large industrial furnace. He flips several switches and turns a dial until an LCD screen displays sixteen hundred degrees Fahrenheit. A large door lifts at the near end of the moving hood furnace. The dirty, rolling monstrosity glides down a track toward the concrete pad where Reb's body lies. It stops short, primed and ready to cremate the father of our nonnuclear family after we finish offering our goodbyes and performing the customary Nephilim death ritual.

Surprised by the functioning furnace in this decrepit building, I ask Vic, "How is this still working with the building abandoned?"

"I've got a friend at the utility company," he replies. "She makes sure that the gas and electricity stay on for this very reason. Although this is the first time we've had to use it in a really long time."

"And with luck it'll be the last for a long time," I offer, knowing full well that without a lot of luck things are likely to get far worse.

Mel reaches into her pocket and produces a vial of blood that flows from one end to the other with the movement of her hand. She looks down into her palm at the thin glass tube and its sacred contents, splashed in the dull light of a single fixture that hangs high above the factory floor. A rustling arises as the group rakes through their own pockets for the vials of scintilla-infused blood that we Nephilim are still known to carry. One at a time, hands jut up from the small group, proudly wielding the tubes with their hallowed contents, the tiny organism that fuels our purpose and gives us power. Like opposable thumbs or binocular vision, it's the part of our anatomy that separates us from the rest of creation, that thing that makes us more than natural.

Surprisingly, my vial remains intact and buried deep within my pocket. I lift it high and close my eyes, reflecting on the impact of my brief relationship with Reb and imagining how devastated the others must feel. And it's not just about Reb. In the immediate wake of his death, it's easy to think first and foremost of him, but we lost Pam and Doc today too. On what is the bloodiest day in the memory of the local alliance, we are united in our despair. It's a much-needed catharsis that may not have happened without Mel's transparent leadership. One at a time we say a word or share a story about Reb, then approach his body and pour out our vials in three parts. The first is poured onto Reb's chest and the other two onto the bare concrete to each side of him—one for Pam and one for Doc.

It's the traditional Nephilim sendoff that dates back centuries to the story of twin brothers. Engaged in a harrowing battle, one of the brothers was stabbed through the abdomen and faded slowly, painfully. When his brother noticed he had fallen, he raced to his side and tried desperately to treat the wound, but he was beyond recovery. In the moments before he passed, the brother withdrew the small goatskin in which he kept his blood—the vial of their day. He poured it out onto his brother's chest and said, "My blood will vouch for you, brother. They will know that you stayed true and fought bravely, and I will see you again in paradise." The practice grew throughout their ranks and was passed down through the generations.

Like humanity, none of us Nephilim are privy to the divine secrets of the afterlife, one possible exception being Verdonos. Obviously we know that the supernatural exists, or at least that there is more to the natural world than humans are able to perceive, but we don't vacation on the soft clouds of heaven or talk to our deceased loved ones about what to expect after death. In death, we're cut off from the living, and so we contemplate their fate and our future. We struggle with the same heavy, existential questions that have always burdened all of creation, perhaps us even more so than humanity. Our angelic nature teases us with a glimpse behind the curtain, but our human nature still denies us any definitive answers. We long for the reassurance that our existence transcends the grave to a peaceful, utopian eternity. For that reason, the power of this ritual is not in the scintilla, it's in the symbolism, the stamp of approval of a life well lived and our sacrifice of something precious to mark the seal. Every Nephilim knows of the ritual and many, albeit far less than I once believed, are motivated to live rightly in the hope of receiving such validation upon their passing.

With the eulogies complete and the blood poured out, Mel signals Vic, who pushes and holds a button on a wired remote. The hood furnace hums with electric current, creeping slowly along its track until it envelops Reb and the blood-soaked concrete pad. It jitters to a clamorous stop, jarring the room with a terrible rattle. Vic looks up with an apology in his eyes, then back to the remote where he switches buttons to lower the furnace door. A loud pneumatic whine cuts through the hollow room, causing the children to plug their ears and the adults to cringe. When the door finishes its descent, Vic looks up at Mel, awaiting her approval to fire it up.

A mutual nod, a loud click, a hiss, and the angry roar of an infernal blast mark the erasure of Reb's physical existence from the planet. We watch for several minutes before Mel turns and ushers us outside, noting the hour or two it will take for the cremation to finish. The first spears of morning light pass between gentle, scattered clouds as some feathered early risers twitter away on the factory roof. In an untidy cluster, we stand around eyeing Mel and waiting for her to give an address, but she just stands with eyes fixed on me.

"What did you want to say, Mel?" I ask to get the ball rolling.

She takes a deep breath and says, "I know it's too soon and we all need rest and more time to mourn, but we can't stay here all day and we can't move until we know where we're going." After scanning the crowd she settles back on me. "To know where we're going, we need to designate a new leader."

Another pause passes with little feedback from the group, who just stand and watch her intently.

Mel gestures in my direction and says, "I nominate Ted. His powers are beyond compare, he is smart and wise, he fights with heart, and, most importantly, he's never wavered in his commitment to truth and to our cause. He's the best man for the job, and I would be honored to follow him."

A slight murmur works through the crowd, during which Mel never breaks her lock on me. I return her intense gaze at first, but then look away at the diverse and perplexed faces of our little band of warriors, present and future.

"I'm flattered, Mel, truly, but you're wrong about something. The most important quality in our future leader is not that they've never wavered. Me being a lifelong, dedicated, pious ass hasn't qualified me to lead any more than your failures have disqualified you from leading. I'm not saying this because you need my approval or blessing. I'm just trying to open your eyes to the reality of the matter. The true wellspring of a leader's value and authority is found in the depth of relationships they have with their people. Look around, Mel; these Nephilim already have a leader." For effect, I survey the group again who, despite the fact that I'm talking, are still turned to face her. "You. They're all looking to you, Mel, and so am I."

Their heads bounce in agreement and Vic shouts, "You the one, Mel!"

Her cheeks flash with color during a proud smile that's as short-lived as it is beautiful, and I can't help but hope to see it again soon.

I continue, "So, leader of the alliance, what's the plan?"

She takes a moment to regain her composure and plan her words before she starts.

"First, I'll just say that I don't think I deserve the privilege of leading you all, but I will do everything in my power to live up to who Reb was and to justify your faith in me. As you know, Reb was like a father to many of us, and I've always thought of you all as family, but under the circumstances I think it's time for our family to grow. It's time for us to stop operating like a family business," she says, knowing this idea is far more radical than any they've considered before. She closely watches their expressions and finds only faithful agreement.

Building momentum, she says, "What happened yesterday at Carver and in Port Ellis were only the first volleys in the war that we've prepared for with zealous dedication. These forces of evil have always existed and they've always known about our little band of do-gooders, but they've left us alone until now, which begs the question: Why now? What's changed? Why have we suddenly suffered their wrath? The answer is that until now, they didn't fear us. They thought we were harmless, insignificant, not worthy of their time and energy. Yesterday's attack was the confirmation that we needed, the validation of our might! It was a message from our enemy in no uncertain terms that we…are…dangerous, and even they can see the threat their foolish pride has created. They ignored us to their detriment, and we became strong."

At this, the group is fired up, hooting with excitement. It's a notable distinction to be worthy of attack, to be enough of a threat to evoke fear in one's enemies, and during the chaos of the day they had not considered this truth. Now, with its realization, the sting of the day's loss is a little more bearable, the spirit of the group is a little more formidable, and it's growing more so with her every word.

"Better still, we are not alone. Now is the time to link up with the other alliance camps, to bolster our forces and share our discoveries. Now is the time to take the fight to them before they can figure out what to do about us. They may have hundreds of mangy, devilish baboons, but we are guardians of truth, beings of great renown, and we are legion!"

Like wildfire, an uproarious reaction sweeps across the crowd, drawing applause and victorious howls. The kids play along, jumping and cheering as the adults respond to Mel's rousing speech. Looking down to the concrete, split by the insidious growth of gnarly weeds, she points at them and continues.

"We will be the weeds that refuse to die, that sprout another stem each time one is plucked up. They can trample us, cut us, and burn us down, but we will return, a never-ending nuisance, because our roots run deep and we refuse to accept failure, even unto death! We will earn the honor of the scintilla poured out in tribute to our lives and we will pass gloriously into the afterlife."

Mel finishes her speech to continued clapping and cheering. She moves through the group hugging and encouraging her followers, and I take the opportunity to slip back into the factory without notice.

The dark room still rumbles with the roar of the furnace, drowning out the hubbub outside. Sitting on the dirty floor, I draw my knees to my chest, exhausted and suffering physically and emotionally. I stare thoughtlessly at the steady glow that splashes against the scorched viewing window on the end of the furnace. The whoosh of the flames lulls me into a deep trance, looking without seeing and listening without hearing. My mind empty, my will absent, I sit still and silent in the peaceful dark until the swelling intensity of the furnace's glow pulls me back into my body. Its brightness lands hotly against the back of my eyes with solar flares that whip like tentacles from its white, glowing center. I snap my eyelids shut for fear of going blind but, as if made of glass, they block nothing. I clasp my hand across my eyes, but again the light shines through as if there's no hand at all. It's when I turn my head to the floor and the light follows, centered in my vision, that I realize it's not a product of my vision at all, but something injected straight into my mind. The celestial orb continues to grow until it washes my world in pure light and renders me blind to my surroundings.

"Theodonis," calls a voice that resonates in my ears as if coming from my own throat. "Theodonis, do not be afraid."

But I am afraid. I'm afraid because the last time I heard a voice from an invisible being, it was in the days leading up to a siege against my people. I'm afraid because I'm blind, dumb, and broken, helpless in the presence of some supernatural power that knows who I am. With any luck, this is nothing more than the hallucinations of my wounded body slipping into blood-deprived lunacy.

"Reb?" I ask almost sarcastically. It doesn't sound like his voice, but my mood is souring in my weariness and whatever this is, I'm not sure I'm interested.

He responds in a balanced, methodical cadence and perfect enunciation. "No, I am not Reb, but I know him and I know you too. It was I who told Reb of Verdonos's true identity and warned him of Verdonos's approach. The legends about him are more accurate than you would expect up to the point of his confrontation with the demons; that is where his lie began. They did not kill him, but offered him an opportunity. They were struggling to corrupt the Nephilim, because even those who were disposed to bad behavior were reluctant to openly deal with demons. They needed someone who was Nephilim, who could seduce them without sounding the alarm of conscience so loudly. It was one of the demons' conditions when they let him live despite his trespassing that his true identity must remain hidden and that anyone who discovers it must be killed. Their desire to conceal his true identity was necessary to hide the unnatural act, the spiritual war crime they committed. In exchange for being their god of deceit amongst the Nephilim, he was spared execution, given greater powers, and granted immortality."

As the angelic voice speaks into my mind, a small spark builds steadily into a rippling flame, angry and resentful. If the voice I'm hearing is truly an angel, then he has all the power needed to defeat Verdonos and his underlings. More than that, he's a personification of all the angelic abandonments and failures that so many Nephilim have endured, and he's at it again. The fire in my chest surges beyond restraint.

"Stop. If you know all of this, why haven't you intervened? If you know that he's Verdonos and that he's been behind all of this, why haven't you stopped him?!" I shout. "If you had, Reb and the others would still be alive! Your warning sent Reb to his death!"

"Ted, I understand your passion, your anger, your resentment, but you know far too little to speak so freely. It was never the design for angels and humans to procreate, but here you Nephilim are for better or worse. It changed the natural order of things millennia ago when angels gave in to their lust. You are not supposed to exist, but since you do there are rules. I am forbidden from interfering directly in any human or Nephilim matters, and so are the demons."

"What about Verdonos's demon baboons? They had no problem attacking me and killing Doc and Pam."

"Those creatures are as much demons as humans are angels. They are merely ravenous wolves, dark creatures of violent instinct, but they have no demonic status," the voice states frankly in its yet unvarying cadence. "Angels and demons battle each other, but we dare not kill your kind or that of humans, especially in the human plane. From the spirit rift we guide and encourage, and demons tempt and afflict, but even this very conversation treads dangerously across the blurred line between our roles. Verdonos, despite his unnatural powers, is Nephilim and I cannot kill him. The penalty for such an act would be unthinkable. Likewise, you have little to fear from demons. This Nephilim war is yours to wage, but the repercussions will be felt by every living thing on Earth."

"So, why tell me? Mel is their leader. Shouldn't you be sharing this with her?"

"Mel is their leader, as she should be. She is the one the alliance needs. But you are its champion, Theodonis, and these words are for you so that you may understand the gravity of your role in this world. The uniqueness of your scintilla is no chance mutation, it is a new design. You are the future of the Nephilim.

Reb knew that, and that is why he eagerly chose death for your sake."

A footstep echoes off the factory walls and for a moment the voice pauses as if to listen. I crane my head toward the door, but I still see nothing but white light in all directions. The steps grow nearer, rushing his disciplined cadence as he finishes.

"Theodonis, you have only begun to discover your potential. Continue to train, searching the limits of your power and taking note of every detail, no matter how insignificant. These Nephilim are important. Protect them, fight alongside them, and teach them, but do not get too close. Your purpose is greater than theirs, your destiny inevitable. When the time comes for you to move on, you must let nothing hold you back."

With his final word, my eyes are afflicted with overwhelming itching as if sprinkled with a thousand grains of sand. I blink to shield them and, thankfully, my world goes dark. I clench my lids tightly together and rub my eyes to combat the ruthless itching.

The footsteps reach my side and stop as Mel sits on the ground next to me. "I was wondering where you went. You okay?" she asks, then continues without waiting. "Before you answer that, I mean because you were just in here talking to yourself with your eyes peeled open and totally white like they were rolled to the back of your skull. That, and because of Reb, of course."

"You saw that, huh?"

She gives a sideways snicker and says, "Yeah, I saw."

We exchange exhausted laughter and I respond to her question. "Yeah. I'm okay. As good as I can be with three dead friends, a stab wound, and a bullet hole in my neck," I say with a breathy huff.

She takes my filthy hand in hers and stares ahead at the hot, yellow furnace window. We sit quietly, our shoulders falling heavily with each shallow breath. Tipping slowly toward me, she rests her head on my shoulder and wraps her other arm around the middle of my back.

Do not get too close.

I turn to her and say, "He spoke to me."

"Reb?"

"No, not Reb. His angel contact. He was speaking to me when you came in. That's why my eyes were…white. That's who I was talking to."

"Well, good. I'm sure his message was exactly what you needed to hear. Anything you need to share with the alliance?"

"He told me more about Verdonos and the angels and demons," I answer, seriously considering withholding the rest. After a few seconds I say, "He said some things about me too."

"Whatever he said about you was for you, Ted. I won't ask and I don't want you to tell me," she declares before I can say any more.

A little relieved, I nod and turn back to the furnace.

A second later, Mel pulls me close and I feel the velvet-soft warmth of her lips against my cheek. She presses her kiss just firmly enough to make her affections clear, but not so much as to demand a response. I smile and look at her from the corners of my eyes as she pulls away. She smiles back, elated and a little embarrassed, and that's when I turn my head and lean in, landing a passionate kiss squarely on her scarlet lips.

Do not get too close…let nothing hold you back.

We separate and exchange a look of wonder and possibility. She jumps up and extends her hand to me, and I take it in my tingling grasp.

EPILOGUE

"Less than a week after the disappearance of beloved CEO and philanthropist, Jan Lucero, Pentastar Pharmaceuticals' Board of Directors has named an interim CEO," vibrates the news anchor's voice through the old Crown Vic's tinny speakers. "In a prepared statement, acting Chairman of the Board, Bjorn Jansen, announced that VP of Marketing, Darren Woodruff, will be taking the reins of the struggling pharma giant—"

"I know Darren," I tell Drake, both of us transfixed on the radio unit.

"What do you think?"

"He's woefully underqualified—"

"Kinda like you, huh?" Drake jabs. "You think they're gonna steamroll him with the Fosillix trial?"

"I don't think so. He's a yes-man, but with Jan gone and Bjorn calling the shots, I think they just want someone they can control, someone who will just be grateful for the title and pay."

Bjorn now speaks through the car stereo, a recording from this morning's press conference. "This has been a challenging time in this company's proud history of helping people find hope and health in the midst of affliction. Over the last few weeks, our Pentastar family has suffered from its own series of tragic losses and affliction. It started on October twentieth with the suicides of Vice President of Operations, Dave McConnell, and Operations Manager, Joel Donovan. Three days later, two of my fellow board members, close friends of mine, Thomas

Sanford and Stacy Meyers, were brutally murdered during a board meeting that I attended. The deeply troubled killer was one of our own, but due to the ongoing investigation I'm unable to provide further details. All I would like to say on the matter is that if the individual responsible is listening to this, please do the right thing. Turn yourself in and tell the truth—"

"*Truth?* That's a joke, right?" I ask rhetorically, looking below my raised left eyebrow at Drake. "He just said Dave committed suicide even though Jan confessed to having Harvey murder him!"

Drake shakes his head in disbelief and continues listening to Bjorn's lies. A cool breeze dawdles dumbly through the car's open doors as I lean forward and prop my forehead high on the contoured plastic dashboard. The sound of the children roaring aggressively while they train with Mel and Vic in the nearby field tempts me away from Bjorn's deceitful droning. Only the naive hope that something redemptive has come from all this calls me back to the sounds of the radio.

"Three days ago, our CEO, Jan Lucero, who has worked tirelessly to bring the revolutionary Alzheimer's drug Fosillix to market, was reported missing. We have been working closely with the Port Ellis Police Department and have offered all of the resources at our disposal to assist them in their efforts to find her. If you have any knowledge of her whereabouts, please contact the Port Ellis Police as soon as possible.

"Lastly, in the wake of all this darkness, we have spent a lot of time evaluating our relationship with our customers and patients—our extended Pentastar family. I'm sure you're all aware of the Fosillix drug trial events and the pending litigation. While our participants were made fully aware of the risks of participating in the trial—"

I mumble into the stippled plastic, "More lies."

"—and signed legally binding liability waivers, it has always been the vision of this company to make lives better, not worse. We will not ignore the negative impact that the trial had on some participants' health and have reached a settlement with the lawsuit plaintiffs in the generous amount of seven hundred fifty million dollars."

The recording stops and the anchor takes back over the broadcast to segue to the next story. My head still propped on the dash, I twist toward Drake who spins the volume knob low then raises his arms and locks his fingers behind his head. He reclines slightly and emits a pronounced sigh.

"Well, at least the trial participants will get paid. And Jan got what she had coming. You happy with that?" he asks.

"I'm not sure it matters. What's done is done. I'm glad the patients and their families will be compensated but, as usual, the truth stays buried. Pentastar will come out of this looking benevolent and squeaky clean, and the only lesson they've learned is how to better handle this situation when it happens again. And it *will* happen again. It doesn't feel like justice."

Drake says, "Yeah…it's not justice. It could've turned out worse for the patients though."

I try to embrace the outcome as a victory, but like a bad organ transplant, my spirit responds with rejection on a molecular level. Any scenario that leaves the lies intact and the guilty unpunished would evoke the same primal response. The masses remain blind and make decisions they might make differently if they knew the truth. Their minds are manipulated, their free will bound and gagged.

Drake stirs and shifts, searching for a comfortable position, but there's something more than the cramped confines of the driver's seat fueling his restlessness. His closed eyes suggest he's attempting a power nap, but I can tell he'd settle for pretend sleep. I can't read his thoughts, but it's obvious that his brain is running hot, nagged by a burdensome notion. However, if I've learned anything about Drake over the last few weeks it's that he's not going to open up just because I ask him to; he has to want to talk. I watch and wait, and he rewards my patience much sooner than I expected.

Without opening his eyes and with a downcast tone, Drake says, "They just left me."

"What do you mean?"

"Back in the gym at Carver. Doc went down first. Pam burned her ammo quick then fought hard while I sent every bullet I could before I pulled my baton ready to fight. They didn't even bother with me, they just swarmed her." He pauses, hardening his countenance to keep from breaking. "I jumped in and tried like hell to save her, but one of those things threw me against the wall and I got knocked out. When I came to, the only thing left of any of it was her blood, smeared and dragged around the floor. The room was empty."

I sit up from the dashboard, wanting to offer some words of reassurance, but all the phrases that come to mind feel like hollow platitudes. His eyes open halfway and stare blankly through the windshield. He draws a deep breath to continue, so I say nothing yet.

"I couldn't save her, Ted. I fully meant to die in that gym. I was ready."

"I know you did. I sensed it when we said our goodbyes."

"Those damn creatures wouldn't even give me the honor of a meaningful death. I was just a pest to be swatted away. The worst part is that they were right. No matter how hard I punched, kicked, and swung my baton, I couldn't make a dent. I've never felt more powerless. I can't explain it, but at least if I had died with Doc and Pam I wouldn't feel like I failed them."

"You don't have to explain it, Drake. I get it. But if you had died, then you wouldn't have shown up on the roof of Milburn Tower and put more holes in Verdonos than anyone else in the history of the world. You saved us. If it weren't for you, they would all be dead"—I gesture at the rest of the group training in the field—"and I'd be wishing I was. If it makes you feel any better, Verdonos and his horde won't make the mistake of letting you live next time. Underestimating you was the worst choice they could've made," I say, nodding with a hint of a smile.

I notice Mel and Vic on approach and flick my head their direction so Drake sees them too. Climbing out of the car to meet them, I step into the unseasonably warm afternoon sun. I squint and shield my eyes with my hand, and for a second it looks like the radiant light is emanating from Mel.

Still fifteen feet away, she asks, "So, what did they say?"

"They're paying off the trial participants but they're maintaining their lies and aren't taking responsibility for anything. Dave is still a 'suicide.' I'm still the suspect of the double homicide of Thomas and Stacy. Jan is a beloved dreamer, leader, and now victim."

"Well, I guess something's better than nothing," she says. "I'd love to help you finish what you started there, Ted, but things are different now. You understand, right?" As I nod, she looks past me to Drake, who has climbed out of the driver's seat and is leaning on the roof of the car. "What did your friend say about Tyson?"

"They locked him up, but he's already been released. They can't really do anything with him until they catch Ted and convict him. If Ted's found innocent, then Tyson wouldn't be guilty of any crime."

"Well, that's not going to happen. Tyson's going to stay free because they'll never find Ted, and even if they did, Ted is innocent, and the truth still matters."

"It matters to us, at least," I state firmly.

Mel smiles and says, "And we will be the spark."

I look away to my right at the short caravan of vehicles that brought us to this Columbia Basin prairie. An old conversion van and two compact sedans stand before a backdrop of scabby, rolling hills that stretch to the base of low, jagged mountains. It's beautiful in its barrenness. An untouched biome of purest life, each petal, tendril, and insect serves its purpose or the ecosystem suffers. I love its simple complexity. Vic breaks the silence, asking, "Mel, how much longer until the others are here and we can head south?"

"Four of them will be here tonight, eight more tomorrow morning."

"Not exactly the army we need," Drake notes. "If they really do own every seat of power, we're not just fighting other Nephilim, we're potentially fighting every army in the world."

Mel's head bobs in agreement. "That's why we're heading south to join forces with an old friend. He's been hard at work for five years winning converts and training up warriors."

"How many are we talking about?" I ask.

Mel fights a smile as she responds, "Hundreds."

*"The Nephilim were on the earth in those days—**and also afterward**—when the sons of God went to the daughters of humans and had children by them. They were the heroes of old, men of renown."*

Genesis 6:4

"And the angels, the children of heaven, saw and lusted after them, and said to one another: 'Come, let us choose us wives from among the children of men and beget us children."

1 Enoch 6:2-3

"And all the others together with them took unto themselves wives, and each chose for himself one, and they began to go in unto them and to defile themselves with them, and they taught them charms and enchantments…"

1 Enoch 7:1-2

"And there arose much godlessness, and they committed fornication, and they were led astray, and became corrupt in all their ways"

1 Enoch 8:2-3

ABOUT THE AUTHOR

Phil Scott Mayes is the author of Verity Rising, the first installment of the supernatural thriller series, Gods of Deceit. A writer of provocative, philosophical fiction, he keeps readers on the edge of their seats while challenging them to confront their worldview. His stories will keep you thinking long after you close their pages and lay down your head.

Though writing is currently a part-time pursuit, he pours himself into each line with a passion that borders on obsession. An avid fan of horror and thriller genres, his works are down-to-earth, relatable, and gritty interpretations of supernatural and science fiction themes.

Born and raised in Michigan, he now resides in New Mexico with his wife and three children.

Made in USA - Kendallville, IN
1235671_9781735142203
02.17.2021 1240